About

Marguerite Kaye wri_____
her home in cold and u_____
Regency Rakes, High_____
published over fifty b_____
not writing she enjoys _____ (but only on
the level), gardening (but only what she can eat) and
cooking. She also likes to knit and occasionally drink
martinis (though not at the same time). Find out more
on her website: www.margueritekaye.com

When **Virginia Heath** was a little girl it took her ages
to fall asleep, so she made up stories in her head to
help pass the time while she was staring at the ceiling.
As she got older, the stories became more complicated,
sometimes taking weeks to get to the happy ending.
Then, one day, she decided to embrace the insomnia
and start writing them down. Twenty books and two
Romantic Novel of the Year Award nominations later
and it still takes her forever to fall asleep.

Regency Christmas Scandals

MARGUERITE KAYE

VIRGINIA HEATH

MILLS & BOON

First Published in Great Britain 2020
By Mills & Boon, an imprint of HarperCollins*Publishers*
1 London Bridge Street, London, SE1 9GF

www.harpercollins.co.uk

HarperCollins*Publishers*
1st Floor, Watermarque Building,
Ringsend Road, Dublin 4, Ireland

REGENCY CHRISTMAS SCANDALS
© 2021 Harlequin Books S.A.

A Scandalous Winter Wedding © 2018 Marguerite Kaye
His Mistletoe Wager © 2017 Susan Merritt

ISBN: 978-0-263-30274-5

MIX
Paper from
responsible sources
FSC® C007454

This book is produced from independently certified FSC™ paper to ensure responsible forest management.

For more information visit: www.harpercollins.co.uk/green

Printed and bound in Spain
by CPI, Barcelona

A SCANDALOUS
WINTER WEDDING

MARGUERITE KAYE

Prologue

London, February 1819

Kirstin Blair curled up in her favourite armchair in front of the fire and poured herself a cup of fragrant tea. It was a new blend, a gift from one of her oldest friends, the Marquis of Glenkin, but while the smoky brew was undoubtedly as refreshing as any Ewan had previously supplied, tonight she might as well have been drinking dishwater. As she settled in her seat, the rustle of the letter secreted in her dressing gown pocket proved too difficult to resist.

She opened the missive once again, staring down at the bold, decisive masculine handwriting. The maelstrom of emotions she had been keeping at bay all day overtook her, making the delicate Sèvres teacup shake in its saucer. She set it down, closing her eyes, lying her head back on the wings of her chair.

She'd never seen his script before. She'd had no inkling, when she broke the seal this morning in her office, of the explosive contents of that single sheet of expensive pressed paper. Scanning the signature first, as she always did, she'd thought her eyes deceived her, but a second appraisal of it left no room for doubt.

Cameron Dunbar. There could not be another with that particular name.

The shock hit her afresh as she stared at the letter. It was not that she'd thought him dead, more that she had so effectively written him out of her life it was as if he had never existed. She rarely permitted herself to recall any detail of that fateful night.

As she struggled to repress the confusing and almost unprecedented smart of tears, years of practice allowed her to draw a thick black curtain over the memory. She would not cry. She had barely shed a tear in the darkest of times. She had taught herself to concentrate wholly on the positive, to look forward not back.

'Onwards and upwards,' she whispered to herself now, but the words which had so often inspired her, and many of the women she had aided, failed to work their magic on this occasion.

Cameron Dunbar. He was unquestionably an outrageously handsome man, but it was not his classical good looks which had drawn her, it was his smile. He had one of those intimate smiles, a smile seemingly intended only for her. Despite the fact that they had been surrounded by strangers, that the carriage had been pungent from the succession of boiled eggs one passenger had consumed at regular intervals, and ripe with the sweat from another, and regardless of the fact that they had been sitting diametrically opposite each other, that smile had enveloped them in a bubble of their own. She'd found herself smiling back, something quite alien to her reserved nature. It should have been a warning that most certainly should have been heeded.

Kirstin's eyes snapped open. Cameron Dunbar's easy charm was of no interest to her. On the other hand, the letter which lay in her lap, whatever its mysterious request turned out to entail, might prove to be a very lucrative business opportunity. If she chose to accept it. Not that she would. She would be a fool to have anything to do with the man who had, albeit unwittingly, come so close to destroying her. She had saved herself, living by her considerable wits, reinventing herself, working hard to create the myth behind which she now flourished, to establish the flawless reputation she now enjoyed. There was no need to conjure up this ghost from her past.

On the other hand, business *was* business. Despite the fact that her alter ego was besieged every day with enquiries, such was the complex nature of her extremely discreet and niche service that only a very small percentage of these commissions could be accepted. Making the impossible possible required her to ensure that she never failed, but the need to make a handsome living that would safeguard her future meant she was not in a position to reject any approach out of hand.

But this particular prospect she most decidedly could not investigate, far less take on, for she could not possibly meet Cameron Dunbar face-to-face.

Yet it was impossible to deny that she wanted to, given the incontrovertible evidence that he was alive. She found herself intensely curious as to how his life had turned out, more than six years on, and what his circumstances were. And she wanted to know what desperate bind he had found himself in that he was compelled to seek her expensive and exclusive assistance. Not that he could have any idea at all who it was he'd actually written to.

Which thought gave her pause. A small smile played on her lips as she poured herself a fresh cup of tea. Taking a sip, she nodded with satisfaction, relishing the smoky blend of this second cup. Cameron Dunbar had written to her alter ego. Even if he remembered Kirstin from that one night over six years ago, he had no reason to connect the two of them. And, actually, there was a reasonable chance that he wouldn't even remember that night, for a man as handsome and as charming and as charismatic as Cameron Dunbar must surely have had many such nights since. That illusion of intimacy between them, that feeling she'd had, the reason she'd allowed herself to be carried away, that *she* was special, that his behaviour was every bit as out of character as hers was exactly that, an illusion.

Seeing him again would change nothing, Kirstin told herself, but the logical approach which ruled her life, a legacy of her mathematician father, failed to hold sway. Her world was quite perfect, as far as she was concerned, and most importantly of all it was *hers*. She had no desire whatsoever to change it, and plenty of reasons to protect it from the eyes of the world. So it made no sense to her that from the minute she'd opened that letter a persistent niggling voice had been urging her to meet the owner of its signature.

Relentlessly analytical, Kirstin probed deeper into her own motives. It was not only blind curiosity which drove her, though that did play a small part. She wanted to prove to herself that the path she had chosen was the correct one. That her defiance of convention had been vindicated. That the smooth, impenetrable face she presented to society was the best form of protection from the judgement of the world for those she held most dear, allowing the life of splendid isolation which existed behind the façade to blossom.

There was no place there for Cameron Dunbar, but nor was there any room for doubts. Thanks to this letter, he'd temporarily escaped from the mental prison she'd locked him in. She needed to see him one more time, to assure herself that he was completed business, then put him back in his cell and this time throw away the key.

Besides, from a business perspective she had an obligation to meet him, at the very least to discover what it was he sought and whether she could provide it. If she could, well and good. She would match a deserving subject to his requirements and there would be no need for them ever to meet again. If not, there would be no harm done.

Kirstin set down her empty teacup. She folded up the letter. All she had to do was to find a way for them to meet once, a meeting that would allow her to see him, to question him, but which would grant him no such reciprocal privileges.

The Procurer always dressed in black. Understated but expensive, her working clothes could be those of a rich widow or a discreet and exclusive Covent Garden madam—there had been a deliberate irony in Kirstin's choice of her assumed title. She was also aware that black outfits, severely tailored, suited her particular form of beauty. Though the notion of using seduction to achieve her goals repelled her, she would not be such a fool as to deny the power of a pretty face. It was unfair, but there were times, especially before her reputation was fully established, when her good looks had worked to her advantage, opening doors which might have otherwise remained firmly closed.

Today, despite the fact that her appearance was irrelevant, for Cameron Dunbar would not see her, she dressed with great care, scrutinising herself in the mirror. The black velvet military-style full-length pelisse with its double row of braid, tight sleeves and high collar showed off her tall, slim figure to perfection. Black buttoned half-boots, black gloves, a poke bonnet trimmed with black silk and a large black velvet muff completed her outfit. What little showed of her face was pale, save for the pink blush of her full lips, and the grey-blue of her heavy-lidded eyes which even today betrayed nothing of the turmoil raging in her head.

Kirstin smiled the enigmatic smile of The Procurer, relieved to see her alter ego smiling back at her. Cameron would not see her, but if he did, he'd see what everyone did: The Procurer, a beautiful, aloof and powerful woman, with an air of mystery about her, a woman with a reputation for making the impossible possible.

Satisfied, she made her customary farewells and left her house by the discreet side door. It was a short walk to Soho Square, to a very different world from genteel Bloomsbury, though The Procurer, whose business relied upon her being extremely well connected, had several dubious contacts who lived nearby. St Patrick's Church was located on the corner.

Kirstin checked her enamelled pocket watch. Five minutes to eleven, the appointed hour and the first test she had set Cameron Dunbar, insisting he be prompt.

This first hurdle she had, with an unaccustomed nod towards letting fate decide, set herself. If he was too early, or was already inside the church, their meeting was not meant to be.

She waited, ignoring her racing heart, standing in the shade of one of the churchyard's leafless trees, a location she had earlier selected for its excellent view of the entrance porch. She would give him just five minutes' leeway. Her pocket watch gave off the tiny vibration which alerted her to the hour, but before she could begin to manage her disappointment at his failure to materialise he appeared.

From this distance, Cameron Dunbar looked unchanged. Tall and ramrod-straight, he still walked with that quick, purposeful stride which made the capes of his dark brown greatcoat fly out behind him. He wore fawn pantaloons, polished Hessians, and a tall beaver hat which covered his close-cropped hair so that she couldn't see if it was still as black as night.

He stopped at the steps of the church to check his watch, thus unknowingly passing her first test, and the breath caught in her throat at seeing his face in profile, the strong nose, the decided chin, the sharp planes of his cheekbones. He was still the most ridiculously handsome man she had ever seen. She was relieved, for the sake of her ability to breathe, that he was frowning rather than smiling as he snapped shut the cover of his watch, returned it to his pocket and entered the church.

Kirstin stood rooted to the spot, staring at the large wooden door of St Patrick's. Her heart was beating so fast she felt light-headed, her stomach churning, making her thankful she had decided against attempting breakfast. He was here. He was, even as she stood watching, making his way down the aisle, following her precise instructions, oblivious of the fact that she and The Procurer were one and the same.

Part of her wanted to flee. She had not expected this meeting to feel so momentous. She was afraid that she might betray herself with all the questions she dared not ask.

Did he remember that night at the posting house? Did he ever think of her? Did he ever wonder what had become of her? What direction had his own life taken?

This last question she, with her many contacts, could have easily found answers to, but until that letter had arrived she had preferred to know nothing, to persist with the illusion she had created that he did not exist.

But now! Oh, now she was afraid that this myriad of feelings she couldn't even begin to unravel, which she'd had no idea had been so long pent-up, would rise to the surface, would be betrayed in her voice. She was afraid that she would not be able to maintain her façade. She was afraid that he would recognise her. She was even more afraid that she would, in her emotional turmoil, spill out enough of the truth for him to guess the rest.

No! A thousand times no! The consequences could not be contemplated, never mind borne. She would never, ever be so foolish. The knowledge calmed her, allowing her rational self to take charge once more. She would satisfy her curiosity. She would learn enough of the man and his situation to ensure that there could never in the future be any seeds of doubt. She would decide whether his case could be taken on and, if so, she would find him a suitable helpmeet. Then she would never see him again.

The Procurer now firmly in charge, Kirstin squared her shoulders and made her way inside the church.

Cameron Dunbar stood in front of the baptismal font set in an alcove off a side aisle. The church appeared to be deserted, though the sweet scent of incense and candle wax from the morning mass hung in the air, along with the faint tang of the less than genteel congregation. Feeling slightly absurd, he made his way to the confessional boxes ranged on the left-hand side of the aisle, entering the last one as instructed.

The curtain on the other side of the grille was closed. He sat down in the gloomy confined space and prepared himself for disappointment. The Procurer's reputation for discretion was legendary, her reputation for being elusive equally so, but he had, nonetheless, expected to meet the woman face-to-face. Part of him questioned her very existence, wondering if she wasn't some elaborate hoax. Even if she was more than a myth, he wasn't at all convinced that he could bring himself to explain his business, especially such sensitive business, in such circumstances.

Sighing impatiently, Cameron tried to stretch his legs out in front of him, only to knock his knees against the door of the wooden box. If he had been able to think of another way to proceed, any other way at all, he would not be here. He hadn't even heard of the woman until two days ago. Max had assured him that everything said of her was true, that her reputation was well-deserved, but Max had also refused to divulge a single detail of his own involvement with her, save to say, primly, that the matter had been resolved satisfactorily.

Cameron trusted Max, and his problem was urgent, becoming more urgent with every day that passed.

How long had he been sitting here? The blasted woman had been so precise about his own arrival she could at least have had the decency to be punctual herself. On the brink of breaking another of her list of instructions by peering out of the confessional into the church, he heard the tapping of heels on the aisle. Was it her? He listened, ears straining, as the footsteps approached. Stopped. And the door on the other side of the confessional was opened. There was a faint settling, the rustle of fabric as The Procurer sat down—assuming it was she and not a priest come to hear his confession.

The curtain on the other side was drawn back. It made little difference. Cameron could see nothing through the tiny holes in the pierced metal grille save a vague outline. But he could hear her breathing. And he could smell the damp on her clothes and the faint trace of perfume, not sickly attar of roses or lavender water, but a more exotic scent. Jasmine? Vanilla? What kind of woman was The Procurer? Max hadn't even told him whether she was young or old.

'Mr Dunbar?'

Her voice was low, barely more than a whisper. Cameron leaned into the grille and the shadow on the other side immediately pulled back. 'I am Cameron Dunbar,' he said. 'May I assume I'm addressing The Procurer?'

'You may.'

Again, she spoke softly. He could hear the swishing of her gown, as if she too was having difficulty in getting comfortable in the box. The situation was preposterous. Confessional or no, he wasn't about to spill his guts to a complete stranger whose face he wasn't even permitted to see.

'Listen to me, Madam Procurer,' Cameron said. 'I don't know what your usual format for these meetings is, but it does not suit me at all. Can we not talk face-to-face, like adults? This absurd situation hardly encourages trust, especially if I am to be your client.'

'No!' The single word came through the grille as a hiss, making him jerk his head away. 'I made the terms of this meeting very clear in my note, Mr Dunbar. If you break them—'

'Then you will not consider my case,' he snapped. Cameron was not used to being in a negotiation where he did not have the upper hand. But this situation was in every way unique. 'Very well,' he conceded stiffly, 'we will continue on your terms, madam.'

Silence. Then her face moved closer to the grille. 'You must first tell me a little about yourself, Mr Dunbar.'

Though he must know nothing of *her*, it seemed. It stuck in his craw, but he could not risk alienating her. She would not, he sensed, give him a second chance, and if there was any possibility that she really was as good as Max averred, then he had no option but to play the game her way.

'If you're concerned that I can't afford your fee,' Cameron said dryly, 'then let me put your mind at rest. Whatever it is—and I've heard that it is anything from a small fortune to a king's ransom—then I have ample means.'

'A king's ransom?' the woman on the other side of the grille whispered. 'Now, that is an interesting proposition. What would you pay, Mr Cameron, to release the current King from his incarceration?'

'A deal more than I'd pay for his son were it he who were locked away. I'd much prefer a madman on the throne to a profligate popinjay. Though the truth is I doubt I'd put up a penny for either.'

'You are a republican, then, Mr Dunbar, like our friends in America?'

'I'm a pragmatist and a businessman, and I'm wondering what relevance my politics can possibly have to the matter under discussion?'

His question caused her to pause. When she spoke again, her tone was conciliatory. 'I take many factors into consideration before agreeing to take on a new client. I was merely trying to establish what sort of man I would be dealing with.'

'An honest one. A desperate one, as you must know,' Cameron replied tersely. 'Else I would not have sought you out.'

'You have told no one about this meeting? Not even your wife…'

'I have no wife. I have spoken to no one,' Cameron replied, becoming impatient. 'You are not the only one who desires the utmost discretion.'

'You may trust in mine, Mr Dunbar.'

'So I've heard. You must not take it amiss if I tell you that I prefer to make my own mind up about that.'

'You are perfectly at liberty to do so. Though I would remind you that you came to me for help, not the other way around.'

'As a last resort. I am not a man who trusts anyone but himself with his affairs, but I cannot see a way

to resolve this matter on my own. I desperately need
your help.'

Her silence spoke for her. He must abandon his reservations, must throw caution to the wind and confide
in this woman, no matter how much it went against the
grain, else he would fail. The consequences of failure
could not be contemplated.

'You must believe me when I tell you I do not ex-
aggerate,' Cameron said. 'This could well be a matter
of life and death.'

Many of the people who sought The Procurer's help
thought the same, but there was a raw emotion in Cameron Dunbar's voice that gave Kirstin pause. Hearing
his voice, knowing that the man who had quite literally changed the course of her life was just inches
away, had been more overwhelming than she could
ever have imagined.

The urge to throw back the door of the confessional,
to confront him face-to-face, was almost irresistible.
She had not expected the visceral reaction of her body
to his voice, as if her skin and her muscles remembered
him, and the memory triggered a longing to know him
again.

She was frustrated by the grille which kept her identity concealed, for it kept him safe too, from her scrutiny. Images flashed into her mind when he spoke,
vivid, shocking images of that night that brought colour flooding to her cheeks, for the woman in those images was a wanton who bore no relation to the woman
she was now. This had been a mistake. She could not
help Cameron Dunbar, yet she could not force herself
to walk away.

'I will listen,' she found herself saying. 'Though I make no promises, I will hear you out.'

And so she did, with a growing sense of horror, as Cameron Dunbar told his story.

When he came to the end of it, Kirstin spoke without hesitation. 'I will find someone suitable who will assist you. Tell me where you may be reached.'

Chapter One

Handing her portmanteau to the hackney cab driver, Kirstin gave the address of the hotel where Cameron Dunbar had taken up residence. It was by no means the grandest establishment in London but it was, she knew, formidably expensive, not least because it had a reputation for offering the utmost discretion, which suited certain well-heeled guests. She wondered how Cameron had come to know of it. The friend he had mentioned, Max, who had recommended The Procurer's services, no doubt. She remembered Max. A difficult, but ultimately satisfying case, and the first one in which Marianne had been involved.

The cab rattled through the crowded streets and Kirstin's heart raced along with it. It was not too late to turn back, but she knew she would not. Her farewells had been said.

'We'll be fine,' Marianne had told her with a reassuring smile, and Kirstin hadn't doubted it, having come to trust her completely over the years in both business and personal terms. But it had been a painful parting all the same, astonishingly difficult to pin a smile to her face, to keep the tears from her eyes. 'Go,' Marianne had said, shooing her out through the door, 'and don't fret. Concentrate on completing this case, which sounds as if it will require all of even your considerable powers. It will be good for me to have the opportunity to be in charge, stand on my own two feet.'

Marianne, discreet as ever, had refrained from asking why Kirstin was taking on this case personally, something she had never done before, though it was Marianne who had, albeit inadvertently, put the idea into Kirstin's head, when she had pointed out that Kirstin possessed exactly the attributes the client had specified.

As The Procurer, Kirstin could have found another suitable female, she always did, but it would have taken time, and Cameron had none to spare. It therefore made perfect, logical sense for her to make the momentous decision to step into the breach, she told herself as the cab neared her destination. It was clear to her, from the sketchy information Cameron had provided, that the situation, though not necessarily a matter of life and death at present, could, if unresolved, easily become one.

Though had it been any man other than Cameron Dunbar who had come seeking her help would she have acted in a similar fashion? No. Kirstin's habit of being brutally honest with everyone, including herself, was ingrained. She would have moved heaven and earth to find a suitable female candidate, but she would not have dreamed of offering her own services. She was here to help Cameron Dunbar resolve his terrible predicament, but she was also here for her own reasons.

It meant depriving another woman of the opportunity to make a fresh start for herself, but after their wholly unsatisfactory meeting the day before yesterday, Kirstin had been forced to acknowledge that she too needed a fresh start. Far from letting her close the door on the man, it had merely served to let him stride through. She had to know more about him, and she had a very legitimate reason for needing to do so. The time would come when she could no longer field questions with feigned ignorance, and it was not in her nature to lie.

More than six years ago she had taken the decision to be true to herself, to live her life in her chosen way, independent of everyone, answerable to no one. In order to continue to do so she must reassure herself that her decision was the correct one, which meant excising Cameron Dunbar from the equation.

And keeping him completely in the dark while she did so.

Kirstin smiled grimly to herself. It was hardly a difficult task for one who made a living from extracting information while offering none in exchange. She must assume that Cameron would remember Kirstin Blair, but he would have no idea that she and The Procurer were one and the same. The Procurer's own unbreakable rules that no questions could be asked, no personal history need be revealed, would protect her, and the notion that she would ever confide in him of her own free will—it was ludicrous. Kirstin, as Marianne had once said, could give lessons in discretion to clams.

Reassured, confident in her decision, as the cab came to a halt and the hotel porter rushed to open the door, she turned her mind to the coming reunion, telling herself that her nerves were everything to do with her determination to prevent the matter becoming one of life and death, and nothing at all to do with the man she was going to be working with in close proximity.

In accordance with the letter from The Procurer, which had arrived yesterday, Cameron had reserved a suite of rooms in the name of Mrs Collins. He had instructed the Head Porter to inform him when this lady, whom he was to claim as an old acquaintance, arrived, and to issue her with an invitation to take tea with him.

His own suite overlooked the front of the hotel. Unable to concentrate on the stack of business letters which had been forwarded from his Glasgow office, Cameron had spent the last two hours gazing out of the window, monitoring every arrival.

He had no idea what to expect of Mrs Collins, though he had formed a picture in his head of a smart, middle-aged woman with faded hair, a high brow, intelligent eyes. The relic of a man of the church, perhaps, who had worked in London's slums, or with London's fallen women, and was therefore no stranger to the city's seamy underbelly, but who had also solicited London's society for alms. At ease with the full gamut of society, Mrs Collins would be tough but compassionate, not easily shocked. The type of woman who could be trusted with confidences and who would not judge. Since her husband had died, she would have been continuing with his good works, saving lost souls, but she'd be finding her widowed state confining, he reckoned, and since she'd always had a penchant for charades, which they'd played in the vicarage every Christmas, the need to assume various disguises would appeal to her.

Cameron nodded with satisfaction. An unusual combination of skills, no doubt about it, which made it all the more surprising that The Procurer had found someone to suit his requirements so quickly.

He leant his head against the glass of the tall window, impatient for her to arrive. The ancient female dressed in a sickly shade of green matching the parrot she carried in a cage, whom he had watched half an hour ago emerge from a post-chaise, could not be her. Nor could this fashionable young lady arriving with her maid, one of those ridiculous little dogs that looked like a powder puff clutched in her arms. A hackney cab pulled up next, and a slim female figure emerged, dressed in a white gown with a red spencer. She had her back to him as she waited for her luggage to be removed, yet he had the impression of elegance, could see from the respect she commanded from the driver and from the porter rushing to meet her, the assurance with which she walked, that she was a woman of consequence.

Intriguing, but clearly not his Mrs Collins.

Cameron turned his back on the window, inspecting his pocket watch, debating with himself on whether to order a pot of coffee. A rap on the door made him throw it open impatiently, thinking it was the arrival of yet more business papers.

'I've been sent to tell you that your acquaintance has arrived,' the messenger boy said. 'She's happy to hear that you are staying in the hotel, she says, and she would be delighted to join you for tea.'

'Are you sure? When did she get here?'

But the boy shook his head. 'Nobody tells me nuffin', save me message. Head Porter says to expect her with the tea directly,' he said. 'If there's nuffin' else...?' He waited expectantly.

Cameron sighed and handed over a shilling. He must have missed Mrs Collins's arrival. Or perhaps there was a side entrance.

A few minutes later there was another soft tap on the door. He opened the door to be confronted with the elegant woman who had emerged from the hackney cab.

His jaw dropped, his stomach flipped, for he recognised her immediately.

'Kirstin.'

He blinked, but she was still there, not a ghost from his past but a real woman, flesh and blood and even more beautiful than he remembered.

'Kirstin,' Cameron repeated, his shock apparent in his voice. 'What on earth are you doing here?'

'I wondered if you'd recognise me after all this time. May I come in?'

Her tone was cool. She was not at all surprised to see him. As she stepped past him into the room, and a servant appeared behind her with a tea tray, he realised that *she* must be the woman sent to him by The Procurer. Stunned, Cameron watched in silence as the tea tray was set down, reaching automatically into his pocket to tip the servant as Kirstin busied herself, warming the pot and setting out the cups. He tried to reconcile the dazzling vision before him with Mrs Collins, but the vicar's wife of his imagination had already vanished, never to be seen again.

Still quite dazed, he sat down opposite her. She had opened the tea caddy, was taking a delicate sniff of the leaves, her finely arched brows rising in what seemed to be surprised approval. Her face, framed by her bonnet, was breathtaking in its flawlessness. Alabaster skin. Blue-black hair. Heavy-lidded eyes that were a smoky, blue-grey. A generous mouth with a full bottom lip, the colour of almost ripe raspberries.

Yet, he remembered, it had not been the perfection of her face which had drawn him to her all those years ago, it had been the intelligence slumbering beneath those heavy lids, the ironic twist to her smile when their eyes met in that crowded carriage, and that air she still exuded, of aloofness, almost haughtiness, that was both intimidating and alluring. He had suspected fire lay beneath that cool exterior, and he hadn't been disappointed.

A vision of that extraordinary night over six years ago flooded his mind. There had been other women since, though none of late, and never another night like that one. He had come to think of it as a half-remembered dream, a fantasy, the product of extreme circumstances that he would never experience again.

He wasn't at all sure what he thought of Kirstin walking so calmly back into his life, especially when he was in the midst of a crisis. Were they to pretend that they had no history? It had been such a fleeting moment in time, with no bearing on the years after, save for the unsettling, incomparable memory. Cameron supposed that it ought to be possible to pretend it had not happened, but as he looked at her, appalled to discover the stirrings of desire that the memories evoked, he knew he was deluding himself.

'Cream or lemon?' Kirstin asked.

'Lemon,' he answered, though he habitually drank his tea black and well stewed, a legacy of his early days on-board ship.

He held out his hand for the saucer, but instead she placed it on the table in front of him, drawing an invisible line between them and bringing him to his senses. Whether they acknowledged their history or not, it had no bearing on the reason she was here now.

'Are you really the woman chosen for me by this infamous Procurer? Do you know what it is I need from you? What has she told you of me? The matter—'

'Is one of life and death, you believe,' Kirstin answered gravely. 'To answer your questions in order. Yes, I am here at the behest of The Procurer. She has outlined your situation, though I will need to hear the details from you. I know nothing of your circumstances, save what you have told her.'

'She has told me nothing at all of you. Is Collins your married name?'

'My name is what it has always been. Kirstin Blair.'

'You're not married?' Cameron asked. It was hardly relevant, yet when she shook her head he was unaccountably pleased as well as surprised. Because it would be impossible for them to proceed if there was a husband in the background, or worse in the foreground, he told himself. 'I'm not married either,' he said.

She nodded casually at that. Because she already knew from The Procurer? Or because she had deduced as much from his appearance? Or because she was indifferent? This last option, Cameron discovered, was the least palatable.

He began to be irked by her impassive exterior. 'You do remember me, I take it?' he demanded. 'That night…'

The faintest tinge of colour stole over her cheeks. She did not flinch, but he saw the movement at her throat as she swallowed. 'This is hardly the time to reminisce.'

Their gazes snagged. He could have sworn, in that moment, that she felt it, the almost physical pull of attraction, that strange empathy that they had both succumbed to that night. Then Kirstin broke the spell.

'It was more than six years ago,' she said pointedly.

'I am perfectly aware of how many years have elapsed,' Cameron snapped.

He had never disclosed his reasons for having made that journey to anyone. He had been interested only in trying to forget all that he had left behind during the trip south, and he had succeeded too, temporarily losing himself and his pain in Kirstin. He'd thought the mental scar healed.

It had been, until Louise Ferguson had written to him as a last resort, begging for his help in the name of the very ties she'd so vehemently denied before. Compassion for her plight diluted his mixture of anger and disappointment that she should turn to him only *in extremis*. He was long past imagining they could be anything to each other, but it forced him to acknowledge that he had, albeit unwittingly, been the root cause of her past unhappiness. There was a debt to be paid.

Doing what she asked would salve his conscience and allow him to put the matter to bed once and for all. He wouldn't get another opportunity, and he needed Kirstin to help him, so he couldn't afford to allow their brief encounter to get in the way. It was the future which mattered.

Cameron swallowed his tea. It was cold, and far too floral for his taste. He made a mental note to stick to coffee, and set the cup down with a clatter.

'I recall, now, that your Procurer's terms specify that there should be no questions asked, either you of me, or me of you. It's a sensible rule and allows us to concentrate on the matter that brought us both here,' he said, deliberately brusque as he leaned back in his seat, crossing his ankles. 'However, I am paying a small fortune for your assistance. I think that gives me the right to ask what it is about yourself that makes The Procurer so certain you will suit my extremely demanding, if not unique, set of requirements.'

Kirstin poured herself a second cup of tea, deliberately avoiding Cameron's gaze. It was more taxing than it ought to be to maintain her poise, but she was determined he would not see how much this face-to-face encounter was affecting her. Those eyes of his, such a deep, dark brown. She could feel them on her now, sense his rising impatience. An understandable emotion, in the circumstances. Extremely understandable, she thought guiltily.

Determined to keep her mind focused on the matter at hand, she peeled off her gloves and untied her bonnet. Cameron had every reason to question her suitability. Her first task was to reassure him—which fortunately she could easily do, by telling him the truth.

'I have worked closely with The Procurer for many years. I know her and her business intimately,' she said. 'She requires the utmost discretion from her employees, and has never had the slightest cause to question mine. As her trusted assistant, I have access to her extensive network of contacts. I am required to mix with a most—eclectic, I think would be the best description— range of characters, in a number of guises. I have the facility to win over the most unlikely people, from all walks of life, and extract confidences from them. You could call it the quality of a chameleon.'

She permitted herself a thin smile.

'Whatever you wish to call it, the net result is that I am expert at finding people who do not wish to be found. I am also, as you requested, a woman of good standing, and so able to enquire after the whereabouts of a young and innocent girl without it being assumed my purpose is nefarious—something you could not do. Though I must ask you, Mr Dunbar, if you have considered the possibility that she has already encountered another with just such nefarious intent?'

Across from her, Cameron was frowning deeply. 'I have not said as much to the young lady's mother, but it seems to me, unfortunately, a possibility which must be investigated.'

'I am relieved to hear that you have not discounted this.'

'I'm more or less a stranger to London, but I'm a man of the world.'

'Then we shall deal well together, for I am a woman who prefers that a spade should be called a spade.'

He laughed shortly. 'Though you look like a woman whose sensibilities are very easily offended.'

'Precisely my intention when I assumed this guise. I have dressed as a lady of quality, because only a lady of quality would be accepted as a guest in this hotel, Mr Dunbar. One should not judge by appearances, though fortunately, for the success of our mission, many people do.'

'Do you think we'll be successful?'

Though he asked her coolly enough, there was just a

hint of desperation in his tone. With difficulty, Kirstin resisted the urge to cover his hand, one of the few gestures of sympathy she ever allowed herself to bestow. It was even more difficult to resist the urge to reassure him, but that was one rule she never broke.

'I will do everything in my power to help you, but it has been over a week now. You must face the fact that the damage may already have been done.'

The pain in his eyes told her he had already been down that path, far further than even she had. 'We must succeed,' he said. 'Mrs Ferguson is relying on me to find her daughter.'

'She cannot possibly blame you if you fail.'

'Believe me, she will, and she won't give me another chance.'

Kirstin frowned, wondering if she had missed something significant he had said in the confessional two days ago, but her memory was prodigious, she missed nothing. 'Another chance to do what?'

'Pay my dues.' Cameron dug his hands into the pockets of his coat, looking deeply uncomfortable. 'The woman believes that I owe her, and in all conscience I think she has a point. If I can restore her daughter to her then we can both get on with our lives unencumbered.'

Only now did his mode of address strike her as odd. She should have noticed it before. She tried to recall what Cameron had told The Procurer in the confessional, and realised he'd said nothing at all of his relationship with Mrs Ferguson and her daughter, save to inform her of the blood tie.

'You don't know your sister well enough to call her by her first name, yet she turned to you when her daughter disappeared?'

Cameron got to his feet, making for the window, where he leaned his shoulder against the shutter. 'Mrs Ferguson is only my half-sister, making Philippa my half-niece, if there is such a thing.'

'You do realise that a failure to disclose salient facts renders your contract with The Procurer null and void?'

He rolled his eyes, but resumed his seat opposite her. 'It's a long story, and I can't see how it's relevant, but until Philippa disappeared I had met her mother only once. I've never set eyes on Philippa myself. This is her.' He produced a miniature, which depicted an insipid girl with hair the colour of night. 'There's no portrait of the maid, but according to Mrs Ferguson she is a pert chit with ginger hair, from which we can infer a pretty redhead.'

'You think that if you can restore Philippa to her mother, your sister will be grateful enough to—to nullify some previous debt?'

'It's not about money.'

No, nothing so simple, Kirstin deduced from the slash of colour in his cheeks. She would have liked to question him further but, like Cameron, she was bound by her own rules. There was a very big difference between history which had a bearing on this case, and bald curiosity.

'And if you fail?' she asked carefully.

'I cannot fail. I've never met the girl, but having seen the mother—she's in a terrible state—I can't let her down. Can you imagine what she must be feeling, to have her only child disappear like that, from right under her nose?'

A shiver ran down Kirstin's spine. 'No,' she said, catching herself, 'I do not want to imagine, and nor does it serve any purpose. What we must do is try to put an end to her suffering. That is why I'm here.'

'I was, as you'll have noticed, somewhat taken aback when you turned up, but I'm very glad you did, Kirstin—Miss Blair—Mrs Collins. Curse it, I've no idea what to call you.'

He smiled at her then. It was a rueful smile. A smile that acknowledged their brief shared history, and acknowledged, too, that it was exactly that. History. Yet that smile, the warmth of it, the way it wrapped itself round her, brought it all back as if it were yesterday...

December 1812, Carlisle

He had boarded, as she had, at the White Hart Inn in the Grassmarket at Edinburgh, jumping into the coach at the last minute, squashing himself into the far corner, apologising to the stout man next to him, though it was he who was overflowing both sides of his allotted seat. The new arrival was swathed in a many-caped greatcoat, which he was forced to gather tightly around him. His legs were encased in a pair of black boots with brown tops, still highly polished, no mean feat having navigated Edinburgh's filthy streets. When he took off his hat, clasping it on his lap, the woman sitting next to Kirstin gasped. The man looked up—not at the woman whom Kirstin had decided must be a housekeeper en route to a new appointment, but directly at Kirstin. In that brief glimpse, before she dropped her gaze deliberately to her lap, she saw enough to understand the housekeeper's reaction, but she was irked and no little embarrassed, mortified that he might think the involuntary reaction had emanated from her. He was handsome, far too handsome to be unaware of the fact, and no doubt accustomed to having women of all ages gasping at him. Kirstin wasn't about to add to their number.

But as the coach lumbered across the cobblestones of the Grassmarket towards the city gate and the road south, she found herself sneaking glances at the Adonis in the far corner. He sat with his head back on the squabs, his eyes closed, but the grim line of his mouth told her, as did the rigid way he held his body, that he was not asleep. His hair was black, close-cropped, the colour like her own, showing his Celtic origins. He had a high brow, faintly lined, his skin tanned, not the weather-beaten hue of a Scot who worked outdoors in the assorted forms of rain which dominated the four seasons, but a glow borne of sunshine and far warmer climes. His accent had been Scots, west coast rather than east, she thought, it was difficult to judge from his few terse words, but he obviously spent a deal of his time abroad. To his advantage too, judging by his attire, which was expensive yet understated. A businessman of some sort, she conjectured, discounting the possibility that he was a man of leisure, for such a man would certainly not travel on a public coach. This gentleman was obviously accustomed to it, managing to stay quite still in his seat despite the rattles and jolts of the cumbersome vehicle that had everyone else falling over each other.

She wondered what it was that he was thinking to make such a grim line of his mouth. Was he in pain? Angry? No, his grasp on his hat was light enough. Upset? There was a cleft in his chin, which was rather pointed than square. It was the contrasts, Kirstin decided, which made him so handsome—the delicate shape of his face, the strong nose, the sharp cheekbones. His brows were fierce. She was speculating on the exact colour of his eyes when they flew open and met her gaze. Dark brown, like melting chocolate, Kirstin thought fancifully before she caught herself, and was about to look away when he smiled directly at her, and she had the most absurd sensation that they were quite alone. She smiled back before she could stop herself. It was the housekeeper's disapproving cluck which recalled her to her surroundings.

For the next few miles, Kirstin doggedly occupied herself with weaving histories for the other passengers, a game she'd played to pass the time ever since she was a lass sitting at the back of her father's mathematical lectures, too young to understand the subject matter which would later enthral her, for she had inherited his logical brain, so instead occupying herself by studying his students. The tiniest details were her raw materials: the type of pencil they used to take notes or the paper on which they wrote; whether a muffler was hand-knitted or silk; which young men wore starched collars and cuffs, and which wore paper; those who fell asleep because they'd spent the night revelling, and those who struggled to keep their eyes open because they worked all hours to pay for their studies.

As the coach proceeded on its journey south, this pastime kept Kirstin's eyes directed anywhere but at the far too handsome and interesting man for the most part, though several times, when she strayed, she met his studied gaze. She was used to men looking at her, admiring and lascivious in equal measure, but this man seemed interested in a different way.

Was he speculating about her reasons for making this long journey unaccompanied? Was he wondering who she'd left behind, who was waiting at the other end to meet her? No one, and no one, she could have told him. He wasn't really interested, why should he be, it was wishful thinking on her part, but she decided to indulge in it all the same, because what was the harm, when her entire life now lay before her, waiting on her choosing her path?

She had taken the bold step of quitting Edinburgh, with no ties to keep her there now that Papa had given up his long struggle with illness. She had nothing save his small legacy and her wits to live on, and only the kernel of an idea, a chance remark made by her friend Ewan, who was now so happily married to Jennifer. She'd laughed, dismissing their praise for her match-making skills, for she had never intended them to make a match, and had seen them merely as the ideal solution to each other's practical problems. Was she a fool to think that she could assist others in a similar fashion?

Her excitement gave way, as it had regularly done since she'd started planning this new life of hers, to trepidation. How was she to go about setting up such a bespoke service? With neither reputation nor references, save the unintended one she'd extracted from Ewan, how was she to persuade anyone to employ her? She closed her eyes, reminding herself of the qualities which would make her successful, reciting them like an incantation. Trepidation gave away to anticipation once more. She opened her eyes to find the handsome man staring at her brazenly and this time she responded, smiling back, because there was no harm in it, and because they'd never see each other again after today, and because it gave her the illusion that she was not completely and utterly alone.

They had crossed the border from Scotland into England well over an hour ago. It was a mere ten miles from Gretna Green to Carlisle, but the snow was falling thick and fast now, making progress excruciatingly slow. Through the draughty carriage window she could see the huge flakes melting as soon as they touched the ground, for it was not cold enough for snow to lie, though it was making a quagmire of the road, a white curtain obscuring the driver's view.

The coach hit a rut, rocked precariously, jolted forward, rocked the other way, then came to a sudden halt, catching everyone by surprise, throwing them all from their seats. Save, Kirstin noticed dazedly, the Adonis, who was wrenching the door open and leaping lithely down. Seconds later her own door was flung open and she was pulled from the chaos in the coach into a pair of strong arms.

He did not set her down immediately. He held her high against his chest, carrying her bodily away from the coach, from the plunging horses and the frightened cries of the passengers, to the side of the road. And still he held her, the snow falling thickly around them. 'Are you hurt?' he asked, frowning anxiously down at her.

Kirstin shook her head. 'No, and I'm perfectly capable of standing on my own two feet, thank you very much.'

He let her go reluctantly, it seemed to her, though her irrepressibly logical brain told her she was being foolish. His hands rested on her arms, as if she required his support, and though she was quite unshaken and perfectly capable of supporting herself, she made no move to free herself as she ought. It was possible, she discovered with some surprise, to think one thing and to do quite another. 'How soon, do you think,' she asked, 'will we be able to resume our journey?'

He shrugged his shoulders. 'Depends on the damage, but probably not till morning. Luckily we're only a short walk from the next posting house. They have rooms there—not smart, but clean enough.'

'You've stayed there before?'

'A number of times, travelling on business. Likely they'll be able to repair any damage to the coach there too, and you'll be on your way in the morning.'

'Won't you be travelling with us?'

'I'm Liverpool bound. I have a ship waiting—though it won't wait, that's the trouble. I'll have to hire a private chaise if I'm to get there in time now.'

'So you are a businessman with foreign interests,' Kirstin said, nodding with satisfaction. 'I had guessed as much.'

'Am I so transparent?'

'Only when you choose to be, I suspect. And I am, if I may be so bold, a very good reader of small clues. Your clothing, your tan, your familiarity with public transport, though I'm not sure, now I think about it, why you should be taking a coach from Edinburgh to Liverpool. Assuming you had just concluded business in the port of Leith, would it not have been quicker to go by boat?'

'Now there, your logical assumptions have let you down, I'm afraid. I had no business in Leith.'

'Oh.' Kirstin felt quite deflated. 'I was so sure— what then brought you to Edinburgh? Your accent is 'faint, but I am pretty certain it is Glaswegian, Mr—I'm sorry, I don't know your name.'

'Dunbar. It is Cameron Dunbar,' he answered, but his attention was no longer on her. He was frowning, the tension she had noticed when first he boarded the coach thinning his mouth.

'I beg your pardon if my question was unwelcome,' Kirstin said. 'I didn't mean to sound so inquisitive.'

He blinked, shook his head, returned his gaze to hers. 'It was a—a personal matter, which brought me to Edinburgh.' He forced a smile, a painful one. 'I'd rather not talk about it.'

'Of course not. I'm very sorry.' Embarrassed and at the same time disappointed, Kirstin stepped away, turning her back on Cameron Dunbar and her attention to the coach, where the remaining passengers were being helped out by the driver and the groom. 'We should go and help them, let them know that there's an inn nearby.'

'Leave them to it.' He spoke brusquely, caught her arm, then dropped it with a muttered apology. 'Excuse me. I only meant that there's no need for you to become embroiled. The coachman is more than capable. Come, I'll walk with you to the inn, then you can have your pick of the rooms before the rush.'

'Thank you, Mr Dunbar, that is very thoughtful.'

'It's not really. I'm being selfish, for it means I can have your company to myself for a little longer. I don't mean—I beg pardon, I didn't mean to presume—I only meant…'

He broke off, shaking his head, looking confused. Whatever this personal business of his had been, it had unsettled him. 'I suspect you're not quite at your normal self-assured best,' Kirstin said, tucking her hand into his arm.

'No.' She was granted a crooked smile. 'I'm not.'

'No more am I, to tell the truth. This journey to London I'm making, it's going to be the start of a whole new life for me, and there's a part of me absolutely terrified that I'll make a mess of it. Though of course,' Kirstin added hastily, 'my feelings are perfectly logical since the odds are stacked against me.'

Cameron Dunbar laughed shortly. 'Has anyone ever told you that you're a very unusual woman?'

'I think you told me so just a moment ago. Though actually what you said was that I was surprising.'

'You are both. And a very welcome distraction too, if you don't mind me saying.'

'Compliments are most welcome, just at the moment.'

They walked on in the growing gloom, through the sleet and the mud. She could not read his expression, though she sensed he was frowning. Twice, he gave the oddest little shake of his head, as if trying to cast off unwelcome thoughts. Relating to this painful personal business of his, she assumed. It seemed that beauty in a man was no more a guarantee of happiness than it was in a woman. There was, of course, no reason to assume it would be. She had not thought she could be so facile.

As they approached the welcome lights of the inn, and a dog started barking, Cameron Dunbar stopped, turning towards her. She assumed it was to bid her goodnight. He once again proved her wrong. 'Since you are in the market for compliments, I find your conversation both endearing and distracting, and I'm very much in need of distraction right now. Would it be too much of a liberty to ask you to take dinner with me?'

It would be wrong of her to dine alone with a complete stranger, she knew that. But she too was a complete stranger to him. And he was not the only one in need of distraction. 'I'd like that very much,' she said simply.

'Thank you, Mrs—Miss—I'm sorry, I haven't even asked your name.'

'It is Blair. Miss Kirstin Blair.'

Chapter Two

London, February 1819

Kirstin shook herself from her reverie. Now was categorically neither the time nor place to recollect the past. Cameron was staring at her, his brow lifted quizzically. 'I'm sorry,' she said, 'what did you ask me?'

'How should I address you?'

'Kirstin will be fine, at least while we are alone. In company—well, it very much depends on the company, and that is likely to be rather varied.'

The wintery sun streaming through the windows of Cameron's hotel suite illuminated the dark shadows under his eyes, the furrow of lines between his brows, the grooves at the sides of his mouth. His skin was drawn tight around his eyes. Pity stirred in her breast. She knew little of him, but such a successful businessman as he must be finding his helplessness difficult to endure. Another man would have blundered on, useless if determined, too proud to ask for help, but Cameron Dunbar had quickly put his own ego aside. She admired him very much for that.

Once again, the urge to touch his hand was overpowering but it was not sympathy he needed. 'We must devise a plan,' Kirstin said briskly. 'Though I do not recommend you share the details with Mrs Ferguson, you will want to reassure her that you are taking decisive action. But first, let us review what you know.'

'I know nothing more than what I've already told The Procurer, and I presume she has already passed that on to you?'

'Of course, but it is my experience, Mr Dunbar, that details often emerge in the retelling that have been overlooked.'

'Can't you bring yourself to call me Cameron?'

No, she wanted to say, because it implied an intimacy she didn't want to acknowledge. But if she refused, he'd wonder why and she didn't want him speculating. So Kirstin shrugged, as if it mattered not a whit. 'Very well, *Cameron*, let us start with your initial involvement in this matter. Mrs Ferguson wrote to you, I believe?'

'An express delivery to my main office in Glasgow. The one piece of good fortune in this whole sorry affair is that her letter found me there. I spend a great deal of my time abroad, looking after my various business concerns, though Glasgow is my home, in as much as any place is. I set off for London immediately, catching the mail coach which had delivered my letter on its return journey, but even so, it has now been over a week since Miss Ferguson disappeared with her maid from the Spaniard's Inn at Hampstead, the last stop on their journey south. Unlike me, Mrs Ferguson's preference is to travel in easy stages, and she certainly wasn't going to take the risk of crossing the heath at night. Little did she know it would have been safer to risk a highwayman than…' He cursed under his breath. '…than whatever befell the pair of them. Two young lassies with not a clue of the ways of the world. It doesn't bear thinking of.'

'Then don't, for it serves no purpose save to upset you. Let's concentrate on the cold hard facts.'

Cameron grinned. 'A woman after my own heart.'

Caught unawares, Kirstin only just bit back her answering smile. 'A woman after saving your niece's life, and that of her maid,' she said tersely. 'Recount for me now, as accurately as you can, what Mrs Ferguson told you of the events of that night.'

'She dined with Philippa in a private salon. She had a headache from the day's journey. Philippa saw her to her room and brought her a sleeping draught.'

'Did Mrs Ferguson request that she do so?'

'She did. She was in the habit of taking one every night. Apparently she is a very poor traveller. If Philippa planned to run off,' Cameron said, grimacing, 'she could easily have done so, knowing she could rely on her mother being comatose. A possibility Mrs Ferguson is all too alive to.'

'And which must be consuming her with guilt,' Kirstin said. 'If she'd been awake, she might have heard that something was afoot, yes?'

'Her exact words.'

'I will need to hear them from her own lips,' Kirstin said. 'If you are more or less a stranger to her, it's possible there are salient facts she's unwilling to reveal to you.'

'Even though it might jeopardise my chances of finding her daughter?' Cameron shook his head.

'I'm sorry, but it is vital that we are blunt with each

other—you don't know her, Mr—Cameron. She could be concealing something.'

He got to his feet to shovel a heap of fresh coals onto the fire. 'You're right, I don't know her, but I'm a fair judge of character. Her desperation to find Philippa is genuine. If she's concealing anything then she's completely unaware of the fact. Which was your point, I know,' he added ruefully. 'Very well. Item one on our list, a meeting with Mrs Ferguson. She's lodging at a friend's house—the friend is in Paris—as she regularly does, apparently, on her shopping trips to London.'

'Thank you.'

'But let me make something clear, Kirstin.' He sat down again on the sofa beside her, his knees brushing her skirts. She inched away from him, an action he noted with a sardonic lift of his brow. She'd forgotten that he was as observant as she. 'I need your help. In your areas of expertise, I will bow to your experience. That is what I'm paying for. But ultimately, I am in charge.'

She stiffened. 'I am aware that you are the client.'

He laughed, shaking his head. 'A client who trusts your professional judgement implicitly.'

'In certain areas.'

He tilted his head to one side, studying her as if he was seeing her for the first time. She stared back at him, her brow faintly raised, subjecting him to her well-practised piercing look which never failed to intimidate. Until now. 'Being given orders does not sit well with you,' he said.

'Nor you, I suspect.'

'Your suspicion would be well founded. We will work most effectively if we collaborate, but the final

decision will be mine. Those are the rules of engagement I agreed with The Procurer.'

'Then those are the rules we will abide by.'

'I am relieved to hear you say so. Have you always
worked for her? Since coming to London, I mean? You
never did tell me what your plans were, though you
told me you had some.' Cameron held up his hands.
'I know, I know, no questions.' He sighed. 'Look, this
situation might be familiar territory for you, charging
to someone's aid, taking control, doing whatever it is
you do, but I feel as if I've walked into someone else's
dream. Or nightmare, more like.'

'Thank you kindly for the compliment.'

'You know what I mean, Kirstin.'

She could tell him it was the same for her, but it was
hardly what The Procurer would call a salient fact.
Instead, she finally allowed herself, for just a fleeting second, to touch his hand. 'You realise the odds
suggest that, even if we find the girls, they may not
be unscathed.'

Cameron flinched. 'You take a very grim view of
the situation.'

'I find that it is better to err on the side of pessimism.'

'Sparing yourself the possibility of disappointment?
So you prefer to stack the odds? Isn't it against your
mathematical principles to do so?'

This time it was she who flinched. That Cameron
had recognised her was not really surprising. That he
recalled anything at all of their conversation though—
now, that was unsettling. She didn't want him to remember her, unguarded, confiding, such an aberration
of her character before and since. As to her mathemati-

cal principles, she had discovered for herself that life
was no respecter of those. 'It is not a question of disappointment, rather one of preparing to deal with the
worst,' Kirstin said.

Cameron slumped back on the sofa, looking quite
exhausted. His eyelids fluttered closed. His lashes
were coal black, shorter than hers, but thicker. Though
he had shaved this morning, there was already a bluish shadow on his chin. A lick of hair stood up from
his brow, marring the smooth perfection of his crop
and in doing so managing to make the perfection of
his countenance even more breathtaking. In repose,
his lips looked sculpted. They had been soft, the first
time he'd kissed her. Gentle. Persuasive. She had tried
other kisses since, but none compared with the memory of his, so she'd stopped trying. At her age and
in her circumstances she ought to be past wanting
any kisses. Looking at Cameron's mouth, those perfectly moulded lips, Kirstin found to her horror that
she was wrong.

She looked away hastily as he opened his eyes. 'You
are understandably weary. We will continue this conversation later, when I am settled in my own suite.' She
made to get to her feet, but he was too quick for her,
grabbing her wrist.

'I *am* tired, and the many dire possibilities regarding what fate befell Philippa and Jeannie, her maid, *are*
grim indeed. I've contemplated them, Kirstin, trust me.
But life has a way of defying the odds. I will find them.
I have to find them, because failure is not an option.
So we will keep searching until we do. Those are my
terms. Under The Procurer's rules, you are obliged to
adhere to them. Go away, unpack, think about it. And

if you aren't willing to make that commitment, then you can pack up again and go.'

Cameron closed the door on Kirstin, and immediately rang the bell. He needed strong coffee, and a good deal of it. If ever there was a time for ordered thoughts, calm thinking, it was now, and his head was all over the place. Retreating to his bedchamber, he splashed cold water over his face, automatically smoothing back the cow's lick in his hair. His face gazed back at him in the mirror as he rubbed himself dry with a towel. He looked a good five years older than his thirty-five years, thanks to the tribulations of the last week, while Kirstin seemed hardly to have aged at all since he'd first met her.

A knock on the door heralded his much needed coffee. He sat down to inhale the first cup in one scalding gulp and immediately poured another, the perfect antidote to the flowery water that passed for tea in this hotel. Though Kirstin had seemed to enjoy it, and by the way she'd oh-so-delicately sniffed the leaves, it would seem she considered herself a bit of a connoisseur. What age would she be now? Thirty-one, -two? It didn't seem possible, but he clearly remembered her telling him the night they met that she was twenty-five.

She *had* changed. She had not aged, precisely, there were no lines marring the perfection of her skin, but there was something about her, an edge to her that hadn't been there before. Experience, he supposed—though what kind? She was not married. It could not possibly be for want of being asked. More likely her very obvious desire to do no one's bidding but her own had kept her single. Bloody hell, but she was as prickly as a hedgehog. It would take a brave man to get any-where near her. She'd been very different that night. Ex-cited, anxious, elated, frightened in turn. In extremis.

As had he been, for very different reasons—emotionally battered, the hopes which had been so recently raised, quite devastated. He'd barely had a chance to come to terms with what he'd read in that letter, only to be told that there could be no coming to terms, no answers to his questions. Not ever. The future had taken on a bleakness he'd not known since child-hood. Kirstin had been like a beacon of light, smiling at him across the coach. He couldn't exactly credit her for turning his thinking around, but she'd been a respite that night, and her enthusiasm, her desire to embrace her future—yes, some of that had rubbed off on him. He'd used the memory of their moment out of time as a talisman in the months that followed. It had sustained him through some dark times.

What would she say if he told her so? She'd be too dumbfounded to say anything, most likely. They had quite literally been ships that passed in the night. She had made it very clear this afternoon that she didn't want to remember anything about it. Yet still she had come here, at The Procurer's behest, knowing she'd be meeting him. Was she simply indifferent, intent upon doing a job for which she would be handsomely rewarded? She was expensively garbed. She had done well for herself, which wasn't surprising. He'd never met any woman, before or since, quite like her. She was exactly what he needed. What's more, he was confident that she'd do exactly what she promised, everything in her power to help him. If she chose to stay.

Cameron cursed. He shouldn't have issued her with

an ultimatum, it was guaranteed to rile a woman like her, so reluctant to take orders from anyone! Yet he'd been right to say what he did, and he had the right, it was written into his contract with The Procurer. If he must have an accomplice, and he was long past the stage where he refused to acknowledge he did, then his accomplice must be wholeheartedly committed to finding Philippa and her maid. Whatever state they found them in, they *would* find them.

He poured himself the treacly residue of the coffee. There was a plate of biscuits on the tray. He bit into one, screwed up his face, coughing as he forced it down. Coconut. He couldn't think of a flavour he detested more, though he must be in a minority, judging by the small fortune he'd made importing the dried version of it in the last year. If they were using it here for the biscuits, it must be getting even more popular. He made a mental note to ask his agent to organise another shipment, then he retrieved his leather-bound notebook from the stack of business papers and set his mind to reviewing his notes. Every little detail mattered, Kirstin had said. When she returned, when she accepted his terms, as she must do, for he could not fail at this first hurdle, then he would be as well-prepared as it was possible to be. Unlike all those years ago.

December 1812, Carlisle

The snow, Cameron saw with relief, was turning to rain outside the window of the private salon. On top of everything else, missing his ship from Liverpool would be the final straw. These last few weeks, since that life-changing letter had finally reached him, having followed him halfway round the world and back again, he felt as if he'd been through the mill. And in the end it hadn't turned out to be a life-changing letter after all. Not a new chapter in his life, but a book closed for ever.

'Ach!'

It wasn't like him to be so fanciful. Leaning his head against the thick window pane, he screwed his eyes shut in an effort to block out the memory, but the words echoed in his head all the same.

You cast a blight over my childhood. You were responsible for making my father's life a misery. I don't want to see you or hear from you ever again.

It hurt. Devil take it, but it hurt. All the more because he hadn't had a clue, until he'd met her, of just how unrealistic his hopes had been. The desire to belong he'd buried so deep for so many years had resurfaced. He wasn't sure he was up to the task of digging a new and final grave for it.

'Mr Dunbar? Excuse me, but perhaps you'd rather take your dinner alone after all. You don't look like a man fit for company.'

Cameron opened his eyes, turning away from the window. Miss Kirstin Blair was hovering in the doorway, a vision of loveliness in a grey wool travelling gown, looking not at all discomfited by his obvious distress, but instead eyeing him in what he could only describe as an assessing way, as if he were some conundrum she wished to resolve.

'I've not changed my mind.'

'There's no need to be polite,' she said. 'An idiot could see that you are troubled.'

He couldn't help but laugh at this. She had a very

singular way of expressing herself. He held out his hand. 'Come away in, please. I won't pretend that I've not got a lot on my mind, but I can say in all honesty that now you're here I'll be able to forget about it for a while. I've ordered dinner. Will you take a glass of sherry while we wait for the food to arrive?'

'Thank you, I will.'

She sat herself down on one of the chairs by the fireside, stretching her boot-clad feet towards the hearth with a contented sigh. He'd known her for an extraordinary beauty from the moment he'd set eyes on her. Without her bonnet to shade her face, her cloak to conceal her figure, by the bright glare of the candelabra on the mantel Cameron could not detect a single flaw. Yet she had none of the airs of a beautiful woman, that assumption they all shared that they would be looked at and admired. He couldn't believe, however, that she was oblivious to her charms.

He handed her a glass of rather cloudy sherry, taking the seat opposite her. She inspected the drink, taking a suspicious sniff and immediately setting the glass aside.

'I would advise against it, Mr Dunbar. It is either the dregs of a keg, or the leavings of a decanter left open too long. It will be revoltingly sweet, if I am not mistaken, for the sugar has crystallised.'

'I'm sure you are right, Miss Blair,' he answered, 'but it is all they have, and I am in sore need of a drink.'

'You'll be in sore need of a restorative in the morning if you drink too much of that muck.'

'I'll take my chances. Believe me, I've drunk a great deal worse. I have not your delicate palate.'

'Obviously not.'

There was a glimmer of a smile in her eyes that brought to mind what it was that had first drawn him to her when he'd first boarded the coach. 'You prefer your sherry to match your wit, Miss Blair.'

'If you mean dry, then you are quite correct, Mr Dunbar.'

He laughed, tipping back the glass and swallowing the contents whole. It was, as she had predicted, far too sweet, and quite disgusting, but it served its purpose and warmed his gullet.

He poured himself another. 'I hope the wine I've ordered will be more to your taste.'

She raised a sceptical brow. 'Do you know anything at all about wine?'

'I ought to. I do a deal of trade in it.'

'Then I must presume your customers are not particularly discerning.'

'Aye, well, it's true. I reckon most of them prefer quantity to quality.' He settled back in his chair, making no bones about studying her. She did not flinch, she did not blush, she returned his gaze evenly. 'What are you doing, travelling alone on the public coach, may I ask?'

'You may, but I'd far rather you told me first what you *think* I'm doing?'

'By using my powers of deduction, as you did? Is that a game you like to play, Miss Blair?'

'I do, though it's usually a game I play for my own amusement.'

'Ah, now, there you've given me another clue, though a surprising one. A woman as beautiful as you cannot possibly lack company.'

'True, if I was inclined to value company because

the company valued only my face, and nature must take the credit for that.'

'A great deal of credit, if you don't mind my saying so.'

'It is simply a matter of ratio and proportion. What Luca Pacioli called *de divina proportione* and Leonardo da Vinci used to great effect. Of chin to forehead. The spacing of the eyes. The alignment of the ears with the nose. The symmetry of a profile. If any of those factors vary from the optimum, then beauty is skewed. My face has no variation, thus it is, mathematically speaking, perfectly beautiful. I hope you are not going to make the obvious mistake of assuming, however, that what is on the outside reflects what is on the inside?'

'Nor am I going to join the ranks of your admirers who, I assume, make the mistake of feigning interest in what goes on behind that perfect visage. Lovely as it is, and I will not deny that I do find you very lovely, would you believe me, Miss Blair, if I tell you that it was rather your air of—it is not aloofness exactly. I'm not sure how to put it, but you strike me as one who coolly observes, if that makes sense?'

To his astonishment, she blushed, and, judging from the way her hand flew to her cheek, she was just as astonished as he. 'My father taught me that observation and deduction are the key cornerstones of any scientific field.'

A tap at the door announced that dinner was served. As the servants set the table with steaming dishes and decanted the wine, Cameron took the opportunity to study his dinner guest. She had spoken impassively, but he was not fooled. His inadvertent compliment had touched her, and her discomfort touched a chord in him.

His own dark looks had been the source of endless whippings in his early years, an unnecessary effort to forestall any vanity taking root. Taking their lead from those who had wielded the whip, his peers had turned on him, forcing him to become tougher, to use attack as the best form of defence. As an adult, when those same dark looks had attracted a very different kind of attention from women, he'd been first incredulous and then—yes, just as Miss Kirstin Blair was now—he had resented it. No one looked beyond his appearance. Save this most surprising woman, now helping herself from the dish of mutton stew with undisguised hunger.

'Dare I ask if you wish to try the wine?' Cameron poured her a half-glass and handed it to her.

She took a cautious sip and nodded her approval. 'It is not that I am a connoisseur, as you suggested,' she said, smiling at his obvious relief, 'it is simply that I have a very sensitive palate.'

'Another gift from nature. Is there no end to her bounty?'

Miss Kirstin Blair chuckled. 'I have no talent for drawing, no ear for music and no patience for fools.'

'You can't blame nature for that.'

She considered this as she took another sip of wine. 'It is an interesting question, isn't it? How much we are formed by nature and how much we form our own nature. Would I be mathematically inclined were it not for my father? I would like to think so, but since I cannot wipe my mind clean and start afresh it is impossible to be certain. Do you take your business acumen from your own father, Mr Dunbar?'

'I doubt it,' Cameron replied shortly.

'He was not business-minded?'

'I have no idea.' Nor ever would have now. The vast wasteland that was his heritage would remain empty for ever.

Kirstin Blair was studying him above the rim of her wine glass dispassionately. 'I seem to have the knack of inadvertently touching on what you least wish to discuss,' she said. 'Though it seemed a natural enough question, given the direction of our conversation...'

He was obliged to laugh. 'As I recall, our conversation began with you asking me to tell you what I have deduced about you.'

'Yes, I did, so feel free while I help myself to some of this excellent capon.'

'Firstly, you are not afraid to defy convention, since we've already committed several social *faux pas*, two complete strangers, dining alone together.'

Her eyebrows shot up. 'Really? You think me a rebel?'

'Not exactly.' Cameron pushed his half-finished plate to one side. 'You do not, I think, set out to be different, but your combination of clear thinking and the expression of that thinking without any attempt to moderate it makes your personality even more singular than your looks.'

'Singular? That is not, I think, a compliment. It might be construed as meaning *odd*.'

'It's the unvarnished truth, just as you prefer it. Am I right?'

'You are.' She propped her chin on her hand. 'Tell me more.'

'You cannot be too much in the habit of socialising,

else this habit of yours, of speaking your mind, would have been curbed—unless you are in the habit only of socialising with similar-minded people.' Cameron frowned at this. 'Since you've told me that you take your mathematical inclinations from your father, then I wonder if he is perhaps a professor at the university in Edinburgh?'

Her half-smile faded. 'Was.'

'Oh, I'm so sorry.'

Kirstin shook her head, looking studiously down at the table to avoid his eyes. 'He had been ill for some time and died peacefully in his bed, as he wished to do, a month ago.'

She met his eyes again, almost defiantly, making Cameron think the better of offering his condolences. 'I presume,' he said instead, 'that this loss is the reason for you setting out on this new life of yours, then? You have no other ties to keep you in Edinburgh?'

Her expression softened, and he knew he'd said the right thing. 'Very good. My mother died when I was a child. I've no other kith or kin. Go on.'

But Cameron shook his head. 'I'll quit while I'm ahead, if you don't mind. Aside from guessing your age, which I'd say was three or four and twenty...'

'I'm twenty-five.'

'There, you see, I should have held my tongue. As to this new life of yours, that you're excited about and afraid of in equal parts, all I can say is that it must be something like yourself—unconventional—and nothing so predictable as a post as a governess or a teacher. Unless you've found an institution which accepts female mathematicians?'

'I did not even attempt to look. Aside from the fact

that few men believe women capable of understanding even the most rudimentary forms of logic, I do not have any formal qualifications. Being a female. It is a vicious circle.'

'Aye, I can see that it is.'

'I'll tell you the truth,' Kirstin said. 'I've no complete idea myself of what this new life of mine will be, save that it will be, as you said, unconventional. You are an excellent observer.'

'A high compliment, coming from one such as yourself.'

'Are you teasing me?'

'I wouldn't dare.'

She laughed at that. 'Beneath that very handsome exterior—and don't pretend you don't know how very handsome you are—there lurks a personality which could, I suspect, be very intimidating if you chose. I think you would dare almost anything, Cameron Dunbar.'

'Do you now?' he said, taken aback by this. 'You don't seem particularly intimidated, if I may say so.'

'No, but that is because you have not tried to intimidate me, being in need of my company to distract you.'

'And because I've taken a liking to you, let us not forget that. I've never met anyone like you.'

'The feeling is entirely mutual.'

'Do you believe in fate?'

'It is not a logical concept.'

'No, but sometimes we humans defy logic.'

Kirstin smiled at that. 'You think it was fate which brought us together today?'

'If it was mere chance, then it was a very fortunate

one. I would not have liked to miss this opportunity to get to know you, however briefly.'

'And you have,' Kirstin said, 'or do—know me, I mean—better than most of my acquaintance, even though we've barely met and are no sooner getting acquainted than we must part. It must be getting late.'

Cameron consulted his watch, exclaiming in astonishment at the hour. 'It's after ten.'

'Why haven't they been to clear the table?'

'Reluctant to interrupt us, I suppose, and plenty else to keep them occupied, looking after the rest of our coach party.'

'They will probably all be abed by now. We make an early start in the morning.' Kirstin pushed back her chair. 'We should bid each other goodnight.'

Cameron too got to his feet. 'We should, though I'm loath to do so.'

'Lest your demons return?'

'You've well and truly banished my demons. I'm much more likely to be kept awake thinking of you, if you want the honest truth.'

He hadn't meant to speak so bluntly, but the words were out before he could stop them. Yet instead of looking affronted, Kirstin widened her eyes as they met his, and in that instant the mood between them changed, became a meeting of minds subsumed by a rush of unmistakably mutual desire.

Chapter Three

London, February 1819

I will find her. I have to find her, because failure is not an option. So we will keep searching until we do. Those are my terms. Under The Procurer's rules, you are obliged to adhere to them.

Kirstin replayed Cameron's words over and over in her mind. As he had pointed out, these were The Procurer's rules of engagement—her own rules. She'd assumed they would protect her from Cameron asking awkward questions, but she hadn't counted on them working against her.

Were they too onerous? She thought back to the women who had played by those very rules over the years, women who had, by doing so, saved themselves, bought themselves independence, a new life, a fresh start. Their success had been richly rewarded, but at what cost? She had never considered this aspect of her vocation. She took account only of the facts: that the woman had the appropriate skills, a determination to succeed and too much to lose to fail.

Those had been the foundations of her own success. She had assumed those other women would be similarly driven and willing to do whatever it took, no matter the collateral damage.

Except she was now the one in the firing line. Had she demanded too much of them? Cameron had the right to keep her here until his search was successfully completed. Kirstin, staring at her unpacked portmanteau, wasn't at all convinced she could commit to that, no matter how urgent and worthy the cause.

Though there were actually two causes, she reminded herself, his and hers. If she left now, there could be no turning back, no other opportunity to know him and to use that knowledge to ratify the life she had chosen.

He had disconcerted her so far. It wasn't only that she still found him fiercely attractive, it was the man himself, so honourable, so assured, and so—so *likeable*. Dammit, he even had a sense of humour!

If only he'd been different. Arrogance, a common trait in many men as successful as Cameron, would have provoked an instant dislike. Even if he'd been less inclined to listen to her, more determined to have his own way, it would have helped. Instead, to add to all his other disconcerting qualities, he was happy to accept her advice and solicit her opinion. Though he was paying through the nose for it, she knew from past experience it did not necessarily mean he would take it. There was steel at the core of him that made it clear he would not hesitate to take control should he deem it necessary.

Which thought made her shudder, for if he knew the truth, and had the inclination to act, a man as powerful as Cameron Dunbar could easily realise her biggest fear. So he must never, ever guess the truth.

Did this mean she should leave, disappear for ever from his view, to protect her secret? And by doing so learn to live with the questions his reappearance had raised? Impossible. Kirstin sat down on the bed and undid the buttons of her spencer. She had no choice but to stay here and do what she had commanded all those other women to do.

All or nothing. It would be challenging, but when had she ever shirked a challenge? It required her to commit herself wholeheartedly, to lay aside her other responsibilities for the first time in six years. Marianne would relish the challenge of taking charge. It might even prove oddly liberating.

A knock at the door heralded the delivery of a note from Marianne. Scanning it, she smiled to herself. In the grand scheme of things this was welcome good news.

Kirstin opened her portmanteau and began to unpack.

'I have decided to stay and abide by your terms until we find Philippa and Jeannie,' Kirstin said brusquely as she took a seat once again in Cameron's sitting room an hour later.

He sat opposite her, making no effort to disguise his relief. 'Thank you. Any delay while The Procurer finds someone to replace you could prove fatal to my chances of success.'

'But what if they are never found?' she asked gently.

'I prefer to operate on the assumption that they will

be. For what it's worth, I am convinced Philippa is alive. I feel it. Here.'

Cameron put his hand over his chest. Kirstin knew where his heart was. She'd laid her cheek on his chest and listened to it as she'd watched dawn come up through the post house bedroom window, the solid, regular beat counting out the seconds and minutes until they must part. She'd thought him asleep until he'd slid his hand up her flank to cup her breast, until he'd whispered, his voice husky with passion, that there was still time for...

She dragged her mind back to the present. 'Your instincts in this case are correct.'

'What do you mean?'

She permitted herself a small smile. 'As soon as I accepted your offer I took the liberty of getting in touch with a man who, quite literally, knows where the bodies are buried in London and its environs. I have received word from Mar—my assistant that he has been in touch. There have been no suspicious deaths fitting the description of your niece and her maid. Trust me, if there had been, this gentleman would know. So we can safely assume that they are alive, for the time being.'

Cameron stared at her in astonishment. He laughed, an odd, nervous sound. He shook his head. And then a smile of blessed relief spread across his face. 'Thank you,' he said fervently.

'That does not mean—'

'I know, I know. But still.' He dragged his fingers through his hair, staring at her in something of a daze. 'It's a very positive development.'

'Yes.' She permitted herself another small smile. 'Yes, it is.'

He had taken off his coat and rolled up his sleeves. There were fresh ink stains on his fingers, though the stack of papers on the desk seemed to her undisturbed. Either he was very neat, or he had been working on something else. The fact that he was no longer tense, and seemed more relaxed to her presence, patently in charge of the situation, led her to the conclusion that the 'something else' was his notes. She was quietly pleased when he proved her correct by opening the leather-bound notebook on the table in front of him.

'I've been thinking...'

'As indeed have I,' Kirstin intervened. 'Before we proceed, I have some questions for you.'

Cameron closed his notebook on his lap, rested his arm on the back of his chair and angled himself towards her. 'Ask away.'

Kirstin took out her own notebook. 'Your half-sister, Louise Ferguson,' she began in clipped tones. 'Firstly, how did she know where to contact you, given that you'd had only one previous encounter?'

'I'm not difficult to find, Kirstin, my name is well-enough known in trade circles. She wrote to my main place of business in Glasgow, as I said, and fortunately for all concerned I was there.'

'But why you, Cameron? You are, by your own admission, a virtual stranger to her.'

'Because her husband is dead and she has no other close male relatives. Because she doesn't want anyone she knows involved. Because she knows enough of my reputation, it seems, to be sure that I have the means that she does not, to pull whatever strings are necessary. And because,' he concluded with a bitter smile, 'she was pretty certain that I'd leap at the chance to help her. As I said, and as she pointed out, I owe her.'

'You do not resent the fact that she turned to you in her time of need when she'd previously estranged herself from you?'

He had not flinched at her bald statement, but she was watching him very closely. There was the tiniest movement, an involuntary tic at the corner of his mouth. It did hurt him that the woman was using him. Of course she couldn't exactly be blamed for doing so, she was a mother in desperate fear for her child's life, but all the same it didn't cast her in a particularly favourable light. While Cameron— There could be no denying that Cameron was a very honourable man.

'I was angry, of course I was, but I can't blame her,' he said, unwittingly echoing Kirstin's own thoughts. 'She's desperate. Not only to find Philippa, but to keep her daughter's disappearance quiet. When I suggested getting the Bow Street Runners involved she almost had a fit.'

'Why? Surely publicising her daughter's disappearance would make finding her easier.'

'Aye, but it would also mean that everyone would know, and Mrs Ferguson isn't sure that either of them would recover from the scandal of it—whatever it turns out to be.'

'So she turned to you, knowing you would help, knowing that you had the means, as you call it, to do whatever was necessary, and knowing that you'd have no option but to be discreet, being unknown to any of her family and friends?'

'My desire for discretion in this matter has nothing to do with my social circle or the lack of it,' Cameron replied tersely, 'and everything to do with my desire to protect the reputation of an innocent young girl, her maid and her mother.'

'My own desire is to understand the circumstances of this case. It was not my intention to upset you.'

'You did not,' Cameron retorted. Though it was clear that she had.

'It is in the nature of these contracts that the client— in this case yourself—is forced to reveal a good deal of his life and his personal circumstances,' Kirstin continued carefully. 'Sometimes things which he would prefer to keep to himself.'

'I am aware of that, and I am doing my best to be candid with you. I am also very much aware that the obligation is not reciprocal.'

'For very sound reasons. You can have no idea of the circumstances under which my—' Kirstin broke off, astounded to detect a quiver in her voice. 'It is a very necessary term of all The Procurer's contracts,' she repeated coolly. 'My—our—The Procurer's aim is to protect the women whom she employs from judgement, from assumptions, from any sort of knowledge which could be used against them.'

'Are they always women?'

When Kirstin remained silent, Cameron rolled his eyes.

'Fine, forget I asked.'

'Yes,' she answered, surprising herself, 'The Procurer chooses always to employ women. Those in need of a blank slate, deserving of a fresh start, who have been judged and found wanting through no fault of their own. I dare say there are many men in such a situation, but it is her experience that woman have fewer opportunities to re-establish themselves.'

'I had no idea that The Procurer was a philanthropist.'

'She is not,' Kirstin snapped, confused by having confided even this much. 'In her view, women don't want charity, they simply want the opportunity to earn a second chance.'

'And you clearly agree with her?'

'Yes.'

'It's an admirable ethos. You are fortunate to work for such a like-minded woman, though I must admit I'm surprised that you work for anyone. When we first met—'

'As I recall, I was not specific at all about my plans.' She waited, allowing the silence to serve as her rebuke, before continuing. 'What was the purpose of Mrs Ferguson's trip to London?'

'To purchase her daughter's trousseau. Philippa has, I understand, made a very good match, one heartily approved of by her family.'

'And one which would be endangered if it were discovered she had run off—*if* she has run off. Has it occurred to you that the two might be connected?'

Cameron wrinkled his nose. 'That the match is to her mother's rather than to Philippa's taste? Certainly Mrs Ferguson is mighty keen on it.'

'Do you know how Philippa feels about the match?'

'Mrs Ferguson says she is perfectly content with the arrangement.'

'Though you don't know Mrs Ferguson well enough to be sure she's not either lying or in denial?'

Cameron sighed. 'You're in the right of it there. I

don't. And the lass is just seventeen, hardly old enough to know her own mind, let alone be married.'

'Perhaps she does know her own mind but has not the strength of character to defy her mother. What type of person is Mrs Ferguson?'

'You'll be meeting her in due course, would you not prefer to form your own opinion?'

'I will, but I am interested in yours.'

'Even though I hardly know her?'

'You are a good judge of character and, as a businessman, accustomed to making rapid assessments. Your powers of observation,' Kirstin said with a wry smile, 'are almost as acute as my own.'

'A high compliment indeed! Mrs Ferguson struck me as a forthright woman, not one given to outright lies, though very sure of her own opinion. If her daughter is unhappy, either with her choice of husband or with the idea of such an early marriage, then she has either said nothing to her mother or her mother has discounted her daughter's views as having less value than her own. But I'm only surmising, Kirstin.'

'It is all you can do for the present. Do you have any notion of what the girl's relationship with her mother may be?'

'Better than the relationship Mrs Ferguson had with her own mother, I hope,' Cameron retorted. Seeing Kirstin's surprise at this, he shrugged. 'Mrs Ferguson certainly cares for her daughter. Her distress, I am sure, is genuine. I'd guess the relationship is dutiful rather than loving. It could be the daughter is keeping secrets from her mother. Aye, it could easily be the case.'

'It is likely to be the case. May I ask what you meant when you said—?'

'No!'

The single word was spoken like the crack of a whip, making Kirstin flinch.

'It has no relevance to this matter.' Cameron tempered his answer. 'Now, if you have finished with your questions, I'd like to discuss my ideas on how we should proceed.'

She'd guessed from the start that he could be intimidating, but she'd had no idea until now that she would be susceptible to it. She had no clue as to how he did it, for he was not scowling, was not looming over her, it was rather that he seemed to have turned into a version of himself carved from granite.

Kirstin resisted the impulse to shiver and forced a small smile. 'Please do,' she said. 'You have my full attention.'

Cameron picked up his notebook with relief. As he recalled it had been exciting, that night they'd met, playing a guessing game of who they were and what their stories were. But now Kirstin's powers of observation and deduction, as she called them, were making him uncomfortable, and the feeling was obviously mutual. It was not surprising, given the time that had passed, that they both had secrets they didn't want to reveal. It was odd, he'd felt he'd known her that night, but the reality was, despite what had occurred between them, they were all but strangers.

'Philippa and Jeannie disappeared from the posting house overnight,' he said. 'Naturally Mrs Ferguson was distraught when she woke to find the pair of them gone. The landlord made enquiries, but no one saw them leave. He offered to contact the authorities, but Mrs

Ferguson demurred. By this time she'd calmed down and had begun to think through the consequences. Believing the disappearance would turn out to be the result of girlish foolishness, she told the landlord some tale of forgetting that alternative arrangements had been made and continued her journey, thinking that the girls would turn up themselves at the house in Mayfair, suitably repentant. Unfortunately she was wrong, and the girls did not turn up.'

'So Mrs Ferguson turned to you?'

Cameron nodded, tapping his pencil on the cover of his notebook. 'Obviously we must go to the Spaniard's Inn and make discreet enquiries ourselves, one or both of us. I've not done so yet simply because I didn't want to prejudice things—frighten someone off, or even alert them to the fact that a search is being made, making our task more difficult.'

'Yes, that was wise of you.'

'Philippa could have run off. She could have eloped. She could have been lured away by one of those dubious persons who haunt the inns on the outskirts of the city in search of innocent flesh.' Cameron winced. 'Or she could have been abducted for some other reason. I think that covers all the options.'

'I think we must also assume that, wherever they are, Philippa and her maid are together.'

Cameron shuddered. 'I sincerely hope so. It's bad enough trying to follow one trail, let alone two.'

A faint frown straightened the line of Kirstin's brows. Her eyes were intent, focused completely on him. He had a flashing memory of that same intent gaze fixed on him as she lay naked beneath him, but he pushed it ruthlessly away.

'Then a visit to the posting house is top of our list, I reckon,' Cameron said. 'I think that must take priority over anything, even your meeting with Mrs Ferguson.'

'I agree. Two young girls with no knowledge of London cannot have disappeared into thin air without assistance. Whether they planned to run off, or whether they were forced into it, someone at the posting house must have seen something.'

'So we travel there tomorrow. In what guise?'

'We'll need to think carefully about that.' Kirstin tapped the end of her pencil against her bottom lip. 'It seems to me that we have a number of questions to ask Mrs Ferguson before we can begin to eliminate any of the possibilities. Whether Philippa had another beau, for example. Or what possible reason there could be for abduction—are Mrs Ferguson's family wealthy? Is Philippa herself an heiress?'

'I don't think so, but I don't actually know.' Cameron winced. 'We can add that to the list of questions to ask Mrs Ferguson, but aside from that I'm afraid I don't know what else we can do until we've visited the Spaniard's Inn.'

'After which I hope that some of my contacts will be able to help us.'

'More of your dubious sources? You'll write to them?'

Kirstin gave a snort of laughter. 'They are not the type to commit what they know to paper. I doubt some of them even know how to write. I will contact whichever of them I think can help, and I will let you know if there is anything to report.'

'If you're going to meet them…'

'Then I must do so alone. It's not that I don't trust

you, but they will not. My contacts tend to be cagey, suspicious of strangers, and with good reason.'

'I don't want you risking your neck.'

'It's my neck, and you are paying me very well to risk it.'

'No,' Cameron said flatly. 'I'm paying you to help me, but not at any cost.'

She sighed, rolling her eyes theatrically. 'Allow me to know my business. I have been running it successfully for more than six years.'

'Running it?'

'Running my part of it.'

'For more than six years? Since you first came to London, then. You have worked for The Procurer all this time?'

'Yes. Now, if we are done here, I would like some time to order my thoughts, so if you'll excuse me.' She got to her feet.

'You'll join me for dinner?'

Kirstin looked as startled by the invitation as Cameron was in issuing it. 'I don't see that we have any more to discuss until—'

'There is the matter of how we are to set about our enquiries in Hampstead.' He hesitated. 'Though we could resolve that matter in the morning, if need be. It's not that. We're going to have to work very closely together. I thought it would be a good idea to have a companionable dinner together, that's all, but if you prefer to dine alone then please don't feel obliged to join me.'

He had the sense that she was weighing up a list of pros and cons, though her expression remained bland enough, making it impossible for him to guess which way the decision would fall until she shrugged.

'Very well, I will join you for dinner. At least I can be certain that the sherry provided by this establishment will be drinkable.'

Kirstin was not surprised to discover a note from Marianne in response to her own earlier missive, assuring her that all would be taken care of for however long she must be away, and that regular updates would be sent. Though she knew it was illogical to require reassurance, since she had been gone less than a day, she was reassured.

Feeling foolish, but unable to stop herself, she kissed the footnote before hiding the papers in the lining of her portmanteau.

Business done, Kirstin turned her mind to dressing for dinner. She had a weakness for beautiful clothes, one of the few guilty pleasures she indulged, and consequently owned a great many more gowns than she had the opportunity to wear. As The Procurer, her various toilettes were designed to be unmemorable, and though she could afford to have them beautifully made in the most expensive of fabrics they were, nevertheless, her work clothes, worn by her alter ego not her true self.

Her true self stared back at her in the mirror as she prepared to dine with Cameron, wearing a crimson evening gown that was far too elaborate for the occasion but which, now she had put it on, she could not bring herself to change.

The plain silk slip was narrow, falling straight from the high waistline, making the most of her tall, slim figure. The overdress of sarcenet had a fuller skirt, weighted down with a border of silk, adorned with a bunch of blowsy crimson silk appliqué poppies. A narrow sash was tied at the back, where the tassels were designed to swish provocatively when she walked. The scalloped edges of the décolleté were both demure and inviting against the swell of her bosom, and there were just a few inches of her upper arm showing bare between the puffed sleeves and her long white kid evening gloves. Her hair was piled high on her head in a severe arrangement which drew attention to her neck and her shoulders. She had darkened her lips with carmine, thickened her lashes with kohl.

Studying herself in the mirror with her accustomed detachment, she was satisfied with the overall result. Allowing her disguise to slip for a second, Kirstin smiled gleefully, executing a little twirl which sent her skirts and the tasselled belt whirling out. She had designed the gown herself, and as ever the discreet Madame LeClerc had brought her drawings to life with flair and French chic. It was a preposterous purchase, justified by a vague notion of wearing it to the opera, which had never been fulfilled nor was ever likely to be, but she was glad of it now. The sophisticated yet alluring woman in the mirror was utterly unlike the Kirstin Blair of six years ago.

Doubt assailed her once more. Her contrariness confused her. Her dress was provocative, but she had no wish to provoke, and certainly no intention of this dinner ending as the last one with Cameron had.

Her ruthless honesty forced her to admit that this was not entirely true. At a very base level she still desired him in a way that she'd never wanted any other man. Was the solution to indulge that passion? Was that why she had dressed herself thus? To tempt him to make love to her in the hope that it would be a failure, in the hope that she would discover her memory at fault?

With a frustrated growl, Kirstin turned away from the mirror. It was a ridiculous idea, and utterly illogical. Of course she wasn't thinking such a thing. Nor did she care, not one whit, whether Cameron found her attractive or not. She wanted to make a good impression—yes, she would admit that much, it was a reasonable enough ambition. She was wearing this gown because it flattered her, because she loved it, and because she wasn't likely to get an opportunity to wear it again soon, and there was nothing more to it than that.

'I have no idea what type of food you prefer,' Cameron said apologetically as he held Kirstin's chair out for her. 'I think I might have ordered far too much.'

'Provided you did not order porridge and bannocks, in tribute to our joint heritage, I am not particularly fussy.'

He laughed, pouring her a glass of red wine, having dismissed the servants. 'I was raised on gruel rather than porridge, and it never came with a bannock as far as I remember. May I carve you some of this guinea fowl?'

'Please.' Kirstin took a cautious sip of the wine before giving a little nod of satisfaction.

'I am pleased to see that my taste in wine meets with your approval.'

'Knowledge you must have acquired later in life, if your origins are as humble as you imply.'

'I fared no better nor any worse than everyone else in my situation.'

Kirstin helped herself to some artichokes. Her hand hovered over the dish of peas, but she decided against them with a wrinkle of her nose and instead took some of the parsley buttered carrots.

'I forgot to ask, what age is Mrs Ferguson?'

Cameron wasn't at all fooled by her casual manner. He spooned some of the disregarded peas onto his plate beside the pigeon to buy himself some time. He could tell her he didn't know, which was true—he had no idea at all of Louise's exact age—but that would only encourage Kirstin to probe further, and her probing into his past was not his notion of getting to know one another.

He cut into his pigeon, which he noted with satisfaction was cooked through. He didn't care for bloody meat, though he knew in some eyes it made him a culinary heathen, when in fact it signalled the pauper he had been, for whom meat had been a rare treat, boiled for hours to provide stock for soup, providing another meal. Some might call it thrift, for him it had kept belly from backbone.

He lifted his glass again, and found Kirstin's eyes upon him. 'You wish to know whether my half-sister is older or younger than I?'

'Older, is what I would hazard. If Philippa is seventeen, unless Mrs Ferguson was also a child bride…'

'You have guessed correctly.'

Kirstin studied him for a moment longer, making it clear that his brusque tone was noted, before forgiving the peas their wrongdoings and taking a spoonful. 'You don't wish to talk about your family.'

It was a statement, not a question, and she was right,

which irked him. 'Why don't you tell me about yours instead?'

'There is little of any note to talk about,' she answered, with a little downturned smile. 'I never knew my mother, who died when I was very young. I have no siblings, older or younger, known or unknown to me. Until I left Edinburgh I lived a singularly unexciting and somewhat secluded life.'

'Though there must have been someone, surely, an aunt, perhaps, who had a hand in raising you?'

'No—at least I suppose there must have been a nurse when I was an infant, but I have no memory of any other females save the servants. It was always just Papa and myself.'

Which explained a great deal, Cameron thought. 'So you never missed your mother?'

'One does not miss what one did not have.'

No, but it didn't stop you imagining what you were missing, and idealising it too. 'You were lucky,' he said, 'to have a father willing to take on the rearing of you on his own.'

'He was my father. He loved me.'

'The one does not follow automatically from the other. Not every man considers a bairn a blessing.'

She flinched at that. 'What about you?'

He shrugged. 'I've never wanted a wife, never mind weans. The life I lead is not one that lends itself to fatherhood, and I've no desire to change that life.'

'Would you have to change it so completely?'

'Aye, I reckon.' He smiled wryly. 'Your father and I would be in accord on this, if nothing else. If you go to the trouble of bringing a child into the world, then you've a duty to do the very best you can to take care of it. In my mind, that means being there, not disappearing off abroad for six months or a year at a time in search of new commodities and trade deals.'

Cameron picked up his wine glass, swirled the contents thoughtfully, then set it down again untouched. 'That's my life, Kirstin, and I love it. If I had to give it up I'd come to resent it, and that's the truth.'

'So you've no interest in having children?'

'I've no room for them, and no desire to make room,' he said vehemently, 'but, judging from that fierce frown you're casting in my direction, I assume you think differently.'

She started, looked momentarily confused, then made a conscious effort to smooth her brow. 'I find your honesty refreshing on a subject so many people equivocate about.'

'Maybe so, but that's not all you were thinking. Do *you* want children?'

She smiled, the Sphinx-like smile that she used, he now realised, when she had no intention of revealing a single one of her thoughts.

'I am not married and, like you, have no desire to change my single state.'

He threw back the remnants of his wine, choosing to accept the non sequitur at face value. 'It's a strange profession you've chosen, if such it can be called, though I remember you said, didn't you, that you were set on an unconventional life? It seems you've achieved that, all right. Has it proved, unlike your Edinburgh days, to be exciting?'

Kirstin, clearly as happy as he to change the subject, laughed. 'It could not be more different.' She poured herself another glass of wine, pushing the decanter across the table to him, twirling the crystal glass between her fingers. 'Is your life exciting? Trading in—? I don't even know what you trade in, save wine.'

'Spices, perfumes, precious stones, mined gold, tin and copper. Coconut. Coffee. Cocoa. Whatever there's a market for. The more exotic the better—I enjoy the challenge of being ahead of the pack in what I can supply. Although I've had my share of disasters. A Greek wine flavoured with resin called *retsina*, which I quite liked, did not go down well with the wine merchants I trade with. And my experiment with a dried spice made from the chilli plant was not very well received either—one of the men who sampled it claimed he could taste nothing else for a month.'

'I am hazarding a guess that you found this chilli spice rather tasty,' Kirstin said.

'Aye, I did, which is just as well, for I've enough of the stuff in my warehouse in Glasgow to season my food for the rest of my life and then some.'

'Did you lose a great deal of money over it?'

Cameron shrugged. 'Where's the fun in playing safe? I make far more than I lose.'

'Your ships must travel across the globe to trade in such exotic goods.'

'And I with them. Persia, Algiers, St Petersburg, Naples, Constantinople, Damascus.' Cameron grinned. 'The more exotic and the more dangerous the better, as far as I'm concerned. I'm not the type to sit in his office at the Trades Hall waiting around to see what goods are unloaded.' He laughed. 'I'd die of boredom. So, to answer your original question, my life is quite exciting. I enjoy the fact that I am my own man.'

'You are fortunate that you can be.'

'I've worked bloody hard, Kirstin, to get where I am.'

'Then that is something else we have in common.'

He studied her under the guise of taking a sip of wine. 'I reckon we've more in common than you think. Variety must be the spice of life in the work you do for The Procurer.'

She smiled at that. 'Very true, and it is one of the things I enjoy most—expecting the unexpected.'

'For me it is the thrill of the chase, closing a deal that everyone else thought impossible. Which, now I come to think of it, is what your employer claims to do, doesn't she? Make the impossible possible?'

'It is a well-founded claim.'

'I'm sure it is. You've no need to get so prickly.'

'I wasn't.'

He raised an eyebrow at this. She was forced to smile. It wasn't much of a smile, but it was enough to make him catch his breath. He'd been trying very hard not to stare at her, at the smooth, beguiling expanse of cleavage revealed by her gown, at the way the filmy fabric clung to her, the way the colour complemented the crimson of her lush lips.

She had painted them with carmine. It was a shocking thing for any lady to do here in England, though he'd seen it used to some effect in other countries. It made her seem exotic. He wondered if it was a foible of hers, or whether she'd done it for some other reason. She had made it so clear she didn't want to be reminded of that night, yet what else was he to think of now that he had allowed himself to look? Now that she was looking back at him and the air between them seemed to crackle with the memory?

The urge to touch his own lips to hers was almost

irresistible, but he could not risk losing her. Cameron pushed back his chair and rang the bell to summon a servant to clear the table. 'We still have to make plans for tomorrow.'

Kirstin got to her feet and went to the window, pushing back the curtains, leaning on the ledge to gaze out. The little tassels on the belt of her gown flicked provocatively against the curve of her bottom. For a woman so slim, he remembered she had a delightfully round bottom.

Cameron groaned inwardly. *Don't think of her bottom!*

'When I was waiting for you to arrive,' he said, 'I pictured Mrs Collins as a vicar's widow.' He tried to conjure her again, that smart, middle-aged relic of the church with faded hair. Comely. A bit wrinkled.

Kirstin turned around. Beautiful. Smooth. Her hair black as night. And her mouth curved into that cool, mocking smile that was so very deceptive, because her kisses weren't at all cool. 'Were you disappointed?'

'You were certainly not what I was expecting.' He told her what he had expected, describing the imaginary Mrs Collins in detail, in an attempt to distract himself.

It didn't work. His description amused her. And intrigued her. Her eyes sparkled. Her lips curved into a half-smile. 'It's an excellent solution.'

'What is?'

'A cover story for tomorrow, our visit to the Spaniard's Inn. The Reverend Mr Collins travelling from Scotland with his wife en route to a new life in America, stopping off in the metropolis to stay with—with...'

'The Archbishop of Canterbury?'

Kirstin burst into a peal of laughter. 'I was imagining the reverend as a man of the High Kirk.'

'A wee bit too strict and zealous even for the archbishop, you mean? A fire and brimstone man, is he, who disapproves of singing so much as a psalm?'

'And who thinks that dancing is a sin only second to fornication.'

'Oh, no, dancing is much worse, for it is done in public.'

Kirstin's lip curled. 'It would be funny were it not true. Though they are a dying breed, there are still a fair few of those hypocrites preaching, determined that we shall all be punished and go to hell for our sins, determined that no good can ever come of what they see as an evil world, full of temptation.'

There was an edge to her words that took him aback, though it also struck a chord. 'I must confess I gave up on the church at an early age, thanks to one such man.'

'Yes? I wonder if I was more or less fortunate for it to have taken more than a quarter of a century for my illusions to be shattered,' Kirstin said. 'My father's faith was of a gentle sort, but I found, in the end, that even the gentler sort will not forgive a sin which is unrepented.'

He could ask, though she would not answer, what this sin was. He had the impression that she had entrusted him with something momentous, that her doing so was some sort of challenge. It was the way she was looking at him, defying him to question her, and yet— and yet there was something else. She had surprised herself.

'I don't think our Reverend Collins is such a man,'

Cameron said gently. 'I think our Reverend Collins is a kind man who does not judge, who inspires his congregation rather than terrifies them.'

He was rewarded with a tremulous smile. 'And Mrs Collins,' Kirstin asked, 'is she a little church mouse, or...?'

'Oh, no, Euphemia is—'

'*Euphemia!* Oh, Cameron, surely not?'

He grinned. 'You don't like it?'

'Euphemia...' She considered this, biting her lip. 'Actually, I think it is perfect. She is not a church mouse, no, not at all, but a rather formidable woman, I think.'

'With a heart of gold, surely?'

She chuckled. 'And a light touch with a sponge cake. Though I beg you not to put that to the test, for I am one of those women who can burn a boiled egg.'

'Which explains your slenderness.'

'And my appetite, when faced with a repast such as you have provided tonight. For which I should have thanked you before now.'

'I merely ordered it. I didn't cook it.'

'Can you cook?'

'Yes, believe it or not, I can. I learnt through necessity, in my early days aboard ship.'

'You were a ship's cook?'

Cameron chuckled. 'I was a cabin boy.'

'From cabin boy to one of the country's leading merchants?'

'I would not say that, exactly.'

'Because you are modest. If you were not one of the country's leading merchants, you could not afford my fees.'

'The Procurer pays you well, then?'

To his surprise, Kirstin looked uncomfortable. 'Yes.'

'There's no shame in it. A man—and even a woman, in my radical opinion—should be proud to be able to make their way in the world by their own ingenuity, and you, I reckon, are particularly ingenious.'

'I will happily admit to that. I'd even go so far as to admit that we have that in common too. I am proud of having made my own way, just as you are, though I have not reached the heady heights of success you have attained.'

'I'm a man. It's much harder for a woman to excel.'

'Though very unusual for any man to recognise that fact.'

'That sounds like The Procurer talking.'

'We speak, on the whole, with one voice.' Kirstin smiled at him. 'And you and I have spoken enough for tonight, I think. It's getting late.'

'It is.' Though he didn't want her to go, didn't want to lose this cocoon which they'd somehow wrapped themselves in, of confidences and understanding. He was a man who neither needed nor sought company, but Kirstin's company was different.

'So it is settled, then. Tomorrow we will travel to the Spaniard's Inn as the Reverend Collins and his wife, Euphemia.'

'It is settled.'

Their eyes held. The air seemed to tense. He took a step towards her. His arm reached for her of its own accord. Her hand grabbed his wrist, halting him in mid-air, and he heard the sharp intake of her breath.

'Cameron.'

He had no idea what she meant. A warning? An invitation? He could not breathe. She lifted his hand to her mouth, touched his knuckles with her lips.

There was a sharp rap on the door. They sprang apart as the servant he had summoned arrived with a tray and Kirstin, looking utterly appalled, turned and fled in a flutter of red, leaving him staring down at his hand and the crimson imprint of her kiss.

Chapter Four

Kirstin slammed the door of her suite shut and turned the key before rushing towards her bedchamber, turning the key in that door too, and leaning against it, as if she were trying to keep a demon at bay, which in a way she was.

Her heart was beating wildly. Her cheeks were flushed, not only with shame but with shameful desire. Dear heavens, she couldn't believe what had happened and, even more mortifying, she couldn't believe that she was standing here wishing that it had not stopped there.

With a noise that sounded ridiculously like a child denied a longed-for treat, and completely unbecoming for a thirty-one-year-old woman, she began to undress, fumbling with the fastenings and ties that had been so cunningly designed for a female without a maid, finding them infuriatingly complicated. She had to be out of this dress, and now. A tearing sound made her curse, but she struggled on regardless. Serve her right for wearing the damned thing. Hadn't she known the effect it would have on Cameron? And hadn't she hoped it would have exactly that effect?

Tugging the gown down over her hips and stepping out of it, Kirstin cursed again. Stupid of her not to take account of the fact that it might have that same effect on her. Though it hadn't been the damned dress, had it? It had been bloody Cameron Dunbar!

'Oh, God.'

She slumped down on the bed, tugging at her hairpins. If only he hadn't looked at her like that. If only she hadn't returned that burning gaze of his. She ought to have remembered how it had been before. That look, the heat of it, and the rush, like some sort of fatal chemical surging through the brain. Desire. Every bit as fatal. It had happened that first time, and it had happened again. Though this time they had not kissed. Not like the last time...

December 1812, Carlisle

'You've well and truly banished my demons,' Cameron said. 'I'm much more likely to be kept awake thinking of you, if you want the honest truth.'

The honest truth was that she was like to do the same, Kirstin thought, though she'd never have dared speak so plainly.

Her mouth went dry. She couldn't take her eyes off him, for his words changed everything between them, turning what had been lightly flirtatious into something weightier, more dangerous. Desire. Though she'd never felt it before, she recognised it for what it was, rooting her to the spot, coursing through her blood, a dark, delicious temptation that whispered seductively in her ear that it should not be denied because the opportunity would never present itself again. She knew it was wrong, she knew it made no sense, but as she stared into Cameron's eyes and saw them darken, reflecting exactly what she was thinking, Kirstin cast caution to the four winds.

She stepped into his arms and his arms wrapped themselves tightly around her even before the distance was closed. She could hear his breathing, rasping, fast and shallow, just like hers, could see from the rigidity of his mouth, of his hands on her waist, how close to losing control he was, and it was, heaven help her, the most heady, powerful feeling, knowing that she could make him take that final step.

And so she did. One hand on his shoulder. The other hand resting on his hip. She lifted her face for his kiss, parting her lips, closing her eyes. There was a second when he resisted. And then his mouth claimed hers and she was lost. Lost without words, without reason, surrendering to the sensation of his mouth on hers, the heat between them, his tongue touching hers, setting her alight, his hand cupping her face, his fingers tugging through her hair, his other hand roving over her body, her back, her bottom, her waist, her arm, brushing the side of her breast.

She was a quivering, gasping, moaning creature, following his lead, running her fingers through his hair, feeling the roughness of it where it was short-cropped at his nape, his skin hot to her touch, and the unexpected silkiness of it where it was longer. She could feel his muscles tensing beneath his coat, under her flattened palms. She traced the line of his spine down to the indentation at the base, and as his hands curled over her bottom, pulling her tight against him, she felt her hands on the tightness of his rear and the thick, astonishingly hard length of his arousal against her belly.

She had never lost herself like this before, and sought only to lose herself further, the wanton creature that must have been dwelling inside her waiting to be released, making her nip at his bottom lip, shiver when he moaned in response, making her arch her back, pressing herself more urgently against him, through all the layers of her travelling gown and her petticoats, a primal instinct to press the insistent thrum of her own arousal against his.

He swore violently, a word she had heard only in the stables, and pushed her away.

'I did not mean—you must believe me when I tell you that I did not—do not...' He shook his head, his eyes dark, his lips swollen from their kisses. 'You'd better go to bed before we do something we'll both regret.'

'Will we?' She was already beyond regret. Her body was like a racehorse, mid-race, at full tilt towards the finishing line and unstoppable. 'Is it what you truly want, Cameron?'

'No.'

'No more do I.'

'Kirstin, do you know what you're saying?'

Her lie was instinctive. 'Yes.'

'Are you sure?'

This time there was no need to lie. 'Certain,' she said.

Hampstead, February 1819

The Spaniard's Inn, situated opposite the toll house, had reputedly once been the haunt of Dick Turpin amongst many other notorious highwaymen. Less than two hours' travel from London, it was an extremely popular posting house, for many travellers the last stop before the metropolis. The Reverend Mr Collins and his wife Euphemia arrived at a relatively quiet time, in a hired post-chaise in the middle of an unseasonably sunny morning.

Cameron was dressed in a shabby black coat patched at the elbows, with breeches, woollen stockings, heavy boots, his adopted profession's requisite neckcloth and a shallow-crowned hat bare from brushing. The outfit, acquired that morning by Kirstin at a second-hand market, exuded an odour which made him wrinkle his nose, though he did not, as she had first feared, refuse to don it, insisting only on his own linen.

The correspondingly shabby brown gown and grey jacket which she wore came from the same market, as did the oversized poke bonnet which obscured her face, and the truly hideous plaid shawl woven in what she could only describe as shades of rotting straw, which she'd draped around her shoulders. What little of her hair showed had been greyed with powder, while her face was the colour of a woman who spent much of her time outdoors, skilfully achieved with greasepaint.

As the chaise pulled up at the front of the inn, Cameron grinned. 'Are you quite ready, my dear Euphemia?'

'Indeed,' Kirstin said primly, rummaging in her cavernous bag, knitted by an unknown and highly unskilled hand in a shade which she had named seaweed. 'But you, Reverend, are not. Put these on.' She handed him a pair of pince-nez. 'And, pray, if you can, refrain from smiling.'

He put the glasses on his nose, eyeing her over the top with his brows raised. 'I thought I was to be a jovial man of the cloth.'

Kirstin couldn't repress a snort of laughter. 'Kindly, not jovial. Sober, verging on the funereal.'

Cameron put his hands together, casting both his mouth and his eyes downwards, and let out the heavy sigh of a man who had lost a sixpence and found a penny. 'Like this?'

'Much better,' Kirstin said, stifling a giggle. She produced a bible from her bag. 'Put that in your pocket. I am sure you will find an appropriate opportunity to consult it.'

'You think of everything. May I say that you look quite—quite Euphemia-like?' Cameron said. 'It requires only a scowl—ah, perfect.' He swung open the door and leapt down, turning to help her. 'What *is* that smell coming from my coat?' he asked, as she stepped onto the cobblestones beside him. 'I've been trying to put a name to it, but for the life of me cannot place it.'

'Wet dog,' she told him, making a show of straightening his waistcoat in a wifely manner as their empty chaise trundled round the corner to the stables. 'If only you would hang your coat up as I have time and again asked you to, my dear, then our hound would not have the opportunity to make his bed on it.'

She could feel him shake with laughter, but she dared not meet his eyes lest he see her own amusement. Though she had not for a moment lost sight of the reason they were here, and the urgency of their mission, she was enjoying herself, relishing the role she was playing and the playing of it alongside Cameron.

'Goliath,' he said to her as he held out his arm for her to take.

'I'm sorry?'

'The name of our hound, my dear. How can you have forgotten when you named him yourself, don't you remember? Even as a puppy he was so very large.'

'And so very smelly.'

'The disadvantage of having such a very sensitive nose, my dear Euphemia. It is to be hoped that the landlord is not similarly endowed, or he will be in no way inclined to prolong our little chat. Shall we?'

The Spaniard's Inn was a square building of three storeys with two tall chimneys and a shallow roof. The windows on the ground floor were shuttered, and those on the second adorned with window boxes which were at this time of year empty. The narrow hallway which they entered was panelled with dark wood, the bare boards scuffed and pitted. A glimpse into the taproom on the left showed a large chamber similarly panelled, empty save for two draymen propping up the bar.

'Landlord's out back, Reverend,' one of them informed Cameron. 'George!' he bellowed. 'There's a vicar here to see you. Hope you aren't going to confess to watering down your ale!'

The summons was not needed, for the landlord was already bustling down the hall, drying his hands on his apron. A tall spare man, with a thin band of grey hair which made his tonsure look like an egg rising from a scarf, he had a mournful moustache to match and would, Kirstin thought, have made an even better man of the cloth than Cameron.

'Reverend.' The landlord, assimilating Cameron's appearance with the eye of a man who made his living from such lightning assessments, sketched the shallowest of bows. 'How may I be of service?'

'Collins is the name, and you can help me with a wee cup of tea for myself and my wife, my good man,' Cameron said in a thick Glaswegian accent. 'Have you a room fit for my good lady, sir?'

'If you'll come this way, madam… Reverend Collins. I'll have my wife tend to you.'

Clearly concluding they were not worth his valuable time, the innkeeper abandoned them in a small room at the back of the inn looking over the stable yard, clad in the ubiquitous dark wood panelling. A fire smoked sulkily in the grate, above which a watercolour of the Spaniard's Inn hung.

'Dick Turpin and Bess, I presume,' Kirstin said, eyeing the one-dimensional figure on a horse depicted, pistol raised, in the foreground of this dubious masterpiece. 'Though it could just as easily be Bessie the cow he's sitting on. I've never seen such a bovine horse.'

Cameron, pulling the bible from his pocket and setting it down on the one table the room possessed, looked up at this. 'I would refrain from saying so, however. I suspect the artist must be kin to the landlord. Why else would a work of art worthy of a five-year-old be on display?'

'A five-year-old would at least have got the number of windows right,' Kirstin said, joining Cameron on the wooden bench set into the wall behind the table, which was the room's only seating. 'Even I could have done better than that.'

Opening the bible, Cameron clasped his hands together and lowered his head, as if in prayer. 'And you, by your own admission, have no talent for art.'

'No.' Kirstin eyed him curiously. 'Have you?'

'What?'

'A talent for drawing?'

'As a matter of fact I do, though I'd call myself a draughtsman rather than an artist. I like to draw maps. Not sure where I get it from. Why do you ask?'

She wished she had not, now, for it forced her to recognise what she had always known, yet never allowed herself to acknowledge. A person was made up of two halves, inheriting traits from both sides of their heritage.

'Kirstin?'

And this person, seated beside her, unlike almost every other person she encountered, had a most unnerving ability to read her thoughts.

She gave herself a shake and picked up the bible. 'Shall we pray together, my dear?'

'What for? A decent cup of tea?'

His irreverence made her smile, but the quizzical look he drew her made it clear he knew she was equivocating.

'Not that I'd know a decent cup of tea, mind,' Cameron added, showing an even greater understanding of her character by choosing not to pursue the matter, a fact that was a relief and a worry at the same time.

Fortunately for Kirstin, the landlady chose this moment to arrive with the tea, decent or otherwise. 'Reverend… Mrs Collins, I am sorry to keep you waiting,' she said, putting the tray down. 'I am Mrs Crisp. I've brought you a piece of my currant cake, but if you'd prefer something more substantial…'

'No, no, Mrs Crisp, this looks affie good,' Cameron said, getting to his feet and resuming his broad accent.

'If you can spare us a wee minute of your precious time, my wife and I would like a word.'

'You would?'

'Sit ye doon, sit ye doon. Why don't you take the second cup?' Cameron retrieved a chair from the far corner of the room and pressed the surprised Mrs Crisp into it. 'You pour, Euphemia, my dear. I'm sure this good lady will welcome the chance to get aff her feet for a moment.'

'Well. Thank you very much. May I get you an ale, or…?'

'Nae, nae. I'm fine, thank you, I'll just have a wee bit of cake. I'm right fond of cake, am I not, Euphemia? Though you'll not take it amiss, Mrs Crisp, if I tell you that my wife, in my most humble opinion, makes the very lightest of sponge cakes of anyone in all of the British Isles. The receipt is the most closely guarded secret in the parish we've left behind, but if you ask her nicely I'm sure she'll tell you.'

'Mrs Crisp is not interested in cake ingredients,' Kirstin said, biting her lip and kicking Cameron sharply under the table.

'Ah, but indeed I am,' Mrs Crisp said, taking the cup which Kirstin handed to her. 'Though I make a very good fruit cake, my own sponges often fail to rise. Do tell me, what is your secret?'

What did one make cakes with? Kirstin's mind was a complete blank. 'Why, nothing but air,' she replied.

'Air?'

'Good Scots air, Mrs Crisp,' she said firmly. 'That's the secret of a nice rise. Now, before my husband allows his stomach to make him forget his manners, I'll have him say a wee prayer.' She smiled sweetly at Cameron. 'Say grace, my dear.'

He bowed his head. He clasped his hands together. 'Grace,' Cameron said solemnly, and took a large bite of currant cake. 'Delicious, Mrs Crisp, quite delicious. I don't think we'll taste anything as good as this in the New World.'

'You are bound for America, Reverend?'

'Indeed we are, Mrs Crisp, a new congregation, a new country. We're fair excited about it.'

'Though one thing is bothering us,' Kirstin said, leaning confidentially towards the landlady. 'We've said our goodbyes to all our friends back home save one. A Mrs Ferguson. She's one of my oldest friends. I don't suppose, with so many people coming through this lovely inn, that you'd remember her? We missed each other, you see, and I'm worried that we'll miss each other again—that she'll have been and gone before we reach the city ourselves. A woman of my age, though much better dressed, she—'

'I remember her well, Mrs Collins.' Mrs Crisp looked decidedly uncomfortable. 'Did you say you are good friends with the lady?'

'Oh, aye, very good friends. The pair of us were at school the'gether.' Cameron was not the only one who could thicken his accent. Kirstin assumed a worried look. 'Don't tell me that something happened to her?'

'No, no. That is…' Mrs Crisp got up, checked the door of the parlour and came back to the table. 'I will be frank with you, Mrs Collins, Reverend Collins, my husband and I are rather at odds on this matter.'

'This matter? You are putting the wind up me, Mrs Crisp.'

'No, no. There is naught—at least that is what Mrs
Ferguson assured my husband. For myself, I would
have been inclined to call the authorities, no matter
what she said, but she would have none of it, and one
must assume that the woman knows her daughter well
enough.'

'Her daughter?'

'This is a respectable inn.' Mrs Crisp crossed her
arms over her sparse bosom. 'There are some,' she said,
her voice lowered to a whisper, 'where young women
are preyed upon, where young girls from the country
are indeed— Well, suffice it to say that the work they
are offered and the work they are given bear little resemblance to each other. You understand me, Mrs Collins, Reverend? I am sorry if I offend...'

'Och, not at all,' Cameron intervened, touching Mrs
Crisp's arm sympathetically. 'Euphemia and I have
long worked in the poorest of parishes. We are sadly
very much aware of the vices young lassies can be
drawn into. Though I do hope you are not going to tell
us that Mrs Ferguson's lass...?'

'No, no. Goodness, no. What I'm trying to tell you
is that she could not have been—nor her servant. We
are most vigilant about keeping a respectable inn and
a respectable courtyard.'

'Despite your historic associations with the highwayman standing guard over the mantel?' Cameron
said, with a perfectly pitched smile.

'Oh, that thing. My husband's mother painted that.'
Mrs Crisp returned his smile with a grim one of her
own. 'A better judge of his fellow man than Mr Crisp
there is not, but when it comes to his mother I'm afraid
he is blind.'

As is his mother, if her artwork was anything to go by, Kirstin thought irreverently, as Mrs Crisp embarked upon a clearly long-suppressed description of her mother-in-law's many failings.

'Aye, you've many a cross to bear, but if you don't mind,' Cameron interjected as the landlady drew breath, 'I'd like to return to the subject of Mrs Ferguson's daughter.'

'Ca—Caleb! You forget yourself, my dear.'

Only by the faintest tremor did Cameron betray himself. 'My wife, Mrs Crisp, only uses my given name when she wishes to castigate me. And quite rightly too, my dear,' he said, with a soulful look at Kirstin. 'I spoke out of turn. I merely know how anxious you are yourself to hear more regarding your friend.'

'A perfectly understandable sentiment,' Mrs Crisp said, 'I'm sorry to have to tell you this, Mrs Collins, but I'm afraid that your friend's daughter has run off.'

'No!' Kirstin clasped her hands together in horror. 'What do you mean? Pray, tell me quickly.'

Mrs Crisp needed no urging, pouring out a highly coloured tale, though it was one which, Kirstin noted, varied very little from what Louise Ferguson had already recounted to Cameron.

'And yet,' Kirstin said, as the woman finally came to an end, 'you say my friend decided against calling the authorities? I find that most...'

'Strange? As indeed did I, Mrs Collins. One minute she's creating a right hullabaloo, demanding that my husband question our staff as if they were not to be trusted, and the next she's changed her tune entirely, and it's all, "Oh, I think I've made a mistake"..."Oh,

I remember now, there was an arrangement!" Shall I tell you what I think?'

'Please do.'

'I think there *was* an arrangement, but it was made by the young lady herself, and her mother, though she might have had an inkling, certainly would not have been party to it.'

'You think an arrangement of a—a romantic nature, Mrs Crisp?'

'That I do, Mrs Collins, that I do.'

'But what makes you conclude that as an explanation for her disappearance rather than something more sinister? Though of course I do not doubt the respectability of your inn...'

'As indeed you should not, but I will allow it's a natural enough question. I will tell you why. It is because of Tom.'

'Tom?' Kirstin repeated blankly.

'One of the stable hands.'

'And what tale did Tom tell?' Cameron asked.

'That a man asked him to take a note to the young Scottish lady who was expected off that day's coach.'

Beside Kirstin, he stiffened, though his expression did not change. 'And did Tom do as he was bid?'

'He did, Reverend, I'm afraid to say. At least, he gave the note to the young Scottish lady's maid, and I must assume that she passed it on to her mistress—her young mistress, Miss Ferguson, I mean.'

'What did Tom suppose was the purpose of this note?'

'Tom is one of those boys who has a way with horses and not a thought for much else in his head,' Mrs Crisp retorted waspishly. 'I doubt he supposed anything much. In fact I know he did not, for when my husband questioned him, at Mrs Ferguson's behest, he never saw fit to mention the note. My husband, you see, asked only if anyone had seen either Miss Ferguson or her maid leave the inn, and Tom did not see them. He saw only the note.'

'Yet he thought to mention it to yourself—when, exactly?'

There was an edge in Cameron's voice now, that made Mrs Crisp's eyes widen. She swallowed, eyeing him less conspiratorially and with some fear. 'Reverend, you must understand Mrs Ferguson was adamant…'

'When, Mrs Crisp?'

'Two days later. Though my husband was content to let the matter drop…'

'His lips being sealed by a douceur, yes?'

'How did you—?'

'Please understand, Mrs Crisp, I am concerned only for the girls. Mrs Ferguson is a woman of some—some strength of personality. I understand that well enough,' Cameron said more gently. 'It's her way or the highway, as we say in Glasgow.'

'I've never heard that expression.' Mrs Crisp's lips twitched. 'It describes her perfectly.'

'So, although your husband let the matter drop, you were worried?' Kirstin prompted.

'The young lady seemed so nice, and the maid—well, she was cocky, as some of these girls are, when they are raised above their station, but I could see no real harm in her. A pair of country mice, that's what they were when it came down to it, and innocent as a lamb, the young lady was. I simply couldn't believe she'd run off with some man—but there, I was wrong. For when I asked around myself Tom remembered the note, and who else would be sending a note like that save a lover? So Mrs Ferguson was right after all, to try to hush the matter up. What a scandal! What that poor woman must be suffering. I don't know what would be worse, tracking the girl down before she is married or letting her marry in haste and repent at leisure.'

'You think they were headed to Gretna Green?'

'Where else?'

'Have you evidence to back that notion up, Mrs Crisp? Did one of your men actually see the carriage?'

'No.' The landlady shook her head. 'No,' she repeated, 'no one has said so.'

'But you suspect…?' Cameron said.

'But you think…?' Kirstin said.

'I think I've said more than enough. Speak to the farrier. He has been dropping all sorts of hints, in the hope of a reward, I'll wager. Whether there's any substance to his nods and his winks—well, I leave it up to you to find out.'

Mrs Crisp got to her feet. 'He's a big brute of a man, and one with a very high opinion of himself and of his worth too. He charges us well above the going rate for the work he does. Were it not for the fact that we could not do our business so well without him— There, but I've said more than enough. You are welcome to talk to him, though I doubt you'll get anywhere. I only hope that you being a man of the cloth, Reverend Collins, will prevent him taking his usual measures with those he doesn't wish to pass the time of day with. Don't say I didn't warn you.'

* * *

It was late afternoon when they arrived back at the hotel. The back stairs to which Cameron had been granted access, having duly greased the Head Porter's palm for the privilege, allowed the reverend and his wife to avoid the main reception area. His generosity had also resulted, he was pleased to note, in the arrival of a servant bearing a tray of refreshments within five minutes of their return.

Kirstin, looking genuinely grateful for the pot of revoltingly fragranced tea, sank down on the couch and poured herself a cup. 'So it is clear, from what the farrier told you,' she said, 'that the two girls were abducted.'

Cameron helped himself to coffee and dropped down into the chair opposite her, stretching out his legs in their prickly woollen stockings. 'Very clear. He saw the maid waiting across the road at the toll booth. "Yon one with hair the colour of a cock's comb," is what he said, so it must have been Jeannie. Anyway, assuming it was a lovers' tryst, the farrier kept an interested eye. It was not until the coach pulled up that he became suspicious. For a maid to have a lover with a coach and a pair struck him as unusual.'

'Though he did nothing about it,' Kirstin said, undoing her shawl and pulling off Euphemia's bonnet. The movement released a puff of powder from her hair, the grey at the front making the rest look even more midnight glossy than ever.

'There was nothing to be done at first, he claimed.' Cameron cast off the reverend's hat and loosened his necktie.

'And when poor Jeannie cried out, while she was

struggling to get away from the two men pulling her into the coach…'

'The farrier dared not intervene. He's a big brawny man, but he feared they would be armed,' he said, with a sneer as he recalled the man's initial bravado, and how easily it had been destroyed.

'If only Philippa had been as timid she would not have tried to save her maid, which is what I think must have happened.'

'Aye. That note which the landlady mentioned, the one intended for the young Scottish lass, it must have been for Jeannie, though who wrote it I have not an idea.'

'Whoever it was, Jeannie must have told Philippa, and Philippa was intrigued enough to follow her to catch a glimpse of this lover. Do you think Jeannie had a lover, Cameron? And if she did, what was he doing waiting for her at the Spaniard's Inn? If he followed her from Scotland—' Kirstin broke off with a sigh. 'It makes no sense. It is much more likely that Jeannie was meeting a relative, isn't it? Or perhaps a friend. Though why she should meet anyone in such a clandestine way…'

'Perhaps we'll get something from Mrs Ferguson when we meet with her tomorrow morning. We may have more questions than answers now, but we've made progress, of a sort. We know that what we're dealing with is definitely an abduction, and not a random one either.'

As he stretched across to set his coffee cup down on the tray, the sleeves of his second-hand coat rode up, revealing the bruised and bloody knuckle which

had, to his great satisfaction, so easily made the farrier crumble.

Kirstin gasped in surprise. 'You hit him!'

Cameron grinned. 'More than once. I find that with
some people the direct approach is much more effective.'

'I thought you wanted me to stay outside so that you
could talk with him man to man.'

'Which is exactly what I did, in his own language,'
he retorted. 'It's nothing.'

'It's not nothing.' Kirstin jumped to her feet. 'I have
some salve. Give me one moment.'

She was gone but a few minutes, bustling back in
with a small tin of something and a washcloth.

'Let me see.'

He held out his hand meekly for her inspection,
amused by her concern, but more than happy for her
to make a fuss over his grazed and swollen knuckles
if it meant her touching him.

It hadn't occurred to him that she might have misin-
terpreted his desire to talk to the farrier man to man. It
had seemed so very obvious to him from the little the
landlady said that the farrier would require roughing
over rather than coaxing or bribing with coin.

Kirstin had poured the contents of the hot water
kettle into a saucer, and was now dabbing cautiously
at his hand with the towel. 'Does that hurt?'

'No.'

'Is this your only injury?'

He chuckled. 'If I told you he'd thumped me on the
chest and that I'd a huge bruise…'

Her head whipped up. 'Cameron, you have not—
Oh, you are teasing me.'

He smiled at her. 'Do you mind?'

'I take it that the farrier came off the worse from your encounter?'

'He'll have been looking for a steak from the kitchen for his eye.'

'How revolting. A pack of ice would serve the purpose just as well.'

'It wouldn't, actually. A steak brings the swelling down much more quickly.'

'What on earth do *you* know of such things?'

Cameron shrugged. 'You don't learn to be handy with your fists without taking part in a few fights.'

'And you are? Handy with your fists, I mean?'

She was not revolted by this. Far from it, she seemed rather taken with the notion.

'Oh, very,' Cameron said airily, though the truth was he'd not had cause to hit a man for a long time, until today. But it seemed that a skill so hard-learned was not easily forgotten, and he was enjoying the effect of his toughness on Kirstin. Who'd have thought it?

'You should have seen the look on the farrier's face, when the Reverend Collins planted his fist on his jaw. *Just because I'm a man of the cloth*, I told him,' Cameron recounted in his best Glaswegian growl, '*it disnae mean that I can't take care of masel.*'

Her eyes were fixed on his. He was not imagining the flare of heat there, he was sure of it, and as he leaned towards her, she leant towards him.

'I suppose that working in such a rough parish as we did, you got into any number of fights.'

'And you, my sweet Euphemia, were always there to bind me up and kiss me better.'

The towel she'd been holding dropped onto the floor. 'I'm not so sure that Euphemia is sweet.'

'Och, but she is. She puts on a good front to the world, mind, but when they are alone Euphemia and—and...'

'Caleb,' she reminded him, with a smile that caught his breath. 'When they are alone...?'

'When they are alone...' He trailed his fingers down the line of her jaw to rest on her shoulder and she leant in, closing the tiny gap between them. 'She is the sweetest...' He kissed her brow. 'The very sweetest...' He kissed the tip of her nose. 'The very, very sweetest Euphemia you can imagine.'

He kissed her mouth. He meant it to be a simple kiss but as their lips met, and he felt the sharp intake of her breath, their lips clung, and their kiss turned into something much more complex.

She tilted her head, and her mouth opened to his, and his head whirled. There was an echo, the fleeting memory of their kisses all those years ago, and then it was gone and he was firmly in the present, drinking in the taste of her, his blood singing in his veins as their tongues touched, as their kiss deepened, as she twined her arms around his neck, as he felt the brush of her breasts against his chest, as he inhaled the odd mixture of powder and greasepaint and second-hand clothes and a feral, heated undertone that must be desire.

Blood surged to his groin as their tongues danced together, as their breaths mingled, shallow and fast, as they pressed themselves uncomfortably together on the sofa, not wanting to move lest they break the kiss, yet wanting so much more.

And then the wanting sharpened, and the kiss

ended, and they were left gazing into one another's eyes, dazed, confused, letting each other go, reality coming back slowly as they sat up, as their breathing calmed.

Kirstin picked up the towel from the floor and folded it neatly in her lap. She reached for the little tin, opened it, and started spreading salve on his knuckles, concentrating only on that, the touch of her fingers light, determinedly impersonal, and the kiss faded like a dream.

'Put some more of this on tonight, before you go to bed,' she said, letting his hand go and snapping shut the tin.

'Thank you.'

She smiled at him awkwardly. 'I feel sure Euphemia would insist on binding your knuckles, but I feel equally sure that you would resist.'

'I reckon you're right on both counts.'

'And I reckon it's time we pack Euphemia and Caleb away, before they do any more damage.'

She got to her feet, shaking out her skirts. Despite the fact that she was still more or less in costume, she was no longer Euphemia but cool Kirstin. 'You'll likely need a bath to rid yourself of the smell of wet dog, so I'll leave you to it.'

Cameron opened the door for her, but as she made to step through, he caught her wrist. 'What did we do with Goliath? He was a smelly beast, but a loyal one, I hope he's not missing us too much?'

She smiled at that. 'I doubt he's missing us at all, living the doggie dream as he is now on your cousin's farm. I think you are missing Goliath more than he is missing you.' She touched his arm lightly. 'We'll get another dog in the New World. Something smaller. And sweeter-smelling.'

And with that she whisked herself away to her own suite, leaving Cameron smiling softly, thinking to himself that a collie would be a good substitute, before the whistling of a messenger boy in the corridor brought him back to reality and he shouted after the lad to bring water for a bath as soon as it could be arranged.

Chapter Five

As she ate a solitary breakfast alone in her suite the following morning, Kirstin realised, with disbelief, that this was only her third day at the hotel, a mere five days since her assignation with Cameron in the church. So much had happened it felt like weeks had passed.

Today she would meet Louise Ferguson, the half-sister who meant so much to Cameron that he would go to the enormous expense of employing The Procurer in order to help her, and yet who meant so little to him that he had no desire to see her ever again afterwards. What form of debt did he feel he owed her, since it was clearly not financial?

She poured a second cup of tea. The curious nature of Cameron's relationship with Louise Ferguson was none of her concern, though perhaps it was indicative of his general aversion to family ties? He had been quite unequivocal on the subject over dinner two nights ago. There was no place in his life for a wife, never mind a child.

She sipped her tea. They were the words of a man

who knew himself very well, and was ruthlessly honest about what made him tick. Kirstin smiled thinly down at her empty plate and absent-mindedly began to butter another bread roll. A man after her own heart, in that sense.

But as she broke off a piece of the bread and popped it into her mouth, her smile faded. She had the proof she had sought. She had done the right thing six years ago, for all concerned, including Cameron, whose sense of honour would oblige him to do what he was not inclined to do if he ever found out. So he must never, ever find out.

For a moment, cold fear clutched at her heart, making her shiver violently, but Kirstin was not given to wild imaginings. She took a deep, calming breath. She reminded herself that she was The Procurer, the keeper of secrets, that there was no reason whatsoever to fear her secret might be discovered.

Her heart slowed. Her fingers unfurled their tight grip on the handle of her teacup. She had made the right decision. She need never question it again. The future she had planned was assured, and hers alone to shape. And so she could—not *enjoy* the situation, as such, given the circumstances, but relish it, knowing it was safe to do so.

She smiled. Now that the burden of her doubt was lifted she could admit to herself that she was not averse to spending some more time in Cameron's company. Free from other responsibilities, she could be herself, just for a while. It would be a novel experience. She would devote her energy to resolving this dreadful situation, and if, in the process, she and Cameron shared some laughter, a little danger, relished the thrill and the challenge of pitting their wits against this unknown abductor—well, then, where was the harm?

Soon enough they would go their separate ways. She might never get the chance to escape reality like this again. *Certainly not in the company of this particular man*, a little voice reminded her as she began to get dressed. But Kirstin brushed it aside, because that was precisely the point. This situation was a one-off.

She had rehearsed her argument that it would be best if she spoke to Louise Ferguson on her own, but when Kirstin tapped on the door of Cameron's suite an hour later he pre-empted her.

'I've already heard the tale straight from the horse's mouth, so to speak,' he said. 'A fresh pair of ears might pick up some undiscovered nuances.'

It was exactly what Kirstin had been about to say herself. From the moment Cameron had been forced to confide in her through the grille of the confessional he had placed Philippa's safe return above all else, but it struck her afresh how few men in his situation would have confidence enough in their own judgement, and indeed in hers, to delegate such a crucial task.

'I agree,' she answered, 'and I very much appreciate your sparing me the need to say so.'

He was sipping one of his endless cups of coffee, his gaze fixed firmly on her. It made her edgy, the way he looked at her as if he was reading her every thought, even though she knew that was preposterous. She would not think about that kiss yesterday. She would not allow a kiss to make things awkward between them, especially when it had been Euphemia and Caleb who had been doing the kissing, not Kirstin and Cameron.

'I am also hopeful that Mrs Ferguson may feel she can confide in a woman more easily than a man,' Kirstin said, trying to keep her mind fixed firmly on business.

To her relief, Cameron nodded, dropping his gaze. 'She knows why I've engaged your services. I won't deny she was dubious at first, terrified that you'd be indiscreet, but she made her own enquiries into The Procurer's reputation and seems reassured. It also helps that you come bearing the good news that Philippa is still alive.'

'As far as we know. I cannot give her any false hope.'

'Though you will not paint the picture blacker than necessary? She is a mother, and her only child—'

'I understand perfectly, I assure you—' Kirstin cut herself short, curling her fingers into her palm. 'I will not alarm her any more than absolutely necessary,' she said calmly, unfurling her fingers before Cameron could notice.

Louise Ferguson received Kirstin in the drawing room of her temporary residence in Mayfair. She was the kind of woman for whom the epithet *well-groomed* might have been invented. Tall, austere, in a grey-striped day gown. Kirstin could initially spot no resemblance to Cameron in her wide-spaced hazel eyes, fierce brows and rather prominent nose. It was the sensual mouth and the dimple in the centre of her chin which betrayed their common ancestry, as did the thick black hair which she wore in a complicated coiffure high on her head.

She rose slowly to her feet when the decrepit retainer announced Miss Blair, greeting Kirstin with a look which mingled surprise with trepidation. 'You will take tea,' she said, in a voice which brooked no dissent.

'Thank you.'

Kirstin took her seat on the opposite side of the table by the fire. The other woman's eyes were tinged with red under her skilfully applied powder. She had worried away at the skin at the side of her right thumb to the point where it was bleeding.

'I am pleased to report that your daughter,' Kirstin said without preamble, as her hostess began the process of pouring and measuring, 'is, if not safe, at least still alive, according to my sources.'

Louise Ferguson gave a little gasp, dropping the silver measuring spoon. 'How do you know? Are you sure?'

'I am afraid I can't tell you how I know, but I am as certain as it is possible to be. Philippa and Jeannie have not met an untimely death.'

Louise Ferguson's chest heaved. She clasped her hands tightly together, tilting her head back, widening her eyes, but tears tracked down her cheeks untrammelled.

Kirstin watched helplessly as the woman tried to regain her composure, resisting the impulse to intervene, recognising in the compulsive swallowing, the shuddering breaths, the lips drawn tight into a grimace, all the signs of an iron will tested to its limits.

She knew implicitly, for she would have felt the very same herself, that Louise Ferguson would not appreciate sympathy. Accordingly, she busied herself with the making of the tea, noting with approval that the leaves were of excellent quality. Silently, she pushed a brewed cup across the table when, with a last shuddering breath, Louise Ferguson gave a little nod, dabbed her cheeks, and wetted her lips.

'Forgive me,' she said.

'A perfectly understandable reaction. Take some tea.'

The woman did as Kirstin bade her, adding a soupçon of milk with a relatively steady hand and sipping gratefully. Her cheeks remained pale, but the taut lines of her face softened as she nodded, accepting a second cup.

'Assuming that Mr Dunbar has explained the circumstances of my daughter's disappearance, Miss Blair, you will understand why I must shoulder the blame.'

'You certainly are partially culpable.'

A gasp and a small splutter of laughter greeted this remark. 'You do not mince your words.'

'You strike me as someone who, like myself, prefers her truth unvarnished,' Kirstin replied coolly. 'If you had not taken a sleeping draught Philippa would not have found it so easy to sneak out of the inn. Whether she would still have done so had you been awake or sleeping lightly is another matter, and a futile source of speculation. We cannot change what has happened. We can only aspire to repair the damage and get your daughter and her maid back safely.'

Such blunt talking might easily have estranged her from Louise Ferguson and destroyed any chance that Kirstin had of gaining her confidence, but since nothing could assuage maternal guilt, no matter how irrational, what Philippa's mother needed most was to feel that she was contributing to finding her daughter.

Kirstin was relieved to see that her strategy was the correct one. Louise Ferguson straightened her shoulders, clasped her hands on her lap and took a deep breath. 'What can I do to help, Miss Blair?'

'Please, call me Kirstin. May I call you Louise?' She waited for the other woman's assent before continuing. 'Now, tell me exactly what happened that night, omitting no detail, no matter how trivial or irrelevant you think it may be.'

'So you see,' Louise concluded, 'whichever way you look at it, I deserve a large portion of blame. I knew that Philippa was not nearly so keen on the marriage as I was, but I was certain that I knew what was best for her. She was, quite naturally, given her tender years, a little anxious about swapping the protection of a parent for a husband, but as I explained to her numerous times, it is the most natural thing in the world and has served society well for generations. I thought she had come to accept it. She was so excited about coming to London, about having a whole new wardrobe of gowns. But clearly I underestimated the strength of my own daughter's resistance.'

'You seem very certain that Philippa has run off to avoid an unwanted marriage.'

'It is the obvious conclusion, given the facts.'

'Your brother and I—'

'Half-brother.'

Which intervention told its own tale, and made Kirstin resentful on Cameron's behalf. But that was another irrelevance, for the moment.

'However you wish to refer to him, the point is that we paid a visit to the Spaniard's Inn yesterday, where a number of new facts emerged which change things somewhat.'

She proceeded to recount the salient details of what they had discovered. The effect on Louise was momentous.

'Philippa did not abscond? You are certain of this?'

'Completely.'

'That—that *blasted* Jeannie!' Louise jumped to her feet, wringing her hands. 'That pert chit wields far too much influence over my daughter.'

Perhaps because, Kirstin thought, Philippa had been starved of any other influence save her mother in her young life. She had never attended school, and seemed to have no friends of her own choosing, reading between the lines of all that Kirstin had heard today. She didn't question Louise Ferguson's love for her daughter, but it was clear that her certainty that she knew what was best might feel suffocating.

Kirstin's own conscience pricked her. Wasn't *she* just as guilty of such certainty? She dismissed this ruthlessly. The circumstances were radically different.

'Louise,' she said carefully, 'can't you see that Philippa acted with the purest of motives, from a desire to protect her maid, who is also her friend, without thinking of her own safety?'

'Would that she had thought first, we would not be—'

'But we are in this situation,' Kirstin said firmly. 'And now we must try to remedy it. It seems reasonable to me to assume that the note Jeannie received was not from a lover—unless some man followed her south from Scotland?'

'No, that does not make sense,' Louise said, frowning. 'She has been walking out with my neighbour's second footman for a few months now. It's a respectable match, and one that I understand from Philippa they are eager to formalise as soon as possible, much to my daughter's chagrin. Jeannie will most likely not be her maid once she is married.'

Louise set her cup aside. 'I've informed Kenneth— that is Philippa's betrothed—that Philippa has been somewhat under the weather and cannot write, in case you were wondering. Heaven forfend that I should force her into a marriage she truly does not want, but nor do I wish to close down the option should she change her mind. It is an excellent match. No matter what you think of me, I only…'

Louise's voice trembled. Kirstin allowed herself to touch her hand in sympathy. 'I am here to help you, not to judge you. If you could concentrate on what else you know about Jeannie, any connection at all with London…'

Kirstin sat quite still, her face a careful blank as Louise did so. Following a series of frowns, nods, and little shakes of the head, she finally looked up. 'Heather,' she said triumphantly. 'Heather Aitken.'

'Who the devil is Heather Aitken?' Cameron demanded, as Kirstin recounted her conversation with Louise some hours later.

'According to Louise, another cocky chit of a maid with ideas above her station. She and Jeannie started work for the Ferguson family on the same day. They are the same age, and bosom buddies, it seems. Heather had not the patience to gain the experience that would earn her promotion, so about a year ago she left Edinburgh for London. "In this city, demand is such that any servant, no matter how lazy, may easily be elevated"— I use Mrs Ferguson's own words here, you understand.'

'And she thinks that this Heather Aitken and Jeannie might have kept in touch?' Cameron said eagerly. 'Does she know where we might find her?'

'I'm afraid not, but that is of no consequence. If she is in London, I will track her down easily enough.'

He looked suitably impressed. She treated him to The Procurer's trademark enigmatic smile, hiding the absurd little rush of pride his admiration gave rise to. She didn't need anyone to tell her how good she was at what she did, her reputation spoke for her. There had, over the years, been grateful letters thanking her, but she never permitted her clients or the women she matched with them to meet her once a contract was completed.

All the same, it was pleasant—very pleasant—to have her unique set of skills acknowledged face-to-face, as it were. Provided she did not become complacent or, worse, vain! And provided she remembered that this particular situation was unique and could never be repeated, for it contravened all The Procurer's well-established rules.

'Heather Aitken is, according to Louise, an ambitious young woman,' Kirstin said brusquely, dragging her eyes away from Cameron's answering smile. 'She will have set her sights on what is known as a superior household, and one therefore likely to use a well-established and respected employment agency.

That will be my starting point. The world of domestic service is a close-knit one, even in a city as large as London. I have already set enquiries in motion.'

'How long…?'

'Impossible to say, but a day…two at the very most. My assistant is aware of the urgency of the matter, I assure you, and is making use of every resource at my disposal.'

'And there is nothing more to be done in the interim?'

'I don't think so,' Kirstin replied. 'This is our best— our only—lead.'

'I'm impressed with your efficiency. I take it, then, that you arranged all this with your assistant immediately after your visit to Mrs Ferguson? Presumably you have an office nearby?'

Cameron's tone was offhand, but Kirstin was not going to fall into the trap of revealing any details of her business. Many had tried to discover them and failed in the past.

'Until we can speak to Heather I'm afraid there seems to me very little else we can do to progress matters, other than have someone interview this under-footman whom Louise says is courting Jeannie.'

'Leave that with me. You are not the only one with contacts. What's more, mine happen to be in the right part of the country. I'll have an express sent to one of my men in Glasgow. I know it will take time,' he added as she opened her mouth to protest, 'but we can't leave any stone unturned. He's just the man for the job. His name is Tommy Devine. I have known him since we were boys. You could say he is the closest thing I have to a brother. We went our separate ways for a wee while, for he has no head for figures and was sent to work in a shipyard while I was learning to be a ledger clerk. But when I went into business for myself I sought him out, and he's been my right-hand man ever since. Is there anything else you'd like to know about him?'

'I only need to know that he has your trust and complete confidence,' Kirstin said stiffly.

'I'm offering you the opportunity to indulge your curiosity about me without needing to reciprocate.'

'I know you are. It's very magnanimous of you. Is this Tommy Devine taking care of business, then, while you are here?'

'As much as I allow him to,' Cameron answered wryly. 'It's not that I don't trust his judgement, I simply prefer to make my own decisions.'

'Now, that is something I do understand. When one has grown a business from the start, nurtured it, cared for it, it is very natural, I think, to be protective of it.'

'Is that how you feel?'

'I can't discuss business. The Procurer—'

'It's you I'm interested in, not The Procurer,' Cameron snapped, the teasing light fading from his eyes. 'Is that such a crime?'

Kirstin shook her head, feeling like a hypocrite. When Louise, highly relieved to have been able to be of some assistance in finding her daughter, had become voluble over a luncheon of smoked salmon and eggs scrambled with cream and chives, Kirstin had encouraged her to talk, telling herself that everything she could discover of the girl's home life was potentially of value. Once the subject of Philippa's short and rather mundane life had been exhausted Louise had turned to her own life, and it would have been so easy, by way of some skilfully placed questions, to lead her on to the subject of Cameron. Kirstin had resisted, but it had been a very close call.

She had tried, but had not been able to persuade herself that his history had any bearing on the case, though the fact that she had tried to twist the facts to satisfy her curiosity appalled her.

The question was, what to do about it? She could keep quiet, but her innate honesty made that option repellent. Guilt and shame made her want to hang her head, but she forced herself to look him straight in the eye. 'No, it's not a crime, Cameron, especially when I cannot deny my own curiosity regarding you. I have to confess that I came very close to encouraging Louise to talk about you over luncheon.'

He stiffened. 'It would have been a futile exercise. Mrs Ferguson knows next to nothing about me.'

'Precisely.' Colour had flooded her cheeks. Now she felt it fade just as quickly. 'I wanted to understand how it is that you and your half-sister are strangers to one another.'

'The one topic on which I was not forthcoming,' Cameron said. 'It didn't occur to you that it is a chapter of my history I wish to keep private?'

'I have no excuse to offer.'

In fact she had one very valid excuse, but she would not use it, even to salve her own conscience. The questions she had almost asked had been to satisfy her own curiosity, and for no other reason. Cameron remained silent, giving her no clue as to his thoughts.

'I am deeply sorry,' Kirstin continued, striving to recapture her usual cool, professional tone. 'You may be assured that I will make no further intrusions into your personal affairs.'

He smiled faintly down at her then, shaking his head before touching her cheek lightly. 'Don't be so hard on yourself. You didn't pry when you could have. Anyway, I'm flattered.' Seeing her confusion, he broadened his smile. 'It proves that I intrigue you enough to make you interested in me. Which I suspect makes me an exception.'

Kirstin blinked up at him. 'You are an exception to almost every rule. But that does not mean I have any desire to—'

'But you do, don't you?'

He slid his fingers in a deliberately sensual movement up her arm, to rest on the bare skin at the nape of her neck. Though she tried to ignore it, she couldn't disguise her shiver of response.

'More than six years since that night,' Cameron said, 'and our desire for one another is every bit as powerful. You, who take such pride in being honest with yourself, should admit that much. But it's the only thing that's unchanged. We didn't know each other then. We barely know each other better now. We are both very different people.' He dropped his hand, stepping away from her. 'Till tomorrow, Kirstin...'

December 1812, Carlisle

Though Kirstin's kisses made his head spin, made his body thrum with desire, Cameron reluctantly tore his mouth from hers. 'You'd better retire to your room before we do something we'll both regret.'

'Will we?'

Her lips were swollen with his kisses. In the candle-light, it seemed to him that her eyes burned with the same desire which made him ache with wanting.

'Is it what you truly want, Cameron?'

He could not lie to her. 'No.'

'No more do I,' she said softly.

His mind was befuddled. Her words were so confident, seemingly so at odds with her experience—or lack of it. Had he misjudged her?

'Kirstin, do you know what you're saying?'

Her gaze did not falter from his. 'Yes.'

Yet still he sought further assurance. 'Are you absolutely sure?'

'Certain.'

She spoke with such confidence his conscience was salved. With a groan, Cameron pulled her into his arms again, kissing her deeply. She responded without hesitation, pressing her body against his, twining her arms around his neck, opening her mouth. Their tongues touched, sending such a flame of desire through him that he stopped thinking, surrendering completely to the frantic urging of their bodies.

He had no idea how they reached her bedchamber, but as she closed the door, locked it, he asked once more, his voice hoarse and ragged, if she was certain she wanted this.

She laughed, a guttural, sensual sound that made the hairs on his neck stand on end and made his already throbbing shaft achingly hard.

'Far more than you, by the sounds of it.'

The challenge implicit in her words stripped him of the last vestige of self-control. He pulled her back into his arms, tight against him, leaving her in no doubt of the strength of his arousal.

'That's not possible.'

Kisses gave way to touch. Hands frantic, tearing at clothing, eager to find skin. His mouth on the hollow at the base of her throat, tasting the warm, feminine scent of her, while he undid the fastenings of her gown, sliding it down her arms, letting it drop to the floor, revealing her slim body sheathed in clinging undergarments.

The swell of her breasts above her corset and chemise made him catch his breath. He traced the shape of them with his tongue and his hands, then the delightful dip to her waist, the even more delightful shape of her bottom, her shallow breathing, her soft moans, rousing him further, urging him on.

She fell back onto the bed, pulling him with her. Her hands roved over his shoulders, his back, under his shirt, tugging it free from his breeches. He yanked himself free of it, eager for the sensation of skin touching skin, her eyes feasting on his body in an echo of the way he drank in hers, her hands echoing his touch.

Loosening her stays, the ribbon at the neck of her chemise, his mouth found the hard peak of her nipple. She arched under him as he sucked and licked, and he slid his hand up her leg, finding the opening in her pantaloons, the warm, soft flesh of her inner thighs and the damp, soft curls covering her sex.

She stilled under him for just a moment, but even as he hesitated in response she pulled him down towards her again, her lips meeting his in a drugging kiss. He stroked his way inside her, the wet, hot, tightness of her making his erection pulse and throb in anticipation. She was moaning beneath him, her body bucking under him as he stroked her to her climax.

This was no time for finesse, and he had no wish to delay completion for either of them. Her hands grabbed fistfuls of the bedcovers, her eyes closed as she came. The sight of her, unravelled and ecstatic under him, almost sent him over the edge. He kicked himself free of his boots and breeches...

London, February 1819

Cameron groaned, running his fingers through his hair. Why was he tormenting himself with the memory of that night? He poured himself a glass of port, wrinkling his nose at the cloying sweetness of it as he knocked it back in one draught. What he needed was a wee nip of whisky, but here in the south they considered the *uisge beatha* gut-rot, comparable to cheap gin, the tipple of the great unwashed.

Doubtless a great many of them would consider *him* a product of the great unwashed. There had been a time, way back, when he'd been trying to prove himself, when he'd have agreed with them. It made him smile now, the memory of those days, when the height of his ambition had been to return in triumph to Garrioch House, to parade the trappings of his success in front of those who'd been determined he was doomed to be a failure. He never had, thank God, realising just in time, on the eve of his planned visit, that the only person he needed to prove himself to was himself.

Cameron sighed, went to pour himself another glass of port then thought better of it. He didn't need to prove anything to Kirstin either, but he did want her to—to *understand* him, he supposed, with a wry smile. To know what made him who he was rather than rely on assumptions. He never talked of the past, and if Kirstin had asked him outright he *would* most likely have blanked her, but in time…

Time. Aye, and there was the rub. If he was to get to know Kirstin at all he'd need time they didn't have. And he did want to get to know her. Now she'd walked back into his life, he wanted to know if there was more to whatever it was that drew the pair of them together than mutual physical desire.

It had been a while since he'd been interested in a woman, physically or otherwise. Too long, now he came to think of it. There had been a fair few women in his life, and there could have been a lot more if he'd been so inclined. For some reason the fairer sex had always liked his dark looks, and his allure only increased when it was supplemented by his success and personal wealth. Trouble was, he'd become bored with their attention. None of those women seemed interested in who he was beyond good looks and affluence.

Frowning out at the twinkling lights of the city, he tried to recall his last affaire, and was startled to discover that it had been at least a year ago, more like two. He'd been starting to believe himself past caring, that his business provided all the stimulation he needed, but Kirstin was proof that his appetites had merely been dulled, not extinguished.

Kirstin, who wasn't a whit interested in his looks, but who was, against her will, it seemed, interested in his life. She baffled him. If she'd wanted to forget that one night, why had she taken on the task of helping him find Philippa? It was all very well for her to claim

that she was the best person to help him—and likely
she was—but she had *chosen* herself for the role, for
not even The Procurer could have coerced her. So why
elect to meet him again, and then pretend that it was
nothing more than coincidence?

Leaning his head on the window pane, Cameron
closed his eyes. It wasn't that he'd been pining away
for her for six years. He'd thought of her, but that night
had, even at the time, seemed like a dream, the pair of
them characters in some romantic drama, not real. He
wasn't daft enough to think that Kirstin epitomised
his perfect woman, and anyway, she was no more the
same person she'd been six years ago than he was. But
there was still something between them, and she knew
it too, no matter how much she might want to deny it.
They were two of a kind. Like drawn to like.

Well, one thing he'd always enjoyed was a challenge, and one thing he'd always been was persistent.
He would take a trip to the docks tomorrow, see what
was coming in, what was in demand. That way he
wouldn't feel his day was wasted. And he'd ask her
along. Show her a bit of his world and tell her where he
came from, see if he could get her talking a bit about
her own background.

With a satisfied nod, Cameron selected a sheet of
writing paper and dipped a pen in the ink. He had an
express to send to Glasgow.

Chapter Six

When she received Cameron's note early the next morning, Kirstin had barely started breakfast. He had decided to take an impromptu trip out to the docks, the missive informed her, and wondered if she would like to accompany him. Surprised and delighted to be able to escape the confines of the hotel, and for a reason entirely unconnected to their sombre task, she hurriedly finished her toilette, donning a full-length pelisse of crimson velvet braided with black, matching bonnet, black half-boots, and black gloves. A quick glance through the window revealed a winter sky the colour of pewter, and sent her back to the wardrobe for her black velvet muff before she hurried out of her suite.

'I reckoned we could both do with a diversion,' Cameron told her when he joined her in the hotel lobby, 'while we wait for Heather Aitken to be located. It's as good an excuse as any to take the pulse of London's current import market.'

He was dressed for the elements in a greatcoat and beaver hat. 'Ready?'

Pulling on his gloves, he made for the front door of

the hotel, but when she stopped at the kerb, expecting him to summon a hackney, he shook his head. 'We'll walk down to the river, take a skiff from there.'

Though he was making an effort to slow his pace for her, she struggled to keep up with him as he led the way unerringly towards the river through St James's Park to Westminster Bridge, unable to disguise the fact that she was considerably out of breath when they arrived.

Cameron eyed her with some amusement.

'A lady, even one in my profession, is seldom called upon to run,' Kirstin said defensively.

He laughed. 'I've never run from anyone or anything in my life. I learnt very early in life never to turn my back on a fight.'

He turned away from her to the riverside steps, where a small skiff was waiting. He conferred briefly with the grizzled old salt in charge, before holding out his hand to help her. 'Be careful, the steps are slippery.'

Seeing her settled as comfortably as it was possible to be on the narrow seat in the stern, Cameron cast off, rock-steady despite the violent pitching of the small boat as their oarsman steered the boat out into the Thames.

'Why did you have to learn to fight so early in life?' Kirstin asked, as he settled beside her.

'I grew up in a place called Garrioch House, in the east end of Glasgow. It's a home for foundlings.'

It took a great deal to surprise her, but this admission made her jaw drop. 'Foundlings! But Louise—'

Cameron put a finger to her lips. 'Let's just enjoy the river trip.'

The sky was lowering. The surprising speed at

which the little craft travelled made the hull lift out of the water then descend with a dull thud, and sent an icy spray into the air.

'*Enjoyable* would not be my first choice of adjective,' Kirstin said, as the boat crested another wave and would have jolted her out of her seat had Cameron not put his arm around her, smiling down at her as he anchored her against the shelter of his shoulder.

'I always think you see a city in a whole different light from the water. Stop thinking about whether you're going to lose your breakfast and look around you.'

'Fortunately, I did not get the chance to eat breakfast,' she answered, trying to do as he suggested.

It *was* an odd way to see the city she knew so well towering above her, for the tide was very low. As they rounded a bend of the Thames, Somerset House came into view, and behind it the crowded district of Drury Lane could just be glimpsed. On the south side the buildings seemed an unstructured mass, a warren of lower-lying houses, wharves and offices contrasting with the more elegant architecture of the north bank and its plethora of church spires. There was the vivid green square of Temple Gardens, while all seemed brown on the other side, and though it must be a figment of her imagination even the air seemed gloomier, the chimneys belching blacker smoke.

The river itself was alive with traffic, from the smallest of rowing boats to skiffs like the one in which they travelled and bigger craft, all vying for space, their oarsmen calling to each other, their passengers too and even, in one passing yacht, a dog yapping in the prow.

'It is busier than Bond Street.' Turning, Kirstin

found Cameron watching her. 'How is it that there are not more accidents?'

'There are too many as it is,' their oarsman interjected gruffly, glancing briefly over his shoulder. 'Young fools who don't know the tides, old lags who forget they're not as strong as they used to be, and rich fools, too drunk or in too much of a hurry to realise that the river has no respect for money or bloodline. But you're safe enough with me. I was born with the Thames flowing in my veins. You'll excuse me now, though, I need to concentrate. We're coming up to Blackfriars.'

The bridge spans seemed impossibly crowded but they negotiated their way through safely. St Paul's Cathedral loomed on the left-hand side, and on the right Southwark Priory. As the narrow, irregular arches of London Bridge came into view the skiff veered towards the north bank and Cameron got to his feet, ready to tie the rope to the iron ring on the wall by the foot of the stairs.

'It's far too risky to go any further downstream,' he explained, helping Kirstin out. 'The tide makes running under the spans of the bridge extremely dangerous.'

After tipping their oarsman, who was already negotiating a fee with someone looking to make the journey back to Westminster, he tucked Kirstin's arm in his. 'Stay close, and if you've a purse on you guard it well.'

It was on the tip of her tongue to tell him that she had been in every dodgy district that he could dream of when she took a quick look around her and changed her mind. She thought of London, high *and* low society, as her world, but this environment was quite alien to her.

'I've never been here,' she said, gazing in awe at the mass of sailing ships jostling for space, tied up two, three abreast.

'It's known as the Pool,' Cameron told her. 'Every cargo must dock here to be inspected by the Excise men.'

'Thieving and pilfering must be rife here, given the temptation,' Kirstin said, looking askance at the rows of open warehouses, the stacks of goods waiting on the quayside to be moved. 'Is it similar at your wharves in Glasgow?'

'Smaller scale, but aside from that not much different. I've found that if you pay your men a fair wage temptation tends to be easier to resist.'

Kirstin chuckled. 'Don't bite the hand that feeds you? A shrewd tactic. I would expect no less from you.'

'Come, let's take a walk around, see what imports are doing well.'

They made their way towards the busiest part of the docks, past the Tower, weaving along quays and wharves, Cameron stopping every now and then to exchange words with a stevedore, with ships' crew and even with an Excise man.

He adapted seamlessly, Kirstin noticed, to each man, his manner, his speech and his accent modulated for each conversation, not enough to appear condescending but sufficient to gain respect. She was impressed, the more so for recognising the same chameleon-like technique she used herself. Though she was content to remain in the background and simply to observe, there was never a moment when Cameron was not aware of her, keeping a careful eye, watching her for signs of boredom.

The Procurer, she knew, was sometimes called The Sphinx. Cameron was the first person she had ever known who could read her most inscrutable expression. It was disconcerting, and made her at times deeply uncomfortable, yet today she felt it bound them, and she rather liked the novelty of it.

They wove their way along the docks towards Wapping, where Cameron steered them towards the large river basin.

'I had a brief acquaintance with this district of London last year,' Kirstin confided with a shudder. 'One of the few commissions which I regret taking on.'

'Because you failed?'

'No, but I will admit,' she said with a wry smile, 'that it was a close-run thing.' She surprised herself then, perhaps because Cameron did not press her, by telling him a little of the difficult nature of the case.

'What happened to the young woman?' he asked.

'I have no idea.'

His obvious astonishment made her hackles rise.

'Such women sign up for the opportunity to make a fresh start for themselves,' Kirstin said, unable to keep the defensive note from her voice. 'It is up to them what they make of it.'

'But aren't you curious?'

'I know, because The Procurer pays her fees promptly, that they have succeeded. I have no desire to know anything else.'

'If it was me,' he said, 'I'd want to know.'

'Well, I'm not you,' Kirstin said.

But he had once again made her uncomfortable by seeming to read her thoughts, since she *had* been wondering, since taking on this role herself, about those other women. What good would it do, though, to seek them out?

'What is that building?' she asked, pointing at the large edifice looming up in front of them, taking up most of one side of the massive, obviously recently created square dock.

'Tobacco Dock,' Cameron answered, his look telling her he was perfectly well aware that she was changing the subject. 'These are the warehouses for storing tobacco—as you can see from the size of them it's a very profitable trade, though not so much as a few decades ago. There was a time in Glasgow when the traders were known as the Tobacco Lords. I remember them, when I was wee, at the Exchange, mincing about in their scarlet cloaks, silver buckles on their shoes, looking down their noses at everyone as if they owned the place. Which I suppose they did, mind you.'

'Even when you were wee, then, you haunted the Clyde docks?'

'Not so much the docks but the river, the ships—it was a window onto the world.'

'Escape,' Kirstin said softly, deeply moved by the image this conjured up. 'Is that what you were after?'

'Aye.'

Cameron was staring off into the distance, perhaps picturing another dock, on another river, many years before. She tried to imagine him, a foundling, with heartbreaking good-looks, dreaming of another life, far from whatever brutal reality he'd endured, and her heart wrenched. 'Was it so very bad?'

He gave himself a shake, blinked, looked down at her with a twisted smile. 'I survived. No, more than that, I flourished against all expectations. You'd probably say I succeeded against the odds, and I wouldn't disagree with you in this case.'

'Will you tell me your story, Cameron?'

'Why do you want to know? As you've been at pains to point out, when we find Philippa we will go our separate ways once again. What difference would it make?'

Looking into his eyes, the strangest feeling took hold of her. Yearning. There was no other word for it. A longing for something she couldn't even begin to define mixed with a sharp, unmistakable and undeniable pang of desire. She forgot that they were standing in the middle of a crowded dock. Turning towards him, she reached her free hand up to caress his cheek. 'It makes all the difference in the world to me.'

He looked at her strangely, then caught her hand. He turned it over, pressing a fervent kiss to her palm. She could feel the heat of it even through her glove. He didn't kiss her mouth, but the look he gave her was enough to make her shiver as if he had.

Then he smiled crookedly, taking her arm again, and heading towards the tobacco warehouse. 'In that case, how can I possibly deny you? You'll need tea to sustain you, though. Come on.'

The Prospect of Whitby tavern lay at the far end of Wapping High Street, right on the Thames. Cameron secured an ornate wood-panelled private room on the top floor, with a view across the river to Rotherhithe and Bermondsey. It was, according to the landlord, the same room in which the diarist Samuel Pepys had once dined, a fact that Cameron found singularly underwhelming but which seemed to impress Kirstin. He ordered an early dinner to be delivered later, and coffee, tea and a platter of bread and cakes to keep them going in the meantime.

Kirstin, having discarded her coat and hat, warmed her hands at the roaring fire, leaning over just enough to give him a delightful view of her rear, and the desire which had caught him unawares a few moments before gripped him again. What was it about this woman that made him want her so much? Was it simply the result of his months of abstinence?

What did it matter? he thought impatiently, hurriedly glancing away from the enticing view as she stood upright and made for the tea tray. What mattered was that he did, and the feeling was mutual. What they would do about it—if anything—he had no idea. But he was damned if it would be nothing.

The coffee she poured for him was like tar, the way every sailor liked it. The landlord knew his clientele. Cameron took a happy gulp, wincing as it burned its way down his throat and into his gut. Kirstin, waiting for her tea to do whatever alchemy it did in the pot, shook her head at his impatience and poured him a second cup.

'Garrioch House?' she prompted, when they had been sitting opposite each other for a few silent minutes.

'Aye, Garrioch House. My home. For the first twelve years of my life, at any rate.'

Now that it came to it, although he wanted to talk about it, there was so much he didn't want to remember, aspects he preferred not to recall, details his memory had coloured and distorted over the years.

He decided to stick to the bare facts. 'A home for

foundlings, it was—and still is to this day, like enough. I was handed into their care when not more than a few days old. Whoever left me gave them my name and a small purse of money, but nothing else.'

'Whoever left you? You mean it wasn't your mother?'

He shrugged. 'Unlikely, given what I know now. A nurse, a midwife, a maid, or simply some poor messenger paid to deliver me, it could have been anyone.'

'And there was no other information to indicate your identity?'

'From the minute I was handed over to Garrioch House, my identity was fixed. I was a bastard.'

'Cameron!'

'What would you prefer? Illegitimate?'

'I prefer— I prefer…' Kirstin swallowed. To his surprise, her eyes held a sheen of tears. 'I prefer not to use any such term. A child should not be condemned for the lack of a piece of paper declaring her—his parentage.'

'True, but unfortunately neither society nor the law would agree with you.'

'Then both are wrong,' she said fiercely. 'You should not be punished for an accident of birth, Cameron.'

'Though punished I was, nonetheless.'

'You mean physically? That's outrageous!'

'Physically, mentally. It's the way of the world, I'm afraid.'

'But not now, surely?' Kirstin leaned forward, her perfect brow deeply furrowed. 'Now you are a successful businessman, a man of status, your own man. You're not going to tell me being illegitimate still affects you now?'

Of course it didn't. That was what he'd have said to anyone else. But Kirstin wasn't anyone else.

'I have no family, no heritage, and in the eyes of society and the law I am stigmatised for ever by my illegitimacy. I cannot change that. I had come to terms with it though,' Cameron admitted reluctantly. 'It's why the letter knocked me sideways.'

'Letter?'

'From my mother.'

He leaned back, closing his eyes, fighting the gut-wrenching pain which the memory of that day could still elicit. His hands gripped the arms of the chair. For a moment he was back there, on the doorstep in Edinburgh's New Town, Louise Ferguson's words ringing in his ears.

Then there was a soft touch on his arm, the rustle of skirts, and he opened his eyes to find Kirstin kneeling beside him.

'I had no idea this would be so painful for you. I am sorry I asked.'

He sat up, covered her hand in his. 'I've never spoken of that day to anyone,' he said.

'You don't have to speak of it now.'

'I want to. The letter was from my mother. Sheila Ferguson.'

'Louise's mother?'

'She was married to Louise's father some years before she had me, and remained married to him for over forty years despite my very unwelcome appearance. When she wrote, he'd been dead a year.'

He could see her beginning to piece the sorry little tale together, but she made no effort to speak, for which he was grateful, as he was grateful for the comfort of her hand, clasped so firmly in his.

'It didn't say much, the letter. Only that she was my mother, that she'd managed to trace me through the records at Garrioch House for they kept the name she'd given me. She wrote that I was the result of an "indiscretion", and though she'd been forced to give me up she'd never stopped thinking of me and wanted to meet me.'

'Oh, Cameron, that is— What did you feel?'

'Angry that she'd left it so long. Disappointed that I had incontrovertible proof that I was, as I'd always been told, a bastard. Wildly curious as to the other half of my parentage, and at the same time desperately determined to dampen any curiosity of any sort. I was thirty years old, a self-made man with my own business, content with my life—' He broke off to rake his hand through his hair. 'And yet I still needed to know. Does that make any sense to you?'

Her cheeks were flushed. He'd have put it down to the heat of the fire had it not been for the fact that she had suddenly dropped her gaze to their clasped hands.

'What have I said?'

She shrugged and shook her head. 'It doesn't matter. Please carry on.'

'Sheila Ferguson—my...my mother—was ill when she wrote to me. Dying, though I didn't know it. The letter was sent to my offices in Glasgow, but I was abroad. It took many months to reach me. By the time I read it and made my way to Edinburgh—'

His voice cracked. He coughed. His eyes smarted. *Devil take it, after all this time!*

'She was dead,' Cameron finished baldly. 'I never got the chance to meet her.'

'But you met Louise instead?' Kirstin said ominously.

'Aye.' He managed a crooked smile. 'Louise, who informed me that I'd ruined her father's happiness and destroyed her parents' marriage.'

'How on earth did she come to such a conclusion?'

'I asked her that. She had grounds,' Cameron said, looking deeply troubled. 'It seems that my mother had an affaire. Or, reading between the lines of what Louise told me, something more than an affaire. She was planning to leave my father for her lover, but he abandoned her. She was expecting me. She had no one to turn to, nowhere to go. Her husband, Louise's father, agreed to keep her on, but the price she paid for respectability was to give me up.'

'Dear heavens. How absolutely awful. But why does Louise blame you?'

He sighed heavily. 'It's not so much that she *blames* me, Kirstin, as hates my guts. My mother wasn't only planning to leave her husband, she was leaving her daughter behind too.'

Kirstin's eyes widened in shock. 'So in Louise's eyes your mother chose you and her lover over Louise and her father?'

'Aye. You see now why I feel I owe her?'

'I certainly see now why she wants nothing to do with you. What I don't understand is how she comes to know such a thing? She must have been a child when it happened.'

'Her father, the good, saintly man, saw fit to en-

lighten her one day. He sounds like a right vicious—
Well, whatever his reason, he told her.'

'Oh, Cameron, that is absolutely awful. So this is
the debt that Louise claims you owe her, then? That is
why you are so determined to move heaven and earth to
find her daughter? Because by your innocent birth you
ruined her childhood and made her feel rejected? Yet
still, however she suffered, I can't help feeling it was
nothing, *nothing* compared to what you endured. You
have been economical with the details of your childhood, but I know it must have been utterly miserable.'

'It's not a competition to see who suffered the most.'

'No, because no matter what she suffered it does not
compare to…' Kirstin caught his hand to her cheek.
'You are an honourable man, while Louise…'

'Is simply a mother desperate to find her child.'

'Yes. Yes, you're right,' she said looking stricken. 'I
beg your pardon. I take it, then, that she wanted nothing to do with you?'

'I neither saw nor heard from her again until
Philippa disappeared. It took me a long time to come
to terms with it, but I do understand her feelings. And
I've no expectations of them changing,' he added hastily. 'I don't want her to feel obliged or grateful.'

'But if she came to know you…'

'She made it clear that she would not make any such
effort over six years ago.'

'Six years ago?' Kirstin's eyes widened. 'Cameron,
do not tell me that it was that very day—' She broke
off, frowning. 'I assumed you were in Edinburgh on
business. I remember now you said you weren't.'

She got to her feet and made for the window, staring
out at the Thames. 'You said then that I was a welcome

distraction,' she said when he joined her. 'I had no idea that was what you needed distracting from. You must have been in turmoil.'

'And yet distract me you did. In fact you turned out to be far more of a distraction than I ever imagined. Kirstin, you do know that that night was— Ach, I don't know how to describe it, to be honest. I don't even know how it happened. Afterwards, I couldn't quite believe it had, and I had no way of finding you again. You never did leave me a note of your address as I asked you to.'

'I never thought for a moment that you were serious about wanting it. Besides, I didn't have an address at that point.'

'You could have found me, though, if you'd wanted to, couldn't you? It's how you make a living…finding people who don't want to be found.'

She flinched at this. 'That night, we both of us agreed, was a moment out of time, nothing more.'

She was right, and it was unfair of him to press her, yet it mattered. 'So you never thought of me?'

'You asked me that before.'

'You didn't answer.'

She continued to stare in silence at the view. A huge barge sitting low in the water due to its cargo of coal was making its precarious way against the tide.

Finally she turned towards him. 'I thought of you,' she said. 'Happy now?'

He was, suddenly. Happy to have unburdened himself. Happy to have had her as his confessor. Happy that she had taken his part, though he hadn't thought he cared one way or the other.

'I'm happy to be here with you, if nothing else,' he said.

She slanted him an odd little smile. 'Taking dinner alone with me in an inn. Again.'

'It's not the same. We're very different people.'

'You can have no idea how different.'

'Oh, I think I can. You're every bit as beautiful, you've not changed physically, but in every other respect—more than six years of making your own way in life, and making a success of it too. You're a very different woman from the one I met that night.'

'And you? Are you a very different man?'

'I'm my own man now, in every sense. We're both older and wiser, I reckon.'

He traced the gentle plane of her cheek, his hand coming to rest on her shoulder. Though he didn't urge her to, she stepped into his embrace. Desire was like the insistent beat of a drum between them, impossible to ignore.

'I think fate has brought us together full circle like this.'

'And fate will send us spinning off back to our own lives, once our business is complete.'

'Do you think so, Kirstin?'

'I know so, Cameron.'

She spoke with such certainty, yet her eyes burned with the fire which smouldered inside him. He was not interested in arguing with her. Instead he bent his head towards her, pulling her gently to close the tiny gap between them. She could have resisted. She did not. With a soft sigh that gave him goosebumps she slid her hand up to his neck, pressed her body against him, and tilted her face for his kiss.

The touch of her lips on his made him shiver. He curled his fingers into the indent of her waist, striving for control. She went to his head like a good malt. And, like a good malt, she should be savoured slowly, treated with respect.

He kissed her. A deep, slow kiss. His tongue stroking along the tender flesh of her lower lip. He felt her shudder and blood coursed to his groin, and for long, delicious moments their kiss went on and time seemed to stop. Then she sighed again, her body moulding itself to his, her fingers in his hair, her hand sliding under his coat-tails to rest on the small of his back, and his own hand slid down to the curve of her bottom, and he was lost.

They kissed, his hands roaming over her body, cupping her breasts, the throaty moan she gave in response making him achingly hard. She pulled him tight against her, and his own guttural cry in response startled him. Still they kissed, staggering back against the table, where she braced herself, wrapping one leg around him, impeded by her skirts, driving him mad with frustration.

Her hands slid under his waistcoat, tugged his shirt free from his breeches, fluttered over the skin of his back. Her own clothes were a barrier to the yielding skin beneath. He yearned to tear them from her. And still they kissed, panting, clutching, until a sharp rap at the door sent them springing apart and the dinner Cameron had ordered, and neither of them could have given a damn about now, arrived.

The door finally closed on the waiter and Kirstin, who had been staring determinedly out of the window while the various dishes were laid out, turned around and burst out laughing. Cameron had tucked his shirt in, but his necktie was askew and his hair looked as if he'd been standing in a gale.

'I suppose he might have imagined that you were shadow-boxing and lost,' she said.

Cameron grinned. 'Were it not for the fact that you were so obviously trying to look invisible. He's obviously well used to it, though, for not only did he knock very loudly, he waited for about five minutes before entering the room.'

'I cannot believe that we allowed ourselves to— I am thirty-one years old, for heaven's sake, well beyond such antics.'

'Well beyond? You don't mean that, surely?'

Flustered, she sat down in the chair he held out for her. 'I have not— I am not— I don't—' She concluded, mortified to hear herself sounding more like a fifty-year-old spinster than a mature woman of the world.

Cameron sat down opposite her, busying himself with lifting the lid from several platters. She knew that his silence was a tactic designed to force her to fill the gap. Well, two could play at that game!

'I will have some of that pie, if it is rabbit, please. And the winter greens.'

He served her, filling his own plate with the same food before pouring them each a glass of wine. Cameron raised his glass in a silent toast. She took a delicate sniff of hers before taking a deep swallow. He was eating with relish, not making a pretence as she was, and she was horribly conscious of his eyes on her, watching as she cut up a piece of rabbit saddle into tiny pieces.

She loved rabbit. The gravy of this pie was delicious, flavoured with mustard and thyme, and the crust a flaky golden brown. She lifted a piece to her mouth, then set it down with a resigned sigh.

'I have no difficulty in attracting men, but most men I meet are not interested in me, only in my looks.'

'Have you considered that some might be, but you refuse to let them see past that lovely exterior?'

Startled, Kirstin set down her knife. 'None of them has tried particularly hard.'

'Because you didn't want them to.'

He was right. It irked her that he was right. 'I am perfectly content on my own, Cameron.'

He poured them another glass of wine, though Kirstin didn't remember finishing her first one.

'Speaking for myself, I've been celibate for almost two years,' he announced.

Kirstin's jaw dropped, and Cameron laughed.

'So you kissed me out of desperation?'

'I was desperate to kiss you, but that's an entirely different thing. Why did you kiss *me*, Kirstin?'

She shrugged, pushing her almost untouched plate to one side. 'You kissed me, so I kissed you back.'

He reached for her plate, then stopped himself with a rueful smile. 'Force of habit. So you were just being polite?'

Force of habit. Because every scrap of food had mattered in Garrioch House. Which meant he must have gone hungry most nights. It hit her then, the true extent of his trust in her. He had confided details of his past which many would consider shameful, confident she would not judge him.

Deeply moved, she saw how insulting her own response was now, saw that she had been batting away his questions, thinking to protect herself, when all he was trying to do was to know her a little better.

'Good manners didn't enter into it. I wanted to kiss you, plain and simple,' Kirstin admitted.

Cameron had been about to take another sip of wine. He set his glass down carefully, but she held up her hand to prevent him from speaking.

'I wanted to know if it would be the same as before.' She twirled her empty glass on the tablecloth. 'That doesn't mean that I have been pining for you all this time. I thought of you. For a while. But then I—I had other matters to occupy me.'

'Your business?'

She shrugged. It was not a lie to fail to contradict something.

Cameron got to his feet. 'Come and see the view, now that the light is fading.'

She joined him at the window. The Thames was turning from brown to silver and pewter. Lights twinkled on the wharves over on the south bank. The river looked perfectly still, the few craft which remained at sail seemingly becalmed.

'The tide is turning.' Cameron took her hand. 'So you kissed me to see if it was as you remembered?'

She curled her fingers around his. She wasn't obliged to explain, but she found she wanted to—to offer a quid pro quo for taking her into his confidence.

'Not to discover if it would be as delightful as I remembered, but to discover if it would be as delightful as I imagined it would be.'

His hand tightened on hers. She saw the flare of heat in his eyes and felt the answering heat in her own blood.

'And was it?' he asked.

'The jury is still out,' Kirstin said, twining her arms around him. 'I think more evidence is required.' And with that she pressed her lips to his.

Lying alone in her bed much later that night, Kirstin touched her hand to her mouth, closing her eyes, shivering at the memory of those kisses. There had been none of their earlier urgency, none of that frantic clutching, the quest for more intimate contact.

Those kisses had been slow, lingering, passionately restrained. It wasn't that they hadn't wanted to make love, but neither of them wished history to repeat itself. And so they had kissed. And talked. And kissed. And then they had taken a hackney back along the river and across the bridge, and now she lay here alone, still tingling and aroused, but in a strange way sated.

It meant nothing, of course, Kirstin's irrepressibly logical mind reminded her. She sat up in bed, suddenly anxious. Of course it meant nothing. She didn't want it to mean anything, couldn't allow it to. Most likely that was why Cameron had resisted attempting to make love to her properly too. The whole point of her coming here, taking this commission on, had been to eradicate any trace of him from her life because...

Kirstin inhaled sharply. There it was. The root of her anxiety. She reached for Marianne's latest missive, still lying on the nightstand, and lit a candle. The footnote was short, but beautifully printed in pencil. Eilidh had bestowed three kisses this time. One more than yesterday. Did this mean her daughter was missing her more?

It had only been four days. Coming up for five. But

they had never been apart for more than a few hours before. Guilt washed over her. For long stretches of these past few days she had not thought of Eilidh at all.

Eilidh. The light of her life, the *raison d'être* for everything that she had achieved, her biggest, best achievement of all. From the first moment she had held her in her arms Kirstin had been overwhelmed with a love so profound that it scared her. For more than five years she had thought of her daughter as unique, special, loved all the more for having only a mother, with no need for a father. But today, listening to Cameron's description of his own illegitimate childhood, had given her pause for thought.

But no! A thousand times no. She would never, ever think of Eilidh in that way.

Though society would. Which was why an insidious, persistent voice had urged her to keep Eilidh hidden from society, wasn't it? And why she had, whenever the child had asked her, avoided every question about her parentage. Kirstin screwed her eyes shut but the tears flowed anyway. It didn't matter that she would not countenance that her child, conceived out of wedlock, was tainted. Others would condemn her for that, if they ever found out.

So they must not find out. If necessary she *would* lie to Eilidh. And she would continue to lie to Cameron, because heaven knew what his sense of honour, and the memory of his own childhood, would compel him to do if he ever found out. He'd want to give his daughter a name. A home. A life of his choosing. And Kirstin knew him well enough now to be afraid that he'd find a way of making it happen, no matter what she wanted. Or he.

Chapter Seven

'It turns out that Heather Aitken's move to the metropolis was not an unqualified success. As a consequence, Mar— my assistant struggled to track her down,' Kirstin informed Cameron the next day. 'Though she did indeed find employment as a chambermaid in a reputable household, she was dismissed for what the employment agency describes as "overfamiliarity with the eldest son of the house".'

'I suspect it will have been the other way around,' Cameron said dryly. 'Regardless, it will have cost her not only her livelihood, but her good character. A fatal blow to her employment chances.'

Kirstin eyed him with surprise. 'What do you know of such things?'

'I do have house and staff of my own.'

'Is it a very large house, then?'

'It's not a cottage.' Cameron shrugged. 'I don't know what you consider large. It's a manor, I suppose you'd call it, with a home farm, gardens—a lot more gardens and land than I've been able to do much with so far. Set in the outskirts of Glasgow, to the east.'

'I can't imagine you as lord of the manor.'

'I don't spend much time there, in all honesty. The farm and gardens provide employment for graduates of Garrioch House and other similar establishments. The options for foundlings are limited unless they have a particular facility, like I did for numbers, which is why they sent me to learn accounts.'

'A skill which has stood you in very good stead, I presume?'

'Very, though I hated sitting in an office totting up numbers in a ledger.'

'Did you run off to sea, then, and become a cabin boy?'

'I used to help the purser, and things just developed from there.'

'To the extent that you now have your own fleet? Tell me, do you take on orphans to crew your ships as well as to farm your land?'

'Aye, but don't go thinking I'm some sort of noble philanthropist. I give them a fair chance. It's up to them what they make of it.'

'A philosophy I can certainly empathise with.'

'Aye.' Cameron was frowning. 'Talking of wasted opportunities, where has this Heather Aitken ended up?'

'Deep in debt to an infamous moneylender.'

He cursed softly under his breath. 'Stupid wee lassie. She should have stayed in Edinburgh. God knows what will become of her.'

'I think we both know what's most likely,' Kirstin said brusquely. She could never be hardened to such cases but she had become reconciled, a long time ago, to the fact that she could only help a select few of them.

'She is living in St Giles, one of the most notorious rookeries in London. I think we will arouse less hostility there if we enter in the garb of the Rev and Mrs Collins. I'm afraid that you will have to put up with smelling of wet dog for a few hours.'

'Goliath,' Cameron said, with the ghost of a smile. 'It's a small sacrifice if it leads us closer to Philippa. Am I to assume that you know your way around this place?'

'I've been there before, quite recently, actually. I had a guide then, but I think I remember enough not to have to pay for another. If you will excuse me, I will go and get into costume. I suggest you do the same. I'll be back in fifteen minutes.'

The odour of Goliath, Reverend Collins's mythical hound, wafting from Cameron's coat, was as nothing compared to the stench rising from the gutters of St Giles's rookery. The worst of Glasgow's slums bore no comparison to this place, where the tall, ramshackle buildings lowering over them looked too rotten and decrepit to support any sort of life, other than the verminous kind.

Beside him, Kirstin was looking steadfastly ahead, ignoring the interest their presence was arousing, but Cameron's hackles were rising. The sharp stares from the gaunt men drinking from pewter tankards outside the rookery's many gin shops were blatantly challenging.

Instinctively, he stared back, with the hard, stony look he had used over the years to face down the bigger, more brutish boys in Garrioch House, the rougher sailors on board the clippers where he had first served, and the brigands who haunted the docks where he did business. If it came to using his fists, he would. Clenching them in readiness, he moved closer to Kirstin, keeping very slightly behind her, the optimum position from which to defend her from attack.

The alleyway they were following narrowed. Fetid air escaped from the cellars, where the hatches had been flung open in search of air, having discharged clutches of small, pale and undernourished bairns who sat, wide-eyed and impassive. Cameron's heart wrenched. He had a purse with him, full of coins, but it would be folly to dispense them now. On the way back, he promised himself.

'I know,' Kirstin said, slanting him a sympathetic smile. 'Only one in a hundred, perhaps less, has any prospect of escaping from here. I came in search of one such. Becky, her name was. A card sharp on the run from the law.'

'And did you save her—? I beg your pardon, did she save herself?'

He waited for the usual rebuff, but it did not come.

'I believe she will, and in rather spectacular style, though I have not yet heard. I sent her to Venice.'

'Venice! I am impressed,' Cameron said.

She permitted herself a tiny smile. 'You are meant to be.'

'I know.'

Another smile greeted this remark, but as they reached a crossroads between two alleyways, her expression became serious. 'It is here, I think. First door, second floor, by the sign of the Laughing Dog tavern.'

'I'll be right behind you, but it might be best if you speak to her first. She'll trust a woman before a man.'

'You read my mind. Are you ready?'

Kirstin mounted the rotting steps, leaving Cameron to check over his shoulder. As he'd thought, a small shadow had parked himself across the way. He waved at the lad, spinning a sixpence high in the air. It was expertly caught, the message acknowledged with a wink. Another sixpence when they left would ensure that they were not set upon.

Hurrying to catch Kirstin, he found her already at the door on the second floor.

'I mean you no harm, Miss Aitken,' she was saying. 'My name is Mrs Collins. I come as a friend, to talk to you of a mutual friend.'

'What friend?'

The door opened a crack. Quick as a flash, Kirstin inserted her foot into it, allowing Cameron to push it open and let the pair of them through. Heather Aitken had retreated, cowering against the furthest corner of the tiny room. A wraith of a girl, with the milk-white skin of one who rarely saw the sun, and a straggle of straw-coloured hair emerging from a dirty cap, she was clutching her hands against her breast, wide-eyed with terror.

'He promised I'd done enough to clear what I owed,' she said. 'Please, I don't...'

'Miss Aitken, we are not here at the behest of Mr Watkins.' Kirstin spoke firmly, approaching the girl as one would a frightened and cornered animal.

'How do you know about him if he didn't send you?'

'I can't tell you that, but you may trust me. I am here for quite another reason.' Kirstin cast her eye about the dingy room. 'Is it too much to hope that you have the makings of some tea?'

'Tea!' Heather Aitken exclaimed. 'Who in the name of the devil do you think you are, to push your way in where you're not welcome and demand a cup of tea?'

'No tea, then. Let us at least sit down and speak civilly.'

Cameron bit back the wholly inappropriate desire to laugh, for there was just a hint of relief in Kirstin's voice. He wondered how many cups of tea she'd forced down her delicate palate in the course of business. A good many, he reckoned, and what was more it was an effective tactic, for Heather Aitken, no longer looking terrified, but slightly baffled and a little bit intrigued, was doing as she was bid and taking a seat at the table. Obviously moneylenders, thieves and murderers did not demand anything so mundane as a cup of tea.

Kirstin took the chair opposite her. There was none for Cameron, but he wouldn't have taken it anyway. Best to keep out of it and let her deal with the lass. He rested his shoulders against the door and watched, fascinated, as she did so.

She took her time, coaxing Heather into recounting what they already knew of her dismissal. The girl's honest outrage at the accusations thrown at her confirmed what Cameron and Kirstin had already surmised, that Heather was an innocent victim.

'They had my name struck off the register at the agency,' she said, 'and the agency made good and sure every other agency knew it. I had to go calling round at doorsteps, but all I could get was daywork, and that doesn't even cover the rent on this place. I know what you're thinking, it's not much of a place, but the door locks and I don't have to share with— Well, Mrs Collins, most of the lassies here, they use these rooms for—for entertaining, if you know what I mean?'

Heather's pale skin flushed scarlet. Kirstin leaned over to pat her hand. 'And you are a good girl, aren't you?'

Heather bit her lip, her colour heightening. 'I'm not so sure about that.'

'Because you borrowed money from Mr Watkins to help with the rent?'

'One of the footmen at the last place I was working introduced me to him.'

'Did he, now? No doubt for a fee.'

'You think?'

'I know,' Kirstin said grimly. 'And Mr Watkins's terms sounded fair to you at first, I expect.'

'I didn't really understand them. I've no head for figures. By the end of the week I owed more than I'd borrowed, but he said it didn't matter, he'd let me carry the payment over, and then...' A tear splashed onto the wooden table.

'Then there came a time when he insisted that you give him all that you owed him,' Kirstin prompted gently. 'And it was a very large amount, quite beyond you?'

Heather nodded. Tears streamed unchecked down her cheeks. The colour had fled, leaving her skin ashen. 'Who sent you here, Mrs Collins? You said you'd come about a friend.'

'I think you know who, Heather, don't you?'

'Is it—is it Jeannie?'

Cameron, who had been quite unable to imagine what this scrap of a lass could possibly have to do with Philippa's disappearance, felt the hairs on the back of his neck rise at this whispered connection. He forced himself to keep very still, for Heather seemed to have forgotten all about his presence, though he wanted to leap across the room and shake the truth out of her. It did not need Kirstin's slanted warning glance to keep him quiet, however.

'Jeannie and you were good friends, I know,' she said, with an encouraging smile at the poor wretch. 'I'm sure that she must have written to you, let you know that she was coming to London. She'd have wanted to catch up on all your adventures in the big city.'

'She thought that I'd done well for myself. She was thinking she might try London for herself, she and her young man, after Miss Philippa got married, for she'd be out of a job then. Mrs Ferguson doesn't like Jeannie.'

'Rather, Mrs Ferguson doesn't like Philippa being so fond of her maid, isn't that it?'

'It is. Jeannie said— How do you know Jeannie, Mrs Collins? I don't think she's ever mentioned you.'

'I'm very worried about Jeannie, Heather.'

A fresh fall of tears dripped onto the table. 'Jeannie is a— She can take care of herself much better than I can.'

'Is that what it came down to, Heather? A choice, Jeannie or you, when you couldn't pay Mr Watkins?'

'He sent a woman to see me. Mrs Jardine, she called herself. She said that I must—that I must—that I must pay my debt back to Mr Watkins by...' Heather covered her face with her hands and sobbed. 'I can't say it. Don't make me say it.'

'Then I'll say it for you. She told you that you must work off your debt in her brothel,' Kirstin said, in a clipped tone very different from the gentle one in which she had hitherto spoken. 'And you, Miss Aitken, were so desperate to escape her clutches that you handed your friend on a plate to her instead, am I right?'

'I thought that— I wasn't sure that they'd find her. I thought that maybe she'd get away—that Mrs Ferguson would…'

'If Jeannie had somehow managed to escape from whatever trap you set for her, don't you think you'd have heard from her by now?'

'She doesn't know where I am. Nobody does.' Heather was pale, shaking, her voice tremulous. 'She thinks I'm still working at the big house where I was first employed. One of the girls there, she brings me my letters.'

'And has there been one from Jeannie to let you know she's in London? No, of course there hasn't.'

'Who are you?'

'I am here at the behest of Mrs Ferguson. This gentleman here is Philippa's uncle.'

'Philippa? What has Miss Philippa to do with this?'

'Miss Philippa, being so fond of Jeannie, tried to save her, and in the process was abducted with her.'

'Merciful heavens. Dear God, what have I done?'

Heather began to sway in her chair and would have toppled to the floor had not Cameron caught her. He set her down on the bed, which was tucked under the eaves of the room. Though her eyelids fluttered, she remained in a deep swoon. He stared down at her slight frame, torn between pity and fury.

'There's no point in being angry with her,' Kirstin said, getting to her feet. 'She was faced with a terrible choice. Self-preservation almost always wins out, in my experience.'

'What should we do with her?'

'Were you thinking of handing her over to the authorities?'

'No! I meant how might we help her? If we leave her like this, she's like to fall further down the road to ruin.'

Cameron turned to the wan figure, now trying to sit up on the bed. 'Listen to me, Heather Aitken, I've no time to deal with you right now, but if, God willing, we find Philippa and Jeannie safe and well, I might consider offering you gainful employment in Glasgow. I'm promising nothing, but you had better make sure you don't do anything stupid in the meantime. Do you understand?'

Brushing aside Heather Aitken's startled promises and belated thanks, he took Kirstin's arm, hastening back out into the close, down the stairs and out into the alleyway, where he tossed a sixpence at the boy waiting across the road.

'I'm assuming you will be able to track down this Mrs Jardine for us?'

'It should be easy enough, if she is a madam. That was an extremely generous offer you made, Cameron. Especially in the circumstances.'

He turned to Kirstin, halting momentarily. 'I understand why you tend to see things in black and white, but in my experience there's many shades of grey in between. The instinct to survive at any cost—if you'd been raised as I was, you'd understand.'

'You're right, I can't imagine, though I am absolutely certain that you would never choose to protect yourself by betraying someone else.'

'No more than you would,' he said.

She stumbled. Catching her, he caught a glimpse of her face, which had been concealed by Mrs Collins's bonnet, and was startled to see a tear tracking down her cheek, But before he could say anything a shadow across the way caught his eye. Cameron snarled at the man, who immediately ducked into the nearest doorway.

'We need to get out of here. I think we've overstayed our welcome.' Grabbing Kirstin's hand, he began to run, hurling the pennies from his purse at the clutch of waiting urchins until they reached the relative safety of Holborn.

You would never choose to protect yourself by betraying someone else.

Kirstin's own words played over and over in her mind as she prepared for her expedition to Mrs Jardine's brothel that night. A few days ago she would have had no hesitation in agreeing with Cameron, but now, sickeningly, she was forced to admit that it was not true. Though she truly believed that she was doing the right thing for Eilidh, and for herself and for Cameron too, every day that she kept his daughter a secret from him was still a betrayal. She was denying him his right to choose for himself whether to acknowledge her or not.

Which a growl of frustration, Kirstin turned to the mirror and began to hook the row of tiny buttons which fastened her full-length black pelisse. Since leaving St Giles that morning, she had been over and over this in her head a hundred times. Cameron didn't want children, but if he discovered he had fathered Eilidh he would feel obliged to take on a paternal role, and the life Kirstin had worked so hard to build for herself and her beloved daughter would come crashing down.

Cameron might want Eilidh to live in Scotland. As her father, he would have the law on his side, and the right to do so. Eilidh was not—she would never, ever think of her daughter as a—a—she would never allow her to be stigmatised for her unconventional birth, but Cameron would not tolerate what he saw as a huge disadvantage. He'd want to give Eilidh his name, which would mean he'd be forced to *marry* Kirstin, and even if it was to be a wife in name only, for the sake of their child, Kirstin could never tolerate such an arrangement. She would be Cameron's property. He would own her and her daughter, even her business. It simply didn't bear thinking of.

Though Eilidh would have a father.

But Eilidh didn't need a father any more than Kirstin had needed a mother. One loving parent was more than enough. So to think of her keeping his daughter a secret from him as a betrayal was quite illogical.

'Extremely illogical,' Kirstin said aloud to her reflection. The words lacked conviction. She, who prided herself on her honesty, was finding this abstention from the truth deeply uncomfortable.

With a sigh, she did up the last of her buttons, put on her hat and her gloves. The transformation was complete. The Procurer, not Kirstin, stared back at her from the mirror. It was odd, seeing her alter ego like this after what felt like a long gap, though it had still been only a few days. She felt confined, somehow, constrained, as if her true self had been bottled up, buttoned down, hidden under The Procurer's mourning black disguise.

Checking her watch, she saw that the hour was approaching eleven. Butterflies began to flutter in her stomach. Putting her own concerns firmly to the back of her mind, she headed for Cameron's suite.

'Do I pass muster?' Cameron asked, throwing his arms wide. 'Am I the proper rakish dandy?'

He was dressed for a night on the town, in a tight-fitting tailcoat of olive-green, with a high collar and a double row of silver buttons. His shirt points were high and starched, his neckcloth much more intricately tied than was his wont, and set with a diamond pin. Buff-coloured pantaloons showed every contour of his muscular legs, and a pair of highly polished Hessians completed his toilette.

'Your shoulders and your calves are all your own, and I don't think you're wearing a corset to nip your waist in,' Kirstin said, trying not to stare at the way his pantaloons clung to thighs which were clearly shaped by muscle and not padding. 'So, no, you're not a typical dandy, but you do look very much the man about town.'

'And you look as if you are about to attend a funeral. All you need is a black lace veil.' Cameron eyed her with one brow raised. 'A very stylish funeral, if there ever is such a thing. Or—I don't know—there is something about the fit of that coat thing you are wearing. You could be a widow or a—don't take this the wrong way—but a very, very expensive...'

'Courtesan?'

He laughed uncertainly. 'Is it deliberate? It is extremely alluring. You don't look at all like yourself.'

'How am I to take that!'

'Alluring, yet untouchable,' Cameron said. 'As if you are made of jet and alabaster. Usually, you leave me in no doubt that you are flesh and blood. Then you are alluring, and almost irresistible.' His smile faded as he studied her. 'You are nervous?'

'Yes,' she admitted, taken aback. 'If we find them, Cameron…'

'Then we will get them out of there.'

'But how? Such places as Mrs Jardine runs will have men on the door. You will be one against two, perhaps more.'

'Kirstin, when this madam realises that Philippa is gently born with influential connections she'll be desperate to be rid of her.'

'If she has Philippa, don't you think that she'll already know these things?'

'Are you thinking that she might already have rid herself of her?'

'I'm sorry, but the same thing must have occurred to you, surely?'

'Aye, of course it has.' He ran his fingers through his hair, wreaking havoc with his carefully smoothed crop. 'I could see her pressing Jeannie into service, but Philippa—it's far too risky for her. I doubt she'll be there. God's honest truth, I don't want to think about where she'll be if she's not. But we're going to find out, Kirstin. Are you up for it? Because if you're not, I can do this on my own.'

'No.' She gave herself a shake, put her hand on his

arm. 'We're in this together, remember? We will find her. Failure isn't an option.'

His own words quoted back at him conjured up the ghost of a smile. 'Right, then,' Cameron said, 'let's get on with it.'

Mrs Jardine kept a discreet house in Margaret Street near Cavendish Square, a well-established business aimed at the exclusive end of the market. Her boast, in the circles where such things were boasted of, was that she could cater for any taste, however outlandish, if the price was right, and provided it was not downright illegal. Though the boundaries of the law, as interpreted by Mrs Jardine, could sometimes be stretched, for a premium.

Admission to her house was strictly by means of introduction by a previous client, but the matter was too urgent for them to consider the delay of even a day while Kirstin found one such, so she watched from the shadows as Cameron attempted to bluff his way in.

As expected, there were two men guarding the door, dwarfing even Cameron's large frame. Though they closed ranks, blocking his way, they made no attempt to manhandle him. He spoke to them. She couldn't hear what he said, but she could see the impact of it on the watchdogs who did not, contrary to her expectations, simply hustle him out into the street. They stood impassive. Then they separated slightly. Then they conferred. Then one of them departed, returning a few minutes later with a well-dressed woman, presumably Mrs Jardine herself. Cameron spoke again. Kirstin caught the flash of his smile. And then he was ushered in and the door was closed behind him.

Kirstin's heart was pounding, her mouth dry. She had been in dangerous situations before, but not like this, and she had always been alone. Tonight she was part of a team. One, possibly two innocent young girls might be somewhere in that house, desperate to be rescued.

She counted out the minutes carefully, until the agreed fifteen had passed. Then she crossed the road and rapped on the door demanding, in the imperious voice of The Procurer, to be taken immediately to Mrs Jardine on a matter of extreme urgency.

Cameron slipped a banknote to each of the doormen as he followed Mrs Jardine into the house. In the brightly lit hallway, he saw that she was younger than he'd thought at first, not more than forty, and had been a beauty in her day. She was not, as he had in his naivety expected, either painted or raddled, but there was a gauntness to her—the hollow cheeks, the deep-set eyes and the twig-like arms were indicative of poor health.

'Mr MacDonald,' she said, 'I must tell you that this is most unusual.'

'Aye, I know that, and I'm right grateful to you for making an exception for me.' He responded to her rasping tones in the soft lilt of the Highlands. 'I've only the one night to spend in London before heading off to India, and I heard that Mrs Jardine's was the premier facility in all of London.'

'And faced with a long sea voyage to India,' Mrs Jardine said wryly, 'your need is urgent.'

'Very urgent.' Cameron attempted what he hoped was a shy smile. 'I've never been in such a place as this,' he said, in all honesty, 'but I'm hoping it will more than cover my requirements.'

He'd had the banknotes ironed. They rustled enticingly as he handed them over. Mrs Jardine did not count them, nothing so vulgar, but he saw the very slight lift of her brow, and knew from the fact that she immediately slid them into a pocket in her gown that she wasn't going to turn him down.

'It depends what you are after, Mr MacDonald,' she said, 'but that will do nicely for a start.'

'I'm fresh from the Highlands,' he said, still smiling, 'but I'm not wet behind the ears. I reckon that's more than enough, whatever my proclivities.'

A dry little laugh which turned into a hacking cough greeted this remark. 'I refuse to believe a man with your looks and wealth could possibly be as inexperienced as you claim, but that is no concern of mine. I have a business to run. Tell me your pleasure, and we can both get on with our evening.'

'Call me sentimental, but I'm after a lass from my own neck of the woods. A lass to remind me of the home I'm leaving behind, fresh as the Highland air, if you get my drift?'

'I sincerely hope you are not asking me to provide you with a virgin, Mr MacDonald.'

'Could you, for a price?'

'No,' Mrs Jardine said baldly. 'Let me give you the benefit of my vast experience of the world,' she continued sardonically, 'to one who claims to know nothing of it. If someone tries to sell you a virgin, you can be certain that the flower has already been plucked. Such girls are rarities, and never available on the open market, not even from such exclusive houses as this.'

'Where, then, might one look?'

He knew the moment he spoke that he'd been too eager. Mrs Jardine narrowed her eyes. 'I think it might be better if you looked elsewhere for your entertainment tonight.'

She made to hand him his notes, but Cameron shook his head, pushing the money away. 'Away, now, I was only curious. Like I said, all I'm after for tonight is a wee Highland lass to remind me of home.'

The madam pursed her lips, studying him for long, anxious moments. Cameron remained smiling encouragingly, until she shrugged, sighed. 'Very well. I do have such a girl, as it happens, arrived from the north quite recently. Are you averse to red hair, Mr MacDonald? I know that some men…'

Though his belly lurched, he remained calm. *Jeannie*, he thought, *dear heavens, it can only be Jeannie.* 'As it happens, I have a particular predilection for red-heads, Mrs Jardine.'

'First floor. Second room on the left. Luckily for you she is free. It's a quiet night. You have half an hour.'

He could feel her eyes on him as he made his way up the stairs, but his mind was already on the girl behind the door. She would be frightened, terrified, even. He'd have to reassure her, explain who he was. Half an hour to calm her, to find out where Philippa was, and to come up with a plan to get her out of there, and Philippa too if she was here. And all the time, Kirstin would hopefully be keeping Mrs Jardine occupied. If things went to plan.

When he reached the top of the stairs, the corridor stretched before him, six doors on either side. Was there a girl behind each? Were they willing, or had they no choice? He understood now, a little, why Kirstin was forced to see the world in black and white. Those few she could assist. The vast numbers she could not. He hadn't realised until now how invidious it must be for her to make such momentous decisions.

As he passed the first door on the left, his footsteps slowed. He stopped outside the second one. Should he knock? Aye. He did so. There was no answer. He turned the handle, easing the door open. She was sitting on the bed with her back to him, a slight figure wearing nothing but a shift, with bright red hair rippling down her back. He felt sick.

'Jeannie?' he said, closing the door and leaning his back against it.

'You can call me whatever you fancy, sir, since you're paying for the privilege,' she said, turning round. Not a Highland accent but pure Glaswegian.

'I'd like to call you by your real name, lass,' Cameron said, 'what is it?'

'Moira.'

'Moira! Oh, Cameron, your heart must have sunk to have your hopes dashed like that,' Kirstin said.

It was very late, late enough for dawn to be imminent, and they were once again in Cameron's suite.

'It was a blow, I'll admit it.'

He was sprawled in a wing-back chair, having discarded his jacket, the high starched collar of his shirt wilting, the carefully tied neckcloth askew. There was a bluish shadow on his cheeks, and darker shadows under his eyes. He looked utterly dejected.

Sitting across from him, still in her tight-fitting pelisse, though she had taken off her hat and gloves,

Kirstin was bone-weary. What would it be like for them to retire to bed together? To lie wrapped in one another's arms, to feel the reassuring beat of a heart, to drift to sleep still entwined, to wake slowly to the comforting warmth of another body, and to know that all it would take would be the gentle caress of a sleepy kiss to…?

'It would be better if we talked in the morning.'

Her eyes flew open with a start.

'You're exhausted,' Cameron said, 'we should…'

'No, this is too important. I'm perfectly fine.' She sat up, wide awake now. 'So, once you were convinced that Jeannie wasn't among the other girls, what else did you learn from Moira?'

'That two other girls had arrived a few days after she did, one a redhead like her. But they were kept apart from the rest of them, and were there only for one night. I asked her where she thought they'd gone, but she clammed up. I reckon she knows something, but she was too feart—so that's it, that's all I have. I hope to heaven you're going to tell me you have been more successful?'

'A little. More importantly, it ties in with what you were told.'

'Kirstin!' Cameron leaned forward eagerly. 'I knew you wouldn't let me down. Go on.'

Moved by his faith in her, she allowed herself to lean over and touch his hand. 'We will find them, I promise.'

Too late she realised she had broken her own rules, but she was well past maintaining The Procurer's carefully neutral front, incapable of pretending that this contract was like any other. She desperately wanted to find Philippa and Jeannie, not only for their own sakes but for Cameron's. She couldn't bear to see him so tormented. 'We will find them,' she said again. 'I promise.'

He gripped her hand. 'But how?'

'There is a club. A club so secret that not even I, with all my contacts, have heard tell of it. One whose members are so powerful and influential that, even though I threatened her with closure, and being sent to gaol for several counts of abduction, Mrs Jardine was still too frightened to talk about it.'

'Could you have her place closed down?'

'The Procurer could.'

'Tell me more about this mysterious elite club,' Cameron prompted.

'They convene six times a year at a secret location for the ritual deflowering of certified virgins,' she said, her horror when Mrs Jardine had confessed this still raw.

She saw her own disgust writ large on Cameron's face.

'There are precedents. Hellfire clubs such as the one founded by the Earl of Sandwich in the last century, where gentlemen of distinction met to indulge in what seems to me common debauchery dressed up as solemn ritual.' Kirstin made no attempt to keep the scorn from her voice. 'From the little I could winkle out of Mrs Jardine, these men will pay a king's ransom for an unsullied maiden, and are ruthless in protecting their anonymity.'

Cameron was staring at her in open disbelief.

'I know,' she continued, 'I found it difficult to credit too, but Mrs Jardine's terror was genuine, believe me.'

'Why, then, would she choose to hand Philippa into their clutches?'

'She had a choice.' Kirstin's voice hardened. 'When she discovered that her henchmen had captured not only a servant but a young girl of breeding, she was horrified. She could, of course, have done the decent thing and let Philippa go, but that would have put her nefarious trade at risk, so she chose to profit from her unexpected windfall instead.'

'We have enough on her to close her down.'

'Which is why she confessed to me what she had done. But we have bigger fish to fry at the moment.'

'Aye.' Cameron thumped his leg with his clenched fist. 'Though it sticks in my craw, we've far more important things to worry about. What the hell do we do now?'

'You're going to have to leave it with me again,' Kirstin said. 'It won't be easy. The fact that I have never heard of this exclusive club means that its members must be from the very top echelons of society. Members of the Government, the aristocracy, perhaps even minor royalty. But I have a few grateful clients who move in such circles. They may be able to shed some light.'

'If you're right about this club's attitude towards anyone who crosses them, they'll have to be very grateful clients indeed.'

'Trust me, they are,' Kirstin said, with more confidence than she felt. 'In the meantime, I did find out one piece of relatively good news. This club meets every second month, on the first Saturday. The sacrificial lambs are kept in a safe house somewhere, and they are exactly that—safe—until the allotted date.

Philippa was not taken until after the last meeting. It is thirteen days until the next one, so we have almost two weeks to find her.'

'Do you think Jeannie is still with her?'

'All I know is that the pair of them were taken together, but clearly Philippa would be by far the most valuable. Whether Jeannie will feature in whatever despicable ritual they plan to enact, I have no idea. She could have been sold on, or more likely sent abroad, I'm afraid, to guarantee her silence.'

He swore under his breath. 'It disnae bear thinking of, does it? So we'll not—for tonight.' Getting to his feet, he held out his hand. 'We're both gubbed.'

'Gubbed?' Kirstin laughed softly. 'I've not heard that expression before, but it describes exactly how I feel.'

He pulled her into his arms and she did not resist, surrendering to the comfort of his reassuring bulk, wrapping her own arms tightly around his waist.

'We'll find them,' she said grimly.

He kissed the top of her head. She tilted her face up, and he kissed her lips. A soft, gentle kiss. Then he let her go.

'We will. Together, we're a match for anyone. Goodnight, Kirstin.'

Chapter Eight

'Thank you for putting me in touch with the Marquis of Glenkin, it was an inspired idea,' Cameron said over dinner the next night. 'I met with his man of business today and, having pored over the books, I'm more than happy to take his various trading interests off his hands.'

'Ewan inherited his father's estate in Argyll about seven years ago, and it takes up a lot of his time, which is an issue now he has a growing family of three boys. He will be delighted to be relieved of the burden and to know it is going to be in safe hands.'

'So you get to help your old friend, while I get to expand my little empire, and everybody wins. Genius! I take it that he's the one who keeps you supplied with your precious tea? How do you come to know a marquis?'

'He was once a mere student of philosophy and mathematics. My father taught him. I've known him for ever.'

'Well, I appreciate the introduction. I'll continue to keep you in tea by way of thanks.'

'There is no need. I was happy to—'

'I'd like to, Kirstin.'

She bit her lip, lowering her eyes to her dinner, shifting slivers of roasted pork from one side of the plate to the other. Cameron waited, knowing that she was debating with herself on whether or not to explain her apparent ingratitude. When she did, he rather wished that she had decided not to.

'When we've found Philippa,' she said, 'there will be no reason for us to remain in contact.'

'Unless we wish to.'

Emotions flitted across her face, but too quickly for him to read them.

She shook her head. 'That is not possible, whether we wish it or not.'

Not possible. An odd choice of words. Why wasn't it possible? He had already worked out that the blame could not be laid at The Procurer's door, for it was obvious that Kirstin and The Procurer were one and the same. He had been waiting for her to trust him enough to tell him her secret, but he was growing impatient.

'Tell me how you got on today.'

Kirstin pushed aside her plate. 'I have been trying to track down someone who can tell us about this secret society and, I'm sorry to say, so far with little success. Either the men I have spoken to really know nothing, or they are like Mrs Jardine, too afraid to speak out. There is what I can only describe as a wall of silence regarding the existence of this club, which confirms what we already surmised—that the membership consists of very influential men.'

Cameron pushed back his chair. 'It's driving me up the wall to have to sit about twiddling my thumbs while Philippa is locked in some room or attic some-where, wondering what the devil is to become of her—or, worse, imagining the ordeal she's to face, if they've told her why she's there. And as for Jeannie, she could be anywhere.'

'It might not feel like it, Cameron, but we are mak-ing progress. I promised we would find them, and we will.'

He leaned his forehead against the cool of the window-pane. Lights winked from the houses across the street. A carriage pulled up at the hotel, and a doorman hur-ried out to help the old gentleman who descended from it unsteadily.

'You can't know that.'

'Come on, no defeatist talk, remember?'

He turned to face her, unwilling to keep up his cha-rade of ignorance any longer. 'You've clearly exhausted your own contacts. Don't you think it's time you ad-mitted defeat, Kirstin, and asked for help from the very top?'

'What do you mean? I don't know anyone who has better—' She broke off, her eyes suddenly wary as she realised the import of what he had asked her. 'You mean The Procurer?'

Cameron said nothing. He had deliberately left her with two choices. She could lie, or she could confess. He dearly wanted her not to lie, but if he had been a bet-ting man he'd have put the odds no higher than evens. Her expression remained quite impassive, but he knew her well enough. She had lowered her lids to hide her eyes. Her hand had strayed to her empty wine glass, twisting it around on the tabletop. When she gave that tiny little nod that told him she'd reached a conclusion he felt slightly sick.

'You have guessed, then,' she said.

Her tacit admission took the wind out of his sails. Taken aback by how much it meant to him, but feigning indifference, Cameron shrugged, returning to the table, pouring the dregs of the wine into their glasses. 'What have I guessed?' he asked, determined not to make it easy for her.

'That there is no— That I...' Her hand shook just the tiniest fraction as she took a sip of wine. 'You know that I am The Procurer.'

When he nodded, she laughed, an odd, strangled sound, and then drank the last of her wine. 'How did I betray myself?'

'By being you,' Cameron said, unable to resist smiling at her. 'You are so very much your own woman, you don't behave like someone who is answerable to another. I was never convinced that you could be anyone's assistant. And then there is your own assistant. Mar...? Margaret? Marjory? Marion?'

'Marianne. You thought it strange that an assistant should have an assistant, I suppose?'

'It wasn't only that. You spoke of her with such assurance, with the air of one accustomed to command.'

'What else gave me away? How long have you known?'

'My suspicions have been growing with every passing day. The way you talk about The Procurer from such a position of intimate knowledge of her methods and philosophy, almost as if you can read her thoughts, which of course you can. You are probably not aware, but latterly you have almost lapsed into speaking in the first person when referring to her. There's one thing that puzzles me, though.'

'What is it?'

'Why are you here, Kirstin? I mean, why you in person and not another woman? My understanding of The Procurer is that she is a—a puppet master—or should that be mistress? You told me yourself, her business is to match women—other women—with her clients. So why didn't you do that with me?'

'Do you wish that I had done?'

'No.' Impulsively, he leaned across the table to touch her hand. Her own gesture. 'Don't fob me off.'

She smiled crookedly, twining her fingers around his for a moment, before pulling her hand away.

'That first meeting in the confessional was meant to be our last.' She pushed her chair back with a sigh, wandering restlessly to the window, where she stood gazing out, her back to him. 'I was curious about you, but I had no intentions of taking on your case. But when you explained why you had come to me, I knew I had to help. I fully intended assigning someone else, as I always do, but when I discussed the matter with Marianne she pointed out in passing that I had the perfect set of skills to assist you.' She turned back to face him. 'It was the right decision, Cameron. There really is no one with better contacts to help deal with such a delicate and sensitive issue.'

She had not answered his question. He knew it. She knew it. She would not lie, but it had already cost her very dear to trust him this far, and there was a risk that if he pressed her, she would simply clam up.

A discreet tap at the door brought the servant with their tea and coffee, buying Cameron some thinking time. When they sat down by the fire, he decided to quit while he was ahead.

'I'm fascinated,' he said, 'will you tell me how you came up with the idea of The Procurer in the first place?'

She smiled at him gratefully, and he knew he'd done the right thing.

'It's not a tale that I've ever told anyone.'

'Then honour me by making me the first.'

Kirstin sipped her tea, trying to compose herself. The initial shock of realising that Cameron had found her out had given way to a strange kind of elation. He had not been incredulous, he had not been sceptical, in fact he'd hardly even been surprised that she and her alter ego were one and the same. She was, despite herself, flattered, but she was also wary.

He had apparently let her off the hook by asking her for The Procurer's history, but that didn't mean he wouldn't come back to his question as to why she was here. For a fraction of a second she considered telling him the truth, but it was the kind of inexplicable impulse people felt when standing on a ledge, the urge to leap into the abyss. If he asked again, she would have to fob him off. She hoped he wouldn't ask again.

'It was Ewan, the Marquis of Glenkin, who gave me the idea,' she said, 'albeit inadvertently. He was my first unofficial case, so to speak. He was desperately trying to avoid a marriage parade, and he needed a woman to pretend to be his affianced bride to get him off the hook.'

Remembering the day Ewan had come to her, distraught, and recalling her own excitement as the idea had formed in her mind of a radical solution, Kirstin settled down to tell Cameron the tale.

'I had no idea that Ewan and Jennifer would actually make a match, thinking only that my friend could sore use the fee she earned to set herself up independently, but that's what they did. And as far as I know they are blissfully happy to this day,' she concluded some time later. 'Ewan jokingly said I should consider becoming a matchmaker, and that's what I do—match problems with solutions, though marriage is never the intended outcome.'

Cameron smiled. '*Making the impossible possible.* It's an excellent selling point.'

'It's more about matching extraordinary skills to extraordinary requirements. The Venetian case I mentioned, for example. The young woman from St Giles, the card sharp. My client required her to help bring about the downfall of a certain man in order to avenge his father's death.'

Cameron's jaw dropped. 'If you are trying to shock me, you've succeeded. How did it turn out?'

'The young woman went to Venice about three months ago, and as far as I know is still there, so I don't yet know.'

'You don't worry sometimes that you are sending some of these females you rescue—?'

'Who rescue *themselves.*'

Cameron looked troubled. 'Who, in order to rescue themselves, have to place themselves in real danger, by the sounds of it.'

Kirstin stiffened. 'You think I ask too much of them? That I take advantage of their desperation, their lack of alternative options?'

'No!' Cameron swore under his breath. 'I don't think you either cruel or heartless, but I do wonder if you expect others to live up to your own very high standards. You would admit that the service you provide is unique. I'm merely trying to understand it better.'

It was obvious that he was speaking in earnest, but Kirstin was torn, because *not* explaining herself, her thoughts, her actions, to anyone, ever, and most particularly since coming to London, was one of the founding tenets that had sustained her. She would not be judged, yet here she was, contemplating exposing herself to Cameron's scrutiny, hoping he would see things her way.

'I'm sorry. I ask too much of you,' he said contritely, interrupting her thoughts. 'You have already entrusted me with a secret which no one else in London possesses—save presumably this Marianne of yours—I have no right to ask for more.'

'No. I want to speak. Now that you know, I may as well tell you the whole story.'

And so she did, from the beginning, the words tumbling out. She told him of her early successes, her near failures, and the outpouring was such an immense relief that she wondered why she had never, until now, felt the urge to speak. Cameron listened, saying very little, though his eyes never wavered from her.

'So, you see, the service I provide truly is unique, and my reputation for never failing has been extremely hard-earned.'

'Which is why you can charge such a premium,' he said, 'and, more importantly, why you have to be so certain that you have identified the right woman for the task.'

'Exactly. I do ask a great deal of them, but I go to a lot of trouble to ensure that they are suited in the first place. Finding the ideal candidate can sometimes be the most time-consuming aspect of any case.'

'I'm not surprised,' Cameron said wryly. 'Not only must she be deserving of a second chance, but possess the rare skills necessary for the task. Have you ever failed?'

'In the sense of not finding a perfect match?' Kirstin pondered this. 'There have been occasions when my client's requirements seemed impossible to satisfy, but I have found that there are many ways to look at a problem. What they think they require and what will actually work are often quite different. The harder task for me is to assess whether the female concerned has the nerve and resolve to succeed.'

'And that is the real key to your success. Your impeccable judgement. Some might even call it intuition. That's what makes you pre-eminent. You conduct face-to-face interviews with the candidates on their own turf. You know by the time you meet with them that they have the skills, but you assess their moral fibre and whether they, like you, are prepared to risk all or nothing. Have I that right?'

She nodded, unable to speak because a very inconvenient and illogical lump had formed in her throat.

'You don't like to think of yourself as a philanthropist, but you are a bit of a crusader, in your own way, aren't you? These women who get a second chance, you feel strongly about the injustice they have suffered.'

Her cheeks heated. 'Don't make a saint of me, Cameron.'

He laughed. 'Saints are heavenly and ethereal crea-

tures. You have much more earthly qualities. Thank
you for trusting me with your secret. You know it will
go no further.'

'Of course I do.' Kirstin looked at the clock, startled to see that it was almost midnight. 'I had no idea
it was so late.'

Cameron yawned, getting to his feet and rolling
his shoulders. 'I visited Louise today. I didn't tell her
much, only that we knew Philippa was alive and as yet
unharmed. Louise's friend is back from Paris. She's
told her what has happened. I think it was a relief for
her to confide in someone.'

'And a relief for you, knowing that someone is taking care of her?'

'If—*when* we find Philippa, Louise will be grateful.
She may or may not stop blaming me for blighting the
family by my presence, but there will be no more to it
than that, Kirstin. Do you honestly think that a woman
who would go to such lengths to keep her daughter's
disappearance quiet for fear of scandal, would welcome
a bastard half-brother into the family with open arms?'

'Don't use that word! She ought to be proud to call
you her brother.'

He snorted. 'So proud she still refers to me as Mr
Dunbar. What is your plan for tomorrow?'

'I must give all those I have contacted at least a day
to mull over my request—I am asking quite a lot—so I
don't have any plans as such. What about you?'

'Nothing in particular. In that case, would it be per-
missible, do you think, for us to escape for the day?'

Kirstin hesitated for only a few seconds. 'Yes,' she
said simply. 'We are unlikely to get another such opportunity, for once we find Philippa—'

'Why don't we stop worrying about what happens after we find Philippa? Or even, if it's possible, let us stop thinking about Philippa and Louise and Jeannie completely, just for a wee while, and simply enjoy each other's company. What do you say?'

'I'd like that very much.'

She got to her feet, meaning to say goodnight, but the words died on her lips as her eyes met Cameron's. She stepped into his arms. She lifted her face. And their lips met.

How delightful kissing could be. Just kissing. Though these were not just kisses. The carmine she used on her lips mingled with the honeyed taste of the wine they had drunk. His hands slid over the silk of her gown as he pulled her tight up against him and his breath was a soft, shallow zephyr on her cheek.

She touched her tongue to his, her hands curling into his shoulders, her body arching against him, kissing him more deeply, making no attempt to hide her arousal. The hard length of him was making her belly clench with wanting.

She shuddered when he touched her, his hands on her bottom, sliding up the rustling silk of her gown to the side of her breasts, frustrated by the barrier of her corsets. He buried his face in the hollow of her neck. He kissed the swell of her bosom, licked into the valley between her breasts. She slid her hands under his coat, flattened her palms over his buttocks, urging him closer.

Cameron wrenched his mouth away, panting. Kirstin stared at him, his pupils dark with desire, his cheeks flushed, knowing she must look every bit as dishevelled.

'It's not remotely that I don't want to,' he said.

She smiled at that. 'You have made that perfectly obvious. And I—I won't pretend that I am exactly reluctant either. But you're right. We have shared enough intimacies and revelations for one night.'

'Then let us save some for another time.' He kissed her again, gently this time. 'Goodnight, Kirstin.'

Kirstin slept deeply, waking very early in a warm glow of well-being and with a mild case of butterflies in her tummy. It took her a moment to work out why. She had absolutely nothing to do today, save spend it with Cameron.

She jumped out of bed, pulling on a wrap, and pushed back the heavy curtains. It wasn't yet light, but the sky was clear, suggesting it was going to be one of those cold, dry, crisp winter days so rare in London.

Pulling the bell for tea, she threw some kindling into the embers of the fire in her sitting room while she waited for it to arrive, which it did with satisfying speed, for the hotel kitchens knew her habits by now.

Pouring the first very welcome cup, Kirstin curled up on the hearth rug beside the fire and stared into the flames. She wrapped her arms around herself, trawling her mind for doubts, for regrets, for fears that her confession would be used against her, but she felt nothing save a huge sense of relief. She neither needed nor wanted approval, but she could not deny that Cameron's admiration and his understanding were adding to her sense of well-being.

And then there were the kisses. And the tacit promise of more than kisses to come. She sipped her tea, relishing the memory and the anticipation of what else might happen. There could be no harm in her admitting to herself how much she enjoyed Cameron's company. There was so little time left to them, most likely no other opportunity like today, to take a moment out of time together.

Her face fell momentarily. She would never see him again once they found Philippa. But that, she reminded herself, was the point of her being here.

Why don't we stop worrying about what happens after we find Philippa? Cameron had said last night. Sound advice.

Kirstin turned her mind instead to how they might make the most of the fine winter's day that stretched ahead of them.

Cameron stared around himself in astonishment as Kirstin reined in the perfectly matched pair of black high-stepping horses, drawing the phaeton she had driven expertly to a halt. The mansion before them was built of red brick and white stone, turrets looming high at each corner, and the pedimented entranceway was a colonnaded porch approached by a broad flight of steps.

'Where are we?'

'Osterley Park. The country home of Lord and Lady Jersey,' Kirstin said, pushing aside the rug and jumping lightly down from the high carriage before he had a chance to help her. 'Though they are not in residence, as you can see.'

Indeed he could, now that he looked more closely, for all the windows were shuttered, the double doors at the top of the steps barred. 'What are we doing here, then, other than trespassing?'

She smiled her enigmatic smile, though there was a gleam in her eyes. 'Patience, Cameron, all good things come to he who waits. Remember, I'm The Procurer. I make the impossible possible.'

Kirstin handed the reins over to a groom who had appeared from around the side of the house. The man seemed to be expecting them, Cameron noticed.

'Shall we?' she asked, as the carriage was led away.

He took her arm, allowing her to lead them along a path which headed out of the courtyard and through some mature woodland, giving himself over to the unexpected pleasure of a day which, she had told him at breakfast, required nothing more of him save that he enjoy himself, which made it pretty much a unique occasion, as far as he could remember.

The sky was a perfect winter blue above them, the sun dappling the path ahead through the bare branches of the trees. Kirstin, wearing a long woollen coat of peacock-blue, trimmed military-style with black braiding, and a jaunty little military cap, nestled more closely into his side as they walked.

'How come you to know Lord and Lady Jersey?' he asked.

'I am not particularly acquainted with the Earl. Lady Jersey is one of the patronesses of Almack's, the club known as the marriage mart by the *ton*. They call her Silence, for she is said never to stop talking. Some make the mistake of thinking such prattle must be quite indiscreet.' Kirstin slanted a mischievous smile up at him. 'I know better.'

'She is one of your previous clients, I must presume?'

'Not directly, but she had a vested interest in being

of assistance to one,' she corrected primly, her eyes twinkling. 'As to the detail, I'm afraid my lips are sealed.'

'With a kiss?' Cameron said, unable to resist.

She gave a little gasp as he pulled her roughly up against him and opened her mouth to his. Wrapping his arms around her, he was immediately aroused by the way she melted into his embrace, by the touch of her tongue to his. He closed his eyes as their kiss deepened, the scent of her perfume, her soap, mingling with the earthy smell of leaf mould, the chill air causing little puffs of cold breath to emerge as they dragged themselves apart, gazing dazed into each other's eyes. Then she smiled that smile that made his groin tighten, and the only thing that prevented him from dragging her back into his arms was the tiny shake of her head.

'Patience, remember?'

She took his hand, leading him along the path quickly now, to where it emerged at the side of a large ornamental lake with a small island at its centre. A rowing boat was tethered to the jetty, its oars already set in the rowlocks. He jumped in without hesitation, helping Kirstin aboard, suddenly consumed with such simple joy that he understood what people meant when they said they wanted to bottle a moment and keep it for ever.

Unhooking the rope, pushing off with one of the oars, Cameron began to row towards the jetty visible on the island. Casting off his hat and gloves, he gave himself over to the pleasure of rowing, long, clean strokes, the oars entering the water at the perfect angle, the boat skimming smoothly along with barely a ripple on the lake's surface.

'You've done this before,' Kirstin said.

'Just a few times,' he replied, laughing. 'I taught my-self to row on the stretch of the River Clyde at Flesher's Haugh at Glasgow Green when I was about ten, in one of the Humane Society's boats—they're the people who rescue people from the water. Even then I must have had an idea of making my living from the sea. I earned a few coppers at the docks once I'd got proficient enough, skiving off school when I could, ferrying sailors back to their ships.'

'I'd willingly pay to watch you exert yourself,' Kirstin said with a wicked smile.'

Her overt appreciation of his body, the way her eyes lingered on his thighs, on his arms as he worked the oars, was arousing. While he'd grown tired of his face and his physique drawing admiring looks from women, he'd happily have Kirstin admire him day and night if he could return the favour. He'd thought such base attraction shallow, found it unsatisfying, and it was where there was nothing else.

Would he desire Kirstin so much if she was not an out-and-out beauty? No question but that the answer was a resounding yes. Because he desired Kirstin. The woman behind the beautiful exterior. He wanted her more than he had ever wanted any woman.

Tingling with anticipation, Cameron rowed with purpose, pulling up to the jetty on the island as the sun disappeared behind a bank of cloud. Tying up, making the oars safe, he helped Kirstin ashore.

'What now?'

She made a show of consulting her expensive little enamelled watch. 'Luncheon?'

Laughing at his bewildered look, for all he could

see were trees and shrubs, she pointed him at a track beside a box hedge.

'This way.'

The folly was painted brilliant white. An exotic open-air temple sat atop a bow-fronted frontage. Bemused, he followed as she led the way confidently up a flight of wrought-iron steps into the main room. It was painted forest-green, the lavish cornicing picked out in gold, the same design and colour reflected in the rug which covered most of the floor.

Astounded, Cameron saw that a fire was burning in the white marble hearth, and a meal had been set out under silver platters on the table in the bow window. A bottle of champagne sat chilling in a bucket of ice placed on a silver tray, and two crystal flutes were set on a convenient side table by the sofa.

Shaking his head in wonder, he mouthed one word to Kirstin. 'How?'

'Magic,' she replied, with a catlike smile.

He threw back his head and laughed. 'I'm inclined to think there's a more pragmatic explanation!'

She closed the door, tossing her hat and gloves onto a chair, and began to unbutton her pelisse. 'It occurred to me in the early hours of this morning that I have never once used my contacts to satisfy a personal whim rather than a business imperative. I decided to make an exception in this case.'

She slipped out of her pelisse and placed it on the chair.

'Then I'm very flattered,' Cameron said.

She chuckled. 'You should be.'

He opened the champagne, pouring two frothy glasses, handing one to her. 'A toast,' he said. 'To The

Procurer, for working her magic. And to Kirstin, for a magical day.'

'It is not over yet,' she said.

Cameron touched his glass to hers. 'You're right about that.' Waiting only for her to take a sip, he set both of the flutes down. 'It's not over...not by a long chalk,' he said, pulling her into his arms.

Their kisses made Kirstin feel as if she were quite literally melting. There was, as Cameron had said, a magical quality to the day which surpassed her every expectation when she had planned it in the early hours of the morning. Only because he knew her secret had she dared to weave such magic. Though if he ever found out her deepest, most precious secret...

Guilt flickered on the edges of her mind. Cameron thought he knew her. He *did* know her, better than anyone knew her. This was a moment out of time, to be savoured later, when there were no more such moments. She would not spoil it with such thoughts.

Sipping champagne between kisses, the cold wine made her mouth tingle, and the taste of it lingered on their lips as they kissed again. They were languorous kisses, kisses which could go on for ever and ever, enhancing her sense of anticipation. She forgot all about the real world, forgot everything save her need for more of this.

Their kisses were intoxicating, creating a mutual haze of desire which banished hesitation, creating an urge, a need to carry on and on and on. Cameron was kissing the nape of her neck, trailing kisses along her shoulder as he eased her chemise over her arms, his hands cupping her breasts through her undergarments.

Her corsets were unlaced, and he kissed her shoulder blades. The ribbon of her chemise was undone, and it dropped to the ground with her petticoats, leaving her clad only in boots, stockings, and pantalettes.

He turned her around to kiss her breasts, taking his time, pressing tiny fluttering kisses over every inch of skin, making her toes curl inside her boots with the delight of it, never wanting it to end, straining not to lose control.

She tugged at his coat and he shed it, kicking it aside. His waistcoat followed. And then his shirt. They dropped to their knees, their mouths clinging, their hands roaming. His muscles were taut, his chest heaving under her flattened palms. She pressed her mouth to one nipple, making him moan, then to the other, seeing her own determined grip on control reflected in his eyes.

He eased her back onto a heap of pillows and took her nipple between his lips, his hand on her other breast. It was the sweetest of tortures, making her writhe, pant, moan. She was fast reaching the point of no return, only a last shred of sanity intervened.

'Cameron.'

He sat back abruptly, startled by the peremptory tone in her voice, swearing. 'I'm sorry. I thought...'

'No, no. It's not that I don't— But we can't, in case...' Her face was flaming. 'It was wrong of me to mislead you, to let you think...'

His smile dawned slowly. It was sinful. 'I know we can't take any risks,' he said. 'I have not brought the means to protect us with me, and I presume even The Procurer does not think of everything.'

Her cheeks burned. 'I was not planning this when we set out this morning.'

'We can't safely indulge ourselves,' he said, with another of his sinful smiles, 'but you can.'

'What do you mean?'

He eased her back onto the cushions, laughing softly. 'Can't you guess? No? Then let me show you.'

He untied the ribbon which held her pantalettes in place. 'Trust me,' he said, when she made to protest, pulling them down over her legs, easing her thighs apart.

And then he began to kiss her again, but this time his lips touched flesh which had never been kissed before. The bare skin of her leg above her garter. Upwards his mouth worked, to the soft flesh of her inner thigh. And then inwards, between her legs. She cried out with surprise, and then with guttural pleasure at the unexpected delight of it, at the way his mouth and his tongue teased and tensed her, licking into the most sensitive parts of her, stroking her to new heights of pleasure.

She wasted a tiny moment wondering what it was, exactly, he was doing, and then she abandoned thought, opening up to the sheer delight of it, arching under him, her fingers clutching at the cushions in an effort to make this new pleasure last and last, and then toppling over suddenly, and with force, her climax rippling through her, wave after wave after crashing wave.

Utterly lost in the moment, every instinct urged her to take him inside her. She tugged at his shoulders, pulling him on top of her, pressing pleading kisses to his lips. He responded with deep kisses, his fingers twining through her hair, long escaped from its pins, but when she fumbled for the buttons on his breeches Cameron rolled away.

'There's a point when even my self-control will falter, and I think we've just about reached it,' he said, getting to his feet, holding out his hand to help her up. 'Please don't fret,' he added, kissing her again. 'I found that every bit as pleasurable as you did.'

'I doubt that.'

He tilted her chin up, forcing her to meet his eyes. 'I mean it.'

And she could see, astonishingly, that he did. 'Thank you?' she said doubtfully,

He laughed, kissing her soundly once more before letting her go. 'No, thank *you*. Now, I think we should put some clothes on and sample some of this food before it spoils.'

'You're right. Monsieur Salois, the Duke of Brockmore's renowned French chef, will be less than impressed if we don't do his dishes justice.'

They had climbed a spiral staircase to the rooftop temple to watch the sun sink over the lake before finally quitting the island. On the drive back, wary of danger from highwaymen and roadside blaggards lurking in the growing gloom, Cameron sat on watch, armed with a pistol which Kirstin had produced from a secret panel in the phaeton. Nothing should surprise him about her now, but she was still capable of astounding him.

When they arrived at the hotel, the carriage and horses were handed into the care of another groom, this one clearly Kirstin's own, for he drove the equipage off rather than heading for the mews belonging to the hotel.

'Thank you,' Cameron said, turning to her at the door of his suite, bowing over her hand. 'For a perfectly lovely day.'

'It doesn't have to end here.'

'I don't want it to, but—are you sure, Kirstin?'

'It is a matter of taking appropriate precautions,' she said, and he was surprised to see her blushing. 'You mentioned that you have…'

'I do.' His heart was already galloping, but he forced himself to ask her one more time. 'Is that the only thing you're worried about?' When she nodded, he pressed her hand. 'Give me a minute. I'll join you directly.'

When he did, Kirstin had already taken off her pelisse, bonnet, and gloves. She locked the door behind him. Her hand trembled as she did so.

'Are you sure you're not having second thoughts?' he asked her.

'Not second thoughts, but I can't help feeling nervous,' she admitted reluctantly.

'You're not the only one.'

'It's silly, isn't it? A lot of water has flowed under the bridge since the last time.'

'Kirstin, I'm not interested in reliving the past. I don't want to make love to the woman I met six years ago. I want to make love to *you*.'

She thought this over. He waited. She gave that little nod of hers. Then she came to him, wrapping her arms around his neck. She smiled at him. *That* smile.

They kissed again, but there was none of the languor of those earlier kisses. These kisses were purposeful, urgent. He ran his fingers through her hair as they kissed, pulling out the pins as she unbuttoned his waistcoat. He shed it with his coat onto the floor.

Their kisses had an edge to them now, a raw hunger that could not be sated by kisses alone. Still kissing, leaving a trail of clothing behind them, they staggered together to the bedchamber. He began to unhook her gown. She tugged at his shirt, smoothing her hands over his chest, pressing her mouth to his throat, licking him, making him moan. Her gown pooled at her feet. She stepped out of it and they moved towards the bed.

He stopped thinking as he helped her out of the last of her clothes, lost in the sheer delight of sensation, his mouth on her nipples, watching her eyes flicker shut as he sucked, licked, stroked. She unfastened the buttons at the front of his breeches. He kicked himself free and she stared at him blatantly, examining his chest, his belly, down to his erection.

She reached for him, running her hand up the length of him, curling her fingers around him, making his breath ragged, making him harder, thicker, pulsing in her hand. Then they were on the bed, her legs wrapped around him, their mouths meeting in another deep, hungry kiss, and he slid his fingers inside her. She was so wet. So tight. He stroked her. She moaned. Arched. Muttered his name. More than ready. As he was.

He quickly sheathed himself. She wrapped her legs around him. One last deep kiss, tongue thrusting, and he entered her, pausing, breathing deeply, clutching at the ragged remnants of his control. She tightened around him as he eased further into her, her eyes wide, watching him shudder, feeling him pulse, and then he began to thrust, slow, harder, hard, fast, and she became a wild creature beneath him, her body finding a rhythm with his, matching him thrust for thrust. She cried out as she climaxed, and then he came with a hoarse cry, falling on top of her, his chest heaving, his arms tight around her, before his mouth found hers in one last, delightfully sated kiss.

Chapter Nine

Kirstin watched as her daughter's left hand curled around the pencil, her expression one of intense concentration. Cameron was left-handed. 'Corrie-fisted', he called it, though he could write a passable script with his right hand, having been forced to favour it at school.

Eilidh glanced up, smiled distractedly, and went back to her sums. The little kink in her hair was sticking up as usual. It was the same kink that Cameron had. And her hair, which Kirstin had always thought reminiscent of her own, was also the exact colour of Cameron's. Marianne was forever saying that mother and daughter were the image of each other, but, looking at her afresh, Kirstin could see that the firm line of her daughter's chin did not come from the Blair bloodline but from…

From her father.

Kirstin felt slightly sick. She wouldn't ever be able to look at her precious daughter again without seeing Cameron. Every time she examined the clever, carefully detailed drawings Eilidh made, she would be reminded that she had inherited her artistic ability from her father. And she would wonder, as Eilidh grew older, which of her skills and ambitions and preferences were her own, and which had been derived from the man who would never be part of her life, whose identity she would never be aware of.

A man who decidedly did not want children. A man who would resent his own child for curtailing his freedom.

You can't miss what you have never had, he had said bitterly, referring to his own lack of a father. But the words rang hollow, even though she was still adamant that Eilidh didn't need a father, and equally sure that Cameron didn't want a daughter.

Kirstin stared down at the unread newspaper on her lap. The consequences of that first night with Cameron had been so momentous as to make her reluctant to repeat the experience. Her occasional dalliances with other men had been unsatisfying, but yesterday had proved once and for all that she was not, as she had assumed, beyond passion. When Cameron had left her in the early hours of this morning she had lain awake, replaying every touch, every sensation he had aroused, already longing for more despite the pleasant sated ache of her body.

Such passion could only be transitory in nature, but they did not even have the luxury of that small amount of time. She would miss him, the only person in her life who knew who she was and why her life had turned out this way, for she had told him far more than she had ever confessed to Marianne. Cameron truly understood her. Save that there was something fundamental about her he didn't know.

Guilt gnawed at her as she studied her daughter. She was withholding a fact that he didn't want to hear and it would destroy both their lives if she told him. Her guilt was therefore illogical. Yet it refused to be quelled. But it would, in time. One more thing to inure herself to.

The clock struck the hour and Kirstin smoothed her daughter's hair affectionately. 'Time for tea, young lady. Marianne said she would bring a chocolate cake.'

'Are you staying for tea, Mummy?'

'Yes, darling, but then I have to go out.'

Eilidh nodded solemnly. 'Business,' she said, matter-of-factly, making for the stairs. 'I know.'

A delighted whoop told Kirstin that the cake had not been forgotten. Marianne appeared in the doorway and, seeing the question on Kirstin's face, immediately shook her head.

'Not a peep from anyone on the list you gave me, sorry.' She picked up Eilidh's workbook, flicking through the pages. 'Not a single mistake, as ever. She has a real head for figures.'

'Of course—she is her mother's daughter!' Kirstin said, more vehemently than she'd intended.

'Have you a headache?' Marianne asked, giving her a strange look.

'No. Sorry. I had hoped that we would have news today, that's all.'

Marianne sat down at Eilidh's desk, her slight build only just too big for the chair. A frown drew her fair brows together. 'It's horrible, thinking of those two girls locked up somewhere.'

'Assuming the pair of them are still together. I'm aware I'm asking a great deal of you, Marianne, expecting you to look after the business as well as Eilidh in my absence.'

'I like to think I've earned your trust.'

'More than that. I rely on you.'

'I've been thinking you could rely on me a great deal more.'

'What do you mean?'

'You're turning business away all the time. I could help, Kirstin. Not replace you, never that, but I could become more involved.'

'But what about Eilidh?'

Marianne hesitated. 'You're not going to like what I have to say.'

'Not if you're going to suggest—again—that I send her to school.'

'You know that I'm right.'

'No,' Kirstin said flatly. 'I won't discuss this.'

'Hear me out,' Marianne persisted. 'If you are still convinced I'm wrong then so be it, but you know that I've got Eilidh's best interests at heart.'

'I don't doubt that. Go on, then, say your piece.'

'Eilidh is a very bright little girl. She needs to be pushed more. But it's not just that, Kirstin. She'll be six years old this year. She needs the company of other little girls, she needs to make friends. She needs to learn how to socialise in company other than ours. It's not normal, the way you closet her away.'

'It didn't do *me* any harm.'

Marianne raised a sceptical brow.

'I don't want Eilidh to be normal,' Kirstin said. 'I want her to be exceptional. I think she *is* exceptional.'

'You're probably right. As I said, she's very bright, but—but don't you see you're narrowing her horizons by keeping her isolated from the world? You're not protecting her, you're making her an outsider.'

A lump formed in Kirstin's throat. Tears burned her eyes. She knew, had always known deep down, that this moment would arrive, but she couldn't face it, not yet.

A child should not be condemned for the lack of a piece of paper declaring her parentage.

How adamantly she had spoken those words to Cameron. How certain she had been.

True, but unfortunately neither society nor the law would agree with you, he had replied.

She knew in her heart that he was right. His was the voice of bitter experience after all.

'No respectable school would take Eilidh,' she said grimly. 'And even if they did…' She pressed her hand to her eyes. 'I couldn't expose her to that. Don't ask it of me.'

'You know, you could pretend,' Marianne said gently. 'About Eilidh's father, I mean. Put a ring on your finger, call yourself Mrs Blair. You already dress like a widow most of the time.'

'But it would be a lie,' Kirstin said wretchedly. 'A tacit admission that I had done wrong. That Eilidh was a sin. I would be giving in, don't you see?'

'Sometimes there's no such thing as right and wrong. Sometimes there's no place for principles. Sometimes there's simply doing what is for the best.' Marianne got to her feet. 'Whether you permit me to take on a more significant role in your business is entirely your decision. But regardless, Kirstin, I urge you to consider sending Eilidh to school, for her sake, if not yours.'

'I'll think about it. After this case is complete.'

Marianne touched her arm. 'We won't let it come

between us, you will do as you see fit, but I owed it to my conscience to speak out.'

'And I'm grateful.' Kirstin smiled wryly. 'I think.'

She picked up the newspaper which had fallen on the floor, and was in the process of folding it up when a notice caught her eye.

'Marianne!' She scanned the notice again, her heart lifting. 'Marianne, look at this. I think I may finally have found the key to unlock access to the secret club.'

Kirstin had been gone all day. If she'd had good news to report he'd have heard by now, surely. All this waiting around was driving Cameron up the wall. It left him with far too much thinking time. He was a man who preferred action to words, but he hadn't even dared leave the hotel, lest Kirstin return. He'd answered every scrap of correspondence. He'd drunk far too much coffee. He'd paced the floor so many times he was surprised there wasn't a path worn in the carpet.

As the clock struck six, he closed his eyes wearily, but the moment he did images from last night started playing out, frustrating him in a very different way. He'd been abstinent for too long, that was what it was. He'd forgotten the sheer joy of release, the bone-deep satisfaction afterwards of lying together, skin to skin, slick with sweat.

Aye, right! He had not forgotten because it had never been like that before. Cameron groaned. Last night had had nothing to do with abstinence. Last night, and yesterday afternoon on the island too, had been all about Kirstin. When they'd made love, whatever kind of love they had made, it had been about more than their bodies uniting—not that he'd be such an eejit as to say there had been a meeting of their minds too. What the hell? It had been special, and it was as simple as that.

Cameron rubbed his chin. He needed a shave. And he needed to think about what all this meant. They had their own lives, the pair of them, they lived in very different worlds, and he'd meant it when he'd told her he was happy with his. But now he wasn't so sure. He had a sneaking suspicion that Kirstin had filled a gap he hadn't even known existed. He had a sneaking suspicion that he could easily fall in love with her if she let him.

'Eejit,' he said, aloud this time, just to make sure he was listening to himself.

How could he fall in love with a woman he barely knew? All very well that she'd admitted she was The Procurer, but he still hadn't a clue how she lived, or even where she lived, and each time he'd tried to ask her she'd turned the conversation.

When he took over the tea business from the Marquis of Glenkin he was to send supplies to her place of business, for God's sake! Why was she so obsessively secretive? It couldn't possibly be because she didn't trust him. So what the devil was she hiding?

Twenty-five minutes later, Kirstin walked through the door. She was wearing another crimson gown, this one patterned with large blowsy roses. Silk, it was, of the finest quality, Cameron reckoned, and yards of it too, in the tiny pleats that formed the skirt which swished provocatively as she walked. The bodice, in contrast, was tightly fitting and low-cut, showing off the creamy perfection of her bosom and the long line of her neck. She never wore jewellery. He'd noticed that before. Her clothes were her one extravagance.

'I have news,' she said, helping herself to a sherry.

Her words pushed all thoughts of the future to the back of his mind. His heart leapt. 'Someone is prepared to talk?'

'None of the people I contacted have stuck their head above the parapet. But that doesn't matter. Look at this.'

She handed him a newspaper. He studied the paragraph which had been circled, announcing the coming out ball of Lady Beatrice, the eldest daughter of the Earl and Countess of Crieff. A name had been underlined twice.

'"The Right Honourable Griffith Griffiths, His Majesty's special envoy, who has lately been in Lisbon on business of the greatest import, will be granted the honour of partnering the debutante in the opening dance."' Cameron gave a snort of laughter. 'His parents seem to have been singularly lacking in imagination when they named him. Presumably he has been earmarked as a prospective son-in-law. How can you be so certain that this Griffith Griffiths will be willing to help us?'

Kirstin beamed. 'Don't ask me to explain, but I will ensure that he does. Now all we have to do is find a way to gain access to Lady Beatrice's coming out ball. How do you feel about playing a second cousin twice removed, come all the way from the Highlands?'

Dinner arrived at that moment. Cameron waited impatiently as the waiter set out the various covered dishes, fussing over their placement on the table. Then there was the wine to be opened, decanted, tasted. And then he was distracted, as usual, by Kirstin's careful pondering over each dish, the way she studied every-thing first before making a small selection and arrang-ing it carefully on her plate. She opted for the fish tonight, and a helping of her favourite winter greens. An odd combination. He had a bet with himself that she'd go back for the veal pie.

'Well?' she prompted, once Cameron had filled his own plate with a large slice of pie. 'Do you fancy play-ing a Highlander?'

'I'm a Glaswegian. I won't wear a skirt. And I'm wondering why we have to go to such a palaver in the first place? Can't we simply find out where your man is putting up while he's in town and call on him?'

'The ball is tomorrow night, and he is guaranteed to be there. We won't get a better opportunity. He may turn out be our only hope,' Kirstin said, becoming agi-tated. 'You have no idea how many strings I've pulled, how many favours I've called in, only to be met with a wall of silence. And all the time the clock is ticking.'

'You're right, you're right. So a Highlander I will be, though where I'm to find a plaid in London...'

'As a matter of fact...'

Cameron burst out laughing. 'I might have known you'd be one step ahead of me.' He lifted his glass to toast her. 'Here is to Laird Garrioch and his good lady.'

Kirstin, in the act of helping herself to a slice of the veal pie, looked up, eyebrows raised. 'Garrioch?'

'Of Garrioch House. The best lies are the ones con-taining an element of truth. Now, shall we discuss tac-tics?'

The next night Kirstin wore a simple white evening gown of satin with a gauze overdress, its front panel and the deep border of the hemline embroidered with white wild flowers. The plaid sash, fashioned by an accommodating Madame LeClerc from the offcuts of Cameron's outfit, was formed of tight pleats, worn over her shoulder and across her body, fixed at the waist with a large silver brooch. Her hair was simply dressed, a ribbon formed of the same plaid threaded through it. On her feet were white slippers. Long white evening gloves covered her arms.

Eyeing herself dubiously in the mirror, Kirstin fancied that she looked like a ghost. A Scottish ghost, mind you. She smiled. Rolled her eyes. And made for the door. She was very much looking forward to seeing Cameron in full Highland regalia.

He whistled silently as he opened the door to her. 'Laird Garrioch is a lucky man.'

Kirstin dropped a quick curtsey. 'Thank you kindly. I rather think Lady Luck favours his wife.'

Cameron bowed, but his smile was mocking. 'I've never worn a kilt before, and I hope to heaven never to have cause to wear one again.'

'At least this outfit doesn't smell of wet dog.'

'I should hope not, after what I shelled out for it. I had the devil of a job putting it on, though I was shown the correct way to fold and fasten it several times. You wouldn't believe how complicated it is. I'm wrapped up like a parcel.'

'Then let me examine the goods,' Kirstin said, making a show of inspecting him.

His evening coat was black and beautifully fitted across the breadth of his shoulders, conventional enough, though it had no tails. The high points of his shirt collar and necktie were pristine white, showing off his tanned face, his freshly shaved jaw. A plain black waistcoat was adorned with a single gold fob on which he wore his pocket watch. There were two plaids. The first was, like hers, draped over his shoulder and across his body, though it was much wider, and held in place by a large silver pin. The second plaid formed the kilt, falling to just above his knee, held in place with a large silver-buckled leather belt. He had not gone to the lengths of acquiring a claymore or a dirk, but there was a sporran fixed to the belt, and another silver pin affixed to the front of the plaid to weight it down. Knitted stockings and buckled shoes completed his outfit.

'Turn around,' Kirstin said, 'let me check the pleats at the back.'

He did as she asked, though his expression told her he knew perfectly well she wasn't interested in the pleats. Just as she'd hoped, the plaid swung out to give her a tantalising glimpse of thigh which she knew from last night was well-muscled.

'Well? Do I pass muster?'

She smiled, letting her appreciation show. 'I would not recommend that you take part in the country dancing, however, unless you wish the young ladies to faint.'

Cameron gave a bark of laughter. 'There's no chance of me dancing. I've two left feet.'

'I doubt very much that anyone will be interested in your feet.'

'We're going to stand out like a pair of sore thumbs, the two of us.'

'Which is exactly the point. It will be easier for us to bluff our way in to the ball if we make no attempt to blend in. That's precisely what you'd expect someone without an invitation to do.'

Cameron sighed theatrically. 'Fair enough. I bow to your expertise in the art of subterfuge. What am I to call you, Lady Garrioch?'

'I hadn't thought. Fiona? Mhairi? Annis?'

But he shook his head to each of these. 'Isla. I think that would suit,' he said eventually.

'Remote and forbidding, just like its island namesake, you mean?'

'No, unique and breathtakingly beautiful. What about me?'

'Let's think,' she said. 'What about Conlan? I was once told that in the Gaelic that means hero, or a man admired by all. Most apt.'

Cameron grinned. 'Isla and Conlan. A bit different from Euphemia and Caleb. Though I think we're every bit as loving a couple, don't you?' He slid his arm around her waist. 'In fact I'll wager we've not been married very long at all. Still in the early stages of—' He broke off, his face becoming serious. 'Look at the time. The carriage will be waiting.'

Kirstin's stomach immediately began to flutter with nerves as she picked up her evening cloak.

'Griffiths is to lead the Crieff girl out in the first dance. It's likely his own dance card will be full at least until the first supper. That will be around midnight. We've timed our arrival to be in the worst of the crush, so Lord and Lady Crieff will be less inclined to make a fuss in front of the rest of their guests. Once we're inside…'

'Kirstin.' Cameron put a finger to her lips. 'We've been over this a dozen times. There's no need to go over it again.'

'No. No. You're right. Only…'

'It is vital we get it right. You think I don't know that?'

'Of course you do.' She managed a shaky smile. 'And we will. If we can just get Griffiths alone, I know that I'll be able to persuade him to talk.'

'You are sure?'

Her nerves began to fade. A steely determination took over. 'Oh, absolutely certain. Now,' she said, softening her accent to a lilt, 'are you ready to play the charming Highlander, Conlan, my hero?'

'I certainly am, *mo ghràdh, mo chridhe*,' Cameron replied in a perfect soft burr. 'It means *my darling, my heart*, in case you're wondering. It's useful, isn't it, that I've a boatswain from the Isle of Lewis?'

'Why would a boatswain teach you such endearments?'

He took her hand, tucking it into his arm. 'Och, you never know when they'll come in handy.'

The ball to launch the Earl and Countess of Crieff's eldest daughter into society was being held at their town house in Mayfair. It was easy to spot. A long queue of carriages and sedan chairs was parked outside and blazing braziers illuminated the entrance. As they had hoped, Cameron and Kirstin were subsumed into the long line of guests making their way up the staircase from the reception hall to the first floor, where the Earl, his Countess and their daughter waited to greet them.

Cameron's attire was attracting a great deal of attention, most of it consisting of sidelong glances, though there were a few more brazen stares and several quizzing glasses raised. Deciding that Conlan, Laird of

Garrioch was the kind of man who enjoyed the lime-
light, Cameron returned stare for stare, supplement-
ing them with a smile, a haughty frown, or a wink,
depending on which took his fancy.

'There will certainly be no fading into the background now,' he told Kirstin as they reached the top
step. 'Are you ready, my wee Isla, to face the music?'

'Divide and conquer,' she said, stepping forward
with not a trace of the nerves she'd shown earlier, and
dropping into a deep curtsey before their host. 'Lord
Crieff, my husband has told me so much about you that
I feel we already know each other. How do you do?'

The startled Earl extended his hand automatically.
'I'm sorry...'

'My lovely wife, Isla, Lady Garrioch,' Cameron
said, stepping forward. 'We're not long wed, which
is why news of our nuptials has not reached you from
the Highlands yet. And this must be your good lady.'
Cameron turned to the Countess, taking her hand and
pressing it to his lips. 'I have heard so much about *you*,
my lady, and none of it did you justice. It is an honour
to meet you at last.'

'At last?' Lady Crieff flashed an enquiring look at
her husband, but Kirstin had placed herself at such an
angle that Lord Crieff could no longer see his wife.
'You are...?'

'Conlan, of course,' Cameron said, 'Laird of Garrioch.' He leaned forward conspiratorially. 'We are on
the last leg of our wedding trip, Isla and I. We've been
away from the castle these last three months, where I
know your invitation to the Scottish branch of the family will be waiting, and I said to Isla it would be right
rude for us not to come along to pay our respects. I

can see from the way your husband has taken to Isla that I'm right.'

Since Lady Crieff could still not see her husband, she had no option but to smile and nod. 'You have been on the Continent for your trip?'

'Indeed, indeed,' Cameron said, 'but I'll not bore you with the details while you've so many other guests to welcome. I'll just introduce myself to wee Beatrice— my how she's grown—and then I'll get out from under your feet. Lovely to meet you after all this time. Isla?'

He waited until Kirstin had dropped a second curtsey, then took her arm and, with the scantiest of greetings to Lady Beatrice, they were past the first hurdle.

'Well?' Cameron whispered as he led Kirstin into the crowd of the ballroom, nodding and smiling and making his way determinedly into the middle of the room.

'Fortunately, the Earl is not the brightest,' she said. 'He assumes I am some sort of distant cousin of his wife's.'

'And she thinks I'm *his* cousin—or she pretended to think so,' Cameron said, with a slight frown. 'I wouldn't count on her not following it up with him if she gets a chance. We'd do well to keep out of her way.'

'Fortunately, her time will be taken up with playing hostess at least for the next couple of hours,' Kirstin said. 'Where will we—?'

'Here, for the moment.' Cameron edged them closer to the floor, where couples were beginning to amass for the first dance. 'I want to get a look at our prey.'

'At last.'

It was after midnight and Cameron was getting impatient. Despite informing Lady Crieff, the first time she'd managed to track them down in the crowd, that neither of them wished to dance, she had quite determinedly foisted a partner on Kirstin, forcing him to take refuge in the retiring room set aside for gentlemen. Now, having observed their target escorting Lady Beatrice down to supper over half an hour ago—definitely a match in the making there—they were finally putting their pincer plan into action.

As Griffith Griffiths got to his feet to fetch more champagne, Cameron moved in, grabbing the man firmly by the arm and thrusting it behind his back.

'What the devil? Let go of me this minute or I'll...'

'Haud yer wheesht.' Cameron spoke in a low growl, in the broad accent of the Glasgow docks. 'A moment of your time is all I ask.'

'And if I refuse?'

'That wouldnae be wise.' Cameron tightened his grip. 'Do we understand one another?'

The other man gave no answer, but he made no further protest as Cameron marched him out of the dining room, keeping him close enough so that no one could see he was being forced, smiling genially.

Griffith Griffiths was about his own age. Fair-haired, with pale blue eyes, he had the look of a well-bred horse that passed for handsome amongst his class, and the sense of entitlement that always made Cameron grind his teeth.

'I don't know who the devil you are...'

'The Laird of Garrioch.'

Griffiths snorted. 'Lord Crieff's cousin from the Highlands? Or is it your wife who is Lady Crieff's cousin? Beatrice wasn't very clear—and for a very good reason, I suspect.'

They were in the small corridor outside the parlour he and Kirstin had found earlier. Cameron came to a halt in front of the door, gazing coolly down at his captive. 'Whatever it is you suspect, you're about to find that you're well off the mark.' He rarely had need to use this tone to any of his crew, but when he did, it never failed him.

It did not fail him now. Griffiths turned chalk white and began to shake. 'What…?'

'If you co-operate, there will be no harm done.'

'And if I don't?'

'Best to co-operate,' Cameron said, throwing open the door.

It was a small room, chilly, the grate empty, the only light coming from a candelabra set on a marquetry table. Kirstin stood in the shadow. Cameron closed the door behind the pair of them and let go his hold on Griffiths, but the man had no sooner realised he could run than Kirstin stepped forward and his jaw dropped.

'You!'

Kirstin indicated one of two chairs set out at the little table. 'Sit down, Mr Griffiths.'

As Griffiths did as he was bade, and Kirstin took the chair opposite, Cameron retired to lean the weight of his shoulders against the door, partly to ensure they were not disturbed, and partly to give Griffiths the illusion of intimacy. Until they'd had him captive here Cameron had not permitted himself to reckon their chances of success, but now, his heart thudding, seeing the profound effect Kirstin's mere presence elicited, he began to hope.

'What are you doing here?' Griffiths was staring at
Kirstin as if he had seen a ghost.

Her smile was the sort which could make the blood
seem to freeze in the veins. 'I came to see you. You
do not need me to remind you that you are very much
in my debt, I take it?'

There was not a trace of bravado left in the man.
Casting a frightened look over his shoulder at Cameron, he simply shook his head.

'Nor do you need me to tell you that one word from
me in Lady Crieff's ear will put an end to any preten-
sions you have to her daughter's hand.'

'No. Please, madam—'

'There is a club,' Kirstin interrupted. 'A *gentlemen's* club which specialises in deflowering virgins.
You know of it.'

A statement, not a question. Kirstin waited. Her
face was completely impassive but there was a hardness in her eyes that Cameron had not seen before. She
had glossed over the details of The Procurer's methods
when telling her stories, and he had been too caught up
in her revelations to consider the lengths she must have
gone to in order to succeed. Now he saw very clearly
how ruthless she could be.

There was a sheen of sweat on Griffiths's brow by
the time he had decided to answer. When he spoke,
it was in a whisper. 'The Erotes Club. Men from the
highest echelons.' Griffiths swallowed audibly. 'Some
of the most powerful men in the land.'

'And why do these powerful men require virgins?'

'They represent Diana. The most powerful virgin.
The ritual celebrates a demonstration of power.'

'By men over women. You mean they are violated?

It strikes me as a flimsy pretence to allow jaded degenerates to indulge in depravity.'

Griffiths, his head sunk onto his chest, nodded. 'I'm not a member.'

'You hardly qualify,' Kirstin said disdainfully. 'Where do they keep the girls?'

'What?'

'Where do they keep their victims, Mr Griffiths?'

'I don't know. I...'

'For a diplomat, you are a singularly unconvincing liar. Listen carefully to me,' Kirstin hissed. 'There is a young lady, about the same age as Lady Beatrice, being held by these men. Like Lady Beatrice, this young lady is an innocent in every way, and I venture, like Lady Beatrice, she has only a very vague notion of what to expect on her marriage night. As you sit here prevaricating, she is hidden away in some attic or cellar, terrified. Imagine, if you can, your intended bride in the same situation. I do not ask you to save her from her fate. I ask only that you give me the information to allow me to do so.'

Seeing Griffiths glance over his shoulder at Cameron, Kirstin gave a brittle little laugh. 'And let me assure you,' she said, 'that whatever fate the Laird over there has threatened you with will only be the first painful step in your fall from grace.'

'If I tell you, do you promise never to come near me again? Never to ask, never to mention...'

'Yes, to all those things.'

'How do I know I can trust your word?'

'You already know the answer to that, Mr Griffiths. I am The Procurer, and there is no one more trustworthy in the whole of London. Unless I am crossed.'

Chapter Ten

In order to avoid any further encounter with their inquisitive hostess, they slipped out via a side door which opened onto the mews, completing the short distance back to their hotel on foot. It was almost two in the morning, but Kirstin was wide awake and so too was Cameron, judging by the alacrity with which he accepted her suggestion that they have a nightcap.

Shivering, for she had left her cloak behind, she crouched by the fire, coaxing the embers into life, sinking onto the rug with her back against a chair, watching as he discarded various bits of his Highland outfit with some relief until he wore only his shirt, cravat, kilt and stockings. She unfastened her own sash and put it on the chair behind her.

Cameron seated himself on the hearthrug beside her, handing her a glass of sherry. 'I have no idea what you have on Griffiths, but you scared the living daylights out of him. I wouldn't like to get on the wrong side of you.'

'Don't say that.' She stopped as her voice began to quiver and took a sip of sherry. 'Sorry, I'm being silly. It's been a very difficult night.'

'And you were formidable. Come here.'

Cameron took her glass from her, setting it down beside his on the hearth. Then he pulled her into his arms, tucking her head onto his shoulder.

'We got what we needed, Kirstin. We now know who runs that club, and we know where the girls are likely being held, all thanks to you.'

'I couldn't have done it without your help. I was terrified that Griffiths either wouldn't or couldn't spill the beans.'

'Well, you covered it up so well that even I didn't notice.' He dropped a kiss onto her head, his hand stroking her back. 'As I said, you were formidable. We'll find the girls now. I'm sure of it.'

She looked up. 'It won't be easy. We can't expect to just stroll in and take them away with us.'

'I know these men are secretive for a reason. They have a lot to lose if their activities are exposed, so we must expect the place to be well-protected. We'll need a plan of attack. Tomorrow, I'll watch the house, get the lie of the land. Maybe as soon as the next day I'll be able to hand Philippa back to her mother.'

'And it will be over.'

She would never see Cameron again. She had known this, right from the first day she'd walked into this hotel suite she'd known it, but for the first time she felt the chasm that would be his absence.

'It will be over,' Cameron agreed. 'And when it is, Kirstin, I thought we might—'

'No.' Whatever it was he was going to suggest—another night, another week, another month—it would be both unbearable and utterly untenable. 'No,' she said again, 'this is it, Cameron. This is all we have.'

She twisted around to face him. 'So let's make the most of it.'

She waited, tense and yearning, willing him not to dispute the point, knowing that if he did they would not even have tonight, knowing that if she kissed him he would not resist, but reluctant to persuade him in that way.

He studied her in the firelight, his fingers tracing the plane of her cheek, her jaw, making her tremble. 'I have never wanted anyone as much as I want you,' he said softly.

'It is the same for me,' she said.

No lie. She would miss him so very much. But still she forced herself to wait until he kissed her. When he did, she was momentarily overwhelmed, closing her eyes on the tears which filled them, telling herself it was the culmination of everything making her feel that way, not Cameron. And then surrendering to the sweet, sensual delight of their lovemaking.

It was utterly unlike what had gone before. This time she was acutely aware of their time together ticking away, and she wanted to remember every moment, to etch the memory on her mind for ever. Every kiss was to be savoured. The way their mouths adapted to each other, the slow sweep of their tongues, the sweet dragging ache inside her that their kisses aroused.

She tugged at the knot of his cravat, casting it aside, burying her face in the warmth of his throat, licking into the hollows at the base, tasting his soap, the faint tang of salt, her chin tickled by the soft hairs of his chest. She pulled his shirt out from his belt. 'Take it off.'

He did as she asked. 'Now you,' he said.

But she shook her head. 'Only you,' she said, smiling wickedly, inspired by the way he had kissed her on the island. 'For now.'

She pushed him, a gentle nudge, and he lay back obediently, his eyes lambent with desire. She leaned over him and began to kiss him, tracing the shape of his body with her mouth, licking, kissing his shoulders, his chest, hard muscle, smooth skin, rough hair. She could hear his heart beating wildly. She pulled out her hairpins, letting the thick curtain of her hair trail over his chest as she kissed downwards, tracing the shape of his ribcage with her hands, licking into the dip of his belly, hearing the sharp intake of his breath, the soft muttering of her name, her own heart hammering.

The belt which held his plaid in place stopped her kisses. She sat up to unfasten it, kneeling between his legs. He had kicked off his stockings. Teasingly, deliberately slowly, she ran her hand up one leg, calf, knee, thigh, her fingers just brushing the thick length of his arousal. His chest was heaving. His eyes were fixed on hers. He was utterly in thrall, hers to do with as she pleased. Save that all she wanted was to please *him*.

She dragged her eyes away, returning her attention to the plaid. It was wrapped several times around his body. Deciding against unravelling it, she pushed it roughly aside. He was completely naked underneath. And completely aroused. She touched him, feathering her fingers along the length of him, fascinated by the silky skin, the hardness beneath. She heard him swallow as she curled her fingers around him. Then, driven by the unstoppable urge to know him, she dipped her head and began to lick.

His body became absolutely rigid. Instinct took over as she took him carefully into her mouth. Cameron groaned. She drew him in deeper, astonished at the responsive throb. Fascinated, she explored him with her mouth and her hands, astounded at his response, at her own. He wasn't the only one throbbing. She ached for his touch.

'Kirstin.' His voice was hoarse, a plea.

She lifted her head.

'No more. I want—wait.'

He struggled to his feet, pulling her with him, the plaid unravelling behind him, and wrapped his arms tightly around her. He was completely naked. She was almost fully dressed. She pressed herself against him, thinking to tease, but it was she who moaned in frustration. When he kissed her she moaned again, her head spinning with desire, her whole body taut with barely leashed passion.

'Yes,' he said, though she hadn't spoken, 'I think we've waited long enough.'

Scooping her into his arms, he strode through to the bedroom, setting her down by the bed. The pair of them made quick work of her clothes, falling onto the bed locked together kissing wildly, limbs tangled, hands stroking, clutching, urging.

His fingers slid easily inside her, making her gasp and clench. 'Hurry,' she said, 'hurry.'

He laughed, a throaty sound that sent a frisson down her spine. 'A moment, just one more moment.'

There was the briefest of gaps while he sheathed himself, though it felt like an hour, and then he pulled her back into his arms, rolling her on top of him, easing himself into her slowly, slowly, slowly, but even so she was so aroused, so near the edge, that his first careful thrust almost sent her over.

She tightened around him. He closed his eyes. And then she moved, and he moved with her, fast, hard, deep, each driving the other to completion, her climax triggering his, his hoarse cry mingling with hers as she fell on top of him and their lips fastened in one last deep kiss.

Lying in Cameron's arms, chest to chest, her head beside his on the pillow, their legs tangled, Kirstin was confused by the surge of emotion that brought her to the brink of tears. She put it down to the culmination of momentous events, the strain of her interview with Griffiths, the fact that they were so close to finding Philippa—and to saying goodbye for ever.

Though she would happily have lain there, listening to the beating of Cameron's heart, falling asleep in his arms, she forced herself to get up, turning her back on him and searching for her clothes.

'The hotel staff will be up and about soon,' she whispered, hearing the rustle of the bedclothes as he sat up. 'Try and get some sleep.'

'What about—?'

'We'll talk tonight. I will spend the day trying to collate any additional information I can glean to add to the details Griffiths has provided, and by then, following your observation of the house, you should have a good insight into the challenges involved in rescuing the girls.'

Throwing her gown over her head, she made for the door, bidding him a hasty goodnight and closing it softly behind her before he could say anything more.

Her own bed was cold. Huddling under the covers, Kirstin closed her eyes, but sleep was the furthest thing from her mind.

When they found Philippa she would have made good on her promise and completed the terms of her contract. So why was she worried, rather than excited? As always, Eilidh was at the centre of it. Cameron didn't want a child. Her child didn't need a father, and even if she wanted one—well, Kirstin most certainly didn't want a husband. She'd made many, many sacrifices for her daughter, but that was one she would never make.

Even if the husband was Cameron?

She sat up, plumped her pillows and threw herself back down on them. No, not even then! She would miss him—but working together, being quite alone together in this hotel, it wasn't real. And, yes, in the last few days it had become increasingly clear to her that she'd miss him enormously. But there was nothing to be done about that, was there? When she returned to reality she would see there was no place for him, so the sooner she returned the better.

And that was an end to it. The explanation for those irrational tears. So now she could get some sleep, because tomorrow was a hugely significant day.

Kirstin closed her eyes, taking slow breaths, counting in, holding, counting out. It was the way he'd looked at her, she thought hazily. As she'd unbuckled his belt. So trusting. And the way it had felt...what she had done afterwards. Such a shocking thing to do. Yet all that had been in her mind had been to please him. To show him just how much...

Cameron didn't bother trying to get to sleep after Kirstin left. Making love to her tonight hadn't been a revelation, more of a confirmation. As he lay back, his hands behind his head, the taste of her in his mouth, the scent of her on his sheets, a slow smile crept across his face.

He loved her.

He had never been in love before, never come close, yet he knew without a shadow of a doubt that he loved Kirstin. He felt it in his bones. They were meant for each other.

Fate had brought them together six years ago, but neither of them had been ready to fall in love. The timing had been wrong, so fate had patiently waited and brought them together again when the time was exactly right. He knew it now. It was just a question of persuading Kirstin.

His smile faltered. It wouldn't be easy. She was so determined not to see all the things which were suddenly so clear to him. The reason neither of them had married in the years since they'd first met was because no one else could measure up. That was why their lovemaking was so perfect. It was illogical. It was irrational. But that didn't mean he was wrong. He loved her. He couldn't feel like this if it was one-sided. He couldn't.

Why would she not countenance the possibility of a shared future together? Was it his illegitimate status? But she'd been vehemently dismissive of those who condemned him for that. Was it because *he'd* been vehement that he'd never want to marry? No. It came back to those words of hers. *Not possible*, she'd said. *That is not possible, whether we wish it or not.*

Why the devil not? They both had businesses to run. They were both accustomed to living alone, answerable to no one. At present, they were settled in two different countries. But all of those things were mere practicalities that could be resolved, weren't they? None of them made a future together impossible.

Cameron pushed back the covers and got out of bed, pulling on his dressing gown. He was missing something. There was something crucial she wasn't telling him. But what the devil could it be to make it impossible for her to consider a future in which he played a part? He *loved* her, dammit! And he was sure she could love him, if only she would allow herself to. What was stopping her?

He rang the bell for breakfast and shaving water. It arrived with an express from Tommy Devine, confirming what they now knew, that the maid's footman suitor was still in Edinburgh and innocent of any involvement. The young man had been wondering why he'd not heard from Jeannie, Tommy wrote, and when he'd discovered that she'd not written to any of the servants at the Ferguson household he'd become more worried still.

Cameron folded the missive, frowning. Louise hadn't taken account of servants' gossip, thinking only to silence Philippa's betrothed. He'd better warn her to do something about it, or all her efforts to suppress a scandal would have been in vain. Ought he to tell her that they knew where Philippa was being held?

Draining his second cup of coffee, he decided against this. A vaguely positive report would be best until they had firm news.

It was not yet eight o'clock, but Cameron was eager to be out and finally taking action—even if it would involve a deal of *in*action. He would have plenty of time, while watching the address Griffiths had given them, to think about Kirstin and to plan how to persuade her they had a future. He loved her so much. Far too much to let her go without a fight. There was a barrow-load of obstacles in their path, but he had always liked a challenge.

A foolish grin crept across his face. He was in love. He, Cameron Dunbar, had fallen deeply and irrevocably in love for the first and last time in his life. Who'd have thought it? Certainly not he.

Pulling on his greatcoat, and picking up his gloves and hat, he opened the door of his suite just in time to see a flash of red pelisse disappear down the stairs. Kirstin was going about her business very early too.

Without thinking, he followed in her wake. She walked quickly, and with purpose. If she'd looked back she'd have seen him. He made no attempt to hide himself, but nor did he try to catch up with her. She headed east, obviously a well-trodden route, for she knew the best places to cross, and never once had to check her bearings.

She was going home, Cameron realised with some trepidation. She had been so very careful never to reveal where her home was, she would be furious if she thought that he was spying on her. Which was exactly what he was doing. But some instinct made him decide to continue to follow her all the same.

The house was on Russell Square. Cameron stopped by the railings. A front door painted glossy black was thrown open as Kirstin approached the shallow steps. A little girl came bounding down, wearing a white pinafore, her coal-black hair in pigtails.

'Mummy!' she cried, throwing herself at Kirstin. 'We didn't know you were coming to see us.'

As Kirstin stooped to hug her daughter, Cameron had a clear view of the child's face. His heart lurched. She looked to be about five years old. He knew without a shadow of a doubt that she was his. He knew it in his bones and in his heart.

He looked on, dumbstruck, until the pair made their way into the house. The door closed. His stomach heaved and he lost his breakfast in the meticulously tended shrubbery of Russell Square.

The morning was turning grey, cold and damp, the kind of day that soaked a person through without it raining. The kind of cold that got into a man's bones. Heedless of it all, Cameron walked, heading south in the general direction of his quarry, the house on Half Moon Street. But it was not the future which occupied his mind, it was the past. His head reeling, he made for the quiet of St James's Park. How could Kirstin have kept such a secret from him? A child! *Their* child! He counted out the years and the months. If he was right, she would be six years old in September. *Was* he right? How could he be sure?

Kirstin had told him it was safe, he remembered. He had been careful all the same. But he had not been sheathed. He gazed sightlessly out at the canal, where a group of ducks were circling to keep warm. And then it struck him. The proof was staring him in the face. If the child wasn't his, Kirstin would have no reason to keep her existence a secret. Therefore she had to be his.

He had a daughter.

Now, finally, he understood Kirstin's use of that

word *impossible*. Now he understood why she'd been at such pains to reveal so little of her home life. But why had she kept her child a secret from him in the first place? She could have found him. She hadn't even tried. Why the hell not? She had denied him a say, had decided he'd no right ever to know his child and, what was more, she'd decided that his child had no right to know him.

Seething, he strode along the banks of the canal, crossing into Green Park, his fists clenching and unclenching, walking faster and faster along Constitution Hill, oblivious of the astonished stares of the few hardy souls braving the weather.

Reaching the entrance to Hyde Park, he slowed, his anger began to fade, and reason returned. Six years ago Kirstin had known almost nothing about him. She had not judged his suitability to be a father, she had judged him—what? Unnecessary? Irrelevant? No. She had simply made the question moot, and by doing so had spared him.

And herself?

Cameron took a seat by the Serpentine, oblivious of the drizzling rain which had started to fall. Now the initial shock had begun to fade, he tried to see the situation from Kirstin's point of view. Six years ago she'd been so excited, so full of plans, and confessedly terrified too, of the bold step she'd taken, leaving Edinburgh behind in search of a new life in London. To find that she was pregnant, with no one, never mind a husband, to support her...

He cursed long and fluently under his breath. What she must have gone through. The strength of mind, the resolution—and to have kept her daughter too, when she could easily have given her away, just as his own mother had done.

The tiny glimpse he'd had into their domestic life this morning had made the loving bond between Kirstin and her child obvious. He smiled wryly. It explained The Procurer's ethos—her first test must surely have been to save herself. And what a job she'd made of it. He could see now too, where the ruthless streak which had made Griffiths crumble had its roots.

If only he could have spared her some of what she must have endured, or even helped her, at least.

And, pray, how did he think he could have done that? Cameron forced himself to take a good hard look at himself. Six years ago, how would he have felt if Kirstin had got in touch? He knew what he'd have done, and that was married her, there was no question, but would doing the honourable thing have made either of them happy?

The answer to that was extremely unpalatable but it had to be faced. He would have resented having both a wife and child foisted on him, for they'd have kept him at home. And Kirstin—would she have consented to marriage? And, if she had, would he have permitted his wife to become The Procurer?

'Permitted,' Cameron muttered. Knowing Kirstin now, he would neither wish nor try to order her life, wouldn't dream of deciding what she could do or what she wanted to do. But back then…? Though he'd love to think otherwise, honesty forced him to admit that he'd have tried to force her into a conventional marriage, would have tried to make himself a conventional husband and father. He shuddered. They would both have been miserable.

Droplets of rain gathered on the brim of his hat had started to trickle down his back. Cameron stood up, shaking the folds of his greatcoat. Deep in thought, he began to retrace his steps, heading for Half Moon Street where he would spend the day on watch. There was no point in going over what had happened or what might have happened six years ago, because it was done. What mattered was the future.

He loved Kirstin. He wanted to marry her. He wanted to spend the rest of his life with her. And his daughter.

Good grief, he had a *daughter*! Tears stung the backs of his eyes. He slowed, almost overwhelmed with the love which surged through him like a physical force. He had a family. He would move heaven and earth to be with them. Whatever sacrifices he had to make to shape his world to Kirstin's he would make. He would convince her—

Doubt clutched at him, stopping his thoughts in their tracks. What if he was wrong? What if she didn't care? Saw their time together as nothing more than a brief dalliance? It was possible, even if he didn't want to admit it, for a person to love and not be loved in return.

But this was neither the time nor the place for navel-gazing. He had a niece to rescue! As he turned off Curzon Street, Cameron forced himself to put Kirstin and his new-found daughter to the back of his mind.

Half Moon Street was, according to Kirstin, a rather mixed bag of a district. There were several town houses occupied by those who either disdained the grander and stuffier parts of Mayfair, or were considered unsuitable by the residents. There were genteel apartments for those whose income could not run to a town house.

There were several gentlemen's lodging houses, for the street was conveniently close to the clubs of St James's. And there were a few discreet houses occupied by a few select ladies kept by gentlemen with the means to support two households for very different purposes.

The house which Griffiths had described was halfway down on the left-hand side of the street, with a red door and a knocker in the shape of a lion's head. The lower windows were barred, though so too were the windows in several other of the buildings. The windows of the attic and the second floor were shuttered, but those on the ground and main floor were curtained. The rooms behind were dark.

Frustrated, Cameron looked around for a place from which to spy, but each house abutted the next. He could not stand there all day without raising suspicion. So he'd have to find a hiding place.

'You did *what*?' Kirstin exclaimed.

It was very late by the time Cameron returned, but she had held back dinner for him.

'I hired a room in the lodging house diagonally opposite,' Cameron said, helping himself to a leg of chicken. 'A room at the front, of course. With an excellent vantage point.'

'How did you explain the fact that you had no luggage?'

'I told some tale of it having been lost in transit. The landlady didn't believe a word of it, of course, but she was happy to go along with it when I supplemented my tale with a very generous down-payment. I'll go back tonight, get my money's worth out of that room.'

It was wrong of her to be disappointed. Guiltily,

Kirstin set aside her own inappropriate ideas for how the rest of the night might be spent. 'You'll not see much in the dark.'

'No.' Cameron frowned down at his chicken as if it had offended him. 'How did you spend your day?'

'That's the second time you've asked me that. Is there something wrong?'

'No. Yes. No.' He pushed aside his plate, uncharacteristically leaving it half-full. 'Kirstin, I— Never mind, it can wait.'

'What can wait?'

He stared at her, clearly torn, then shook his head. 'Now is not the time,' he said.

She had the impression he was talking to himself rather than her, for he stared down at his plate again for some time, shifting his dinner about abstractedly.

Finally, he gave a sigh. 'What were we talking about?'

'You are determined to return to Half Moon Street. In the dark. Even though you won't see anything.'

'But I might.' He sighed again, and gave himself a little shake. 'No, I'm definitely going,' he said firmly. 'I want to keep an eye out for any comings and goings,' he added grimly. 'We've no idea how many poor lasses are locked away behind those doors.'

'It's not likely to be more than one or two. What I have managed to extract from my sources, using what Griffiths told us, is that the *gentlemen* of the Erotes Club are very discriminating.' Kirstin gave up pretending to eat. 'They number minor royalty amongst their members. To think that such men— It's disgusting.'

He drummed his fingers on the table, frowning deeply. 'If they find out that you've been sniffing around, they will ruin you without compunction. If they are as influential as you say, they'll know who The Procurer is and where to find her. However we go about breaking into that house, you can't risk being involved.'

He looked exhausted, with circles under his eyes, his jaw dark with stubble. 'They could just as equally ruin you,' Kirstin said, reaching across the table to clasp his hand.

He tightened his fingers around hers. 'It's *my* niece we're rescuing, *my* promise to Louise Ferguson that we're honouring. Two young lassies, Kirstin, and a mother at her wits' end. Compared to that, my business doesn't matter.'

'I made a promise too, remember? To you, Cameron. I'm not deserting you at the last minute.'

'Kirstin, you can't risk all you've worked for.' He pushed back his chair, pulling her to her feet and wrapping his arms around her. 'I can't let you do that,' he said, sounding oddly desperate. 'After everything you've— No, I won't let you.'

She reached up to smooth back his hair, puzzled by his vehemence. 'Then we'll have to make sure that we don't get caught, because I'm coming with you. No,' she said, putting her finger over his mouth when he made to protest, 'listen to me. Philippa doesn't know you, Cameron. How is she to know you have come to save her, not take her away to endure some horrible fate? It will be much better for her if there's a woman there to reassure her—and Jeannie, too, if she is in that house.'

'I hadn't thought of that.'

'And as for those in charge of the Erotes Club— yes, they could ruin us both, I'm not denying it, but we could ruin them too, if we have to.'

'Expose their—their private peccadillos to the public, you mean?'

'Exactly. *If* we are caught—and we won't be—then
we can threaten to expose them. They have even more
to lose than we do.'

His arms tightened around her waist. 'They don't.
Kirstin, I—' He broke off, biting his lip, shaking his
head at her enquiring look. 'Another time. I must go.'

'We'll find a way to get Philippa back safely. We
are so close…'

'I know. It's not that.'

'Then what?'

'Not now. We'll make a rescue plan in the morning.
Try and get a good night's sleep.'

A longing to spend the night sleeping wrapped in
his arms assailed her. Not to make love, but simply
to sleep. She yearned to smooth away his frown and
his worries, and to wake up to his kisses, his tender
smile…

Kirstin untangled herself from his embrace and bestowed her professional smile on him. 'The sooner we
act the better, for the sake of those girls.'

And for the sake of her own peace of mind too.
She could not allow herself to become too attached
to Cameron. Feelings clouded one's judgement. She
could not permit that.

'Until the morning.'

She nodded, was about to head for the door, but
somehow found herself wrapping her arms around him
instead, pressing a fleeting kiss to his lips. 'Good luck.'

There was a distinct and inexplicable wobble in her
voice. Afraid as much of the emotion in her voice as of
Cameron's noticing, Kirstin fled.

* * *

They had spent the morning planning and preparing. Now, on the brink of leaving for Half Moon Street, Kirstin was trying not to panic. 'You really think this will work? Wouldn't it be easier to hire a couple of thugs?'

'Easier if we want all hell to break loose.' Cameron turned from the mirror, where he had been adjusting his cravat. 'And that's exactly what we're trying to avoid.'

'I know that.' She managed a strained smile. 'Don't worry. I won't lose my nerve.'

'That is one of few things I'm not worried about. Come here, sit down for a minute.' Cameron patted the sofa, clasping her hands in his when she sat down beside him. 'The more time we can buy ourselves between spiriting the girls away and our little ruse being discovered the better, right?'

'Right.' It was foolish to be reassured simply by the clasp of his hands and a warm smile, but she was.

'So we will persuade this Mrs Allardyce woman Griffiths says is the housekeeper that we've been sent by her employers, the Erotes Club. The mention of the name should be enough to convince her we are legitimate visitors.'

'But if she is cautious and insists on checking first?'

'Then I will point out how foolish she is being to risk upsetting her paymasters by contacting them unnecessarily when discretion is all. And if that doesnae work,' Cameron said in his broadest Glaswegian growl, 'then I'll batter the life out of the two thugs on the door, and you can take care of the lassies.'

Kirstin shivered. In his guise of a rough Glaswegian, Cameron made her feel fragile, helpless, when she was never any of those things, and he made her feel completely safe, sure that he would never let any harm come to her, though she was in no need of a protector.

'It is to be hoped that we can avoid any physical violence,' she said, unable to prevent herself from pressing a kiss to his knuckles.

'If there is, then you've chosen the perfect disguise, Nurse Grey.' He smiled wickedly. 'I'm tempted to get myself a wee bit bloodied just so you can be my ministering angel.'

'Oh, no, Dr Black, you are quite mistaken, I am no ministering angel,' Kirstin replied in Nurse Grey's clipped tones. 'I'm the stern, cold-baths-and-plenty-of-fresh-air kind of nurse, who tolerates no malingering.'

'But who also has a wee soft spot for Dr Black?' Cameron winked.

'Dr Black, I think you are trying to distract me from the task in hand.'

He kissed her softly. 'Is it working?'

Kirstin sighed, smiling reluctantly. 'Yes. I am much better now. Shall we go?'

He narrowed his eyes, scrutinising her for some moments. What he saw obviously satisfied him, for he nodded, getting to his feet and pulling her with him. 'Aye,' he said curtly. 'Let's get this business done.'

Chapter Eleven

Half Moon Street was eerily quiet in the middle of the afternoon. The pavements were deserted as the hackney carriage pulled up in front of the red door of number nine. Dr Black, in a long cloak, with a tall hat, carrying an old-fashioned swordstick in the guise of a malacca walking cane with an embossed silver top, descended first. Nurse Grey, in a plain brown wool dress and short cape, with a white starched apron and cap to match, emerged behind the good doctor, carrying his bag and keeping her head lowered.

Though Kirstin's heart was hammering, her mind was completely focused on the task in hand, taking her lead from Cameron.

A sharp rap of the knocker revealed a tall, well-built woman of about forty, dressed in a housekeeper's garb. Her smile failed to meet her eyes.

'Yes?'

'Mrs Allardyce.' Dr Black had the plummy, booming, confident voice of a man sure of his station in life and his welcome. 'I take it we are expected? I am Dr Black,' he said, upon receiving a blank look, 'and this is my assistant, Nurse Grey. Please resist making the obvious comment, it has been done to death.'

Taking advantage of the woman's confusion, he pushed passed her into the hallway with Kirstin scurrying behind. The two thugs who guarded the house and its precious contents stood, arms folded, at either side of the stairs, like grotesque and oversized newel posts.

'Gentlemen,' Dr Black said, with a careless nod.

Mrs Allardyce, meantime, had recovered her nerve. 'I am afraid you are under some misapprehension, Dr Black,' she said coolly. 'There is no one here who requires the services of a medical man.'

Cameron clapped his hands together and tutted with just the right amount of condescension. Kirstin, still hovering in the background and taking covert stock of the place, wondered who his role model was, certain that he had one.

'Well, now, Mrs Allardyce,' he continued, dropping his voice to a confidential stage whisper, 'I sincerely hope for your sake no one here is ill, since it is your job to keep them fit and well, and that would constitute a dereliction of duty.' He smiled benignly. 'Rather, it is a matter of my verifying that they are up to specification. For the coming experience. If you take my meaning. This is the first occasion the goods in question have been sourced from a madam such as Mrs Jardine, so the powers that be prudently wish to satisfy themselves as to their suitability.'

'I am not sure I can allow...'

'Now, I am very sure that you don't want me to disclose in front of these fine gentlemen here precisely who sent me, for your—let us call him your benefactor— would not wish his name to be bandied about, would he?' Dr Black's smile became menacing. 'He pays you a great deal for your discretion. You would not wish me to cause him to think that his money has been badly spent.'

Kirstin was not surprised to see Mrs Allardyce wither, but the woman had not earned her trusted place in this hellish house for nothing. She did not dismiss the thugs. Instead she opened the door of a small parlour and indicated that Dr Black should follow.

Kirstin hesitated, but a tiny shake of his head informed her that Cameron wanted her to remain where she was. The door was left open, giving her a view of Mrs Allardyce and Cameron, she remonstrating, he standing his ground, shaking his head, saying little. Though Kirstin's hearing was acute, she could make out only the odd muttered phrase.

The two thugs made no pretence at uninterest, their attention fully focused on the confrontation. Taking advantage of this, Kirstin studied each of them, noting the unmistakable outline of cudgels under their rough coats. To deter unwanted visitors, no doubt. Her mouth was dry. How many girls had been incarcerated here, locked away, kept fed and watered, physically unharmed, but in mental turmoil? What kind of state would they be in when they were finally taken to meet their fate? And what happened to them afterwards? Some of the many questions she had been unable to obtain answers to. With this case, she had for the first time reached the limits of The Procurer's influence.

The booming tone of Dr Black made her start. 'A wise move, Mrs Allardyce. Your caution does you credit, but I fear you might undermine your position were you to trouble your superiors with a spurious query as to my credentials. They are not the type who like to have their actions questioned.' Cameron was shaking the woman's hand. 'I shall inform His Grace that he is being very well served indeed. Now, if you will call off these gentlemen…?'

A nod from Mrs Allardyce and the men stood aside. 'Nurse Grey, if you will bring my bag we will complete our task and be gone.'

He began to stride up the stairs, so Kirstin hurried after him. Cameron paused for a mere second at the top of the landing on the uppermost floor to swear under his breath.

'That was one hard nut to crack, but she decided discretion was the better part of valour. Philippa is in the room at the end of this corridor. Jeannie is with her.'

'They have cudgels, both men,' Kirstin said.

'Better that than pistols.' Cameron raised his voice. 'Hurry along, Nurse Grey, I'm a busy man. I don't have all day.'

There were two doors on either side of the hallway in addition to the one in which Philippa was being held. All four of the rooms, to Kirstin's utter relief, were empty. She knew that any attempt to release other victims would put Philippa's safety at risk, it was something they had both discussed, and a conclusion painfully reached. But she knew that Cameron would have been still tempted, and as for herself—well, she was simply glad not to be put to the test.

'This is the one, Nurse Grey,' Dr Black boomed, throwing back the first bolt.

As he stooped to open the second bolt Kirstin saw that his hand was shaking, fumbling with the mechanism. She touched his arm. Their eyes met briefly. He gave a firm nod and pulled back the bolt, opening the door just wide enough for the pair of them to step through, before shutting it again and leaning his back against it.

The girls, one with raven-black hair, the other with a tangled mop of bright red, were huddled together in the furthest corner of the room. They were dressed in white shifts, barefooted, but while Jeannie's face was a picture of utter terror, Philippa was trying desperately to compose herself.

'What do you want?' she asked, and though her voice trembled there was a touch of her mother's hauteur in her tone. Louise, Kirstin thought, had been very wrong in thinking her daughter lacked spine.

There was no time now for explanations, all that could wait until the girls were safe. 'Philippa,' Kirstin said calmly, 'my name is Kirstin. This man with me is Cameron. We've been sent by your mother, Mrs Louise Ferguson, to take you home.'

Jeannie whimpered and would have come forward, but Philippa caught her, pushing the maid behind her, glaring at Kirstin from under fierce brows exactly like her mother's.

'Why hasn't my mother come herself? We haven't made any trouble. We've eaten our dinners and we've kept quiet and we've not made a fuss, exactly as we've been told to do. So if the ransom has been paid why hasn't Mama come to fetch us?'

Ransom! So this was how the girls were kept in line—with the promise of release. At least they had been spared the agony of knowing their real fate, but it was a hideous lie to feed them.

'Philippa,' Kirstin said urgently, 'there has been no ransom demand. Your mother has had to resort to other

methods to rescue you. I cannot explain right now,
there is no time, but believe me, your only chance of
escape is with us, right now.'

'But they said—'

'Dr Black?' Mrs Allardyce knocked on the door.
'Have you completed your preliminary examination?'

'Get on the bed,' Kirstin said, in a tone which
brooked no argument.

Cowed, the girls did as she bade them, watching
wide-eyed as she removed a fiendish-looking pair of
forceps from the doctor's bag and held them out for
Cameron, who had hurriedly cast off his cloak and
gloves. Jeannie gave a shriek at the sight of the in-
strument, and even Philippa whimpered. No need to
tell them to look as if they'd been traumatised, Kirstin
thought darkly, recalling her own first glimpse of one
of those fearful implements.

She pulled out a towel spattered with pig's blood
from the bag and draped it over her arm. 'Philippa,
your mother has a miniature of you which she keeps in
a blue enamel case,' she whispered. She tried desperately to recall what Louise Ferguson had been wearing at their one and only meeting. 'And she has a ring,
rose gold, with five garnets set in the shape of a cross.
And a gold locket, oval in shape.'

'It has a lock of my father's hair in it. Who *are* you?'

Kirstin heaved a sigh of relief. 'Please do as we
ask, say nothing, and you will be with your mother
very shortly.'

Philippa nodded. 'Jeannie, did you hear that?' she
asked her maid gently. 'Hush, now, do as they say, and
we'll be home soon.'

'Take this,' Kirstin said, pushing a second gruesome towel into Jeannie's hands. 'Hold it here,' she said, 'as if…'

'Dr Black! If you do not open this door…'

'Now, now, Mrs Allardyce, I was trying to preserve the girls' dignity.' Cameron waved the forceps in the woman's face. 'Our very important little miss passes muster, as far as I'm concerned, but I would prefer the absolute certainty a very quick second opinion would provide. Unfortunately, we have a little bit of a problem with her handmaiden. Nurse Grey?'

Kirstin obligingly held up the gruesome towel. She pointed to Jeannie, clutching the second towel in her lap, hoping that Mrs Allardyce was the squeamish type and not inclined to question the exact nature of either Jeannie's complaint or Dr Black's examination.

'Not a handmaiden at all,' Dr Black said, tutting, 'but soiled goods, I'm afraid. You see what a wise decision it was to call me in? She'll make a full recovery, but she's of no use to your benefactor. I'll take her with me, find her a more appropriate home.'

He tapped the side of his nose, then clapped his hands together. 'Nurse Grey, young ladies, let us be off. The sooner we are gone the sooner we will be back.'

'This is most unusual,' Mrs Allardyce protested. 'I am not at all sure…'

'Ah, but you will be, with the benefit of a second examination,' Dr Black said. 'An hour, two at the most, and I'll have her back to you. Better safe than sorry, that's what I say. I've no more desire to upset our paymasters than you.'

Kirstin hurriedly wrapped her short cape around Philippa, while Cameron held out his cloak for Jeannie, placing himself between the girl and Mrs Allardyce so that she did not see Kirstin grabbing the bloodied towel and shoving it back into the bag along with the forceps. Jeannie could barely stand, but Philippa whispered something reassuring in her ear and pushed her forward.

Kirstin led the way, with Cameron at the rear, the two girls sandwiched between them. She fought the urge to run, heading down the stairs at a stately pace, aware of Dr Black still making booming small talk, though the roaring in her ears prevented her from taking in a word.

The thugs were in position at the bottom of the stairs. Kirstin made for the door. One of them rushed in front of her. She had just enough time to wonder frantically if she could lift the heavy doctor's bag high enough to hit him square in the face when he opened the door for her and stood back.

The carriage was waiting. The driver, seeing them, jumped down from the box and lowered the steps. Kirstin discovered that she could still find solace in prayer as she stood back to let Philippa and Jeannie in. She climbed in after them.

Dr Black bid Mrs Allardyce a last fruity adieu and a promise that her helpfulness would be extolled. Then Cameron leapt into the coach, slammed the door shut and it was over.

When they had arrived at the house where Louise was staying Kirstin had firmly refused to leave the coach, not wishing to intrude on the reunion. She completed the business of covering their trail by paying their driver to lose his memory, returning late to the hotel and a note from Cameron, informing her that he was staying for dinner with Mrs Ferguson.

The following morning she received a second note, informing her that he would be wholly occupied for some hours assisting Mrs Ferguson—still Mrs Ferguson, not Louise—complete her travel arrangements north with all possible speed. Understandable, and extremely wise, Kirstin thought. Louise wished to thank her in person, but Kirstin decided against this. Seeing Cameron's face as they'd left Half Moon Street had been all the thanks she needed.

So she wrote her own note, informing Cameron that she was taking a walk in Hyde Park and would see him at dinner. The weather co-operated with her desire for fresh air and solitude, a chill breeze making the few clouds which dared to blot the clear blue winter's sky scud along. The park was virtually deserted. It was too cold for nursery maids and their children, too early in the year for the hoi polloi to take the air and show off their horses, their toilettes and their mistresses, so Kirstin had nothing but the ducks and a few hardy souls taking their daily constitutional for company.

She wandered aimlessly, trying to conjure up the satisfaction of a job very well done, which she had every right to, but signally failing. The case was over. Philippa and Jeannie were both safe and would recover fully from their ordeal in time. Cameron had made good on his promise to Louise, the debt he believed he owed her paid. And Kirstin had made good on her promise to Cameron.

Their time together was almost over. Tonight would be her last in the hotel, for there was no reason to linger there. Tomorrow she would go home to Eilidh, and Cameron—most likely Cameron would escort Louise and Phillipa safely back to Edinburgh.

It was over. There was no point in crying or feeling sorry for herself, especially when she had exactly what she wanted, a happy outcome for the case, and for her the reassurance that she had made the right decision all those years ago, when Eilidh had first been given into her arms.

She would miss Cameron. Dreadfully at first. But it would pass. And she would have no cause to question her decision again. Nor ever to see him again either.

She halted at the edge of the Serpentine, staring blindly at the murky waters as she tried to get herself under control. There was still tonight. They would be together tonight. They would make love tonight. One last time. She would make it memorable. And when morning came—

But she wouldn't think about the morning.

'Kirstin.'

She whirled round. 'Cameron!'

'You didn't call,' he said. 'Louise was very disappointed. She couldn't understand why you were so reluctant—but in the end she wrote you a note.'

'You know that it is my policy to remain in the background.'

'I thought this case was different. Obviously not.' He offered her his arm. 'Shall we walk? It's cold standing here.'

She sighed, doing as she was bade, and they began to follow the path around the Serpentine. She didn't have to explain herself. Yet she couldn't resist. 'I have already broken a great many of my own rules in taking your case on. It *is* different from any other, you're right about that.'

'Then why won't you see Louise?'

'Because she doesn't owe me any thanks. Her gratitude should be directed at you. You're the one who rescued Philippa.'

'We achieved that together, you and I.'

'But I wouldn't have been involved at all if not for you.' She glanced up at him, smiling faintly. 'From the beginning you've put the safety of those two girls over everything. I know you think that it was a—a form of reparation, but you didn't commit a crime, Cameron, simply by being born.'

'So you stayed away in order to ensure that Louise had to heap every scrap of her gratitude on me, is that it?'

'And did she?'

He laughed. 'Almost, but not quite. She was almost effusive. I even got a hug—well, a light patting, which is the next best thing.'

'Did she explain who you are to Philippa?'

'She did.' His expression became serious once more. 'That is one very brave young lassie, Kirstin. She didn't say much about what they'd been through, and insisted that they were never in fear of their lives, well-cared-for, all that, and Louise was happy to swallow it.'

'You think Philippa is protecting her?'

'Ironic, isn't it? Philippa's not one to blow her own trumpet, but I reckon she was a tower of strength to Jeannie.'

'What will happen to her? Louise blamed her for what happened…'

'I reckon she still does, though she dare not say it for

fear of upsetting Philippa. In the short term, all Jeannie wants is to go home to her mammy in North Berwick.'

'And what about Philippa's engagement?'

'That decision, believe it or not,' Cameron said, 'has been left in Philippa's hands. She, clever girl, has chosen to take her time deciding.'

'Goodness, but Louise has changed her tune.'

'She's had a lot of time to think, she told me.'

Kirstin raised a brow. 'She seems to have told you quite a lot.'

'Aye.' Cameron smiled briefly down at her. 'Whether it's relief, gratitude, or whether this whole horrible experience has genuinely altered her view of life, she does seem to have warmed to me.'

'Cameron!' Kirstin stopped in her tracks, beaming up at him. 'That is…'

'Hold your horses. She's not ready to call me brother yet, not by a long chalk. Though Philippa is already calling me Uncle Cameron. Which, let me tell you, sounds mighty strange.'

'I think that where Philippa leads, Louise will follow. I'm so pleased for you.'

'We'll see.'

They turned at the dog leg of the Serpentine and began to head back on the other side of the lake.

'Do you think the members of the Erotes Club will come after us, after yesterday?' Cameron asked.

'I doubt it. I'm not naïve enough to think they'll abandon their activities, but at least we've forced them to cancel their next meeting. Considering all you have achieved, you don't seem particularly happy.'

'For someone who has played a pivotal role, I could

level the same accusation at you. I owe you a huge debt of gratitude in addition to a large fee.'

'I don't want your money, Cameron.'

'Don't be silly, Kirstin, you've earned it, and I signed a contract…'

'I don't want your money. I did this because— Oh, it doesn't matter.'

'It matters a lot.' He stopped as they reached the gates of the park. 'I've wondered from the beginning why you took my case on when The Procurer's business is to find other people to make the impossible possible, not to do it herself. So why am I the exception?'

That look of his, the way his eyes bored into her very soul, made her want to flee. And why was she getting the impression that this was a plea, rather than a question? What did he want her to say?

'I met you because I was curious. I took on the case because I was the best person for the role and time was pressing. I stayed because I desperately wanted to help find Philippa and Jeannie.' All of which was the truth, but not even half of it.

And none of it, evidently, was what Cameron wanted to hear. 'Is that it?' he asked.

'I knew how much finding them meant to you,' Kirstin elaborated a little desperately, 'and—and I— you deserve to be given a second chance. Your sister—I was sure that if only she could forget the past she would realise how fortunate she is to call you her brother.'

He smiled wryly. 'So you did it for me?'

'I—yes. I did it for you.'

She couldn't tell if that satisfied him or not. He looked up at the sky, which was darkening, the sun now completely obscured behind thick cloud.

'Looks to me like we might be in for snow. We should head back to the hotel.'

'I sincerely hope it's not snow, else your journey north—'

'Oh, I'm not escorting Louise.' He took her arm and began to walk quickly in the direction of the hotel. 'I promised I'd visit as soon as was convenient, but now is not in the least convenient. I've business of my own to attend to.'

'Ewan's tea business?'

But Cameron, increasing his pace, seemed not to have heard her.

The evening gown Kirstin wore for her last dinner with Cameron had an underdress of scarlet satin paired with an overdress of sarcenet decorated with silk flowers in every shade of red, the leaves picked out in silver. The neckline was square, the sleeves simple caps, the hem weighted with a border of red and silver beading. It was an outrageously expensive and wildly extravagant gown, one she was unlikely ever to wear again, though the result was worth every penny.

Kirstin painted her lips with carmine, added a light dusting of powder to her nose, and adjusted the velvet ribbon in her hair. Crimson slippers and a new pair of long white evening gloves completed her toilette.

'You look absolutely ravishing,' Cameron said, bowing low over her hand.

'Thank you.'

In a dark blue coat and waistcoat, with tightly fitting fawn pantaloons and a pair of gleaming Hessians, Cameron had dressed with care for this, their last night.

Their last night. She mustn't allow herself to think of it like that.

'You look very dashing.'

'Thank you. Sit down, Kirstin. I've asked them to delay serving dinner.' Taking a bottle from a silver bucket, he began to twist the cork. 'I thought we'd forgo our sherry. Tonight calls for a celebration, a toast.'

He seemed tense. Watching him pour the champagne into crystal flutes, Kirstin was becoming nervous.

He sat down beside her and touched his glass to hers. 'To you,' Cameron said. 'Kirstin Blair, a woman who makes the impossible possible.'

'Cheers,' she said, immeasurably touched and also reassured. She took a sip of the golden liquid, relishing the way the bubbles melted on her tongue, and sighed with pleasure. 'This was a lovely idea.'

But Cameron's smile was perfunctory. He set his glass down, untouched, and Kirstin had a horrible conviction that the night was not going to go to her plan. Her fingers tightened around the stem of her own glass. Cameron's throat was working, a sure sign that he was having to steel himself to say something, and she was absolutely certain that, whatever it was, she didn't want to hear it.

'Cameron...'

'Kirstin.'

The look in his eyes made her heart flutter, then pound. She sat frozen to the spot, allowing him to remove her glass and take her hands in his.

'Kirstin, when I told you that I never dreamed of marriage, I meant it. But that was because I'd never met the right woman.'

'No.' She tried to pull her hands away, but he held her tightly.

'Listen to me,' he said urgently, 'please hear me out.'

Feeling quite sick, she realised that if she did not, the break between them would never be final. Besides, it was every bit as vital to make the break clean for him too. And it would be a test, she thought grimly, of her own resolve, which she could use as a talisman against any future regrets.

'Go on,' she said.

'Six years ago—' He broke off, cleared his throat, released her to take a deep gulp of his champagne. 'Six years ago,' he began again, 'I met the right woman. You.' He smiled at her softly. 'But the time wasn't right for us. You were only just setting out to make a life for yourself, and I—well, I hadn't a clue whether I was coming or going, after that meeting with Louise. So we went our separate ways. And we lived our own lives, the pair of us, and made a success of them.'

'Exactly, Cameron, which is why—'

'When the fates brought us back together this time,' he interrupted, 'we were ready. I didn't know it that first night here, Kirstin, when I went on about my freedom to roam the world and my liking for having things all my own way, but I very quickly realised. You are the one I've been waiting for. You are the only woman for me. I love you with all my heart.'

'No.' Her own heart was beating so hard that she could hardly breathe. 'No, Cameron. Please, I can't…'

'You assume you can't, because you've not thought about it. Think about it now, Kirstin. I'm not asking you to marry me straight away—though that's what I want. And I'm certainly not asking you to give up all

that you've worked so hard for. All I'm asking is that
you think about it, that you give us a chance to see if
we can create a whole new life together. Will you at
least think about it?'

'No!' Panic-stricken, she jumped to her feet. 'No,
Cameron, I can't countenance that.'

'Why not? Don't you care for me?'

'You know I do, but—I told you. I told you right
from the start that we could not—that we could never—
Our situations are far too different for us ever to find
any compromise we could be happy with.'

'You can't know that if you don't try.'

'I don't need to try,' Kirstin said wretchedly. 'I know
it wouldn't work, it's impossible.'

'Why is it so impossible?' Cameron caught her
hands, forcing her to face him, to meet his gaze. 'Can't
you trust me with the truth?'

It was that same look he'd had at the park gates earlier. As if he was pleading with her to tell him something. An appalling possibility crossed her mind. But
that was simply not credible. She tried to think, tried
desperately to recall if she had said one single thing,
made a single slip which could have set him down that
path, but there was nothing.

She shook her head. 'There isn't anything to tell.'

'You know,' he said gently, 'the one thing you're not
any good at is lying.'

He knew. She had no idea how he'd guessed, but
he knew. She was finding it difficult to breathe. She
must have laced her corsets too tight. The room was
too hot. The need to escape was too strong to resist.
Kirstin, who had never failed to face anything in her
life, made for the door.

He caught her easily. He was smiling. Why was he smiling?

'Kirstin, my darling, I know we have a daughter. I know that she is the reason you think our being together is impossible, but you're wrong. I have never been so delighted...'

'Delighted?' She stared at him in utter disbelief. 'You told me that you never wanted children. You said that you would resent them, that you—you cannot possibly be delighted.'

'But I am. When I saw her—'

'When?' Cold anger cloaked her terror. 'When did you see her?'

'The morning after the ball. I was on my way out, heading to Half Moon Street, and I saw you.'

A faint flush tinged his cheeks. 'You *followed* me?' Kirstin exclaimed incredulously. 'You spied on me? You followed me to my home, the home that I have been at great pains to keep private.'

'For a reason I now understand fully.'

'For a reason which I never wished you to know.'

'But I understand that,' Cameron said urgently. 'You were determined to establish yourself, to make an extraordinary life for yourself. Despite what happened between us that night, you didn't know me, could have had no idea whether I'd ignore a letter informing me that I was a father or, perhaps worse, from your point of view, whether I'd force my name on you and dictate how both you and your daughter should lead your lives. Am I right?'

He was so correct that she was astonished and could only nod. 'You see now why it is impossible?'

'I see now why it was impossible six years ago. But now…'

'No,' Kirstin said flatly, 'nothing has changed. I am perfectly happy as I am, and perfectly capable of taking care of my daughter myself. I don't need you.'

Cameron looked as if she had slapped him. 'And my daughter? Isn't she entitled to a father?'

'She doesn't need one. She has no idea who you are, and that is how I intend things to remain.'

'But I love you.'

'That changes nothing,' she said ruthlessly, refusing to see the hurt she was causing, wanting only to escape, to protect her daughter and herself. 'I don't love you. I *won't* love you. There is nothing more to discuss.'

He was silent for a very long time. 'I notice you don't deny that she is mine.'

It was an agony not to relent, but she was fighting for her life. Even so, she would never tell such a dastardly lie. 'Of course she is yours,' Kirstin admitted shakily. 'Why else would I have kept her a secret?'

He studied her, his eyes hardening. 'I won't allow my daughter to suffer as I did for the lack of a name.'

'She has my name.'

'You know perfectly well what I mean. You are so determined to bend the world to the shape you desire, and heaven knows I admire you for it, even though there must have been many occasions when you've paid a heavy price for your uncompromising stance. But it's wrong of you to make our daughter pay the price for your principles.'

'*My* daughter does not suffer,' Kirstin said through gritted teeth.

'What does her school think about her mother, *Miss* Blair?'

'She does not attend school.'

His lip curled. 'So that's how you preserve her innocence? That's how you protect her, is it? By hiding her away? You can't do that for ever.'

'Don't you dare tell me what I can and can't do. *This* is why I did not tell you…'

'You're deluding yourself,' Cameron barked, making no attempt to subdue his anger any more. 'You can't keep her hidden away from the world for ever. The longer you lie to her…'

'I don't lie to her.'

'She may not be old enough to be curious yet, but one day she will ask about me. For such an intelligent woman, you're being incredibly stupid. I can't bear the thought of my daughter going through life tarred as a bastard.'

'She is not—'

'Don't kid yourself. That is exactly what they'll call her. She'll be ridiculed, she'll be bullied, she'll be made to feel that she is worthless. It will be a permanent stain on her character. I speak from experience, as you may recall from my choosing to confide in you.'

'It's not the same,' Kirstin protested, but her words lacked conviction.

'You know it is, which is why you've brought her up in splendid isolation, by the sounds of it. Well I won't stand by and let her suffer. I won't let her endure what I did.'

His peremptory tone made her rally. 'You have no say in the matter. After tonight, I never want to see you again.'

If her words hurt him, he recovered quickly enough. 'After tonight, I am absolutely determined to give my daughter my name.'

'Don't be preposterous. You can't force me to marry you, Cameron.'

'I won't have to. Logic and reason, those tenets you live by, will eventually make you realise that you owe it to your daughter to free her to go out in the world, and to protect her too. It's clear that you love her very much. Loving someone doesn't mean keeping them in a gilded cage, Kirstin. It means…'

He turned away, pouring a glass of champagne with a shaking hand, downing it in one. She watched, unable to move, almost beyond thought, never mind words. *This couldn't be happening.*

Cameron set the empty glass down. 'I'll give you a year.'

She stared at him blankly.

'Twelve months to think about what I've said, to come to terms with the fact that we're going to be married, and then I'll be back.'

'We're not going to be married.'

'You need have no fear that I'll force myself on you, or on my daughter either. I won't interfere with your precious life. I'll give the child my name—you'll allow me that, at least?—but that's it.'

'I would become your property. You would be entitled to my business—the law would give you it all, including my daughter.'

'Do you not understand me at *all*?' he roared, clutching at his hair. 'Can you not get it into your head that I'm not interested in owning you or changing you or— Dear God, Kirstin, have you really no idea at all what I feel for you? I wouldn't change a hair on your head.'

His hand reached out towards her, but he snatched it back. 'You think this is all about the child, don't you? You're quite wrong. It was about you, first and foremost—but there's no talking to you about that. I've done with spilling my guts. Think very carefully about what I've said. I'll be back in exactly a year from now to hear your answer.'

He opened the door for her. Distraught, she walked towards it, wondering if her legs would carry her the short distance to her own suite and the sanctuary of her bed.

'Kirstin?'

She gazed up at him through a curtain of tears.

'Her name,' Cameron said wretchedly. 'I don't even know her name.'

'Eilidh,' she said, as the tears began to cascade down her cheeks. 'Her name is Eilidh.'

Cameron remained where he was, standing by the door, completely numb. A sharp rap roused him from his reverie. He wrenched it open, only to be confronted with two waiters and his very carefully ordered dinner. He sent them away, keeping only the wine, cursing his stupidity. After all, Kirstin only gave second chances to deserving females.

He loved her and yet he had lost her.

With a shaking hand, he poured himself a large glass of wine, gulping down the finest vintage the hotel had been able to provide as if it were ale. Kirstin was gone. Kirstin didn't love him. *Wouldn't* love him.

He stared down at the floor as if into a chasm. He'd

get by without her. His chest tightened. He bit back a huge heaving sob. He'd survive. He poured himself a second, brimming glass of burgundy and tipped it down his throat. Another sob racked his body. No wine, no matter how fine, was a cure for a broken heart.

Cameron staggered to his bedroom, threw himself on the bed and pulled a pillow over his head.

He woke in the early hours of the morning with an aching head but a clear mind. He'd gone over and over what he'd said the night before, wondering if he'd got it wrong, but he hadn't. It was Kirstin who had made it all about her daughter, giving him no option in the end but to follow her lead. The child was all she cared about.

While he had been falling in love with her almost from the moment she'd stepped through the door of this very suite, she had never seen him as anything other than a—a dalliance. She didn't love him. She wouldn't love him. And there was not a thing he could do about that.

Heavy-hearted but resolved, Cameron rang the bell for shaving water and coffee, and set about packing. He would never be happy without Kirstin, but if what made her happy was to be free of him, that was what he'd give her.

Though on one point he was resolute. His daughter. Eilidh. It was a very different kind of pain, the knowledge that he'd never be part of her life. The only thing he could do was protect her from all that he'd suffered. Let her save the grit and determination she'd no doubt inherited from her mother for more worthwhile causes than defiance and covering up her hurt.

Sitting at the writing desk, Cameron dipped a pen in

the ink and pulled a fresh piece of paper towards him. It was a curt note, businesslike in its tone, stating his terms. He folded the thick wad of notes he'd obtained from his bank yesterday and sealed it. Contract completed. Time for him to move on.

Picking up his portmanteau, he gave the porter directions for the rest of his luggage. No looking back at the room where he and Kirstin had made love. Or *he* had made love, to be brutally accurate. No looking back at the table where they'd dined together so many times, or the sofa where they'd sat, sipping sherry. He'd never drink sherry again.

Treading lightly, he pushed his note with some difficulty under the door of Kirstin's suite. Then he made his way down the stairs, paid their bill, and went out into a hackney, headed for the posting house to join his sister and his niece for their journey back to Scotland.

Chapter Twelve

Eight months later, October 1819

Kirstin made a final, wholly unnecessary check of the dining table. The silverware glittered, the crystal sparkled, the napkins at each of the four place settings were crisp and folded into the shape of fans atop the Royal Doulton crockery. She'd lived in this house on Russell Square for four years, and this was the very first dinner party she had hosted. A most extraordinary and momentous event, which had taken her three months to organise. She moved one of the decanters set out on the sideboard a fraction to the left, twitched the curtains, and left the room.

Her little enamel watch told her that her guests were due in half an hour. In the drawing room, champagne was chilling on ice, sherry and madeira had been decanted, and a variety of glasses and goblets were set out on a silver tray. Upstairs, Marianne was reading Eilidh her bedtime story. Her daughter had turned six two weeks ago. Another milestone she had deprived Cameron of.

Her heart lurched as it did every time she thought of him, which was constantly. Every time she looked at Eilidh she was reminded that her daughter was the product of two parents, reminded that one of them was missing out on every aspect of her life. Guilt was her constant companion. But it wasn't the worst of her burdens. Being in love and having thrown away the chance of happiness was the hardest to bear.

Kirstin sank into her favourite chair, resting her head against the winged back, closing her eyes. She'd finally acknowledged that she loved him that fateful morning when she'd woken up heavy-eyed in the hotel to find his note pushed under the door, though she had refused to act on that revelation.

She'd procrastinated for weeks, diverting herself by being insulted that he'd insisted on paying for her services when she had wanted to give them free, as a gift. With anger that he had spied on her, with outrage that he had dared to demand that she marry him, with indignation that he had dared to ignore her very clear declaration that they could have no future once Philippa had been found.

She had refused to allow herself to miss him. She had refused to take his vow to return seriously. It had been bluster. He had been hurt by her rejection. Angry at being thwarted.

But she knew Cameron too well to convince herself of any of those things, and the pain of recognising how her cruel words must have injured him was an agony.

He loved her.

She remembered the first time this fact had fully registered. She had been in discussions with a client, too intent on the subject matter to notice that he'd served her coffee and not tea until she'd tasted it. Assailed by the aroma, and the memory of Cameron drinking his first cup of the day, as he always did, in one gulp, she had completely lost track of the discussions.

Cameron loved her.

He'd poured his heart out to her, and all she'd been able to think about was Eilidh. She'd thought that Eilidh was all he'd been interested in, too obsessed with her own fears to listen.

Cameron loved her.

Later that day, alone in her drawing room, Kirstin had mustered the courage to reflect on their time together. The memories, kept buried for weeks, had been frighteningly vivid, fresh and heartbreaking.

Cameron loved her. He loved *her*—everything about her. He knew who she was under her skin, and he didn't want to change her. He didn't want to put her in a gilded cage.

When you love someone... he'd said, and though he hadn't ever finished that sentence she knew now what he meant. He'd set her free by leaving her, as she'd asked him to do. When he came back it would not be to trap her or to change her. He'd asked so very little of her. How her jibes, her determination not to listen must have hurt him. She'd give almost anything to take them back.

She had known she could not undo the harm done, but she had been determined to find a way to apologise. It would have to be something extraordinary. Something unique. A gift that no one else could give.

The idea which had come to her had been so obvious it had taken her breath away, though how she was to achieve it, she'd had absolutely no idea. But she had known she would find a way.

Because she loved Cameron.

It had come to her like a simple truth, one she had not once tried to deny in the weeks and months that had followed. She loved him with all of the heart she must have convinced him she didn't possess. She loved everything about him, and it was just as he'd said to her, she wouldn't change a hair on his head.

She'd cried then, wretched with guilt and with loss, for it had all seemed so impossible. Even if she hadn't killed his love that night, even if he did still love her, despite her best efforts to stop him, what difference did it make that she loved him back?

They led very different lives. He didn't want to change hers. She didn't want to be the reason he changed his, for then he would blame her if it went wrong, or he would resent her, and their love would twist and warp into something very different.

Eilidh, ironically, was not the problem Kirstin had always imagined, because Cameron was not the man she'd always feared. All he'd asked from her was the right to give his daughter a name. To legitimise her, in society's eyes, for her sake.

From a man who had never had a family, who had gone to such lengths to protect the family who had rejected him, that was a very paltry request. He'd asked for his daughter's given name, but he'd claimed no rights—on the contrary, had promised not to interfere. How much that must have cost him. How wrong she had been, how very wrong, to imagine that he'd take more if it was not given—Cameron, who always put everyone's needs before his own.

Kirstin was wrong to deprive her daughter of a father. She was wrong to deprive Cameron of his daughter. And he was right. She'd finally acknowledged the sickening fact, less forcefully put to her by Marianne too, that she could not force Eilidh to fight her battles against a judgemental society. It was selfish of her and very wrong. Logic and reason, as Cameron had predicted, must prevail.

Next February, when the year was up and Cameron returned—and she didn't doubt he would—she would marry him in name only, for the sake of their daughter.

But Kirstin didn't want to marry Cameron for Eilidh's sake. Yes, she wanted him to be a father, but she wanted—longed, yearned—for Cameron to be her husband. But, given they lived such different lives it seemed as impossible as ever. And yet she was just about to have dinner with three remarkable women who had achieved that feat for themselves.

Her pocket watch pinged the hour. A few seconds later there was a rap on the door. Her dinner guests had arrived.

She got to her feet, shaking out the skirts of her scarlet gown. No black apparel tonight for this momentous occasion, the first time The Procurer had ever come face-to-face with some of the women who had, with her help, rescued themselves. They had achieved it, all three of them, in the most surprising manner. She wanted, desperately wanted, to learn from their experience. To find a way to make the impossible possible, and so grant her heart's desire.

This was one dinner which would not be reported in the press, though it was hosted by one of the most powerful women in London, and her guests, in very different ways, wielded a great deal of power of their own. All three had, thanks to The Procurer's intervention, escaped very different tragic fates.

None of them knew each other. Kirstin had chosen them carefully. They were strong, feisty, in at least two cases, and extremely intelligent women. Each one had been determined to find a way to support herself and live independently. Yet every one of them had married the man The Procurer had despatched them to help.

Kirstin wanted to know why. She wanted to know how. She wanted to know if they were happy. She wanted to know if she could benefit from their experience.

'I am asking a great deal of you,' she said, when the champagne had been poured and the introductions made. 'Perhaps not as much as when we last spoke,' she said with a smile, 'but I am asking you to be completely frank. I'm aware I am breaking my own rules by asking you to share your history.'

'You've already broken your rules by revealing your true identity to us and inviting us into your home, Madam Procurer.' Madame Bauduin, whom Kirstin knew as Lady Sophia Acton, looked at her fellow guests for confirmation. 'I think I speak for all of us when I say that we are very much aware of the honour you do us, Miss Blair, and the trust you have invested in us.'

'And I also speak for all of us, I'm sure,' said fiery-haired Allison Galbraith, Countess Derevenko, 'when I say that anything we can do to assist you, we will do. We owe you not only our lives, Miss Blair, but our happiness.'

'No, you owe me nothing. Whatever you have achieved, you've achieved through your own efforts. I merely provided you with the opportunity.'

'Precisely—when no one else would.' Becky Wickes, the former card sharp who had very lately become the Contessa del Pietro, beamed. 'I'd like to propose a toast.' She raised her glass, and the other two women followed.

'To The Procurer, who makes the impossible possible,' they said, as one.

Deeply affected, Kirstin made no attempt to disguise her tears. 'Would that I could weave such magic in my own case. The one thing I am lacking and cannot have is…'

'Love,' Sophia said softly. 'The last thing I thought I was looking for, if you recall. I cannot imagine living without it now.'

'Being only recently married,' Becky said, with a wicked smile, 'I am not ashamed to say that it's the one thing I can't get enough of.'

Sophia chuckled. 'I've been married to Jean-Luc for almost a year, and I still feel exactly the same.'

'Three years and two little bundles of joy since I was married,' Allison said with a tender smile, 'and with every passing day I find myself more in love with Aleksei.'

'Miss Blair…'

'Kirstin, please.'

'Kirstin,' Sophia said, setting down her champagne flute, 'are you telling us that you are a victim of unrequited love?'

She had never said it aloud, but it was surprisingly easy in the company of these remarkable women, each of whom was quite transformed. 'I am in love,' Kirstin said, 'with a man called Cameron Dunbar. As to whether it is unrequited, there's the rub. He does— or rather did—love me, but I fear I have ruined everything.'

'And you would like to remedy that?' Allison asked.

Kirstin nodded. 'But his business is in Scotland. His life is travelling the world. And mine...'

'Is making the impossible possible,' Becky said, chuckling. 'What is it they say? Physician heal thyself?'

'That is exactly what she's trying to do,' Allison said. 'Ladies, The Procurer wants to learn from our experience. That's what you meant, isn't it, Kirstin, when you said you wanted us to be completely frank with you? I'm willing to bet that we swore to you that all we wanted was the chance to lead our own lives, and yet each of us opted instead for marriage.'

'Marriage *and* independence,' Becky said.

'Kirstin wants to know how that might be achieved,' Allison concluded. 'And the answer is, not without difficulty.'

'And a lot of compromise—which I confess did not come easy to me,' Becky added.

'I think that we would all do very much better discussing this over dinner,' Sophia added. 'Judging by the delicious smells, I think it has arrived.'

'Shall we?' Kirstin got to her feet. 'With your reputation for serving the best dinners in Paris, Sophia, I took the precaution of engaging Monsieur Salois for the evening.'

'The Duke of Brockmore's chef?' Sophia's eyes gleamed. 'I have heard great things about him. Ladies, we are in for a treat.'

November 1819, Oban, Argyll, Scotland

Cameron stood on the jetty where he had been deposited, gazing out at the Isle of Kerrera which was, presumably, his final destination. A small island—he judged it to be no more than four or five miles long— it was dwarfed by the majestic Isle of Mull and, as far as he could see, uninhabited.

Each step of his journey from Glasgow, every connection from post-chaise to ferry, and onwards by pony across drover's roads, had been carefully co-ordinated by the unseen hand of the person who had summoned him here. Unseen, but not unknown.

He knew of only one person capable of orchestrating such a complex trip. Though he had absolutely no idea why he was here, he had been certain, from the moment he broke the seal on her letter, that it was Kirstin he would be meeting.

A little boat was making its way from Kerrera towards him across the choppy waters of the sound, and Cameron's iron grip on his nerves loosened. He had steeled himself to wait the full year before allowing himself to contact her, but he had thought of her every day and missed her more with every passing moment.

Knowing her as he did, he was sure that she would agree to a marriage in name only for the sake of their daughter. Knowing her as he did, he was certain that she would wait until the very last moment to do so. He very much regretted his ultimatum, but she had left him no choice. He had been very sure that she would make good on her vow never to love him.

Then the letter had arrived, and with it hope. He'd tried to manage that hope, but now, as he stepped into the little boat and the taciturn boatman headed towards Kerrera, Cameron surrendered. Kirstin wouldn't bring him all the way to an island on the Inner Hebrides to agree to a marriage of convenience. This wasn't about Eilidh. Nor was she bringing him here to tell him that she wanted nothing more to do with him.

His heart began to hammer as the boatman beached the dinghy and pointed to the track which led up the slope and along the shoreline.

'It's about three miles' walk,' he said. 'You'll know where you're headed when you see it.'

With this cryptic comment he set off again, back to the mainland, and Cameron set off too, glad of the sturdy brogues he was wearing, along the stony track.

The views back to the little fishing village of Oban were spectacular, but he did not waste his time on them, focusing only on walking at a brisk pace which became almost a run. The path wound inland, up and over what he reckoned must be the southern tip of the island. A farm lay in the glen below him, but a wooden arrow pointed him along another path.

The castle loomed suddenly into view, perched on the cliffs—though it was more of a ruined tower than a castle, with half of its roof gone. The approach was a steep scramble down what must have once been a bridge, judging by the crumbling remains.

Kirstin was waiting in the empty doorway, wrapped in a thick black cloak, bareheaded, tendrils of her glossy black hair blowing in the breeze. She was trying to smile, but her eyes gave her away. His heart soared as he looked at her, her expression a mirror of all he'd been feeling himself, so full of hope and yet utterly terrified.

'You came,' she said, by way of greeting.

'Of course I did,' he said, pulling her into his arms. 'How could you possibly have doubted me?'

'After all that I said...'

'Let's not rake over it. I love you, Kirstin, and if you—'

She threw her arms around him. 'Oh, Cameron, I love you so much.'

'Of course you do,' he said, beaming like an eejit, wondering if his heart might burst.'

Kirstin's smile was dazzling. She reached up to smooth his hair. 'Of course I do,' she said softly.

He kissed her. Her lips were salty, with sea or tears or both. She was trembling in his arms, clinging to him as if he might vanish, and he kissed her again, soothing kisses, whispering that he loved her, would always love her, touched to the core by the very fact that this bold, brave, fiercely independent woman needed to be reassured.

'I love you,' he murmured, kissing her forehead, her tear-stained cheeks. 'I love you.'

'I love you too. I love you so much.'

His arms tightened around her. Sheer untrammelled joy filled him as their lips met again, tenderness heating to passion as their kisses deepened. Only the shattering of a slate, blown by a gust of wind from the roof, made them jump.

'Kirstin, my darling, could you not have chosen a more convivial place for our reunion?' Cameron said ruefully. 'Somewhere with a roof, at least, if not a bed.'

She laughed. 'I didn't bring you here to make love to you.' Her face fell. 'After all the terrible things I said to you, I couldn't even be sure that...'

'I thought we'd agreed not to go over that? You were frightened I'd take our daughter from you. You were frightened that I'd start making all sorts of demands...'

'I should have known better—' She broke off, biting her lip. 'I know better now.'

'And I know that we've a lot of talking to do, a lot of sorting out to do. It won't be plain sailing, Kirstin, and I'm not making any promises...'

'Oh, no, please don't. That is one of the things I've been warned against.' She smiled at his obvious confusion. 'You'll be astonished when I tell you who has advised me. But before we talk about the future, Cameron, please let me make up to you for the things I said. Not by making love to you—not yet, anyway—but by telling you why I have brought you home.'

He eyed the castle doubtfully. 'Home? It would take a great deal of work to make this into a home. Were you thinking we should buy it?'

She chuckled. 'I've already bought it. For you. Here, come in under what little shelter there is and read this.'

She ushered him through the empty doorway and into what was left of what must have been the great hall, under the remainder of the roof. The thick parchment she handed him was a deed of sale for the Island of Kerrera and all its goods and chattels.

'Why?' he asked, completely puzzled.

'Until the Jacobite Rebellion of 1745 this was the ancestral home of the Laird of Kerrera,' Kirstin said. 'Finlay Cameron, Laird of Kerrera, to be precise. He fought with Bonnie Prince Charlie at Culloden, and was forced to flee not long after, returning first to Dunbar Castle to rescue his wife and his baby son, Lachlan. They sailed for the East Indies, their passage having been arranged by Lachlan's best friend, a government man playing a very dangerous game.'

'Wait a minute, did you say Dunbar Castle?' Cameron interrupted. 'This is *Dunbar* Castle?'

Kirstin nodded, smiling. 'Finlay and his wife never returned to Scotland, but their son, Lachlan, had grown up hearing such romantic tales of Dunbar Castle that in the early seventeen-eighties he made the bold decision to try to recover his ancestral home. He came first to Edinburgh, to make good on a long-standing promise to his father to seek out the man who had helped the family escape retribution for the Rebellion. John Campbell was dead, but his daughter Sheila was living in Edinburgh.'

'Sheila…' Cameron stared at Kirstin incredulously. 'That was my mother's name.'

'Sheila Ferguson. Née Campbell.' She caught his hand between hers. 'I know that Finlay wrote to her, for he kept copies of all his correspondence and left the copies behind at his home in the East Indies. I have those for you, Cameron. But when he sailed for Scotland the trail went cold. Clearly when they met they fell in love—for she must have loved him, to contemplate giving up her daughter and her husband for him. They would have planned to return, I would guess, to live in the East Indies as man and wife.'

'But my mother didn't elope. My father abandoned her—that is what Louise told me.'

'Your father came north, heading for Kerrera. He made it as far as Oban. The parish records show he died of the plague before he could either see the place of his birth or make good on the promise he'd made to the woman he loved. I'm so very sorry, Cameron. I doubt he even knew of your existence.'

'How did you manage to find all this out? How long has it taken you?' Cameron asked, utterly stunned.

'I started with your name. It was the one thing, you told me, that your mother gave you.'

'So I come from a long line of merchants. The sea is in my blood. I can't believe it—what you've done, it's impossible.' He laughed ruefully. 'Though not impossible for The Procurer. I don't know how to begin thanking you.'

'I don't want your thanks. I want…'

Kirstin drew a shaky laugh. 'It won't be easy, we both know that. We must make no promises we can't keep. We will have to compromise. But it's not about giving up independence, Cameron. It's about finding room in your life for someone to share it with, someone who respects you, and who loves you so much they wouldn't change a hair on your head.

'No, wait,' she said, when he made to speak, 'I'm not finished. I want you to be a father to Eilidh in much more than name. You've already missed out on so much of her life. She's *our* child, not just mine. I want us to be a family, Cameron, all three of us, but before that there's something every bit as important I need to ask you.'

She dropped to her knees. 'I love you exactly that way. I know you love me too, in the same way. We can make it work as long as we have each other. Will you marry me, my darling?'

He was dumbstruck for all of a second. Then he dropped to the ground beside her, pulling her into his arms.

'You can have no idea, my love, of how very, *very* much I would like to marry you. Yes,' he said, kissing her. 'Yes,' he said, kissing her again, 'and yes,' he said, kissing her for the third time, but most certainly not the last.

Epilogue

Excerpt from the Town Crier, *December 1819*

The End of an Era!

We can exclusively reveal to you, our loyal readers, that today marks the end of the reign of the legendary London icon hitherto known only as The Procurer.

The woman who makes the impossible possible quite literally lifted the veil of secrecy from her most exquisite countenance today when she stood before the altar of St James's Church to plight her troth to Mr Cameron Dunbar, Merchant of Glasgow.

In true Procurer fashion, she has been harbouring an astonishing secret—they are tying the knot for the second time! The pair, it seems, made a match the first time around when they eloped to Gretna Green seven years ago.

For reasons they would not entrust even to someone as discreet as yours truly, they kept their marriage private. Today, in The Procurer's own words, they celebrated their love for each other in public.

For the ceremony the bride wore a full-length pelisse of crimson velvet trimmed with swansdown, which perfectly complemented her striking beauty. Her adorable little daughter, playing bridesmaid and carrying a bunch of heather sent all the way from the family's Scottish estate, was identically dressed.

Both daring toilettes were created exclusively for this momentous occasion by the Bond Street modiste Madame LeClerc. The groom, a Scot with rather splendid shoulders and an excellent pair of legs, was disappointingly not clad in the kilt, though the more observant among us noticed a sprig of heather in his lapel pinned there, the clearly doting father informed us, by his little daughter for luck.

A light dusting of snow began to fall as the happy family entered the church, much to the delight of the youngest member of the party. A more romantic winter's day or a more romantic wedding cannot be imagined. I am not ashamed to confess that the magical scene brought a tear to my eye.

Mr and Mrs Dunbar are quitting London with their darling daughter almost immediately, and will retire for some unspecified period to consider their future plans.

Does this mean that The Procurer is lost to London for ever? Watch this space!

'Well, what do you think? Will the piece serve?' Kirstin asked.

Cameron set the scandal sheet he had been reading aside, shaking his head with amusement. 'I think it will serve very well, provided that no one checks the records at Gretna Green.'

'If they do, they will find all is in order,' Kirstin said, smiling at him. 'I am nothing if not thorough.'

He gave a hoot of laughter. 'I should have guessed.'

The door of the hotel suite was flung open and Eilidh burst in. Kirstin watched indulgently as her daughter threw herself into her father's arms. 'Daddy! Marianne says I have to say goodbye now. But you and Mummy will be back very, very soon, won't you?'

Cameron picked her up, hugging her tightly. 'Of course we will,' he said, 'and then all three of us are going to our new house to see in the New Year. Isn't that exciting?'

'In Scotland. Will there be lots of snow?'

'It will probably come up to your chin. We can go sledging.'

'Will Mummy come sledging too?'

Cameron cast an amused glance at a horrified Kirstin. 'No, Mummy will make sure we come home to a nice hot drink.'

'And will you still read me a story in the new house?'

'I'll read you a story every night, I promise.' He kissed her forehead. 'You know I'll really miss you?'

'Yes,' Eilidh said seriously, patting his head, 'but you'll have Mummy and I'll have Marianne and you'll be back quick as a flash.'

He laughed, setting her down reluctantly. 'Quicker than that. Now, go and kiss Mummy goodbye.'

The door closed on Marianne and Eilidh a few moments later. 'I know I'm biased, but she's an extraordinary wee lass. And in that,' Cameron said, pulling Kirstin into his arms, 'she takes after her mother. Have I told you lately that I love you with all my heart?'

'Yes, but I'm more than happy to hear it again.'

'I love you. With all my heart.'

'And I love *you*. With all my heart. And with all my body too.'

'You do, do you?'

Kirstin wriggled free of his hold. 'Come with me,' she said, urging him towards the bedchamber in their hotel suite, 'and I'll show you.'

'Oh, no, Mrs Dunbar,' Cameron said, scooping her up in his arms, 'I think we'll start married life as we mean to go on. Let me show *you*.'

She was laughing as he set her down by the bed, but then he kissed her, and the warmth of her laughter turned to the heat of desire.

The stunning creation of crimson gauze and silver spangles which Madame LeClerc had designed for the wedding ceremony was cast aside as Cameron kissed his way lingeringly down her body, making her pulses jump and flutter, slowly, deliciously slowly, building the tension inside her. He shed his own clothes carelessly, until they were both naked, and she was clinging desperately to the remnants of her self-control, and he was hard, panting, reaching for his sheath.

'No,' Kirstin said impulsively, catching his arm. 'I think we'll start married life as we mean to go on.'

'Are you serious?'

She gazed deep into his eyes, almost overwhelmed by the love which surged through her like a physical force. It terrified her, how close she had come to throwing it all away. 'You have no idea how much I love you,' she said. 'I am very serious, if it is what you want too.'

'Kirstin…' Tears filled Cameron's eyes. 'It is what I want. More than anything, I find. If we are fortunate enough a second time, I can think of nothing more perfect.' He kissed her deeply. Then smiled at her wickedly. 'Of course we may not be fortunate straight away. It may not even be possible.'

'Then I'm looking forward very much to trying to make the impossible possible,' Kirstin replied, pulling him towards her.

* * * * *

Historical Note

I've taken a few liberties with the timings of travel between London and Glasgow. It would probably have taken somewhere between two and three days, even travelling by the mail, but that was far too long for poor Philippa and Jeannie to have been in custody, so I cut their trials just a little short.

Osterley Park, which Kirstin borrows for her day out with Cameron, is a real place. It does have an island, but not the one in my book, which is based on Temple Island further down the Thames at Henley.

You might think that the Erotes Club is a totally over-the-top invention of mine. Absolutely not. I used the Hellfire Club of which Byron was reputedly a member, but there are many and assorted others to choose from far worse than the one I've written about.

If you're Scottish and of a certain age then the comedian Rikki Fulton's Reverend I M Jolly *Last Call* sketches would have been a highlight of your Hogmanay television. Cameron's Reverend Mr Collins is my tribute to him, and a little nod, too, to the fabulous Mr Collins, my favourite Jane Austen character.

If you're interested in reading Ewan and Jennifer's story—The Procurer's first case—then you can, for free! *From Cinderella to Marchioness* is available on the Harlequin website, along with loads of other fabulous free reads. The link is on my website.

Finally, if you're a regular reader of my books you'll know that I like to reuse my secondary characters. In case you're wondering, Madame LeClerc the modiste came to England from France with Serena in *The Rake and the Heiress*, and made a very important gown for Henrietta in *Rake with a Frozen Heart*. Monsieur Salois is chef for the Duke and Duchess of Brockmore in *Scandal and the Midsummer Ball* and *Scandal at the Christmas Ball*. I'm not done with either of them yet!

HIS MISTLETOE WAGER

VIRGINIA HEATH

For Nicole Locke.

My first-ever writing buddy. Thanks for adopting me and showing me the ropes.

Prologue

St George's Church, Hanover Square—
June 1815

Every pew was taken. No mean feat in a church as large and grand as this one, yet hardly a surprise when this was the wedding of the Season: the day when the darling of society, the beautiful only daughter of the Earl of Upminster, married her handsome peer.

Even the sun had come out to celebrate and was cheerfully streaming through the imposing stained-glass windows in an exceedingly pleasing fashion and causing a kaleidoscope of colours to decorate the floor. The air hung heavy with the fragrance of lilacs, Lizzie's favourite flower, and tall vases and boughs festooned the aisle she would soon walk down.

Her wedding dress was embroidered subtly to match and her dainty bonnet decorated with beautiful silk replicas, scaled down to sit in a pleasing fashion. Just as she had always imagined.

In fact, to her complete delight, everything about her wedding to the Marquess of Rainham was exactly as she had imagined it. After all, she had been planning it all since she was ten, right down to the minutest of details because it was the most important day of her life. The beginning of her perfect, happily ever after, exactly six months on from her first meeting with the man she loved with all her heart.

Many in society were surprised by the match, her own dear parents included. Charles did have a reputation as a bit of a rake and had broken more than one heart before he had found his one true love. But as she was prone to point out whenever he was criticised—something which happened with annoying regularity—everybody knew rakes made the very best husbands once they found the right woman, and Lizzie was very definitely the right woman for him.

Dear Charles told her so every single day. From their very first dance he had been the most ardent and attentive suitor, and although Lizzie came with a substantial dowry, he made it quite plain that he did not give two figs for the money. The money meant nothing because he would happily take her with nothing. In rags if need be. Dowries were of no consequence when his heart beat only for her. They were destined to be together for ever. All he cared about was her. Something he proved time and time again with his effusive compliments and daringly longing gazes. It was all so wonderfully romantic. A courtship which had made her the envy of her peers and now she was having the perfect wedding, too. The first bride of June.

'I shall give him a stern piece of my mind later! Be assured of that!' For the second time in as many minutes her father snapped his pocket watch open and stared impatiently at the dial. 'It is the bride's prerogative to be late, not the groom's. To leave us here, hiding in the vestry like common criminals, is beyond the pale, Lizzie. I have no idea what the bounder can be thinking to insult us so grievously.'

She smiled reassuringly at him. At the Foreign Office he was used to being in charge and far too much of a stickler for timekeeping than was necessary, and he had been very vocal with his misgivings about her choice of husband. She had spent much of the last two months reassuring him that everything was destined to be wonderful and her Marquess was not at all what everyone believed. 'Calm down, Papa. Nobody in the congregation is aware that we have arrived, so it hardly matters. There is probably a perfectly good reason Charles has been delayed. He will be here.' Last night, just before he had crept out of her bedchamber window and scrambled down the wisteria, he had blown her a kiss and told her how he was counting the seconds until they took their vows. What difference did a few minutes of tardiness make in the grand scheme of things? Especially when they were about to embark on a lifetime together.

Instinctively, her hand fluttered towards her belly and she suppressed the grin which threatened to bloom. Her father would hit the roof if he knew what she had kept secret from everyone for the last week.

Later tonight, when they were all alone, she would tell Charles about the baby. Her wedding present to him. Made in love almost two months ago, when she had gladly given him her innocence as there seemed little point in prolonging the agony of withholding it unnecessarily. 'We are engaged,' he had said teasingly the first time he had clambered up the wisteria and surprised her in her bedchamber. 'What difference do a few more weeks make? Besides, when a love is as deep and abiding as ours is, a wedding ceremony is merely a formality. I am already married to you in my heart.' As was she. Lizzie knew he would be overjoyed by the news. The perfect end to the most perfect year of her life.

It was the ashen face of her brother Rafe, over half an hour later, which caused the first real doubts to creep in. He came in through a side door, quietly closed it behind him and simply stood, slightly slumped before her.

'He's gone, Lizzie.'

The finality in his voice made her fear the worst. Her darling fiancé was dead? Surely not. She could not bear it. 'What do you mean he's gone? What has happened?' He had been in fine fettle a few scant hours ago. Ardent. No sign of illness or fever. Tears were already streaming down her cheeks as the panic made her heart hammer wildly in her chest. 'Did he have an accident?' Please God, make him not have suffered.

Her brother shook his head and it was then she saw the fierce anger in his eyes.

Anger and pity. For her.

'No, poppet. Nothing so noble, I'm afraid. I don't quite know how to tell you this, so I shall just say it straight out. The scoundrel is marrying someone else.'

Lizzie's knees gave way and her father supported her as she stumbled backwards on to a chair. 'You are mistaken.' The walls started to spin as nausea threatened. 'Charles would not do that to me. He loves me.'

'He left a letter…' A letter that her brother had obviously already read because the seal was broken and the open missive hung limply in his hand.

Callously, it was addressed to no one in particular and had been left on the mantelpiece in his bachelor lodgings at the Albany. Conversationally, it informed the reader that he was bound, with all haste, for Gretna Green with the Duke of Aylesbury's daughter. A drastic step taken because her father had forbidden their courtship a full year before. Of course, they had tried to fight the fierce attraction which had consumed them. However, his love for the obscenely wealthy Duke's plain and awkward youngest daughter was *'deep and abiding'* and for the longest time he had already been *'married to her in his heart'*. Their vows were just a formality because, and this was the most crushing blow, *'his heart beat for her alone'*.

The familiar words cut deeply, slicing through her initial disbelief and shock more effectively than anything else could have. What a dreadful way to discover words which had meant so very much to her had ultimately been meaningless to him all along.

'If we act in all haste, Rafe, we might be able to mitigate the scandal.'

Ever the pragmatist, her father's conversation wafted over her. A message was dispatched to the Duke of Aylesbury. Fevered plans were set in place. Her papa's government connections and high place in society would all be utilised to make everything all right, they would close ranks around her to protect her flawless reputation—yet how could things ever be all right again? She had been jilted.

Jilted!

With every meticulous and carefully laid plan for her perfect future made so thoroughly for so long, she had failed to foresee this terrible scenario. Lizzie had been the silly fool who had fallen for the charming Marquess until a much richer prospect had come along. The pregnant, silly fool who had stood waiting patiently for him at the church, who had believed all his calculated seductions, all his blatant flattery, so blinkered by her love for him that she had not heeded all the well-meant words of caution from nearly everyone in her acquaintance including her own family. The trusting, needy, idiot who did not even warrant the courtesy of a letter of her own from the treacherous scoundrel who had deflowered her, nor a mention in the one her brother had found. Written by the same duplicitous hands which had been all over her body only hours before. Charles must have known he was eloping when he had climbed into her bedroom window, but had used her regardless. Like the true libertine and shameless rake he was. Their fairy-tale courtship and all of his apparently heartfelt declarations whispered intimately in her virgin's bed stood for naught. It had all been a pack of lies and she had fallen for every single one.

Her hand automatically went to her belly again. All at once, the sickly smell of lilacs threatened to overpower her, or maybe it was the catastrophic ramifications of her now-dire situation. Or perhaps that was merely the bitter taste of humiliation and utter, complete betrayal. Total devastation. Willingly, she had given a man her tender, young heart and he had blithely returned it to her bludgeoned.

Shredded into irreparable pieces.

Chapter One

*A London ballroom—St Nicholas's Day,
6th December 1820*

Hal twisted the sprig of mistletoe idly between his fingers and took another cleansing breath of the cold night air. The heat in the tedious Renshaw ballroom was stifling, but then again, as it was quite the crush inside no doubt everyone would laud the evening as a resounding success. There was nothing guaranteed to cause more excitement in town than two hundred sweating aristocrats stuffed into their winter finery and all forcing themselves to be cheerful in deference to the season.

For Hal, it also signalled the start of a month of sheer hell, as now he was the Earl of Redbridge he would be expected to attend every single one of the festive functions between now and Twelfth Night. It was, apparently, a Redbridge tradition, and the only one his mother was determined to continue even though her tyrannical husband was mouldering in the ground, and she had happily ignored all his other edicts since his death last year. In fact, she was so looking forward to it, Hal couldn't bring himself to complain, even though it culminated in him hosting the final, most opulent and eagerly anticipated ball of all at his Berkeley Square house on the sixth of January. Twelfth Night. The official end of the Christmas season.

In previous years, he had always managed to make a hasty exit from the short but frenetic festive season. He had danced and flirted with a few game girls, then disappeared to his club or to a gaming hell or to the bedchamber of whatever willing widow or wayward wife he happened to be enjoying at that particular time. Now he was stuck. Shackled by an ingrained sense of duty to his mother, who was enjoying life to the full now that she finally had her freedom and her period of mourning was over. Although like him, she hadn't seemed to mourn much. His father had been a mean-spirited, dictatorial curmudgeon who criticised absolutely everything his wayward children did. But he had made Hal's gentle mother's life a misery.

Hal had lost count of the number of times he had heard her crying, all alone in her bedchamber, because of yet another cruel or thoughtless thing his sire had done to her. However, if he went to her when she was crying, she would pretend nothing was amiss. 'Pay it no mind, Hal. Marriage is meant to be filled with trials and tribulations.' Something which did not make the prospect of it particularly enticing.

If he went to his father and called him on it, after the tirade of abuse which always accompanied such impertinence, his father would shrug it off as the way of things. A wife was a means of getting heirs. Nothing more. That duty discharged, they were merely doomed to tolerate each other. That was the inevitable way of things. And surely it was long past time Hal stopped sowing wild oats, settled down to do his duty to the house of Stuart and begat some heirs of his own to continue the legacy? And whilst he was about it, he needed to start learning about estate management and how to do *proper* business, which in his father's world usually meant ruining people and feasting off their carcasses in order to amass an even larger fortune than he already had.

'The world runs on coin, Henry, nothing else matters. Or do you intend to be a shocking and scandalous disappointment to me for ever?'

A silly question, seeing as Hal had no appetite for either cruelty or *proper* business. Instead, he had made it his life's mission to thoroughly disappoint his father at every given opportunity as a point of principal, and the single most thorough way of doing that was to be creating frequent scandals. Hal enjoyed the spectacle of his livid father's purple face as much as he did bedding a succession of wholly unsuitable, and gloriously unmarriageable, women. Reckless wagers at the card table came a close second. His father abhorred the careless use of good money on anything so frivolous and unpredictable. Money was for making more money to add to the heaps and heaps they had already, because money meant power and his father adored being powerful above all else. Even if that meant making everybody else miserable or his only son hate everything his father stood for. As the years passed, the gulf between the Earl and his scandalous only son had widened so much there might as well have been a whole ocean between them. A state of affairs which suited Hal just fine. Being scandalous had become so ingrained, such an intrinsic part of his own character, now his father was dead he actually *missed* misbehaving. It was as if a part of him was missing.

It was not the only thing in his life which had changed since he had inherited the title. He also had to run the enormous estate he now owned, something he never expected to relish, and the vast and varied business investments were a constant source of amusement. Because it turned out Hal had a natural talent for making more money by considering investment opportunities his father would never have dared touch, and without having to resort to those abhorrent *proper* business tactics his dreadful father had used, Hal had been feeling a trifle odd for months now. Yet could not quite put his finger on why.

The sad truth was simply having fun really wasn't fun any more. Since he had become the Earl of Redbridge he had found the gaming hells had lost their appeal, as had the bawdy widows and wayward wives. Instead, he found himself wanting to dive into his new ledgers rather than a willing woman's bed. He enjoyed reading the financial news and, to his utter dismay and total disgust, found the debates in the Lords fascinating. All the things his father had wanted him to take an interest in, the very things he had avoided resolutely for all of his twenty-seven years, now called to him and Hal was uncharacteristically inclined to listen. It was beyond disconcerting.

To begin with, he assumed this odd malaise was a temporary condition, brought about by the lack of need to vex his father and the shock of taking on his mantle, but the odd mood had persisted way beyond those unfamiliar, tentative first months. In fact, he hadn't been between anyone's sheets but his own in an age, and apparently out of choice rather than lack of opportunity. The last time he had engaged in a bit of bed sport, Hal had had to force himself and then found the whole interlude wholly unsatisfying. Almost as if something was missing although he could not say what. The widow had been passionate and lustful—two things he had always enjoyed in a woman—yet Hal had not been able to get out of her bed quickly enough and certainly had no intentions of ever going back to it. All in all, his lack of libido was becoming quite worrying. As was his lack of risky, devil-may-care behaviour. If he did not find a way to combat it, Hal was in danger of turning into his cold, dour father and that would never do.

'Are you hoping to find a willing young lady on this terrace to steal a kiss from?' His brother-in-law, next-door neighbour and best friend in the world, Aaron Wincanton, Viscount Ardleigh, stared pointedly at the green sprig in Hal's hand. 'And if you are, should I make myself scarce? I can happily hide somewhere else if I am interrupting a potential tryst.' His friend held aloft two generously filled brandy glasses and did a poor job of blending into the background.

'By all means, join me. There is nobody here I want to kiss.' Too many seasons spent in too many ballrooms had made him quite jaded. Each crop of new debutantes seemed to become sillier than the previous ones, not one of them could converse on any topics other than the banal and he found their blatant, simpering new interest in him since he acquired his title irritating. Especially when they wouldn't give him the time of day beforehand. He had been far too scandalous. But now, he was an earl and they all wanted to be the one to give him his father's longed-for heirs.

'Oh, dear. Have things got that bad?'

'It's all right for you. You are no longer an eligible bachelor. You can breeze in and out of any ballroom unencumbered. I can scarcely make it to the refreshment table without some hungry young miss trying to get her matrimonial claws in me. And do not get me started on the mothers!'

'You are an earl, tolerably handsome, I am told, and a rich one to boot. I doubt you will need the mistletoe, I dare say most of them will happily kiss you quite enthusiastically without it. Even with your womanising reputation.' Hal groaned and stared mournfully in to his brandy, something which made his brother-in-law laugh. 'Is there really no one you find even slightly intriguing?'

'It is hard to be intrigued when they are all so frightfully eager.'

His friend nearly choked on his brandy. 'A travesty indeed! Poor you. All these eager women and no inclination to indulge.' Good grief! Had it become *that* obvious? Things were clearly direr than Hal had imagined if other people were beginning to notice, and that was beyond embarrassing. 'I think I know what ails you?'

'You do?'

'Yes, indeed. Your lack of interest in the opposite sex can easily be explained. You miss the thrill of the chase. We men are born with the inherent desire to hunt for what we need.'

'I hate hunting.' Hal's father had thoroughly enjoyed it and had forced his reluctant little boy to accompany him on far too many of them. He still recalled the first time he had seen a poor, terrified fox ripped to pieces by a pack of dogs and how frightened and appalled he had been when his father had soaked his handkerchief in the still-warm entrails and smeared the sticky blood all over Hal's face. A hunting tradition, apparently, and one he still could not understand. 'You know I hate hunting.'

Aaron rolled his eyes. 'Not foxes, you fool, women! You cannot deny you are a hunter of women. A lone and fearless predator. When they are all so depressingly eager and happy to fall at your feet, you miss the thrill of seducing them.'

'Perhaps.' Without thinking he turned his body to gaze through the windows back into the ballroom and watched the sea of swirling silk-clad young women on the dance floor to see if just one of them stood out to him and inspired him to go seduce them. Then sighed when none did.

'The trouble is,' his friend continued, far too cheerfully for Hal's liking, 'you grew up with Connie.'

'And what, pray tell, does my tempestuous sister have to do with this?'

'She has set a standard you have come to expect from all women.'

'Are you suggesting I yearn for a foul-tempered, flouncing termagant of a woman? Because really, Aaron, I love my dear sister to distraction, but the idea of being married to someone similar terrifies me.' Not that he was looking for a wife. Heaven forbid! The idea of being shackled for life in matrimonial disharmony, like his parents, filled him with dread. Besides, he was still too young to sacrifice himself to the parson's trap. His father had often said all respectable gentlemen had a duty to be married before they were thirty. Hal had another three years to go to thwart that edict and had no immediate desire to become respectable. Not when he still had far too many wild oats to sow. And he would, as soon as he shook off his odd mood. He had every intention of making the man spin in his grave for a considerate amount of time as penance for being so awful. At least another decade.

'Fear not, it takes a *real* man to deal with a woman like your sister and you are not in my league, dear fellow. What I mean is merely this. All those eager girls do not present a challenge to you, which is why you are so out of sorts.' He waved his hand dismissively in the direction of the dancers. 'Therefore I am prepared to set you an *interesting* challenge out of family loyalty, to restore some of your missing vigour. A bit of fun to liven up this laboriously festive social season for the both of us, seeing as Connie has decreed we spend it here with your mother, and your mother has such *exuberance* for society again. Wouldn't you relish a decent challenge? For our usual stakes, of course.'

'I suppose...' It was a sorry state of affairs if a man in his prime was without vigour, yet the plain and simple truth was Hal had not encountered a single woman in well over a year who did not bore him to tears. Even the unsuitable, corruptible ones he favoured were leaving him cold. Although he was prepared to concede fun would be good, if nothing else, as it had been a bit thin on the ground of late. 'What sort of challenge?'

'How many berries are on that sprig of parasitic vegetation you are clutching like an amulet?'

'Five—why?' Because Aaron had a particular gleam in his eye and as their usual stakes involved the loser mucking out the other's stables single-handed, or when

in town just Hal's, as Aaron had cheerfully sold his
house years before, he was understandably wary. Being
bored and being consigned to shovelling excrement for
his brother-in-law's amusement were two very different things entirely.

'Five berries equal the five separate kisses I challenge you to steal. Each one in a different location and
all five before Twelfth Night. Let us call it The Mistletoe
Wager, in a nod to the season.' Their bets always had
names and there had been some momentous ones. The
North Road Race. The Serpentine Swim. The Fisticuffs
Experiment and the ill-conceived and often-lamented
Naked Night in Norfolk, when they both nearly froze
to death trying to brave the winter weather sitting out
in the elements on the exposed beach of Great Yar-
mouth. They had hastily agreed to end that one early
when they simultaneously lost feeling in their gentlemen's areas. The Mistletoe Wager certainly sounded
a lot more pleasant than all its painful predecessors.

Hal felt himself grin at the thought. Five kisses! He
could do that in his sleep. 'To be frank, I think it is only
fair to point out I am so confident of my appeal, I believe you will be ensconced in my well-stocked stable
tomorrow. Challenge accepted!'

'Hold your fire, my arrogant young friend. I have
not set out my full terms yet. There is one more thing
I must insist upon.'

'Which is?'

'I get to choose whom you have to kiss.'

Hal felt his eyes narrow suspiciously. 'No nuns. No
dowagers or ladies in their dotage and for pity's sake
spare me Lady Daphne Marsh. I must insist that the ladies selected have teeth! Rumour has it those clattering

dentures she wears are made with teeth chiselled out of the corpses on the battlefield at Waterloo.'

'Really? I had heard they were carved out of a single walrus tusk... Either way, I agree they are distasteful.' Aaron held up his palm solemnly. 'You have my word. Only eligible, pretty ladies I would have chased after myself, before I had the great good fortune to be forced into marriage with your sister, qualify. What do you say? Shall we shake on it to seal the wager?'

For a few seconds Hal dithered, before he realised dithering was reminiscent of something his staid father would have done. 'On one condition. The ladies you choose can only be selected from within the very ballroom we are currently avoiding. Those are my particular terms.' That would ensure no ridiculous women were chosen. Aaron did like to best him and he would not put it past him to select five girls in the remotest corners of the British Isles just to vex him.

'Agreed!'

Hal thrust out his hand and the two men did their level best to out-shake and out-squeeze the other, as was their custom, for a solid thirty seconds before they stepped back. 'Five stolen kisses in five entirely different locations with five very lucky ladies.' He turned towards the French doors and grinned triumphantly. 'Choose away, dear brother. I feel guilty for accepting such a ridiculously easy bet.'

'Your arrogance astounds me! Do you honestly believe every proper young lady in that room would allow *you* to steal a kiss?'

Hal actually laughed, because really, it was just too funny. 'There will be no need for stealing, I can assure you. I am the single most eligible man at this ball. I am phenomenally wealthy, devilishly handsome, totally charming and, as you have quite rightly pointed out, I'm an *earl*. There isn't a young lady in that ballroom who would *not* welcome my advances. In fact, I dare say a few of them might try to steal a kiss from me with precious little effort on my part this very evening.' Which ironically was part of his current problem. They really were all so predictably eager.

'I refuse to believe you. As the father to two tenacious daughters and husband to a wife of supreme intelligence, I believe you are grossly underestimating the female sex. There must be at least a dozen young ladies currently in the ballroom who are in possession of good sense and taste, and thereby would never consider attaching their lips to yours.'

Hal watched with mounting amusement as Aaron carefully scanned the crowds, his frustration with the eager young ladies beyond becoming more apparent with every passing second. After a full minute, his intense perusal became a trifle desperate, then he straightened and nearly sighed with relief. When he turned back to Hal there was definite mischief in his expression, yet it did not daunt him. 'Who is the lucky first of the five?' Because he fully intended to pluck off one of those white mistletoe berries tonight in front of Aaron's eyes and then ceremonially place it in his hand.

'I don't recall stating there would be five different ladies, old boy.' Aaron was grinning smugly from ear to ear. It was a familiar tactic. Each time one of them proposed a ridiculous wager, the devil was in the detail of the language. Like attorneys they always quibbled about the minutiae of the terms. Hal went back over their conversation himself, preparing to counter, and experienced the first trickle of unease when he realised his irritatingly smug relative was right. There had been no mention of five *different* young ladies which shifted the parameters of the challenge significantly. To steal a kiss from a young lady once was a relatively simple task, by and large. More than that involved actual wooing and Hal had always been scrupulously careful about where and to whom he wooed. And Aaron knew it, too.

'I shall not be selecting five young ladies. In fact, there is only the one. All you need to do is find suitable opportunities and locations to kiss her five times.' He turned and pointed triumphantly through the condensation covered window to the solitary figure sat alone in a corner. 'I choose Lady Elizabeth Wilding.'

'Sullen Lizzie?'

'Now, now. You of all people should know how unfair nicknames can be here in the *ton*. Wasn't your own dear sister known as the Ginger Amazonian for years? A dreadful name which was most unfortunate. If people overhear you calling the poor girl that, the name might stick.'

Hal could almost smell the horse manure and realised he had been ambushed. 'As I recall, dear brother-in-law, it was you who gave my sister that unfortunate nickname, so don't try to use that against me. Besides, she *is* sullen. The sullenest woman in Mayfair. Why, she barely casts me a disdainful glance if we happen to pass on the street. You picked her on purpose, you snake! Everybody knows Lady Elizabeth Wilding loathes all men!'

'How can you say that when the chit was engaged once?'

'And callously called it off on the morning of her

wedding without a thought to the poor groom's feelings!' Everyone remembered that juicy titbit of gossip. It had caused quite a scandal, from what he recalled, as the announcement was made to the congregation as they had waited for the bride and groom to take their vows.

'Marriage is for life, Hal. I believe it shows how sensible she is to have refrained from making the wrong choice. And even you have to concede that the dissolute Rainham was a bad choice. Nobody has seen the fellow in years—probably had to run away from all his creditors. *Brava* to her, I say. It hardly makes her a man-hater to have realised Rainham was a mistake at the last minute—merely choosy. When one has the largest dowry of any young lady in the *ton*, one has to be *very* careful.'

'Ha! By all accounts the dowry is so sweet because her personality is so sour. Her poor father must be so desperate to marry her off to have offered such a ridiculous sum. How many Seasons has she been out now?' Hal prodded Aaron in the chest. 'I shall tell you. Too many and that in itself tells me everything I need to know. Even with the dowry she is resolutely dour. She has not, to the best of my knowledge, entertained the overtures of a suitor in years. Her mouth curls in distaste every time she converses with a single gentleman. And when was the last time she accepted an invitation to dance?' Sullen Lizzie positively glared at any fellow brave enough to get within ten feet of her. Despite her famed beauty, Hal had never bothered being one of them. Gently bred young ladies with pristine reputations were not his type and he sincerely doubted scandalous earls were hers. Kissing the frosty Lady Elizabeth once would be a huge achievement. Managing to do it five times would be a miracle.

'Are you conceding the challenge then, because if you are I shall send a note to my stable master immediately, instructing him to cease all shovelling for the night. I want you to have a decent pile in the morning. We did shake on the wager, after all, and I must remind you that you are both a gentleman and a peer of the realm, and as such duty bound to honour your word. It is a great shame, though. I had hoped you were made of sterner stuff. Lady Elizabeth is a very beautiful woman and, as you previously stipulated, one who is in possession of all of her own teeth.'

Male pride, Hal mused, was a dangerous thing. Everything about the wager told him he would lose so why bother. However, a bigger, primal part of him wanted to best his cocky friend and in truth Lady Elizabeth was a stunningly beautiful woman and it would be no great hardship to kiss her. Unsociable. Unapproachable. Unreachable. Very definitely a challenge for only the finest, most skilled of hunters, and only where women were concerned he was undoubtedly that. 'I wouldn't dream of conceding.'

He watched Aaron's face fall before staring back at him stunned. 'Really? Are you completely sure?' And now his friend sounded nervous, as if he regretted his own choice, too, but was also too stubborn to back down.

'I shall kiss Sullen Lizzie five times in five different locations before Twelfth Night. And you, Aaron, are going to move a veritable mountain once I win and I am going to crack open a bottle of my finest port and watch, gloating, while you do it!' The more he thought about it, the more Hal was convinced Lady Elizabeth Wilding was the perfect candidate to test his superior powers of seduction on. At least she wasn't eager and surely that had to be a point in her favour. Hal would have to be resourceful and tenacious. Like a hunter of old. Already, he could feel the previously sluggish, hot male blood coursing through his veins at the prospect. He clinked his glass against his flabbergasted friend's.

'Let the Mistletoe Wager commence!'

Chapter Two

Lizzie gazed wistfully at the ormolu clock on the Renshaws' opulent fireplace and stifled a groan when she saw the time. It would be at least another hour before her father relented and allowed her to summon the carriage. His insistence that she maintain this silly façade after five long years was beyond tiresome. Initially, he had insisted she return to society to maintain appearances. Her continued presence gave credence to the lie that she had chosen to terminate her engagement to Rainham, as was a woman's prerogative, and therefore she had nothing to be ashamed of. It was necessary, he explained, to keep her scandalous, dirty secret a secret.

Back then, she had readily agreed to keep her baby a secret and spare her family the scandal. The wonderful Wildings had rallied around her, fiercely protective, and their loyalty was something she would always be grateful for. So many girls 'in trouble' were cast out and shunned by their families, even more had to suffer the horrendous grief of giving up their child and never seeing or daring to mention the poor thing again. Fortunately, she had been spared both of those ordeals. For the first year she stayed largely at the family estate in Cheshire with her brother, his wife and their young son Frederick, venturing back into town to keep up the necessary appearances when the need arose, but after her mother had died, Lizzie and George were summoned back to Mayfair to live with her father, something she had agreed to do temporarily because she could not stand the thought of him being all alone.

Aside from the bothersome London Season and the shorter Christmas one, where she was forced into a society which would instantly turn on her if they were ever appraised of the truth, she got to live her life exactly as she wanted to.

Almost.

Yet to all intents and purposes, little George did not exist outside their Mayfair house. Small children, it turned out, were very easy to conceal from the prying eyes of the world. For the longest time it had been surprisingly easy to behave in public as if nothing untoward was going on. Back when he was a baby, Lizzie had only been too pleased to comply. It would have caused the most horrendous scandal for both their family and the Government to have done otherwise. As the most senior man at the Foreign Office, the King's chief advisor on the delicate art of global diplomacy, her father had to be seen to be above reproach and she had not wanted to bring his ambitions to a shuddering halt because of her foolish indiscretion. She had returned to society after her clandestine confinement and nobody was any the wiser. All in all, they had done such a good job that even now, remarkably, her pristine reputation was still intact and, to all intents and purposes, she was just another single young lady on the marriage mart.

Except she wasn't.

Despite her father's steadfast refusal to give up the hope Lizzie would find a suitable man to marry, there was nothing which would ever tempt her to take a trip down the aisle again. Once bitten, twice shy, and Lizzie had been bitten too hard. So hard she was certain she still bore the treacherous Rainham's teeth marks. From the outset, she had rebelled against her papa's misguided belief she would soon snare another man who could be convinced, or bribed by his powerful father-in-law, into claiming the new-born child as his own. Instead, she actively repelled any man who dared to come within six feet of her. And, for good measure, any woman, too. The last thing she needed was allowing anyone to get too close, just in case she inadvertently let slip something which might embarrass her family or, more importantly, bring unwarranted shame and censure on her son.

Heaven forbid she would consider the alternative and marry a man who was shallow enough to be bribed to take on her child. Georgie deserved better than that and Lizzie would never allow him to be an inconvenience to a husband who would prefer her delightful little boy did not exist at all. As a wife, she would be bound by her husband's edicts. What if Georgie was banished to boarding school or some remote property to be brought up by strangers? Unloved and all alone. She would protect him from that with the last breath in her body. No, indeed. The very last thing she could ever risk, for the sake of her beautiful boy, was marriage.

However, her dear papa refused to acknowledge her fears or that the trusting, foolish girl she had been had died the day Rainham had jilted her. What had emerged from the wreckage was a stronger, harder woman who would never be seduced into the merry dance of courtship again, no matter how charming or handsome her would-be suitor was. If she could thank the scoundrel Marquess for something, other than the fruit of his lying, deceitful loins, then it would be for opening her eyes to the harsh realities of life. Lizzie had been a hopeless dreamer then; now she was a realist. Her papa called it pessimism. It was much better to always expect the worst, that way you were guaranteed never to be disappointed. Being at the mercy of fate, or fickle men, was not a situation she would ever allow again.

And, on the subject of plans, soon she would put her most audacious one into action. This would be her last foray into polite society. One more month of maintaining this ridiculous charade for the sake of propriety, and her dear papa's career, before she withdrew from the *ton* for ever. Georgie was not a baby any more. He could run around, talk and asked an increasing amount of questions about everything, the most consistent one causing her the most sleepless nights. *Where is my papa?* There was only so long her darling boy would accept her blithe answer of *far, far away* without complaint, yet she knew she was being unfair to him by keeping him the dark.

Her little boy needed to go to school and experience the sort of childhood all little boys deserved. He needed to play outside, not be restricted to twice-weekly jaunts to Richmond Park with his mother. The infrequent visits with her brother's son were not enough and, as good a grandpapa as her dear father was to George, or no matter how many hours he spent playing with him, her son needed to be with children his own age, not adults. She wanted him to grow up feeling confident and secure in who he was. It was hardly his fault he was the Wildings' dirty little secret.

Her dirty little secret.

After Christmas was done and dusted, and after she had found the right words to tell her beloved father of her decision, Lizzie was going to leave the sheltered safety of their Mayfair house. The spacious cottage in Yorkshire had already been purchased in the name of Mrs Smith with the small inheritance she had been left from her grandmother and via an attorney sworn to secrecy. It was already decorated and comfortably furnished in readiness. The well-paid attorney had seen to that, too. In a few short weeks, Lizzie would, to all intents and purposes, cease to be Lady Elizabeth Wilding for as much of her life as possible.

Instead, she would pretend to be a young widow—lord knew there were enough of them thanks to the carnage of decades of war—and Georgie would grow up like a normal boy, free from the stain of illegitimacy. Nobly fatherless because of Napoleon. Just the two of them. In quiet, peaceful, utter bliss. No more questions. No more lies—all bar that one.

Even so, she dreaded telling her father. He had stepped into the breach all those years ago and still believed his protection was necessary, until she learned to trust again and found a man to relieve him of the duty. Hence, she was at the Renshaw Ball at her misguided papa's request, miserable and beyond bored, and would no doubt have to attend all manner of so-called similar entertainments for the next, interminable, miserable month.

In desperation, he had even taken to approaching potential husbands on her behalf. Sensible, staid men who were nothing but upright and no doubt he had significantly inflated her dowry as bait. Luring them with the enticing scent of money, encouraging them to come and talk or ask her to dance. Refusing to believe her insistence that she was done with men and never wanted another one, no matter how dull, staid and annoyingly persistent the fellows he selected were.

So pathetically, because she could not bear to hurt her papa's feelings, she was hiding in the furthest chairs reserved for the most committed of wallflowers, attempting to be invisible. A sorry state of affairs, indeed, but easier than upsetting her father with yet another argument.

Why couldn't he see that time was running out and the scandal he had vehemently suppressed for years was in danger of blowing wide open? They could not keep George sequestered in the house for ever, or wire his talkative mouth shut, and hell would have to freeze over before she would allow the rest of society to judge her innocent baby based on the circumstances of his birth. Lizzie would never regret George, regardless of how he had come to be in her life, and she was so very tired of hiding him. Poor Papa. His eagerness to find her a husband was beginning to drive a wedge between them and that broke her heart as well. The last five years of nonsense could not be allowed to continue much longer.

'A penny for your thoughts?'

The deep male voice from behind startled her, yet Lizzie hid it instinctively. Sometimes, particularly arrogant young bucks still attempted to flirt with her for sport. Something which was always ruthlessly nipped in the bud. A slow, calculated glance to the side revealed Henry Stuart, the newly minted Earl of Redbridge. Handsome as sin and with a sinful reputation to match. She did not bother hiding her irritation at recognising him.

'Do not trouble yourself, my lord. I can assure you that whatever misguided impulse sent you my way, it was most assuredly futile. I am in no mood to engage in polite conversation or anything else this evening.' She flicked her eyes back towards the dance floor and turned her body away from his, allowing the uncomfortable seconds to tick by. Men were like wasps. If you ignored them, they eventually went away.

She heard the slight creaking protest of wood and realised he had eased his big body into the chair alongside. She gave him her best unwelcoming frown and curtest tone. 'I do not recall inviting you to sit.' This insect clearly needed swatting.

Looking decidedly bored, the Earl glanced at the rows of empty chairs around them and shrugged. 'These seats have been expressly placed here by our hostess to rest upon. I do not recall being told I needed anyone's permission to sit in them. Please ignore me, Lady Elizabeth and, in turn, I shall ignore you as you have made it quite plain you would prefer me to. Believe me, there are a million places I would rather be as well.'

As she could think of no immediate retort to such blatant indifference, Lizzie stared resolutely at the dance floor and her unwelcome companion did the same. Neither spoke. After a full five minutes, she actively considered standing and moving to the opposite side of the room. His continued presence rattled her, although she could not say why. Men did not linger when they had been rejected. As a rule. But moving would alert him to her discomfort and that would never do. 'You can sit there all night. I still will not talk to you.'

'Yet here you are, talking regardless.' He stifled a yawn. 'Fear not, fair maiden, like you, I am hiding. I find these events tiresome.'

'There are many other places to hide, my lord, perhaps you should retire to one of those and leave me in peace. I was here first and, in case I have not made it obvious enough, I am not desirous of either your company or your attentions.'

Only his eyes turned to look at her and they were inscrutable. Very green. Very bored. 'Clearly you have an inflated sense of your own appeal if you have construed my sitting as evidence of my interest in you.' Lizzie instantly smarted at the insult, yet quashed the urge to show it. She could hardly go around dismissing men curtly from her presence, then become offended when one was blessedly uninterested.

'I should still prefer you to sit elsewhere.'

'Believe me, under normal circumstances I would be only too happy to comply with your request. However, drastic times call for drastic measures. I find myself in the unpleasant position of *having* to endure your company and, as I have specifically chosen to sit with you, you might try to be a little honoured by the accolade.'

'Honoured?' Despite the affront, he did, devil take him, have her intrigued. 'And why, pray tell, do you *have* to endure me of all people, when there is a positive ocean of other, more agreeable people here to annoy?'

He gave the room a dismissive scan, then his sea-green eyes locked with hers far more impertinently than any eyes had in quite some time. 'May I be brutally frank with you, Lady Elizabeth?'

He was still regarding her blandly and, much as it pained her, Lizzie nodded. 'Honesty? From a renowned rake? This I have to hear.'

He heaved an irritated sigh, although clearly more at his own situation than at her rudeness, and stared at the dance floor with an expression of complete distaste. 'Since I came into the earldom, I find myself in the hideous position of being *eligible*. Earls, apparently, need wives, and there are a vast number of eager candidates for the position keen to push themselves forward—I confess, I am finding it all rather tiresome.'

'From what I know of your reputation, sir, I would have thought you would relish so much *opportunity*.'

His dark brows drew together and his top lip wrinkled in disgust. 'Opportunity? Are you quite mad, Lady Elizabeth? The only opportunity this whole sorry situation offers me is the opportunity to be caught soundly in the parson's trap! A place, I can assure you, I have no desire to be. Any decent rake worth his salt does not dally with *nice* girls. Everybody knows that!' He shuddered and Lizzie found herself smiling before she stopped herself. At least he *was* being honest.

'All very tragic, yet I am still none the wiser as to why you have singled out this particular corner of the ballroom to hide in, or more specifically why you have to endure being here. With me. Or why I should feel *honoured* in the process.'

He lent sideways to whisper, as if he were imparting some great secret, and his warm breath tickled her ear. It was, surprisingly, a wholly pleasant sensation. 'It is well known, my dear lady, that your *charming* disposition and *sociable* nature are not for the faint hearted. Especially during this joyous festive season.' She watched the hint of a smile linger for a moment on his face, a hint of a smile which was every bit as roguish as he was, saw his broad chest rise, then fall slowly under his crossed, irritatingly muscled arms and felt her pulse flutter at the magnificent sight of him. Her bizarre reaction made her scowl at him in anger. Something which obviously amused him greatly, because the half-smile turned into a full rakish grin, and to her complete shame, that grin did strange things to her insides.

'You have *quite* the reputation, Lady Elizabeth, thank goodness, as I cannot tolerate people *without* a bad reputation. All that goodness makes me nervous. However, I digress, it is your reputation for ill-humoured and barely concealed dislike of polite society which I am in dire need of. A deterrent, as it were. *You*, madam, are the perfect foil for a man in my position. A sullen shield to defend me against my hordes of eager admirers. Nobody will dare to come and talk to me when I am sat here with you. I shall be spared every crushing bore, every ambitious mama and every nimble, nubile, pathetically eager yet dreadfully dull, potential bride.'

When he had first approached her, Hal was determined to charm her out of her perpetual frown. However, at the very last moment he had realised the beautiful and frosty Lizzie would probably be immune to such overt flattery. With her pale golden hair and cornflower-blue eyes, she must have heard every compliment ever uttered and, as Aaron had warned, she was definitely a woman far too intelligent to be won over by flowery words.

At the last second he had changed tack, because he always came up with the best ideas on the hop, and

failed to be charming and was now very glad that he
had. It had been exactly the right move and one which
cemented his belief in his ability to understand women
better than most men. Sullen Lizzie was responding to
his casual uninterest with far more interest than he had
ever witnessed her display before, when really he was
only being honest.

Sort of.

He *was* finding the hordes of admirers tiresome and
he genuinely *did* have no intention of marrying any time
soon, what with all the wild oats which had so vexed
his father still in urgent need of sowing whilst he diligently avoided being respectable.

Her pretty blue eyes, which had been narrowed in
annoyance just a few minutes ago, regarded him with
wary curiosity. 'Have you been encouraged to come
speak to me at the bequest of my father?'

'Not at all. I cannot recall the last time I had cause
to speak to the Earl of Upminster.' An interesting snip-
pet. Clearly her father disapproved of her solitary ten-
dencies if he was actively directing suitors towards her.
'I take it he is trying to marry you off?' For effect, he
scrunched up his face at the word marry and, without
thinking, she nodded before she stopped herself. The
change was quite spectacular. Her slim shoulders stiffened and her back straightened. Her eyes went icy blue.
Her expression became bland. Cold. Even her character
seemed to withdraw deep inside herself until all that
was left was determined, stony indifference. It was like
watching the drawbridge go up on a castle. Hal could
not remember a time when he had spoken to a woman
quite so…guarded before. Getting past all her layers of
defences was not going to be easy and already his con-

science was niggling him that something about this situation was very wrong, but a wager was a wager and, if nothing else, he needed to prove something to himself as well as to Aaron. 'My father used to drive me mad with his demands that I marry.' More truth. What the blazes had got into him?

'I notice you managed to resist him.'

'As have you.'

'My father means well.' There was a note of exasperation in her tone. He watched her lovely eyes wander towards the Earl of Upminster and soften instinctively at the sight of him. There was love there. Loyalty. Then he noticed the way she winced when her father grinned back encouragingly. Clearly he assumed the fact she was talking to a man was a good sign. Even if the man happened to be him. Without realising it, she had shown Hal her Achilles' heel. 'He just does not understand...' She stopped herself. Her plump lips sealed in a flat line.

'He just does not understand that you are not inclined towards marriage. Most people do not understand such a thing could be possible, I suppose, especially for a woman, when procuring a husband is meant to be at the very top of her list of priorities.'

'It does not even feature on my list of priorities.' This was said with such fierceness she quite forgot to put her guard up for a moment. There was fire beneath all the ice, too. Interesting.

'Mine either. No doubt I shall have to succumb one day. Produce the obligatory heir and a spare, but I am only twenty-seven and far too young to settle down.'

'Hence you are using me as a shield to ward off the eager hordes.' The ghost of a smile touched her lips and Hal experienced a strange flutter in his chest at being the cause of it. For some reason, he sensed the stare of another and, when he looked towards it, saw her father watching their interactions like a hawk. 'I wish I had a shield to protect me from my father's enthusiasm for finding me suitors. But alas, he is beyond determined and I fear I am doomed to suffer regardless.'

'Perhaps I can return the favour?' The words were out before he could stop them. However, the opportunity was there, ripe for the picking, and a true seducer took advantage of the moment. Thinking on his feet. 'I notice your father appears to be interested in you talking to me.'

The shutters came down again and her expression became unreadable. 'He will get over it.'

Tread carefully, Hal. 'I think it is fairly safe to say we both have an aversion to marriage. Your father wants you to find a man and half of this ballroom wants me to be the man for them. Why don't we form an alliance against them all?'

'I am not sure I follow, my lord.'

'The way I see it, this dreadful Christmas season is stuffed with potentially awkward and bothersome social functions which we are both duty-bound to attend. Your father is going to bore you with a succession of would-be suitors and, because my mother is determined to enjoy life and I must be her escort, I am going to have to spend a great many hours hiding from the hordes on freezing terraces, if tonight's experiences are anything to go by. Therefore, why don't we pretend to be interested in one another? Your father will be thrilled you have selected a suitor of your own accord, thus one would hope he will leave you alone to allow romance to blossom, and your legendary sullen disposition and my most *obvious* attentions towards you will deter other young ladies from coming after me. And at the very least, we will both have someone like-minded to talk to during all those long interminable hours of enforced gaiety. These affairs can be so dreadfully dull.'

Hal allowed the silence to stretch as he watched her mull over his proposal. To his complete surprise, he did feel a little guilty at how he was trying to manipulate her, but that was far outweighed by the benefits of their unlikely partnership. Even if he lost the bet, which of course he wouldn't, Lady Elizabeth would be an effective deterrent from all those eager young ladies and that, in itself, would make the next month far less painful even if he did end up having to take up the shovel.

'No, thank you, my lord.'

'I wouldn't be so quick to dismiss it out of hand if I were you. Such an arrangement benefits both of us and I suspect the pair of us would rub along quite well. We are both obviously jaded and have a healthy disregard for all this nonsense around us. Think of all the fun we could have.'

'I said no!' The barricade went up again and this time it was unyielding. She sat stiffly, staring away from Hal resolutely. Their brief, enlightening conversation was clearly at an end. Something about her demeanour made him reluctant to push further. He had the distinct feeling if he continued to attempt to whittle down her defences he would do more harm than good. Sullen Lizzie was going to be a stubbornly tough nut to crack and therefore Hal would have to use subtle persistence to get her to voluntarily lower the drawbridge rather than a battering ram to breach the enormous walls she had placed around herself. He sat quietly beside her. Just in case she had a change of heart.

After an age, she stood and he watched, fascinated, as her eyes once again sought her father. The sigh of frustration was audible when the Earl of Upminster beamed at her expectantly across the room and beckoned to her to come and meet the gentleman stood ramrod-straight and eager at his elbow. A far more suitable and sensible suitor than Hal.

'Are you sure I cannot tempt you into an alliance?'

Her step faltered and it was then that he realised he might still stand a chance. 'Absolutely not. The idea is preposterous.' But she was tempted. And for now, that was enough.

Chapter Three

Her father could barely contain his excitement in the carriage ride home. 'Although your choice of fellow leaves a great deal to be desired, it was encouraging to see you finally talking to a gentleman, Lizzie. Are you finally warming to the idea of courting again?'

Of course she wasn't, but she could see the benefits of the outrageous proposal. Having a pretend beau would certainly make the next month bearable. Perhaps refusing him had been a hasty decision? And then again, she had survived five interminable Seasons and five miserable Christmases by herself; she could jolly well manage one last month on her own. 'It was a conversation, Papa. Please do not read anything more into it than that. I am quite indifferent to the Earl of Redbridge's charms.'

Besides, Lizzie had already decided never to converse with the man again despite the allure of a month of peace. He had been far too solid and too tall, smelled far too nice and, for some inexplicable reason, he interested her in a way no man had since her traitorous former fiancé. The lack of charm and flattery had been refreshing. A little too refreshing, and she had found herself breaking her own rules by talking to him. And he was astute. He had immediately worked out her father wanted her to wed, yet he had understood her reluctance to comply. Without thinking, Lizzie had let things slip unguarded out of her mouth. At one point, she had to remind herself midsentence that Henry Stuart was cut from the same cloth as Rainham. A handsome rake. A charmer. Something worth bearing in mind when her pulse kept racing every time he had gazed down at her. As soon as she had reassured herself she was still uninterested, talking to him had been almost entertaining.

Almost. Which was a worry.

The man had a very impertinent way of conversing with her which she had decided she did not like. Leaning close and talking in that hushed, deep whisper had made several pairs of nosy eyes stare at them intently. Something which was made all the more uncomfortable by the irritating fact the whispering had been unsettling, too. Lizzie had not been that close to a man since the last time her wretched former fiancé had scrambled down the wisteria and had no desire to ever be again. Unfortunately, her traitorous body seemed to have other ideas and had covered itself in hundreds of goose bumps when his lips had hovered close to her ear. She sincerely doubted her unexpected reaction had anything to do with the Earl of Redbridge, more likely they were caused by five years of blissful isolation from all things male.

'I know it was just a conversation, Lizzie, however as it was the first conversation you have deigned to grant a man of your own accord in years, and because I saw you smiling once or twice, you will forgive me for marking its significance. Regardless of your indifference towards Redbridge—which I heartily approve of, by the way—your change of heart towards the opposite sex *in general* warms mine. Who knows? You might meet a nice man whom you are not indifferent towards. I know plenty of sterling fellows who would suit you perfectly. One more suitable than Redbridge, of course, as his reputation is unacceptable.' His face clouded briefly as they both inadvertently thought of Rainham. 'I want you to marry, Lizzie. Someone safe and dependable. I promised your mother on her death bed that I would see you settled with a good man after what that blackguard did to you. We both hoped you would find someone sooner rather than later.'

'But I have no desire to marry anyone, Papa. Mama would understand if she could see how happy Georgie is. Throwing a new husband into the mix at this stage in his life would unsettle him.'

'The boy needs a father.'

'No. He doesn't. And certainly not one who would tolerate him at best, or hide him away on some distant estate at worst. Forgive me for disagreeing—but he does not need a father. He has a wonderful grandfather instead.'

She watched his eyes go all misty for a moment before he cleared his throat to try to disguise his emotion by pretending to clear away a speck of imaginary dust. 'But I am not getting any younger. You know how much I worry about you being left all alone in the world when I am gone.' The guilt turned sour in her mouth. He would be devastated when she finally plucked up the courage to tell him she intended to be all alone sooner rather than later and would leave him all alone in the process. They would visit, of course, but it would hardly be the same. 'And the right husband would bring my grandson up as his own. I would make it a stipulation in the settlements.'

Wouldn't that be dandy? Poor Georgie's place in his mother's house would be an enforced legality and no doubt the source of a great deal of resentment. 'Does that honestly strike you as the best outcome? Because it doesn't to me. I am quite capable of looking after myself and my son unaided, Papa. I do wish you would stop worrying about us.'

'Tell me, Lizzie, as a parent yourself, can you ever envisage a time when you will not be concerned with little Georgie's welfare?' He had her there. Probably never was the answer. 'Now be a good daughter and indulge this old man for once. I know what is good for you and I refuse to give up on your mother's last wish. You deserve the love of a good man.' He patted her hand affectionately, his mind made up regardless.

As always. Exactly why she had been forced to go behind his back.

'I have high hopes of this festive season. High hopes indeed.' He had kissed her cheek and practically skipped up the stairs to bed. A very bad sign as he had that twinkle in his eye. The one which he always got when he was intent on matchmaking and, as he had only recently increased her dowry, his buoyant mood did not bode well.

More guilt was piled on afresh and she spent all night questioning the logic of her impulsive decision to refuse Redbridge. Such a bargain only served to give her father hope where none existed and that seemed cruel. Being duplicitous, although it was something she had been forced to do for five long years, was not something which sat well with her, especially when she was doing it to her family rather than the rest of the world. However, her father's attempts at marrying her off were becoming overt in the extreme. Very overt and very extreme. He meant well, she reminded herself. He meant well and he loved her. For that alone she would grit her teeth and endure whatever challenges he threw at her in their final month with as much good grace as she could muster.

Lizzie managed to catch about two hours of sleep before she was woken at dawn by her maid with a steaming cup of chocolate and a report of the weather. 'It's freezing outside, my lady, but it doesn't look like rain.'

'Can you tell the nanny to ensure little Georgie is bundled up against the cold and tell her to inform him if he refuses to put on his gloves again then he will not be flying his kite. And I am sure they have already thought of it, but check the carriage is packed with a few extra blankets.' Knowing her son, he would get cold once he had tired himself out dashing around Richmond Park and if he was too chilly he would not nap on the way home. Something which always made him surly in the afternoons.

As it was every Tuesday and Thursday morning, breakfast was on the table before seven and Georgie was already bouncing in his chair with excitement. 'Come along, young man. Eat your porridge. You know your mama will not leave until the bowl is empty.' Her father was an indulgent grandparent and insisted on eating with them every morning, even if that meant getting up twice a week at such an ungodly hour.

The drive to Richmond took over an hour and the streets were nicely deserted at such an unsociable hour. As the remote park would be, too. Lizzie would be able to spend a blissful few hours outdoors with her son miles away from London and away from prying eyes and be safely back home by early afternoon when the fashionable residents of Mayfair went out. They had visited the huge parkland at Richmond twice weekly for the last six months for the sake of both her own and her son's sanity. It was not as if the pair of them could wander around Hyde Park or St James's. Georgie had never been to either in case he was seen and the scandal erupted. He loved to run free in the countryside, loved to explore wooded nooks and crannies and delighted in all God's creatures, whether that be the smallest woodlouse or the majestic red deer that roamed wild in the open parkland of Richmond.

Soon he would be able to do this every single day and as happy as that prospect made her, it was bittersweet. Part of the reason her son enjoyed these jaunts so very much was regaling the excursion in great detail to his grandpapa afterwards. As soon as they arrived home, her son would boisterously run into her father's study, clamber on his knee and describe every beetle, every twig, the exact strength of the breeze and the hue of the sky. Then he would lie for at least an hour under her father's desk while the pair of them worked in companionable silence—her father on important affairs of state; Georgie sketching childish depictions of animals in the expensive coloured chalks his grandpapa had bought him for that express purpose. She was dreading telling them those days were now numbered, despite the fact it was ultimately for the best.

Her son shovelled in the last spoonful of porridge. 'Come along, Mama! I hope we see the deer again today. Do you know that the Latin name for the red deer is *cervus elaphus*? Grandpapa found it in one of his books. They mainly eat grass and twigs—but apparently they are also partial to moss.'

'Really? Well, that is interesting. What else did you learn about them?' She wrestled him into his coat, then took his hand. Listening to his incessant, excited chatter Lizzie resolutely banished all thoughts of her father's meddling and the Earl of Redbridge's increasingly tempting offer from her mind.

Aaron had been gloating over breakfast. As soon as the ladies left them to their newspapers, he had grinned smugly across the table and recounted the magnificent way Lady Elizabeth Wilding had given him short shrift at the Renshaw ball. 'All that practised charm, your fortune, title and apparent good looks did nothing to sway the lady. You do not stand a chance of winning this bet, Hal. You have no idea what a good mood that puts me in.'

Hal took it all gracefully, but seethed inside. Aaron took the word competitive to new levels and was a gloating victor. The best Christmas present Hal could give to himself was the splendid sight of his brother-in-law wielding a shovel and, by Jove, he had to do whatever it took to ensure it happened. Sullen Lizzie had been interested in his proposition. He had seen it with his own eyes and an alliance between them was the best way forward to fulfil the terms of the Mistletoe Wager. All he had to do was convince her of the benefits. There was a chance that might be better achieved in private than in a public social setting.

An hour later he found himself striding jauntily up the front steps of the Earl of Upminster's Grosvenor Square town house, a house which had always been but a stone's throw from his own, but might have well been on the moon for all the dealings he had had with its occupants, an enormous bunch of flowers in his arms.

He rapped the brass knocker smartly and stood tall, his most charming smile firmly in place and his thick hair freshly combed. The large, imposing butler was a bit of a shock. The fellow looked more suited to prize fighting than domestic service. He positively filled the door frame. 'Good morning. I have come to call on Lady Elizabeth. Please tell her I am here.' Hal handed over his calling card, but kept the flowers. He wanted to see her face when she saw those as he had picked the blooms specifically.

'Lady Elizabeth is not at home, my lord. I shall tell her that you called.' The heavy front door began to close.

'Now, now, my good man, we both know how this game is played. It is barely eleven o'clock so I am sure she *is* home. Nobody goes out this early. Not in Mayfair.' Unless they were on the hunt for the perfect bunch of flowers to give to a guarded yet intriguing occupant of this very house. Hal had had to travel to Covent Garden directly after breakfast for the cream roses. 'Inform Lady Elizabeth that I intend to remain rooted to this front step until she grants me an audience.'

The giant butler sighed. 'Suit yourself, sir, although I must warn you, it will be a waste of your time. Lady

Elizabeth is *genuinely* not at home this morning.' The door went to close again and Hal began to suspect that the man might be telling the truth.

'Can you tell me where she is then?'

'I am afraid not, my lord.'

'Will she be back this afternoon?'

'Yes, my lord. However, she is never *at home* in the afternoons, if you get my meaning.' The butler stared impassively. 'Nor will she be at home tomorrow morning as she is never *at home* in the mornings either.'

'Then you admit that she is, as I suspect, currently *at home* as we speak, yet resolutely *not at home* to all callers regardless as to who they might happen to be.'

'Not at all, my lord. Lady Elizabeth is *genuinely* not at home on Tuesday and Thursday mornings, and not at home *any* other time.'

This clearly called for a different tactic. 'Can I ask what your name is?'

'You can, my lord. I am Stevens, his lordship's butler.'

'You are a vexing fellow, Stevens.'

'I do try, my lord.'

Hal dipped his hand into his pocket and fished out the silver crown he always kept there for emergencies. Covertly, beneath the enormous bouquet he held, Hal flashed the coin at the butler. 'Be a good chap and tell Lady Elizabeth I am here to see her.'

Stevens glanced down at the coin, scowled and promptly closed the door. Hal couldn't help admiring him for it. He liked a man who could not be bribed, it said a great deal about his character. But not all men were as moral, so he wandered around to the mews instead.

However, it soon became apparent that the Earl of Upminster had possibly the most moral staff in Mayfair.

With his bribes increasing from a crown to a guinea to a colossal five pounds, he was similarly turned down by the stable boys, a footman and scullery maid who had been sent out to buy beeswax. In fact, their lips were sealed tighter than Stevens's, who had at least informed Hal she was *genuinely* out and would be back this afternoon—although not for him.

That left him with a bit of a quandary. He was too tenacious to give up, but too lazy to stand guard in the square until she came home. Living less than a sedate ten-minute walk away he did not have to. This afternoon suggested *after* midday and *later* this afternoon suggested after one. He would stand guard from one, bouquet in hand, and meet her when she arrived home. She could hardly tell him she was not at home when facing him, could she?

The Upminster carriage turned in to the square a little past two to Hal's enormous relief. Over an hour of sentry duty in December had rendered his feet and fingers frozen solid, but the expensive flowers thankfully still looked impressive as he walked towards the holly-wreathed front door to greet her.

However, the carriage did not slow and sped past him, its elusive occupant hidden from his view by the tightly drawn curtains, and turned down towards the mews. Hal quickly followed, rounding the corner just in time to see the impressively tall, wooden rear gates slam shut. Frustrated, he dashed back to the front door and knocked again.

After an age, Stevens opened it.

'I know she is at home Stevens, I just saw the carriage return. Kindly tell her I am here.'

'Lady Elizabeth has been made aware of your presence, my lord, and of the fact you have been loitering outside for most of the day. She has asked me to convey a message and was most particular it was issued verbatim.' For effect, he coughed gently, then scowled and bellowed, 'Go away, Redbridge! You are as welcome as a dog with fleas.'

'She said that?'

'She did, my lord. And in that exact tone.'

'Ah.' Seeing as his only option was to try and overpower the butler, something which he was not entirely certain he could do and which would ruin the line of Hal's coat significantly, he had no choice but to admit defeat. 'Can you see that Lady Elizabeth gets these, Stevens.' He thrust the flowers forward. 'And as you are so good at delivering messages verbatim, would you kindly tell her exactly this. My *tempting* invitation still stands.' He winked at the giant saucily and watched the big man's eyes widen. 'Please make sure you wink, Stevens, as that is part of the message, too. Good day to you. It has been a pleasure.'

Chapter Four

The following evening, within half an hour of their arrival at the Benfleet soirée, Lizzie's resolve not to argue with her father lifted surprisingly swiftly and was soon replaced with raging, clawing anger. Because this time, her dear, meddling papa had gone too far.

'I have taken the liberty of filling your dance card for you.'

He had said this so blithely, in the midst of a crowd, which made calling him on it impossible. He had also made sure her partner for the next dance was stood right next to him as well, effectively trapping her because the calculated old politician knew full well she would rather not cause a scene. The 'lucky' gentleman, a slightly rotund fellow with no discernible chin, appeared terrified as he held out his hand, making it obvious to one and all he had been press-ganged into service and was there only on sufferance. She was tempted to feel sorry for him.

With gritted teeth, she allowed him to lead her to the dance floor, all the while shooting daggers at her father. Once this dance was done, they would be having words, and when those words were said she fully intended to go home.

However, being skilled in the art of diplomacy, her dear papa had already anticipated her intent and had successfully managed to render himself invisible. For over an hour she danced stiffly with man after man, trying to catch a glimpse of him, her mood deteriorating significantly every time he failed to materialise. To make matters worse, he had apparently found the dullest men in the whole of Christendom to saddle her with. All so crushingly safe and dependable they blended into the wallpaper. All depressingly in want of a wife with a substantial dowry. When the ancient Earl of Ockendon came to claim her, Lizzie pretended to need to visit the retiring room, fled on to the terrace and shivered behind a statue. Freezing to death was infinitely preferable to dancing with him.

'Isn't it a little cold to be stood out here without a shawl?'

Lizzie spun around and saw the Earl of Redbridge lounging against the balustrade, smiling smugly and looking effortlessly gorgeous. 'Where have you been!' Instantly, she clamped her silly jaws shut. He did not need to know she had been frantically looking out for him.

'Be still my beating heart. You sound astoundingly pleased to see me.' His words grated. 'In fairness,' he said as he shrugged out of his coat, 'I only arrived a few minutes ago. I saw you dancing with someone, looking more sullen than usual, and had been waiting for the opportune moment to rescue you because I am a charitable soul, by and large. But you disappeared out here at speed. At one point, I was certain you were going to break into a run.' He solicitously placed the warm garment over her shivering shoulders. It smelled of him and, despite her better judgement, Lizzie snuggled into it gratefully. He might well be an irritant and a rake to boot, but his thoughtful gesture was kind and not at all what she would have expected from a man like him.

'My father has filled my dance card and I blame you for it!'

'How can I be to blame? I wasn't even here.'

'I chatted with you last night. Then you sent me flowers. It set a precedent and it has given him ideas. He has lined up every dullard from here to Land's End, hoping I will take to one of them.' She tried, and failed, not to notice the way the soft linen of his shirt clung to his upper arms or the way his waistcoat emphasised his broad chest and shoulders. He reached out and plucked the ribbon of her dance card from her wrist and scanned the names.

'Good grief! What a shockingly dour bunch.' To her consternation he then picked up her hand and gently threaded the ribbon back over it. His fingers were warm. Too warm. They were giving her skin ideas. 'As I alluded cryptically to your charming butler yesterday, my offer still stands. I am prepared to lend myself to you as your decoy beau to ward off this sea of dullards if you agree to protect me from my ocean of eager hordes.'

This must have been what Adam felt like when Eve offered him a bite of her apple and, curse him, his proposition was attractive. 'I suppose…for the sake of a month of peace, I could pretend to be a little interested in you.' Good gracious. Lizzie could not quite believe those words had just come out of her mouth, but thanks to her father, what other choice did she have? Her stubborn papa was vehemently determined to get her wed with unacceptable over-zealousness. She was heartily ashamed at being so weak-willed in the face of such temptation. 'But only on the strict understanding that it is all a sham and I would never *really* entertain you as a suitor.' Of its own accord, one of her fingers was jabbing him pointedly in the chest. It was alarmingly solid. His reaction was to smile down at her, unoffended by her insult.

'That's the spirit. I hope you have a talent for acting because nobody will believe it if you continue to glare at me as if I am something offensive stuck to the bottom of your shoe.'

Now that he came to mention it, her facial muscles were beginning to ache from the exertion of her frown. As they always did at these unwelcome social functions. Lizzie scrunched up her face to loosen them and then stared back at him blandly. 'I do not wish to give my father false hope. I should prefer it if you appear more keen than me in his presence. That way, once I terminate our acquaintance he won't be too upset.'

'Agreed. I shall be a simpering, fawning lapdog in front of your father and an amorous suitor in front of your dullards.'

She did not like the sound of that. 'Not too amorous!'

'My dear, you know nothing about the ways of men. When a young lady is being courted and appears uninterested, it means she is still fair game and only spurs the other fellows on. Men are a competitive bunch. It is in our nature. However, when the lady is obviously keen on another, they will retreat. As gentlemen, they are duty bound to do so. It's in the gentleman's code somewhere. Besides, nothing will cool their ardour quicker than the sight of you fawning over another man. We have our pride.'

'My father has increased my dowry to make me more attractive.' Pride and duty would hardly stop the greedy from coveting the money she came with.

'Even more reason why you must encourage my amorous advances in front of them. I am disgustingly rich and, as I obviously do not need your money, they will assume we are *in love*.' She stiffened then and her outraged reaction clearly amused him. 'I understand your reluctance. Really, I do. You are frightened you might forget our arrangement is all a sham and genuinely fall in love with me. A perfectly understandable fear. I am irresistible, after all, and you are bound to develop romantic *feelings*.'

The snort of laughter escaped before she could stop it, because he was amusing if nothing else and that knowing, rakish grin he perpetually sported did suit him. 'There is no danger of *that*, my lord!'

'Then tonight we shall begin our ruse and by the end of the evening we will be the source of much-fevered speculation.'

Lizzie huffed as reality dawned. 'Thanks to my overzealous father, I am doomed to dance with a card full of dullards, unless I conveniently freeze to death first.'

'Fear not, fair maiden, once we go back inside I will shamelessly monopolise you. You'll be spared dancing with another dullard this evening and every evening henceforth. From this point on, the only man you will dance with is me.'

'I thought I was to be spared another dullard.' She

frowned belligerently and he met it with another roguish smile. It tempted her to smile back. Almost.

'Careful, Lizzie. If you are going to be mean to me I shall have my coat back.'

Automatically, her frozen fingers clutched at the garment possessively. Even for December, it was particularly cold. The statue next to them positively glittered with frost. 'I did not give you leave to call me Lizzie.'

'Yet I have called you it anyway. As a special treat, you can call me Hal. Henry is far too formal, especially when a couple is as besotted as us.'

'We are not besotted.' The set-down had less impact with her teeth chattering together. Both his hands came up and began to briskly rub the warmth back into her arms through the fabric of his coat. She wanted to chastise him for his impertinence, but it did feel marvellous. Escaping into the icy night air had been foolhardy in sleeveless silk.

'Heaven forbid! However, we must give off enough of the appearance of it if we are to be left alone. The *ton* loves to watch a blossoming love affair from afar. It makes it easier for them to gossip about it. If we orchestrate this charade correctly, we are guaranteed at least three yards of space at every function from now until Twelfth Night.'

Something which sounded very tempting.

'Where did you find roses in December.'

'I know a fellow in Covent Garden who can get any bloom for a price. Roses, freesias, tulips, lilacs...'

'I loathe lilacs. Be sure to never buy me those when you are pretending to court me.'

'Understood. No lilacs. Not that I would have bought you lilacs, of course, they don't suit you at all. The flowers in your bouquet were chosen specifically because they reminded me of you.'

Lizzie pulled a face. 'Don't tell me—the cream roses symbolise my alabaster skin?'

He grinned back, unoffended. 'Indeed they did, while the tiny pink rosebuds echoed the beautiful sweetness of those luscious lips I *ache* to kiss.'

'How clichéd. And the holly? Your joy at falling hopelessly in love with me at Christmas?'

'Not at all. They are reminiscent of your charming personality. Sharp and prickly.'

She liked the fact he was not trying to flatter her. Since Rainham, she had greatly distrusted it and found herself grinning at his cheek. 'Lady Elizabeth?' A voice called from the French doors. Her persistent dance partner had clearly tracked her down. The unladylike groan she gave made Hal laugh. Lizzie felt the intimate timbre all the way to her frozen toes.

'Dear me…if my ears do not deceive me, I do believe the Earl of Ockendon is ready for his dance. Tell me, is his breath still rancid? Last time I got too close to him, I swear it singed my eyebrows.'

'My father believes I need a safe, sensible man. Upright and above reproach.'

'And to be that he needs to be hurtling towards seventy?'

'I believe the Earl is fifty-something.'

'Good gracious! The man must have had a very hard life.'

'Lady Elizabeth? Are you out here?' The voice was getting closer and instinctively Lizzie went to dart behind her statue again, only to find herself rooted to the spot by her companion's surprisingly strong arms.

'Hiding is not the answer. He will merely bide his time and hunt you down later. Everyone knows Ockendon is desperate for an heir. Lucky you, by the way. To be favoured with his attentions must be the pinnacle of every young lady's romantic ambitions. You need to brazen it out.'

'Surely you are not suggesting I grin and bear it!' The thought of a few minutes twirling in the pungent wake of the man's breath was already turning her stomach.

'Of course not. Remember what I told you. We need to let him see dancing with you is futile…seeing as your heart is already engaged elsewhere. I do believe this is one of those occasions which warrants my *amorous* attentions.'

Lizzie was nowhere near ready for that. There had been no time to prepare. Instinctively, she took a step back. 'I don't think so.'

He quickly closed the distance and whispered again, far too close to her ear. Goose bumps covered her arms. 'Think, Lizzie. Here we are. The stars are twinkling up above. You are wearing my coat…' Those strong arms slowly snaked around her waist and pulled her closer. 'If you gaze up at me with convincing longing, the old fool will assume we are having a tryst.'

Arguing against his logic was prevented by the ominously close sound of another call from her unwelcome beau. 'Lady Elizabeth! Is that you?'

With the most limpid expression she could manage in a blind panic, Lizzie stared longingly up at Hal. He winked encouragingly, then, to her complete shock, dipped his head and pressed his lips to hers.

The sky tilted. Or perhaps it was the floor. Either

way, the experience knocked her off kilter. His arms tightened around her and his mouth moved slowly over hers. It might well have been a pretend kiss, done to give credence to the idea they were engaged in a tryst, but it felt dangerously real to Lizzie. She did not attempt to try and push him away, justifying her actions as a way of discouraging the persistent old Earl rather than enjoying the heady taste of the younger one who held her so possessively. Unconsciously, her own lips began to respond, her eyelids fluttered closed and she found herself rising on tiptoes to press her body against his. More worryingly, she was reluctant to prise herself away. Later, she knew, she would claim this was all part of her act, but for now she was prepared to acknowledge it for what it was.

A revelation.

Because kissing Hal was really, quite something. Not at all how she remembered it with her traitorous fiancé and dangerously addictive.

He was a scoundrel. A rogue. An opportunity had presented itself and, despite the nagging guilt he could not explain, he had seized it. Regardless of the circumstances, Hal's reaction to the kiss was completely unexpected. Every kiss before this had always been merely a prelude. Pleasant, but not earth-shattering. A means to a more passionate and satisfying end. Lizzie's lips were different. Almost as if they had been infused with something addictive, like opium or absinthe, because the moment they had touched his he had quite lost all sense of everything except her. It had nothing to do with passion or attraction, although undoubtedly he was overwhelmed by both of those emotions, and everything to do with a sense of rightness. They melted together, melded and, for once, a kiss was not merely a prelude but a significant event in its own right. Hal had no idea if Ockendon had seen them, if the man still stood there or if he was loudly expounding his outrage. Everything had disappeared except the woman in his arms. It was all strangely overwhelming.

She broke the contact by taking one step smartly back and to his chagrin appeared decidedly underwhelmed by the whole episode. 'I did not give you leave to kiss me.'

'Yet I did it anyway.' Feeling peculiarly shaky, Hal scanned the vicinity. 'I thought it would convince the amorous Ockendon you were unavailable.' Not strictly true. Yes, they had a bargain, but he had been thinking of his wager with Aaron—then had forgotten it instantly the second their mouths had touched.

'The Earl has gone.' Obviously, it had not had the same impact on Sullen Lizzie, because not only was she heartily unimpressed, she was also briskly removing his coat as if she found it as offensive as his kiss. She thrust it at him unceremoniously. 'Never do that again!'

'Perhaps I was a tad over-zealous.' He forced a rakish grin to cover his disappointment at her reaction.

'I am certain there are other ways to bestow your amorous attentions on me without having to resort to that. We should go back inside. The very last thing I want, aside from dancing with foul-smelling old men, is to be ruined by *you*.' She shuddered and then marched back towards the French doors, before stopping briefly to rally him. 'Come along, *Hal*, let's go put on a show.'

Hal tried not to feel offended. He had only sought her out because of the wager, sort of. There had been an odd part of him which had been desperate to seek her out the moment he had arrived at the Benfleet soirée, however he had put that down to his excitement at winning the bet and besting Aaron. Although Hal was trying not to think about the bet because every time he did he experienced something akin to indigestion, churning up his gut and making him feel uncomfortable about the way he was deliberately deceiving her. Then again, his conscience did feel lighter knowing she was also benefiting from the situation, albeit in a roundabout way. He was doing her a favour and favours were noble. Yet despite all that, he had been unexpectedly moved by the kiss. It hadn't been particularly long and by his standards it had been remarkably chaste, yet it had affected him.

Affected him? Now there was something to ponder, he thought miserably as he trailed behind her back into the crowded ballroom. Something was undoubtedly wrong with him. First a lack of vigour, the bizarre allure of controlling his father's estate, the gnawing constant niggle which hinted dangerously at a lack of real fulfilment in his life and now he was going all pie-eyed and wobbly over one silly kiss with a woman who was, at best, ambivalent to him. Or perhaps that was exactly what was wrong. Her unenthusiastic reaction had dented his male pride, ergo he was feeling unsteady.

Hal took a deep breath and let it out slowly. He was overthinking things and that was also very unlike him. Hal preferred to think on his feet. On a positive note, he was one kiss down and she hadn't slapped his face or severed their fledgling alliance upon receiving it. Which in turn meant there would be another opportunity to steal a kiss from her over Christmas. Poor Aaron would be spitting teeth later.

That thought buoyed him and, by the time he got to the refreshment table, Hal was feeling normal. Thankfully, Lizzie spotted an ambitious-looking matron and her daughter a few seconds before he did and slipped her hand possessively through his arm. It had the most staggering effect. One minute they had been prowling towards him with definite intent, the next they suddenly veered off to the right, pretending they were looking for someone else.

'Well saved, my lady. That was close. An eligible man must keep his wits about him at all times. I knew you would be a sterling deterrent.'

'I am glad I could be of service.' She smiled tightly, her eyes locked on something in the distance and gripping his arm with far more force than was necessary. 'I would greatly appreciate it if the favour was immediately reciprocated.' The smile was now so false it might have been painted on to a mask. Hal followed her eyes and spotted a determined gentleman scurrying in her direction and tried not to smile when the first bars of the waltz began. More by luck than judgement, fate was working in his favour.

'I believe this waltz is mine.' The interloper shot daggers at Hal when he saw her arm still looped through his. There was far too much pomade in the fellow's thin hair, either that or it had not been washed in the last week. Patches of his bald pate shone through the greasy strands and the poor chap was at least two inches shorter than Lizzie, a feat in itself when she was barely a few inches above five feet.

'I'm afraid there has been a mistake, old chap. The lady has already promised this dance to me.'

The bald man was outraged. 'It was arranged with the Earl of Upminster himself. I watched him write my name down on her card.' He puffed out his pigeon chest in indignation. 'We are colleagues at the Foreign Office!' One effeminate hand, more suited to clerical work than seduction, shot out and lunged for the card hanging from Lizzie's wrist, but Hal was closer and grabbed it before the upstart did.

For the most part, being blessed with height was something he was always mindful of. Those less fortunate tended to become a little intimidated if one loomed and he was too good natured to want to make others uneasy. However, occasionally a situation called for it. This one did. Pulling himself up to his full six feet and three impressive inches, Hal glowered down at the irritating fellow before him, forcing him to crane his neck up to look directly into his steely glare. 'This dance is mine.'

'No, it isn't. I specifically asked for the waltz. Upminster pencilled me in for it. I demand to see that card!' The pigeon's chest was now so puffed the buttons on his coat were straining around the heavy padding. 'Hand it over immediately!'

There was no need for any words. They were causing enough of a scene without further unseemly conversation. Rather splendidly, Aaron was paying them particular attention behind a potted palm. Hal tried not to look at his brother-in-law. Already, in less than a day since they'd struck the wager, he had stolen one kiss and secured the possibility of many different locations to kiss his lady again. Now all he had to do was choose the right opportunities to do so. That would take finesse. Clumsy, eager overtures would not be welcomed, of that Hal was quite certain. This fair, prickly ice maiden was too guarded. Wary and suspicious of everything, including him. However, she had just insisted he return the favour and save her from another man and that had nothing whatsoever to do with his bet and everything to do with his fortuitous alliance with Lizzie.

With deliberate slowness, Hal lifted it with a smile and slowly tore the offensive dance card into tiny pieces, then sprinkled them like confetti into Mr Pigeon's out-stretched hand. He turned towards his fairly startled-looking new ally and made a great show of kissing her hand.

'You promised me this dance, Lady Elizabeth.'

Chapter Five

There was challenge and amusement in his eyes. Half of the ballroom were watching them, whilst pretending not to. The fevered whispering behind so many hands and raised fans nearly drowned out the orchestra, yet she quite admired the bare-faced audacity of the man. Even though he had already left her completely unsettled after the kiss, and knowing the very last place she would ever find her missing equilibrium was in his arms again, dancing with him was infinitely preferable to the sorry specimen her father had sent. And this was all a charade after all. To her ultimate benefit. The perfect decoy for a month of blissful peace. Her last month of pretence.

'Yes, *Hal*, I did.'

His warm palm came to rest affectionately on her hand. The possessive all-male gesture sending a clear message to everyone in the room.

She's mine.

Lizzie's corset suddenly felt tight at the tingle of excitement it gave her and nerves began to jump in her tummy. Hal took his time leading her to the middle of the floor, obviously used to being the centre of attention and enjoying the spectacle they presented. A tiny part of her did, too—the rest of her was frankly terrified by it all. This was all so bizarre and out of character. She never danced, nor did she ever show any interest in any men, yet here she was, being escorted into the parting sea of obviously shocked couples by possibly the most eligible bachelor in the room. Amongst the openly curious onlookers, she felt the weight of several pairs of female eyes as they glared at her with outright hostility. His hordes. Judging by the amount of dismayed expressions, there were quite a number of them.

'You're supposed to look besotted, not like you are being led to your execution.' The subtle hint from her smiling partner reminded Lizzie theirs was a mutually beneficial arrangement. They were supposed to be protecting each other. She could do this. For peace from her father for their one, final society Christmas. Lizzie forced herself to relax and beamed at him as he took her in his arms.

Once she had got over the fact every eyeball in the Benfleet ballroom was locked on them, dancing with him was quite heady. Of course, she hadn't waltzed in five long years, she reasoned as he glided her effortlessly around the floor, and the waltz was meant to be heady. It had nothing to do with the arrogant, yet amusing, Earl of Redbridge. Despite being completely immune and impervious to men, Lizzie could see what his hordes found so appealing. He was a fine specimen of manhood. Beneath his coat she felt actual muscle—not padding—and he was exceptionally handsome. The dark hair had deep auburn strands running through it, which predictably the chandeliers picked out perfectly.

However, both of those things paled into insignificance when one looked deep into his eyes.

Hal had a way of gazing at her which made Lizzie nervous. As if those mossy depths saw right through her. She did not faze him, when she proudly terrified every other man who had tried to get near her, and that was disturbing and strangely thrilling. In fact, if anything, Lizzie was rather enjoying their new little secret just as she had enjoyed the way he had effectively neutralised her father's matchmaking in one fell swoop by tearing up her dance card so publicly. His menacing glare was like a warning shot. She sincerely doubted any more dullards would venture towards her again this evening. The handsome Earl was the perfect deterrent. Even the prospect of remaining at this ball for the duration no longer seemed tiresome now that he would be close by.

Hal woke in a fabulous mood. It made no difference that he had crawled into bed in the small hours or that his troublesome nieces were playing noisily outside his bedchamber door. He had succeeded in kissing Sullen Lizzie once. How marvellous an achievement was that?

Except, if he was honest with himself, he had thoroughly enjoyed spending time with her. After their waltz, they had stood for the better part of an hour near the refreshment table, both revelling in the pithy comments they were parrying back and forth about the dullards and the hordes. The woman had an excellent sense of humour when she let her ironclad guard down, he had to give her credit for that, and was extremely knowledgeable on a wide range of subjects from literature to politics. The latter was fascinating and proved to be a topic she felt safe discussing. She stopped frowning and became animated. Her father's elevated position in the Foreign Office gave her insights Hal had never considered before and he asked her a million questions to gently pry her out of the hard shell she hid within. For once, he did not flirt or flatter, knowing such things would be wasted on her. Instead they talked to each other as equals and retired back to the wallflower chairs for another hour until her father came to claim her.

The Earl of Upminster had greeted Hal unenthusiastically. He had looked him up and down, narrowed his eyes and then told his daughter he remembered all the names of the *other* gentleman who still wanted to dance with her should she require them. As he had promised, Hal behaved like an ardent and besotted potential suitor while she largely appeared indifferent to him until her father had ostensibly left them to their own devices when his daughter showed no desire to comply. However, in reality this meant he took himself to a spot less than twenty feet away and made no secret of the fact he was watching Hal closely.

The pair of them had subtly laughed about it afterwards and then watched the festive nonsense whirl around them from their blissfully solitary position at the furthest edge of the ballroom. It had been strangely fun conversing with a woman and not trying to bed her— not that he would have minded bedding her if she had been inclined. Enjoying intelligent conversation with her did not render him blind to her feminine charms. If anything, her obvious intelligence and rapier wit made her more attractive.

Lizzie was intriguing. Interesting as well as caustically witty, still very guarded which bizarrely gave her an enticing aura of the mysterious, and she was undeniably the single most beautiful woman in the ballroom. The corkscrew golden curls and animated cornflower-blue eyes tended to draw his gaze, as did her lush mouth when she spoke. Even without the wager those plump, pink lips would tempt him to kiss them. He would still win it, but they both benefited from the association as Lizzie was plainly delighted at successfully thwarting her father's matchmaking attempts. A great weight off Hal's newly discovered conscience regarding women. Or more particularly, his conscience regarding one woman. Her.

Dressed and shaved, Hal had a jaunty spring in his step as he left his bedchamber and scooped up each of his irritating red-haired nieces to hold them wriggling and giggling under each arm. As was his prerogative as naughty uncle, he deposited each one on the ornate curved banister, cocked a long leg over himself, to sit behind them lest they fall off, and began to slide the three of them downstairs.

'Henry!' The ominous tones of his sister Connie did not faze him and he grinned at her as they whizzed past at speed. 'How many times have I told you not to teach them to behave like hellions? The girls are boisterous enough without your help.'

Hal came to a sedate stop at the ostentatious gold acorn at the bottom of the stairs and gave his sister a peck on the cheek. 'As I recall, it was you, dear Sister, who taught me the quickest route down these stairs.'

'We were children.'

'As are Grace and Prudence. Although why you called these two monsters after such ladylike virtues is beyond me.'

'At some point, you need to grow up, Hal.'

He winked at his nieces. 'Never.' For good measure, and to vex his sister further, he roughly tossed a squealing Grace over his shoulder before picking up Prudence by her foot and carrying her upside down into the breakfast room.

'Good morning, Aaron! And if I may say so, what a *splendid* morning it is.'

His brother-in-law glared at him through narrowed eyes over the top of his newspaper while his sister poured them all tea.

'Somebody is particularly jovial this morning. I couldn't help noticing you spent most of the evening intimately ensconced with Lady Elizabeth Wilding. Does she have a bearing on your good mood?' Connie smiled at him hopefully as she placed a steaming cup in front of him. Recently, and to his complete annoyance, she too had made numerous hints about him settling down. 'Absolutely everyone was gossiping about you.'

'Gossip must be very light on the ground if a simple conversation and one dance are being misconstrued.' Hal was pleased he sounded sufficiently bored enough that his sister's face dropped. When she turned back towards the sideboard to fetch her husband's tea, he took the opportunity to flick one plump, white mistletoe berry at Aaron across the table cloth. His brother-in-law's eyes narrowed further as he pocketed the damning fruit. They both knew better than to alert Connie to their wager. She still hadn't forgiven them for causing the shocking scene at the Serpentine last summer. 'Although I believe Sullen Lizzie was quite taken with *me*.' He shot Aaron a pointed looked and stifled the bark of laughter when he saw him practically foaming at the mouth in indignation at being thwarted.

'Sullen Lizzie? What a dreadful nickname. I hope you are not the root of it, Hal. Nicknames can destroy a young woman's confidence.' She shuddered involuntarily at the memory, making her husband scowl. Thanks to Aaron, Connie had been known as the Ginger Amazonian for years on account of her unusual height and vibrant red hair. It was something his brother-in-law still felt guilty about.

'Am I never going to be forgiven for that one, stupid mistake?' Aaron said.

'Of course not, darling. You know I live only to make you miserable.' But the pair of them were staring at each other soppily again, something they did a great deal, and for once Hal found himself envious of their obvious affection rather than baffled by it. It must be wonderful to have a person look at you like that. To know you completely and understand you so well…

Something which brought him up short. What the blazes had got into him? He was not yet thirty and had far too many wild oats still to sow.

The rest of the meal was its usual chaos. His mother arrived, echoing Connie's sentiments about his current interest in Lizzie. Then his nieces made a mess and a lot of noise whilst doing it and the adults were forced to converse across the table in a volume usually reserved for the hard of hearing in order to be heard above it. Hal loved these occasions in the Berkley Square town house as they would never have been allowed in his father's time. The Stuarts and Wincantons had been at loggerheads for centuries before Aaron had married his sister despite the fact their country estates were next door to each other. But now, with Aaron's town house sold and his father festering in the ground, they all gathered here together. The once-cold house almost felt like home.

Except, there was something missing. Something untenable and ethereal which kept niggling at him. Something he kept trying to put out of his mind, yet which kept creeping back in again. His discontent was beginning to anger him, so he tried to ignore it while he ate his breakfast.

When the ladies disappeared to sort the children, Aaron launched like a cannon ball. 'You kissed her, then?'

'I did indeed.'

'I will need details.'

'A gentleman never tells.'

'The pertinent details which allow me to ascertain if the terms of the wager have been fulfilled. Where did you kiss her?'

'On the lips. They tasted like cherries and she smelled of pink summer roses.' Hal sighed for effect because bating Aaron was fun.

'Not details of the kiss, you buffoon. The location!'

'Oh, right. The terrace. I found her shivering behind a statue hiding from Ockendon. And for your information, I believe Ockendon saw us, although there was no mention of needing witnesses in our original terms. As a gentleman and a peer of the realm, you have my word the kiss occurred and I am frankly offended you would think I would lie.'

Aaron appeared disgruntled, but nodded. 'Fair enough. I cannot deny I am disappointed with Lady Elizabeth for allowing it to happen. However, I am reassured by the knowledge that stealing four more is likely to be more problematic. She will see through you in no time, if she already hasn't. Her father appeared particularly scandalised by your association and that will also work in my favour. In fact, if I am any judge of character, she will already be bitterly regretting her lapse in judgement and has already resolved never to go near you again. Mornings have a habit of reminding one of the folly of the evening's mistakes.'

Hal smiled enigmatically as he rose from the table. Aaron did not need to know about the alliance yet or the fact that Lizzie and Hal would be spending a great deal of time together for the sake of their own sanities, lest he try to sabotage it. Such things were always saved and discussed at great length during the required post mortem of a wager. It was part of their ritual, after all, and always done over a good bottle of cognac.

Chapter Six

Lady Bulphan's annual Christmas Concert was always a dull affair. For some inexplicable reason, despite having more than enough money to pay for a proper orchestra, Lady Bulphan thought it was fun to assemble a rag-tag group of musicians, and the world's worst choir, drawn from the ranks of society. At best, their musical stylings were dismal. Famously dismal and after so many years no longer funny. But because Lord Bulphan was one of Prinny's advisers, they were too well connected for anyone to dare to ignore their invitation so the affair, though no longer a crush, was always well attended. The sensible had ready-made excuses months in advance. Lord Bulphan also happened to be one of her father's oldest and dearest friends, so not only were they always in attendance, they had also come early in a show of support.

It was all right for Papa. He was ensconced at the 'secret' card table, known only to those in the inner circle and would remain so for hours and thus spared the pitiful and painful renditions of Christmas carols from the Bulphan Ensemble. They were currently murdering 'Hark! The Herald Angels Sing', or at least that was what Lizzie assumed it was meant to be. It was difficult to tell over the screeching of the ten violins. Ten violins who all appeared to be playing from completely different parts of the score.

To make matters worse, in her attempt to sit as far away from the performance as possible, she had chosen one of the most uncomfortable chairs she had ever had cause to sit upon. And her corset was too tight. In a rare flash of vanity, she had insisted her maid tighten it to allow her to wear this particular blue gown, and Lizzie now bitterly regretted it. Why had she been so determined to emphasise her eyes when she was not intending to attract anyone? At least not consciously. Subconsciously, she had been oddly nervous about this evening, or more specifically about her planned liaison with a certain handsome and charming rake this evening. It was his fault her corset pinched and her mood was foul.

'Good evening, Lady Elizabeth.' She smelled the Earl of Ockendon before she saw him and her misery was complete. 'We missed our dance the other evening.' In deference to the musicians he was speaking just above a whisper and far too close. She recalled Hal's claim the man's breath had nearly singed his eyebrows and sympathised with the comment.

'As I do not recall you either asking me to dance or heard myself accepting it, I shall have to take your word for it.' Lizzie turned her head rudely to focus her full attention on the caterwauling from the choir. Still, he sat in the next chair but one to her. What was it with men and sitting where they were not welcome of late?

Maybe she was not sending out clear enough signals as to her ambivalence to all things male.

'I did not give you leave to sit, sir.'

'You have a tart mouth, madam—but I confess I like that about you. Amongst other things.' He looked pointedly at her bosom and his thin lips curved into a slimy smile. Lord save her! Another reason to regret this uncharacteristically glamourous and exposing choice of gown.

'Your good favour is wasted on me when I find I like nothing about you.'

'Your father wants you wed and I am merely putting myself forward as a candidate for your consideration.'

In horror, Lizzie faced him and allowed her rampant disgust to show in her expression. 'I have no desire to be wed and even if I did, it certainly would not be to you, *my lord.*'

He chuckled and for some reason it sent a chill through her. 'I hope to convince you otherwise.'

'Something that I can assure you will never happen.'

'Never say never, Lady Elizabeth. I am a powerful man who can be very *persuasive.* Perhaps all you need is the right *incentive* to lure you out of spinsterhood?'

There was something about the way he answered, as if there was an underlying threat which made her breath shorten, even as she stared back at him blandly. 'I can assure you I am stubbornly and happily wedded to spinsterhood.'

'And why is that, Lady Elizabeth? Is there some dreadful, deep, *dark* secret which keeps you from committing yourself to Holy Matrimony? Something you keep *hidden*, perhaps? Something that has scandalously been hidden for *years*?'

An odd thing to say, unless… Unease made her spine stiffen. Did he know? The man moved in powerful circles, it was true. Had somebody let something slip inadvertently? Nausea threatened, but Lizzie forced herself to remain unaffected as he watched her carefully. The way his eyes narrowed slightly suggested he might suspect something, but there was enough of a hint of question to reassure her he was still unsure. She needed to speak to her father, but getting up now and rushing to do so would give the game away for certain. All Lizzie could do in the interim was sit impassively and brazen it out.

'You are astute, sir. There is a dreadful deep, *dark* scandalous secret I have been keeping *hidden*.' The knowing half-smile she offered him was borne out of the fierce desire to protect Georgie. Ignoring her acute physical disgust, she leaned closer and fought the urge to gag. 'You see, my lord, I discovered early on that I despise all men and want nothing to do with any of them. Your good self, included.'

'Really? Aside from Redbridge, I presume. You appeared quite partial to him yesterday, as I recall. And then there was that erstwhile fiancé of yours. What was his name?' He tapped his chin thoughtfully, his cold, dead eyes never leaving hers for a second. 'Ah, yes. The Marquess of Rainham. You were quite partial to *him* as well.' His eyes swept up and down her body and lingered on her bosom again. 'Quite…*partial*.'

'Yet I shall never feel partial to you, my lord. Of that I am quite certain.'

'Passion *and* a tart mouth. A splendid dowry…and of course, your *hidden* secrets. What a tantalising package you are, Lady Elizabeth' His thinly veiled threats and coded words hit too close to home for her comfort.

'Go tantalise another spinster, my lord. I am sure there must be someone desperate here who would lower themselves to consider you.'

He chuckled and stared at her bosom again while she fought the urge to dash away and bathe. 'You will make a fine wife indeed, Lady Elizabeth. A fine, young and *fertile* wife…'

'I have been looking everywhere for you.' Hal strode confidently into the fray and smiled at her. Lizzie had never been so pleased to see another person in her life.

'I am sorry I am late, Lizzie dearest. My sister had a hairdressing crisis, delaying our arrival.' Like her own personal bodyguard, he smoothly sat in the tiny chair which separated her from the odious Earl, forming a pleasant-smelling, solid buffer between them. 'Have I missed much, aside from your delightful company of course?'

The easy smile and casual manner did not hide the question in his intelligent eyes. Lizzie had no idea how much he had heard of her whispered conversation with Ockendon, but he had heard enough to be irritated on her behalf. His arms were folded stiffly across his chest, his thighs spread just wide enough to edge the old Earl away and let him know his presence was unwelcome.

Acting bored despite her unsettled nerves, Lizzie smiled at Hal in what she hoped resembled outright adoration. 'You missed an interesting rendition of "While Shepherds Watched Their Flocks by Night". Lady Bulphan pretended to be a shepherdess, complete with crook and stuffed sheep. She acted out the words.'

'Then I am sorry I missed it. Was it as tuneful as

"Hark! The Herald"?' Hal had angled his body ever so slightly towards her. His broad shoulders and back shielded her from seeing Ockendon while effectively shutting him out of the conversation like the ramparts around a castle. It gave her some comfort, though not enough. Her skin suddenly felt dirty and her stomach was churning.

'Sadly, there were no violins.' Lizzie hoped her voice was not as rattled as she felt. For Georgie's sake she had to appear calm.

'None? A travesty indeed, when all ten of them sound quite splendid from the refreshment table. But then again, there is a significant amount of rum in the punch, so I suspect it deadens the ears. Come, let us avail ourselves of a cup or two so that we might enjoy the subtle nuances of the music better.' Hal was on his feet in an instant as if he had known she needed to escape. 'If you will excuse us, Ockendon.' He waved his already crooked arm in open invitation and Lizzie was only too happy to take it. The old Earl's questions and crude insinuations had frightened her and she clung to Hal's arm with slightly shaking legs and a racing mind.

What had he meant by deep, dark secret? *Passionate, partial and fertile.* A coincidental choice of words? She doubted it. It all felt a little too convenient, had been said so pointedly, to have happened by chance.

Hal poured them both a cup of punch, then manoeuvred her towards an alcove, away from anyone else.

'What was all that about?'

'The Earl of Ockendon has put himself forward as a potential husband.' Yet if he knew about her son, he knew she was soiled goods. It had to be the stupid dowry. His talk of being *persuasive* and offering her the right *incentive* hinted at blackmail. Or maybe she was allowing her vivid imagination and over-protectiveness of her child to weave fanciful meanings into his words which were not there. Five years of deception tended to make one paranoid.

'I didn't care for his tone or for the way he looked at you.'

Neither did she. Lizzie still felt violated from the brief episode. The way his eyes had lingered on her bosom, the way they had darkened when he spoke of passion. However, until such a time as her secret was exposed—or wasn't—Lizzie would continue to keep it hidden. 'It hardly matters. It is no secret Lord Ockendon has long wanted a wife young enough to give him heirs.' The shiver was involuntary. Ockendon terrified her. 'I should imagine I am merely one of the many lucky ladies he has approached on his quest. Or perhaps he has exhausted all other possibilities and is now scraping the bottom of the barrel to be considering me?' Those mossy-green eyes regarded her thoughtfully, unsettling her further.

'Maybe he is simply drawn to the unattainable. You present a challenge.'

'I thought you said once a gentleman knows a lady's heart is engaged elsewhere he will cease his attentions towards her. He saw you kiss me. He certainly alluded to it, yet it only appears to have spurred him on.'

'Some gentlemen have thicker skins than others. Ockendon's is clearly like leather. You have my word he will yield once he realises who he is up against.' The serious, steely tone vanished as soon as it started, replaced with the roguish devil-may-care man he usually presented, and Lizzie realised the handsome, flippant new Earl of Redbridge was not quite as superficial as he wanted the world to believe. 'With any luck, with my fortune, title and dashing good looks, he will quickly realise he has no hope for your affections against such a magnificent opponent.'

'I sincerely hope you are right. The man puts my teeth on edge.'

His hand came to rest warmly over hers. 'Do not worry, fair maiden. I shall stick to you like glue all night and if Ockendon comes within ten feet of you I will challenge him to a duel. I promise.' Something about the way he said it made her believe him.

True to his word, Hal did exactly that until her father finally surfaced. Her papa laughed off her fears about Ockendon, refusing to discuss it beyond the trivial, but granted her the excuse of pleading a headache and summoning the carriage early. Because, as he rightly stated, who wouldn't have a headache with the Bulphan Ensemble playing so enthusiastically. Clearly the card game was as lacklustre as the music because he happily accompanied her home.

'Ockendon is harmless, Lizzie, a silly old fool who is barely tolerated in the Lords. You are reading far too much into his words because you are a good mother who wants to protect her son. But let me put your mind at rest. Only Lord Bulphan knows of little Georgie's existence and he would never break my confidence. The servants are too loyal to have betrayed us and we have always been scrupulously careful about any excursions. Besides, poor Ockendon has never had a talent for being particularly charming, I doubt he has the first clue about how to go about wooing a woman. Perhaps the fellow said what he said as an attempt to intrigue you. It's a bit of mild, and slightly pathetic, flirting, I'll wager, and nothing more. A bid to get your attention.' His lack of concern went some way to reassuring her she was imagining things and her father briskly changed the subject. He patted her hand and his demeanour changed from counselling to casual. A little too casual. 'I had the great good fortune to be seated next to Lord Hewitt at the card table and I was heartily impressed by him. He works at the Home Office and by all accounts is doing a sterling job. He is thirty. A perfectly respectable age for a young buck to take a wife and rather fortuitously he is seeking one as we speak. Now there's a catch...'

Lizzie rolled her eyes in exasperation and glared at her father across the carriage. 'I wish you would stop matchmaking, *Father.*' They both knew she only called him Father when she was angry and he bristled. 'I do not want a husband. Not now nor never. Why do you continue to refuse to accept that?'

'You might at least give Hewitt a chance. I am not suggesting you marry him, merely talk to him. You seemed to find it no great chore to chat away to that scoundrel Redbridge all night.'

'I have no interest in him either. He is not the sort to settle down into marriage, therefore conversation with him is blessedly harmless as we are both quite averse to it. That is the full extent of our attraction towards one another!'

'He does not regard you with aversion, young lady. Why, he can barely contain his pleasure at looking at you!'

Did he? Lizzie was quietly pleased with this piece of information until she caught herself. She did not want anyone looking at her covetously, whether they be Redbridge or Hewitt, or, Heaven help her, Ockendon. 'The Earl of Redbridge is a devout rake. I dare say he looks at every woman in possession of a pulse in much the same way. As I have already stated, I am quite immune to his charms.'

'That is as maybe, but can you not see while he is sniffing around you he is scaring off all of the other young men who *might* make you a suitable husband? I selected several for you to dance with the other night and because of him they were denied the opportunity to impress you.'

Thank goodness. Which was exactly the reason she needed Hal in the first place. As usual, her papa was determined to continue in the same vein he had for the last five years no matter what she said. He had promised her mother, after all, and he wasn't getting any younger. They just kept going around in ever-decreasing circles. 'It will take more than one silly dance to convince me that I need a husband, Father.'

He scowled and they both glared at each other stubbornly across the benches until he relented. 'Perhaps you are right, Lizzie. One dance will hardly change your mind.'

Chapter Seven

There was a lull in yuletide entertainments after the Bulphan Christmas Concert. After two days, Hal was practically climbing the walls with boredom. At least he hoped it was boredom, although rather alarmingly he was coming to suspect his restlessness had rather more to do with a curious desire to spend some more time with Lizzie than genuine boredom. Genuine boredom came from inactivity, and there might not be any balls or parties to go to, but he had been inordinately busy.

Estate business had occupied a great many hours, as had his speculations on the Stock Exchange. However, during each of those tasks the image of *her* had floated into his mind and made him forget what he was supposed to be doing. Hal had even dragged himself to a gaming hell in the hope it would distract him, but the card tables held no allure and the hostesses less. He'd left after less than an hour because he could not seem to stop thinking about her. Just as he was now, as he was idly strolling down High Holborn on a particular errand on this dull Thursday afternoon. It was most disconcerting.

It stood to reason he would think of her occasionally. Hal was only one kiss down and still had four more to claim in less than three weeks, but it was not the bet he kept mulling over. It was that kiss. The subtle scent of roses from her perfume. Or the way her eyes sparkled when he said something which amused her. The way she flipped between regarding him with wary hostility to forgetting she distrusted him and became entertaining with interesting, witty conversation. The peculiar sense of unease he had every time he recalled the tense exchange between her and Ockendon. The way she had been skittish afterwards. And scared. Ockendon had frightened her, yet he had no idea why such a confident and vibrant young woman would feel bothered by anything that silly old fool had to say.

Half the time Hal had absolutely no idea what was going on in her head, the other half he felt a strange kinship with her. Lady Elizabeth Wilding was a conundrum indeed and one he was intrigued to understand. To understand her, it stood to reason he would need to spend more time with her. A lot more time. To that end, he was counting the days until the Marquess of Danbury's house party at the weekend. There were exactly two of them.

Hal sighed as he came to Noah's Ark, Mr Hamley's magnificent toy emporium, annoyed with his current leaning towards unnecessary and incessant introspection. It wasn't healthy and this odd mood was not conducive to shopping for his nieces. Melancholy might lead him towards toys which were quiet and sensible and that would never do. He had come here intent on buying something noisy and entertaining for them for Christmas—something special from their naughty uncle.

Something which would drive his sister and brother-in-law mad and whip the children into a state of perpetual excitement and he needed his wits about him to do it. Last year's matching, miniature soldiers' drums, complete with jaunty bright uniforms and a genuine cavalry bugle, had caused mayhem and sent Connie into one of the best temper tantrums Hal had seen in years. By hook or by crook he was duty-bound to top that. The girls were depending on him.

The bell tinkled as he pushed open the door and he took a moment to soak up all the sights and sounds. In deference to the season, shiny boughs of holly edged all the shelves and hung from red ribbons in gay balls from the ceiling. All around him were toys of every kind. Amongst all this bounty, the shop was filled with customers, no doubt all here on the same mission as he was.

Seeking out the perfect gift for Christmas morning.

A few children giggled with excitement in one corner, while their harried parents tried to prise them away from the displays, and every shop assistant was engaged in either serving or wrapping. Clearly, Hal was going to be here for some time. He didn't mind. Shopping for toys was hardly shopping in the literal sense. Literal shopping was painful. Noah's Ark was pure pleasure.

His feet instinctively took him towards the instruments, seeing as they were undoubtedly loud, and his eyes were drawn to the brass trumpets. Connie had loathed the bugle most of all, but were trumpets too similar? He would hate to become predictable. No... Not instruments again. He was turning in a slow circle, seeking inspiration, when a familiar waft of roses brought him up short and, like a dog, he began to sniff the air to locate the source just on the off chance it might be Lizzie. He followed the smell around the other side of a tall cabinet and grinned.

'Hello, fair maiden and woman of my dreams.'

She practically jumped ten feet in the air and dropped the handful of tin soldiers she had been holding.

'Hal!' She appeared horrified to see him and he tried not to be miffed. 'What are you doing here?'

'Hunting down the most unsuitable toys to give to my troublesome nieces for Christmas. So…this is the mysterious thing you do every Tuesday and Thursday when Stevens says you are *genuinely* not at home. You shop.'

She was blinking rapidly and for a moment appeared flummoxed. 'Yes… Yes… I shop. Every Tuesday and Thursday. Nothing mysterious about it at all.'

'Your terrifying butler gave the impression you were doing something far more mysterious.'

Her response was to laugh, somewhat falsely, and blink some more. Puzzled, and keen not to continue talking about a topic which had clearly made her batten down those defensive hatches and pull up the drawbridge once again, Hal crouched down to pick up the soldiers and frowned at her selection. 'You really can't give him these.'

'*Him?* What do you mean *him*?' She had stopped blinking. Now her eyes were as wide as saucers. Obviously, she was unused to being caught by surprise and he had clearly terrified her in the process. And in a toy shop of all places.

'Your brother has a young son, does he not?'

'Yes! Yes, of course… These are for Frederick… My nephew.' She smiled, although it did not quite touch her eyes as he dropped the tiny soldiers back into her palm. She stared down at them mournfully and then appeared confused as his latter comments permeated her thoughts. 'Why can't I give him these? Little boys like to play with soldiers.'

'Of course they do—but those are soldiers from the Netherlands. I am sure they are jolly nice fellows, and they are our allies, but I am certain your nephew would much prefer proper British soldiers when he sends them into battle on the carpet.' Hal reached out and plucked a tiny cavalry officer astride a charging horse from the shelf. 'Look at this fearsome chap. Proper smart crimson regimentals, that splendid black hat and his sabre poised ready to strike down any of Napoleon's army silly enough to stand in his way.'

He handed her the lead figurine and she smiled properly this time. Those beguiling cornflower-blue eyes lit up and caused Hal's throat and groin to tighten simultaneously. Lord, she was lovely. Inside and out. 'I can see you are an expert on little boys.'

'I used to be one, so I suppose that does give me a bit of an advantage.'

'Seeing as you are so knowledgeable on toy soldiers, I wonder if I might trouble you to help me select a few more.'

'It would be my pleasure.' Hal was telling the truth. Spending time with her outside their arrangement was perfectly all right by him, especially as the topic of toy soldiers had apparently done the trick and melted her impenetrable guard. 'How many do you want?'

'How many do I need?'

As he was in danger of gazing wistfully at her—goodness knew where that had come from—and had the ridiculous urge to sniff her perfume and touch her hair, he turned away to study the lead battalions stood neatly on the shelves and pretended to give the matter some serious thought. 'Are you adding to an existing collection of soldiers or starting from scratch?'

'These will be his first soldiers.'

'Music to my ears, fair maiden, and so much simpler. We should start with the basics then.'

'Which are?'

Hal was already picking up men. 'Well, you will need a Wellington. That's for sure. Somebody needs to be in charge. And a Napoleon, else who would be defeated at the end of the game?' He pressed the two toys into her outstretched palm and wished neither of them were wearing winter gloves so that his fingers could graze her soft skin. 'We will need a selection of British officers of all ranks…cavalry…infantry. A few Highlanders. Ignore the fact those soldiers are wearing skirts. They are warriors at heart and put on such a good show for us at Waterloo.' Her cupped hands were overflowing, so he began to gather the others in a pile on the shelf. 'And we are going to need cannons. Lots of cannons.'

'Isn't it all a bit extreme when we only have one Frenchman to fight?'

'You make a good point. Much as it pains me, we are going to have to buy some Frenchies.' He grabbed a handful and scowled at them, and swore he felt himself grow a few inches in height when he heard her giggle.

'You have been so particular about the British troops, shouldn't we take the same care with the French? Won't they also need officers, cavalry and the like?'

'They are the enemy, madam, and need I remind you that we beat them. Thrashed them into surrender because they are a rag-tag, disorganised and dissolute group made up of illiterate, drunken peasants and smelly cheese makers. *Of course* we will not need French officers and cavalry. We have to keep things realistic and the French guillotined all their leaders years ago.'

He really was very charming, especially when he was being irreverent, and Lizzie was grateful he had saved her from purchasing the wrong soldiers. Her son would have noticed instantly that they were wearing the wrong uniforms and it would have given her father the opportunity to point out that this was exactly why her son needed a father. Much as it pained her to admit it, it would never have occurred to her to buy officers or cavalry or an enemy army for them to fight against.

'Thank you.' She felt quite emotional, knowing she would be giving Georgie a Christmas gift he would love. Sometimes being a mother to a little boy was a challenge and getting more so now he was growing. The whole journey to and from their weekly jaunt to Richmond Park, he had talked about nothing else but how much he wanted a proper army to play with. This was what he had meant and she had potentially ruined it because she did not know the difference between the enemies or the allies. Thank goodness she had run into Hal—although he had given her quite a fright.

One minute she had been thinking about him, hardly a surprise when she had been incessantly thinking about him since his impertinent kiss on the Benfleet terrace, and then he had been stood next to her as if she had conjured him with her mind. Looking all windswept and handsome. Then he had saved her again. He had an irritating habit of being in exactly the right place at exactly the right time—something which probably had a great deal more to do with luck than the niggling suspicion that Henry Stuart, the charming and handsome Earl of Redbridge, might be someone she could depend on. 'I think it is only fair I return the favour.'

She was being nice. Towards a man who she was not related to. Whatever next? Yet as out of character as the offer had been, Lizzie did want to do something nice for Hal. He had saved her from one balding dullard, twice from Lord Ockendon and he had just saved Christmas morning. 'You say you are here to find presents for your nieces, a task I am eminently suitable for—seeing as I used to be a little girl.'

'I don't want anything sensible. Or quiet.'

'Why ever not?'

'As the naughty uncle it is my duty to purchase toys which will drive their parents to distraction. Last year it was drums and a bugle. I had to stuff handkerchiefs in each ear to drown out the cacophony and went to bed with a headache.' Hal smiled boyishly, clearly very pleased with himself. 'It was marvellous.'

'Oh, I see. You have not come here to buy gifts for your nieces at all, merely gifts for yourself.'

He appeared affronted at the suggestion. 'My nieces always love my gifts. They are the highlight of every Christmas morning.'

'And are they played with after Christmas?' Because Lizzie had the distinct impression they miraculously disappeared, consigned to the attic with all the other inappropriate toys. His dark brows drew together and after a long pause he huffed.

'Now you come to mention it, no. They aren't.'

'Then wouldn't it be better to choose something different? Something they'll love and their parents can live with? Something truly special which can be played with all year? From their favourite naughty uncle.'

'Hardly a naughty uncle if I am giving sensible gifts. I've been training Prudence and Grace to be hellions since the day they were born. Girls saddled with such pious names should always be a handful.'

Lizzie's mouth curved into a smile at his belligerent expression. 'Although I already know I shall regret asking this question, but how does one train one's nieces to be hellions?'

Mischief twinkled in his green eyes and he leaned towards her, covertly looking both left and right, as if the information he was about to give her was of the utmost secrecy. 'It has been a three-pronged attack. Firstly, I have always actively encouraged naughtiness. Hiding just before they are due to go out, sliding down banisters, inappropriate horseplay. Lots of high-pitched noise—especially when there are guests in the house. I find a bit of quiet praise after the event or a well-placed dare works wonders.' The image of him playing with children came easily. Except, for some reason, she could not picture him playing with any other child except little Georgie. 'Secondly, to be proper hellions, I have made sure their arsenal of weapons is always well stocked. I have invested hours schooling them in the subtle art of practical jokes and taught them to be resourceful with the materials at hand. Jam, cobwebs, flour, et cetera. Creepy crawlies are always good. Connie loathes things with lots of legs and, although he would rather die than admit it, my brother-in-law Aaron does, too. Therefore, I have meticulously shown the girls where to hunt for the best specimens, how to trap them and keep them safe until exactly the right moment. Timing is everything, after all.' His voice dropped to a whisper and Lizzie found her head intimately close as she strained to listen. He smelled of fresh air. Spicy cologne and something heady, wholly him and completely unidentifiable. It was probably the aroma of sin. 'Last spring, totally unprompted, Prudence filled her mother's favourite riding boots up with frog spawn. I cannot tell you how proud it made me.'

The bubble of laughter surprised her and she covered her mouth with her hand. 'Your poor sister. I feel so sorry for her.'

'Don't you dare. It is nothing more than her just deserts. She tortured me as a child. Mercilessly. Being older, she was always so much bigger and used it to her advantage. I have lost count of how many times she overpowered me, rolled me up in the nursery rug and then sat on me. I'll have you know I spent hours incarcerated in that blasted rug. I have suffered violence at that woman's hand and as a gentleman, I could never physically retaliate and she knew it. On one occasion, she then went on to use my father's razor to shave off one of my eyebrows. It took months to grow back and made me the laughing stock of the village. Is it any wonder I now shudder at the sight of a tightly-weaved Persian?'

'Maybe I feel a little less sympathy for your sister now, but I still think you should buy something for your nieces which they will love and continue their hellion training on the sly.'

'I cannot say I am happy about it, but I shall bow down to your better judgement. You were once a little girl after all, as you say, although I doubt you were a hellion.'

'Why ever not?'

He pretended to study her, then frowned. 'You are far too—nice.'

'Good gracious! Your life must be filled with dreadful people if you think I am one of the nicer ones.'

'Actually, my mother is thoroughly nice. My sister Constance is predominantly nice but has moments when she is terrifying, and her husband Aaron is the best friend a fellow could wish for. I am surrounded by decent sorts so I know one when I spot one. You may try to hide your niceness from the world at large, but I know the truth. In fact, I am of the opinion you are really far too nice be associated with a man who is wilfully training his nieces to be hellions.' He gently took her hand and curled it about his arm and began to lead her to another part of the shop. Lizzie tried not to feel content at the closeness or the compliments.

'On the subject of your hellion-training—what, pray tell, is the third prong in your three-pronged strategy?'

'Oh, that is the easiest part.' The wolfish grin made her pulse instantly flutter. 'I make sure I always lead by example. I am, Lady Elizabeth, a *thoroughly* naughty boy.' And Lord help her, that was exciting.

With her guidance, Hal reluctantly bought two beautiful wax dolls of the highest quality. Then he happily allowed Lizzie to select different outfits for the dolls so the girls could play dressing-up games with them. As he walked her back to her carriage, insisting on carrying all the many packages himself, it occurred to her that she had had a thoroughly enjoyable time in his company and was disappointed to be going home.

'You will be at Danbury's tiresome house party this weekend, won't you? My mother is insisting on going.'

Lizzie was trying to avoid it. 'I hope not.'

His handsome face fell. 'Oh, don't say that! I was relying on you to be there and now I am doomed for certain. Please come, Lizzie. The hordes will be there en masse and there are few places to hide at a house in the country, apart from the countryside, of course, and it is frightfully cold. I shall be for ever in your debt.'

'I don't know…' She dithered and he grabbed her hand and stared mournfully into her eyes.

'Have you any idea how dangerous a house party is for a confirmed but deliciously eligible bachelor? I would sooner run the gauntlet than attend one undefended. There will be parlour games. What if they play Hot Cockles? Everyone knows that is merely a flimsy excuse to kiss someone you've got your eye on. Without you as my partner, I will be a target. The hordes will stampede towards me and I might well end up crushed. And then there will be wassailing and there is no telling what danger I will be in once those young ladies are emboldened by alcohol. I shall have to keep my bedchamber door barricaded as I wouldn't put it past a few of the more ambitious ones to visit me in the dead of night and then claim I ruined her. This house party is the single most perilous event of the whole Christmas season because there is literally *nowhere* safe for me to hide. I will be a captive and will hold you entirely accountable if I end up compromised into marriage.'

He gripped her fingers and gave her a pitiful gaze. 'Please come. We have as good as sworn an oath of allegiance to one another. You save me and I save you.' He was sounding increasingly desperate and looking totally miserable. Adorably miserable. 'How about this? Regardless of our arrangement, if you come to the Danburys' I shall owe you a huge favour which you can demand from me any time of the course of my entire life. In the small hours if need be and in the Highlands of Scotland. Or even that desolate place they send convicts in the Antipodes. No distance is too far. I will ride through wind and rain, climb mountains… I am now literally begging you. Throw me a bone… I will be at your beck and call. Just do me this one favour, Lizzie darling.'

Her pulse fluttered at the word 'darling'. It shouldn't have, but it did. 'I'm not sure…'

'But I am at your mercy. Take pity on a poor, irresistible, terrified earl!'

It was only one weekend, she supposed, wavering, and they did have an arrangement. He had rescued her from Ockendon and smoothly extricated her from his vile company and he had just saved her from inadvertently buying the wrong soldiers for her son. 'All right.' It was just two nights away from Georgie and would please her father. 'I shall be there. But under duress.'

His green eyes brightened as his face split in the biggest grin, making him look quite boyish and even more adorable, if such a thing was possible. 'If we weren't in public, I would kiss you!' And rather bizarrely, if they weren't in public, she was sorely tempted to let him. She was still all a quiver at his throwaway use of the word 'darling'. 'Oh, to Hell with it, nobody is looking…' Before Lizzie could stop him, he had opened the carriage door to shield them from view, lifted her off the floor, spun her in a quick circle, then briefly touched his lips to hers. 'Thank you, Lizzie darling! You are a life-saver.'

It had not been anything more than boisterous ex-

uberance brought about by his gratefulness, but regardless, being held in those strong arms for just a few
seconds was quite something. Even the chaste, friendly
kiss fizzed through her system till she felt it all the way
down to the tips of her toes. Her nerve endings were still
tingling when he stepped away. Her lips still tingled as
he helped her up into the carriage. Her thoughts were
jumbled; she didn't know whether to sigh or moan or
laugh, his kiss had scrambled her wits so effectively. It
was rather like being struck by lightning. Quick, unexpected and potentially deadly. Something which made
her feel quite unsettled all the way home.

Chapter Eight

'A message just arrived for you.' Hal's sister Connie
swept into his study, grinning. 'One of the Earl of Upminster's footmen hand-delivered it. Said it was *most*
urgent.' She plopped her bottom resolutely on his desk
before she handed it to him. A clear sign she intended
to stay while he read it. Hal tried to ignore the tickle of
excitement as he stared at the feminine, sloping writing on the front, or the desire to slowly trace the pad
of his index finger over the pen marks. Since he had
waved off her carriage this afternoon he had done nothing but mope. Whilst it had hardly been much of a kiss,
ostensibly done out of opportunism to smugly press the
second mistletoe berry into Aaron's hand, Hal wasn't
fooling himself. At the time, he had not given the wager
a thought, he had simply needed the contact. His body
still hummed from the effect it had had on him and he
was not entirely sure what to make of that fact. Had
she felt it, too? Against all his better judgement he did
hope she might say as much in her unexpected letter.

Unless it was a chastisement?

Or worse.

'Thank you. I shall read it later.' He placed it on the corner of his desk and stared back down at his ledger, hoping Lizzie was not reneging on her promise to attend the Danbury house party after all. If she was, he might have to resort to throwing himself down the stairs in order to sustain a believable injury to get out of going. Without Lizzie it would be dreadful and he was strangely excited about spending time with her.

'It might be important.'

'I sincerely doubt it.'

'It might be from *her*.'

Hal shrugged and began to add up a column of figures in a last-ditch attempt to convince his sister he was ambivalent. It was the wrong move. Connie's hand shot out and grabbed the letter, then she scampered to the other side of the study with it, giggling, just as she had when they were children, banished to the nursery because their father was at home and he found their very presence an irritant. The seal was cracked open before he could get to her and she swiftly sidestepped his attempt to lunge for it.

'That is my *private* correspondence, Connie! Give it back.'

'"Dear Hal…"' She gave him a knowing look as they circled each other like gladiators across the Persian rug. 'That's nice. You are on first-name terms.'

'I'm warning you, Connie!'

'"I have an emergency…" How exciting! And you are the first person she turns to.'

'If you don't give it back…' He lunged again and managed to grab her arm, but being a tall woman and a terminally vexing one, she simply used her other hand to hold his precious letter and read it at arm's length.

'"And you did say that if I had an emergency, no matter where or when it was, you would come and rescue me..." Be still my beating heart. I never thought I would see the day when my irritating little brother would grow up to become a knight in shining armour.'

Desperate times called for desperate measures. Hal hooked his leg around hers and grabbed her firmly around the waist, but despite his best efforts to stop her wriggling, the damn letter remained resolutely out of his reach. With no other option, he seriously considered toppling her to the floor and rolling her up in the rug. 'Give me my letter now, Connie—or so help me!' He tightened his arm around her ribs and squeezed in warning. Hardly an act of war, but what else could he do under the circumstances? She was a woman and, even though she was a termagant and often his torturer, he was morally incapable of physically harming her. Being a human corset was the best he could do.

'"I would be eternally grateful..."' *Squeeze.* '"If you could..."' *Squeeze.* '"Come to dinner tonight. I know..."' *Really big squeeze.* '"It is short notice and I apologise. We always eat promptly at eight. Lizzie."'

When only one hand and her vibrant red head poked unapologetically out of the cage he had formed around her, a breathless Hal finally snatched the note out of her frantically waving and ridiculously long arm and scanned it himself, but that was all there was. Five sentences leaving him none the wiser, but elated. Not only had she *not* retracted her promise to be at the dreadful house party as he had initially feared, she wasn't telling him off for the stolen public kiss and wanted to see him. Hal could not bring himself to care about the particular circumstances although he suspected it might be dullard related.

'Shall I inform Cook that we will be one less this evening?' There were times he wished he wasn't a gentleman so that he could strangle his smug sister. Even physically restrained, she always had something to say. Hal did not bother answering as he let her go and paced to the opposite side of the room to read the letter again to see if he could glean any more from it.

'I believe this is a first for you.'

'I have dined with women before. On numerous occasions.'

'Yes, but I assume on those occasions you dined *alone* with them.' Connie settled her bottom into his vacated chair and began to twiddle with his letter opener. '*This* will be vastly different.'

He should ignore her; he knew that from old. 'How so?'

'Well, for a start, you will be in company.'

Hal had assumed as much. Lizzie was hardly the sort of woman who would ignore propriety and there would be at least one dullard in attendance as well. 'I eat dinner in your company every day and to the best of my knowledge I haven't managed to disgrace myself once. Well, not in the last few years at least.'

'That hardly counts seeing as we are family…' His sister smiled the patronising smile she used when she thought she knew better than him. Unfortunately, damn her, she usually did. 'However, to the best of *my* knowledge, Brother dearest, this is the first dinner you have ever taken with a woman and *her* father. You are going to be on display. Scrutinised. Judged. The Earl of Upminster is a well-respected member of the Government.

Only the best sort will pass muster for his daughter. From what I witnessed at the concert he heartily disapproves of you already. This dinner could be a potentially painful and dangerous affair, fraught with pitfalls. It could ruin your chances like that.' She clicked her fingers for emphasis and stared back at him seriously.

As their alliance was a mutually beneficial sham, brought about by a secret wager with Connie's husband, who was blissfully ignorant of the separate bargain he had made with Lizzie to win his wager with Aaron, it seemed prudent to respond with casual uninterest.

It hardly mattered to Hal what Upminster thought of him. It was not as if he was *really* applying for the position of the man's son-in-law. Too many wild oats, et cetera, but if he appraised his sister of his alliance with Lizzie to stop her vexing him she was bound to tell Aaron, because she told Aaron everything. And if she got wind of the Mistletoe Wager then both he and Aaron were as good as dead because they had both promised Connie faithfully they would never enter into another wager again after the unfortunate incident at the Serpentine.

Good grief! This was all becoming unnecessarily confusing. His sister watched his face carefully as he considered it all, clearly searching his reaction to try to gauge the strength of his feelings for Lizzie.

'If you make a hash of this dinner, her father could forbid Lady Elizabeth from seeing you.'

Which rather put a different spin on things and gave him more to worry about than his complicated deceptions. Lizzie would be at the mercy of Ockendon, he would be chased by the hordes and Aaron would gloat while Hal had to shovel dung.

A quick glance at the mantel clock alerted him to the fact that it was less than an hour until eight. Instantly, he was off the floor and dashing to his bedchamber, determined to make a good impression.

Lizzie wanted to pace the floor of the drawing room or to stare expectantly through the lace curtains to see if Hal was going to come and rescue her. However, as her father's hostess, she was stuck making small talk with the insipid bunch of gentlemen he had foisted on her for the evening. She should have anticipated this scenario the moment her wily papa had conceded that *one dance* would hardly convince her to take a husband. Two paltry hours' notice was all he had given her for tonight's *impromptu*, informal little dinner, as he had sprung it on her the moment she arrived home from the toy shop.

Although it did not appear to be particularly impromptu as far as he was concerned. No, indeed! A great deal of planning had gone into this little shenanigan. Georgie had been fed and was safely ensconced in the nursery and any sign there was a child in the house had been eradicated by the servants before she had learned they were expecting company. Not including her father there were three single gentlemen in total and not one single lady apart from herself. 'This is merely a meeting of colleagues,' he had said by way of explanation. 'An informal gathering arranged in haste so we hardly need to stand on ceremony. None of the gentlemen will expect it.'

They came in all shapes and sizes, she had to give her father credit for that at least, because he had considered variety even if the gentlemen in question were all drawn from the junior ranks of the government. But each and every one was only here for either her dowry or to impress her powerful father. In reality, all three were probably here for both. Lizzie was nicely trapped and doomed to get to know these crushing bores far better than she ever wanted.

Lord Hewitt was everything she had suspected he would be. Sensible, bland and filled with an overwhelming sense of his own importance. Lord Cheshire, on the other hand, looked as though he wouldn't say boo to a goose and blushed pink to the tips of his ears every time he so much as glanced in her direction and the least said about the stick-thin Lord Roseby the better. Like a lapdog he was hanging on her every word, a little too close, a little too cloying. His pale skin had a blue hue about it which made him appear ill.

Blue, pink and bland. A fine bunch of dullards, who would be here for hours trying to *impress* her properly seeing as they had been denied the opportunity on the dance floor. If that wasn't bad enough, her papa was currently listing her virtues like a litany. Intelligent, kind-hearted, accomplished, a sensible household manager, a good hostess… Of course, he was conveniently omitting her other attributes. Ruined. Compromised. Soiled. Comes with additional baggage you will need to find room for. No doubt it would take a significant amount of palm-greasing to erase those stains.

At five minutes to eight, when their butler came in to the drawing room looking harried, Lizzie almost visibly slumped with relief. 'The Earl of Redbridge is on the doorstep, my lord, and he is most insistent he has been invited here to dine.'

'Why, that is preposter—'

'He has, Stevens. Do show him in.' Lizzie stood and smiled sweetly at her father's outraged expression. He was not the only one who could casually lie and scheme on the quiet. 'Seeing as this *impromptu* dinner is a meeting of your colleagues, I didn't think you would mind if I invited someone to converse with when the conversation inevitably turns to state matters. Besides, with the Earl of Redbridge we are now six and six diners perfectly balances the table. You know I hate odd numbers.'

'If you wanted to balance the table, you should have invited some ladies!'

'So should you. Had I been given more notice of this evening's plans I would have. At such a late stage I could only extend an invitation to one of our close neighbours. The Earl resides around the corner in Berkeley Square.'

'There must be a great many young ladies living closer, Lizzie!'

'Oh, there are, but I do so enjoy Hal's company, Papa.' Clearly she had to abandon her original plan to appear disinterested in the Earl of Redbridge's attentions in front of him. However, as her father had taken an immediate dislike to Hal he would likely be relieved when their sham courtship came to its natural conclusion in the new year, so she was hardly giving him false hope and banished the pang of guilt.

'If the gossips are to be believed, a great many women enjoy Redbridge's company, Lady Elizabeth. I am surprised you would tolerate him.'

How marvellous. Lord Hewitt was patronising as well as condescending and bland. Lizzie shot a warning glance at her papa and set her jaw stubbornly. 'If my *chosen* guest is not welcome with the present company,

Father, then I shall take tea with him in the morning room and then eat my dinner alone in my room. On a tray.' The temptation to poke out her tongue and flounce off was enormous.

'Of course he is *welcome*, Daughter. If you have invited him as a guest, then I am sure he has a great many redeeming qualities which make him deserving of a place at *my* table and I should be glad to learn of them over the course of the evening. As I am sure *you* will make every effort to learn about the redeeming qualities of our *other* guests as well.' Lizzie loathed it when her father used his politician's voice. His mouth said one thing, but his tone and expression said quite another.

There was not time to make a pithy retort to that effect as Hal strode into the dining room confidently, clutching the most beautiful bouquet of hothouse flowers, and his eyes locked warmly on hers. A wonderful extravagance which must have cost a small fortune in December and one which nicely told the dullards he had no need of her dowry. Nestled amongst the blooms were pink roses and one single stem of prickly holly. The holly made her feel all funny because she knew he had put it there deliberately. For her.

'Lizzie, you look stunning.' He gave her the flowers and then very slowly kissed her hand, gazing up at her with questioning eyes. She supposed it was right that she should appraise him of the reason for her summons although the feel of his lips on her skin was making casual, coded conversation difficult.

'I am so glad you were able to come, on such short notice, but as you can see, my father decided at the last minute to invite some of his government colleagues and you know how *dull* I sometimes find matters of state.'

'*Ah*…yes.' People could say what they liked about Hal's dubious scandalous reputation, but there was no denying the man was as sharp as a tack. He gave her a saucy wink. 'State matters. Very dull indeed. I am glad I could come to your aid.' He squeezed her hand reassuringly before dropping it. Only then did he turn to the other men in the room. 'Thank you for having me Lord Upminster. It is a great honour to *finally* be here.' She watched Hal's eyes wander towards Stevens before he smiled at the scowling butler triumphantly.

Her father smiled stiffly and Lizzie tried not to be openly amused at how Hal cheerfully greeted his guests and how they responded with barely disguised disdain. Lord Hewitt attempted to look down his nose at him—however, being more than several inches shorter, he had to do so looking upwards which rather spoiled the effect and drew attention to the frightening size of his flared nostrils and the profusion of hair growing within them. Pink Cheshire was clearly intimidated up against such a powerful specimen of obvious, confident manhood and did his best to blend into the wallpaper whilst Roseby began to resemble a ghost stood next to Hal, a pale, reedy apparition who would blow away like mist in a strong gust of wind.

If only they all would.

Thankfully, they were called in to dinner at the stroke of eight. In hopeful anticipation of being saved, Lizzie had arranged a sixth place setting without her father's knowledge and had also had the good sense to swap around the name tags he had placed strategically on the table hours before. Now, the pompous Lord Hewitt was seated next to her dear papa at the opposite end of the table, Hal was sat to her right and pink

Cheshire was to her left. Never having spoken to any of the other men before, it was undoubtedly a stroke of luck she had accidentally placed herself next to the shy one as he was hardly going to dominate her time. That said, the uncomfortable silence around the table as they all waited for the soup was quite painful and as hostess she supposed the task of finding an initial topic of conversation fell to her.

'Are any of you attending Lord Danbury's house party this weekend?'

Both Hewitt and Cheshire nodded, but only Bland Hewitt spoke. 'Indeed I shall—but for the hunting, you understand. Nothing more. I find the typical yuletide entertainments puerile. I am of the opinion silly parlour games should be played by children, not grown men.'

'Oh, I don't know, there is something to be said for the odd parlour game. Occasionally, they can be fun.' Her papa was a great lover of charades and quite ridiculously competitive at all games involving cards. Speculation was a particular favourite because he always insisted it was played for money and tended to be a very sore loser if he lost his. This comment earned him a frown from Lord Hewitt.

'Cards are tolerable, I suppose, as long as money is not wagered, but playing the fool for the entertainment of others is not something I could ever demean myself to do. I cannot abide seeing grown men prance around the drawing room miming words, or groping around blindfolded or humiliating themselves by getting involved in silly, improper games involving women.' His gaze flicked disapprovingly towards Hal. 'I prefer to behave like an adult.'

The pompous tone made her father bristle, but as he

had high hopes of his only daughter settling down with someone sensible and staid he covered it quickly. 'Yes, I do understand your reticence.' Clearly he wanted to give Hewitt another chance, but Lizzie had taken an instant dislike to him and decided to kill her father's forlorn hopes swiftly.

'You are always the first to suggest charades, Father. You always appear to heartily enjoy it.' This earned Lizzie a pointed look from the end of the table, but she was unrepentant. Papa needed to know that she and Lord Hewitt were incompatible. 'And *so* do I.'

'Me, too,' said Hal loyally, immediately getting the gist of what was really going on, 'The sillier the better. I shall enthusiastically join in with every one of Lady Danbury's parlour games if you are playing them, too, darling Lizzie.' Whilst this was said flirtatiously for the benefit of the dullards, he used his knee to nudge hers under the table and Lizzie couldn't stop herself from beaming at him. Of course, to everyone else it appeared that she was encouraging his advances and she did not care. Having Hal here helping to thwart her father's overt matchmaking plans was certainly turning what could have been an awful evening into a passably pleasurable one.

'I might even be tempted to partner you in one or two of them if the mood strikes me.' Lizzie's eyelashes fluttered and she realised, with a start, she was genuinely flirting. Where had that come from? Panic and surprise made them bat quicker and her pulse sped up.

'You surprise me, Lady Elizabeth.' Lord Hewitt tilted his head back a little so he could look down his nose first at Hal, then her. 'I would have thought a lady who was sensible enough to shun frivolous dances or balls would baulk at the prospect of pursuits so banal.'

'Lizzie has a great sense of fun.' Hal gave her a glance filled with complete mischief, as if they were sharing some great secret, which of course they were. 'And she does thoroughly enjoy being twirled about the floor when she is presented with a spirited, handsome and charming partner. Why, at the end of *our* waltz she could barely contain her delight at having danced it.' Thanks to Hal's magnificent public shredding of her dance card, it was highly likely Hewitt and the rest of this motley crew had been prevented from twirling her as well.

Lord Hewitt's eyes narrowed at the subtle dig, then his expression became bland again. 'Do you hunt, Redbridge?'

'I try to avoid it.'

'I suppose it is too gentlemanly a *sport* for you.' Hewitt offered a patronising smile to the table at large and Blue Roseby made no attempt to suppress his chuckle. 'Or perhaps the choice of prey is not to your taste?'

'Careful, Hewitt. There is a lady present. I doubt Redbridge would care to discuss his favourite *sporting* pursuits in front of Lady Elizabeth and her father.' Even Lord Cheshire nodded conspiratorially before he saw her expression and blushed like a beetroot.

How charming! They were all closing ranks to try to make Hal uncomfortable, intent on dredging up his past indiscretions to gain her father's, and probably her, censure in the process. Hot on the heels of her unexpected foray in to flirting with him came the overwhelming

urge to defend him although, to his credit, Hal did not
appear bothered by the barbs or need her help.

'I like a good gallop across the fields as much as
the next man, old boy, but I have never understood the
peculiar excitement which comes from stalking a de-
fenceless animal.'

'Hunting does take a particular strength of character,
I will grant you.' Lord Hewitt took a slurp of his soup
and failed to notice the drop which missed his mouth
and fell on to his intricately tied cravat. 'It is not for all
men. Do not feel bad about not having the stomach for
the *noble* sport.'

'Strength of character?' I see nothing either strong or
manly, or indeed noble, in a pack of over-excited gentlemen, complete with a half-starved pack of snarling
hounds, chasing after a terrified fox or deer and then
revelling in seeing it being ripped apart at the end.'
Hal's amused green eyes were locked on Hewitt's and
did not waver.

'I suppose that is where the pair of us differ, Redbridge. I am clearly a *man's* man.'

Three male heads bobbed in agreement, although
Lizzie was delighted to see her papa's nod was very
half-hearted to say the least, more a twitch than an
actual inclination of the head. He had never had the
stomach for hunting either and was obviously having
second thoughts about his most recent preferred candidate to be his son-in-law. Hal had shown Hewitt up for
the stuffed shirt he was with very little effort. Hal, of
course, managed to appear nonplussed and remained
his usual, good-natured, charming self even though he
was being grievously insulted.

'A *man's* man. Yes, Hewitt, I believe you must be. In

which case, I suppose that makes me a *ladies'* man.' He looked positively delighted at the prospect.

'Or perhaps, in view of your lack of stomach and immature behaviour, you are still a child, Redbridge, in which case, I think we would all prefer it if you were seen but not heard. Even better, neither *seen* nor *heard*.' He chortled at his own tart wit, blissfully unaware that in one sentence, Lord Hewitt had effectively moved her from mild dislike to hating him with a vengeance—and her father knew it. A new tension settled over the table. One only Lizzie and her father were part of.

'Come now, Hewitt,' her father said, 'I am sure you cannot mean that and I am certain you will make a splendid father. Seen but not heard, indeed! That is funny. You sound like a stodgy, old-fashioned and staunch disciplinarian.'

Of all things, this apparently was the one which most offended. Hewitt's self-important expression became outraged. 'I believe discipline is the single most important role of a father, Lord Upminster, and one I intend to take very seriously when I have my own sons. Unruly children grow into unruly adults.' Hewitt glared at Hal as if to prove his point, then continued undaunted spewing more nonsense out of his pompous mouth. 'To avoid bad habits forming, it is imperative to raise one's offspring correctly. Obedience is one of the first lessons they must learn.'

Insufferable man! 'Oh, really, my lord, pray enlighten us to more of your thoughts on child rearing. How, for example, does one teach one's offspring obedience?' Lizzie voice came out silkily and she watched her father wince out of the corner of her eye.

'I am glad you have asked me that question, Lady

Elizabeth, for it shows you are willing to learn and that is a most excellent quality in a young lady. Strict punishments are the key. Spare the rod and spoil the child.' He smiled and nodded as if he were the unquestionable expert on the subject. 'Bed with no supper for mild indiscretions, withdrawal of all privileges…liberal use of the strap.'

'And you would use the strap on young children, too?' Pigs would have to sprout wings and soar through the clouds before she would allow this buffoon anywhere near her son.

'The younger you start, the better.'

Lizzie's father stared at her, looking completely miserable. Pleading with her silently not to lose her temper, but it was too late. Whether it caused a scene or not Lord Hewitt was going to receive a piece of—

'My father used the strap on me daily, for as long as I can remember, and look how I turned out.' Hal's timely interruption made Lizzie pause. 'I have lost count of how many times I went to bed without supper, how much of my allowance was held back or how many things he confiscated. Dear Pater was cold, dictatorial and devoid of all humour.' Hal waved his wineglass conversationally. 'Yet all that rigid discipline failed to achieve what he wanted. We did not respect him. In fact, my sister and I hated him. He had pushed us both so very far away we did not care about his good opinion and made it our life's work to grow up completely opposite to his wishes. Any father who believes sparing the rod will ultimately spoil the child is doomed for ever to be loathed by their offspring and probably blissfully ignored in the long run. However, it does beggar the question: if you wish to be estranged from them for ever, why have the poor children in the first place?' Hal smiled sweetly to the table at large. 'Would you mind passing the salt, please, Cheshire?' He let the silence stretch as he sprinkled some and stirred it into his consommé, tasted it, then smiled as if he had not just said something earth-shatteringly brilliant. 'Lord Upminster, Lizzie was telling me there are reports of Napoleon's health failing.'

'Yes, indeed...' And just like that calm descended over the dinner table again. Hewitt was po-faced and silent for much of the rest of the meal, his flaring nose plainly out of joint. Without him, pale Lord Roseby kept his comments in check and poor Lord Cheshire continued to blush at everything and did not add anything of any value to the conversation over all five of the 'impromptu' courses. A little after eleven, only Hal remained, looking quietly pleased with himself and rightly so. He had been both a subtly attentive suitor, leaving the three dullards in no doubt they did not stand a chance with her, and an intelligent and lively conversationalist who had, frankly, saved the sorry debacle of a meal.

Like her rat of a fiancé, Rainham, he had an immense talent for charming people, yet Hal was refreshingly different from Rainham on so many levels. Despite his outer layer of superficiality, he proved he had an extensive knowledge of current affairs, had a keen interest and perceptive head for business and clearly not only attended many debates in the Lords, but also paid attention. On many topics, he was more informed than the other young men around the table, who should have known better because they were part of the Government. There was so much more to him than ready charm and Lizzie found herself quietly proud of him.

Even her father appeared to have revised his poor opinion a little, although he had practically cemented his bottom on the sofa next to his only daughter and made it quite obvious that was where it would stay until Hal left as well. He had also spent the last fifteen minutes unsubtly flipping open his pocket watch and reminding them of the time.

Something her unlikely comrade found very amusing as he took an inordinate amount of time finishing his second glass of port. With a contented sigh, he placed his glass on a side table and stretched out his long limbs languidly. 'I suppose I should wend my home, too.'

'I shall show you to the door.' As soon as Lizzie stood, her father did, too, and she glared at him. 'I think I can manage seeing Hal out, Papa. I shall only be a minute.'

'I hardly think it is proper to leave you alone with—'

She held up her hand and cut him off mid-flow. 'As I recall, I saw out all three of our other guests alone without any issue. In fact, you insisted upon it.'

'Yes—but your father knew nothing untoward would happen with those fellows.' Hal unfurled his long body out of the chair and elegantly stretched out his spine, his casual and unoffended manner effectively diffusing the situation. 'I am an altogether different kettle of fish and I completely understand your father's concerns. If I had a daughter, and she was being courted by someone like me, I would be exactly the same.' He bent and placed a soft kiss on the back of her hand which made her breath hitch. 'I shall say my goodbyes to you both here. Goodnight, Lord Upminster. I look forward to seeing you again at the Danburys'.'

Her father acknowledged the statement graciously, but soon resumed his over-protective bluster. 'I would appreciate a proper conversation with you this weekend, Redbridge, concerning your *exact* intentions towards my daughter, because I shall tell you straight—I disapprove of your association. If I may speak *plainly* to you, sir, I am afraid your reputation precedes you and my Lizzie needs a sensible man in her future.'

Hal smiled wistfully at this and shrugged in his typical good-natured way. 'Perhaps. However, from what I know of your daughter, sir, with her clever mind and feisty temperament, I will tell *you* straight that Roseby, Cheshire and that pompous fool Hewitt are not in her league and, if I may speak to you *plainly*, too, sir, you do her a disservice by foisting them upon her.'

What a thoroughly splendid thing to say. The urge to kiss him was instantaneous. Only a small fraction of that urge was born out of gratitude. The rest of her simply wanted to melt against him for being so wonderful. Her father's mouth hung slack, he was so taken aback at being so politely chastised. For a second his jaw twitched as if he were about to counter, then he clasped it shut tightly, and simply blinked. Hal was still holding her hand in both of his and brought it back to his lips again. Lingered.

'Goodnight, Lizzie darling. Sleep tight.' And in three broad strides, he was gone.

Chapter Nine

Hal had managed to glean enough of the Earl of Upminster's travel plans over their dinner to know he had
important business to attend to at the Foreign Office
on Friday and therefore would not be leaving for the
Danbury house party until late afternoon. This allowed
Hal to time his own journey to the Danbury estate to
coincide his arrival within a few minutes of Lizzie's.

This did mean delaying his sister Connie, Aaron and
his mother, who had wanted to leave directly after luncheon. They were particularly unimpressed with Hal's
prolonged disappearance after luncheon, which in turn
made the initial atmosphere in his own carriage tense,
to say the least. Of course, the frostiness might also
have something to do with his jaunty festive attire. The
sprig of mistletoe, with its three remaining white berries pinned to the lapel of his coat, did a splendid job of
making Aaron uncharacteristically belligerent. It was
near eight o'clock when they rattled up the Danburys'
drive. Eight o'clock and pitch black; they were all stiff,
starving hungry and absolutely freezing cold.

'Had I known we would be travelling this late into

the evening I would have had additional hot bricks and blankets put in the carriage.' Connie rubbed her hands together to ward off the chill of the brisk night air. 'I really cannot understand what you were thinking, Hal, to have delayed us for so many hours.'

'Oh, I think I know exactly what he was thinking,' said Aaron, glaring at the fancy coach being unloaded just in front of them, the Upminster crest barely visible in the darkness. Connie's eyes followed her husband's and a knowing smile crept up her face when Lizzie's well-turned silk-clad ankle chose that exact moment to appear out of the door. Hal allowed his own eyes to feast upon the sight, purely because he had always had a particular fondness for a good pair of legs regardless of the female they happened to be attached to, and then hastily stared elsewhere when he saw his sister's interested expression.

'Oh, yes…now I think I understand it, too. Come along. Let us not waste the opportunity my lovestruck brother created for himself. We must befriend her.' And she was off, like an arrow shot from a crossbow, dragging their mother by the arm on a determined trajectory towards Lizzie and her father.

But Aaron stood rooted to the spot, his arms folded across his chest and his dark eyes narrowed. A stance which made Hal laugh. 'Now don't be a sore loser, old chap. It is hardly my fault your wife is thrilled with my association with Lady Elizabeth. Look at them all talking. I will lay money on the fact she is already extolling my virtues.' He patted his mistletoe corsage for effect. 'I sense another one of these berries will be gracing your palm imminently.'

'My wife might be extolling your virtues, but I intend to spend the weekend appraising Lady Elizabeth of your true nature.'

Poor Aaron. Hal almost felt sorry for him. 'Do your worst. Not only do I suspect it will not make one whit of difference, I am supremely confident she will happily let me continue to court her. By the ball on Twelfth Night, you will have all five berries.'

'And then what?'

'What do you mean *and then what*? Why, you will be spending January the seventh in my stables, that ageing back of yours creaking from the exertion of an inordinate amount of shovelling.'

Aaron waved this off stony-faced. 'That aside, what are you going to do about Lady Elizabeth? It is morally wrong to trifle with a woman's affections when you have no intention of making a commitment.'

Of course, Aaron's conscience would surface now that Hal was winning the wager—however, Hal had no intentions of telling his friend the devious truth. 'Do you wish to concede the wager?'

'You should be the one to concede it, Hal.'

'I will extricate myself from the situation gently once I win.' The lie tripped easily off his tongue. Lizzie was as opposed to marriage as Hal was, thank goodness, which was the most significant part of her attraction, and their arrangement was concluded after Twelfth Night regardless. 'I have not made any declarations or promises, nor have I even alluded to the prospect of more and, for the record, neither has she. This is merely a flirtation. For both of us.'

'She invited you to sit at her father's table. That is fairly significant.'

The conversation was beginning to make Hal uncomfortable. He couldn't tell the truth, yet pretending he had no conscience over the situation did not sit right with him either. If he and Lizzie did not have a particular and mutually beneficial arrangement, he already knew he would concede the wager. She was too good to be trifled with and if anyone else tried it he would nip it in the bud swiftly and mercilessly, something he never thought he would ever hear himself think about a woman he had no family connection to. 'Lizzie knows what I am, Aaron, and doubtless sees the situation for exactly what it is. Come along. We are appearing rude by not joining the ladies.'

After the flurry of polite hellos and the taking of coats and cloaks, Lord and Lady Danbury came to meet them in the holly-decked hall. Lizzie had come to stand next to Hal as the hosts greeted each guest individually. As they were at the end of the line, the raucous sounds of laughter coming from the crowded drawing room bizarrely gave them privacy. 'I am sorry about my papa's behaviour towards you the other evening. He means well, but has a tendency towards over-protectiveness.'

'Think nothing of it. I am quite used to that sort of reaction, I can assure you. It is probably deserved.' He was lying. It was definitely deserved, although for once he felt a little ashamed of his past. Aaron's reservations were also bothering him.

'Doesn't it upset you? Having everyone judging you and dismissing you as a superficial hedonist?' It hadn't up until now. For years, he had worn the mantle of rake proudly to vex his father. The more scandal he created, the more satisfying his father's explosive reaction was. However, whilst he could not deny his past, Hal realised he did not want that to be how she judged him.

'The *ton* loves to gossip and I give them an outlet to do so. However, compared to some, I fear I am not as great a scoundrel as the gossips make out. I have hidden depths.' What had possessed him to say that? He had meant it to come out as a flippant, flirty remark, instead it had sounded too earnest, because it was true. There were many aspects of his character he kept hidden. His new conscience being one of them. Aaron would have a field day if he knew he was getting to him.

'Oh, I am well aware of your hidden depths.' She was smiling, but not in a patronising way. 'Beneath the layer of boyish charm lies a thoughtful and intelligent man. You are well informed, clearly read the newspapers and not *just* the gossip pages, have a great understanding of commerce and diplomacy...'

'Diplomacy? I wouldn't go that far.' Except Hal desperately wanted the compliments.

'A diplomat knows how to deal with all manner of people, something you manage to do very effectively without causing an argument. Look at how deftly you stopped Lord Hewitt from dominating the conversation with his own silly opinions. Or how you politely chastised my father for foisting those dullards on me the other evening. You were quite wonderful. Your comments hit home, by the way. He has been most introspective about it all since. He even apologised for springing them on me and for promoting Lord Hewitt as a potential suitor. Thanks to you, he learned quickly what sort of a pompous fellow Lord Hewitt is. A man who can achieve all that, so casually and without causing an argument, is very skilled at the art of diplomacy.'

You were quite wonderful. For some reason Hal had

latched on to those words and swore his chest expanded
with pride at the sound of them. At least he hoped it was
pride, although pride didn't tend to make one's heart
hammer excitedly or one's throat tighten with emotion. And why was it he was suddenly unable to look
away from her?

'Oh, look! Our two lovebirds are under the mistletoe.' Lady Danbury's excited voice brought him sharply
out of his daze and simultaneously he and Lizzie both
glanced up. Suspended from the chandelier on a long
piece of scarlet ribbon was a huge ball of mistletoe. 'You
must kiss her. It's bad luck to ignore it!'

'Yes, Hal—kiss her!' Connie joined in the call and
every eye in the hall was suddenly locked on them expectantly. Apart from the Earl of Upminster, who appeared most aggrieved at the suggestion, and Aaron, of
course, who was glaring with barely concealed disbelief at the fickle hand of fate. It was probably that glare
which cut through the sudden and inexplicable nerves
and convinced Hal to go for it. Another berry would
soon be plucked and poor Aaron would be there to witness it all. Although, he doubted that had much bearing on the giant butterflies which were now flapping
away in his stomach.

He looked down at Lizzie, who was a little wide-eyed
and clearly waiting to follow his lead, watched her lick
her lips nervously and felt his own warm in readiness.
'We wouldn't want to court bad luck, would we, fair
maiden?' His voice came out deeper. Softer. Hopeful.

She shook her head imperceptibly and he watched the
tip of her tongue dart out to moisten her lips as her face
tilted up a little. An invitation? He hoped so. Hal would

rather they did not have an audience, although usually something like that would not bother him, but he was damned if he would let such a sterling opportunity slip. His hand came up to touch her cheek of its own accord before his mouth came down to lightly touch hers and, in that instant, everybody else disappeared.

She tasted of home.

Those were the first thoughts which permeated his brain after his body rejoiced at the contact. Warm and comforting, yet at the same time incendiary. The second her lips had touched his, his body had needed more—however, his heart appeared very content to simply savour the peculiarly intimate moment. He felt no desire to hurry nor could he deepen the kiss in public, so he simply stayed exactly where he was, grateful she did not step back either.

'That's quite enough of that!' Lizzie's father tugged her away and shot daggers at Hal through eyes narrowed to slits and the beautiful, sensual spell was broken. 'Come along, Lizzie, we have dawdled in this hall long enough and we both need to change for dinner. We do not want to hold the meal up.'

Her cornflower eyes slanted briefly to his in apology and Hal did his best approximation of a roguish smile to fluster her already flustered father some more, and saw the delicate blush staining her cheeks at being made a spectacle. Then she dutifully followed her father and a footman up the stairs.

She moved with such grace, he noticed, her trim hips undulating slightly in a very pleasing, feminine fashion with each step. At the top she turned and their gazes locked once again, except there was no apology in them this time, more bemusement, making him wonder if their very short, very chaste kiss had had the same effect on her as it had on him. Hal's head was spinning. His pulse a notch too fast. His cravat suddenly far too tight and his body desperate for more.

Of her.

The urge to bolt up the stairs and simply take was extremely unsettling.

All this time he had wondered where his missing vigour had gone and it had chosen this precise moment, when he was on full display in a crowded hall, to suddenly reappear with a vengeance.

He wanted Lizzie.

Good gracious!

Properly wanted her. It had nothing whatsoever to do with his wager with Aaron and he was quite certain this new feeling of actual desire for Lizzie was certainly contrary to the terms of their alliance. Nor did it resemble any of the multiple ways he had wanted women before. Those had been solely about passion. Whilst he most definitely felt that for her, there was also something else lurking inside, something dangerously bordering on affection and emotional need rather than the purely physical.

Good grief! His heart was engaged.

A new startling and unexpected development Hal needed to think about.

Alone.

His suddenly weak knees nearly buckled at the revelation. How the devil had that happened?

'Oh, look!' Lady Danbury decided to clap her hands together at the same time to achieve maximum impact. 'They cannot bear to take their eyes off each other. Look at the pair of them gazing at each other over the banisters! When they are wed, I shall proudly tell everyone the romance blossomed under my very roof!'

The word *wed* made him feel decidedly queasy, but Hal managed a weak smile while he gathered his wits together and tried not to feel guilty to see both his sister and mother beaming at him in excitement as they began to follow another footman upstairs. The only person not beaming was Aaron, whose expression was best described as total incredulity mixed with disgust.

'It staggers me that luck continues to favour you when you really don't deserve it.'

'Don't be a poor sport, Aaron.' Hal took the stairs two at a time with his heart thumping, hoping he appeared nonplussed. 'I did not even see that fortuitous ball of mistletoe and neither did you.'

'Aha! So you admit it was a fluke? Therefore, it doesn't count towards the five.'

'There was no stipulation that fluke kisses were not included, old boy, and well you know it. I am three down and have only two left to go. You are just peeved you did not spot the mistletoe first.'

'If I had, I would have stood beneath it myself and refused to move.'

'It is Christmas, and at Christmas one has to expect mistletoe to crop up somewhere, and thus I am now hopeful a few more stray sprigs will be conveniently dotted around this estate—in entirely different locations, of course, as stipulated in the terms of the wager—although we both know I won't need the aid of mistletoe. I am irresistible to the ladies. I doubt you remember what that feels like now you are past your prime, old boy.'

'I am blissfully married to your sister, not past my prime.'

'If you say so. I am blissfully thrilled that you could be there to witness that kiss. Your face was an absolute picture. Who knew your jaw could fall open that wide? Seeing it has made the inevitable victory significantly sweeter.'

'What are you two whispering about?' Connie was stood looking down at them suspiciously.

'I was just commenting on how splendid the Danburys' mouldings are, my darling. Why, the craftsmanship on the ceiling is positively exquisite.' His friend smiled innocently up at his wife although it was plain she did not believe her husband one bit.

'Oh, really? Miraculously, after five years of marriage, you have a sudden interest in mouldings?'

Aaron threaded her arm through his. 'Five *blissful* years of marriage, Constance. You keep forgetting the word *blissful*. Ah, look! Our bags have arrived.'

His wife suitably distracted, Aaron made a very rude hand gesture to Hal below, then they went left on the landing while another footman waited to escort him and his baggage to the right, explaining Lady Danbury had ensured the single ladies were placed alongside the married couples whilst the bachelors were to be housed at the furthest end of the west wing for the sake of propriety. Although that kept him firmly and gratefully away from the clutches of the hordes, it also neatly separated him from Lizzie which was probably just as well now that his missing vigour had crawled out of its hiding place and still lingered in his breeches.

Hal watched his brother-in-law's retreating back and

could not resist a final dig. 'Oh, Aaron, aren't you forgetting something?'

He sent the third white berry whizzing through the air with such perfect timing, it hit its intended, and supremely irritated, target smack in the middle of the forehead.

Chapter Ten

Lizzie closed her bedchamber door and gratefully sank on to her mattress, feeling more than a little overwhelmed. A silly, innocent kiss under the mistletoe should not have turned her insides into mush and given her body ideas it had no right having. There should be a warning note pinned to Hal, letting all ladies know never to let his lips anywhere near their person as it scrambled the brain. Hours later and she was still flushed from the experience. Hot all over and thankful they had been in company all night and that her father had brought the kiss to an end swiftly, else she probably would have quickly lost all sense of reason, wound her arms around his neck and happily dissolved into a puddle at the man's feet.

And if she was brutally honest with herself, it was not only the intoxicating nature of his kiss which was worrying. The moment she had seen him standing on the drive, six feet and some of glorious, handsome male, a rakish smile on his face and a knowing glint in his eye, Lizzie had been ridiculously happy to see him and more than a little excited at the prospect of spend-

ing the entire weekend in his company. Why she was
having these thoughts, when he was a charming rake
like Rainham, who by his own admission was wholly
against marrying any time this decade, and when she
was a confirmed spinster who had sworn off men for
ever, was a mystery. However, there was no point denying the odd frisson she felt whenever she was near
Hal was attraction and perhaps there was a little affection in the mix. Henry Stewart, Earl of Redbridge, for
all his faults, was very easy to love.

Not love! Lizzie hastily corrected with alarm, sitting bolt upright again...*like*. He was very easy to *like*
and, truth be told, she was in grave danger of liking
him a great deal.

Fortunately, their hostess had seated them at completely opposite ends of the dinner table because Lizzie
had needed the distance. Unfortunately, the pair of them
kept locking eyes during the meal and what was worse
was that a great many of the other diners noticed. Hal's
sister was one of them and clearly delighted at their
interest in one another. When the interminable dinner was over, Lizzie initially avoided him. A situation
which he complied with, as if he sensed her reluctance
or perhaps felt the need for some distance himself. A
sobering thought indeed, especially as the idea he was
attracted to her, too, and similarly avoiding her hurt.
Which was, of course, ridiculous. For an hour, they
were across the room from one another, yet at all times
Lizzie was painfully aware of exactly where he was and
exactly what he was doing.

When two young ladies commandeered him, practically backing him into a corner of the room, Lizzie realised she was being unfair. Her odd mood was hardly

Hal's fault and she had agreed to keep the hordes at bay. Thanks to his well-chosen words to her father, for the first time in years, he was not openly trying to match-make at a social function. A whole weekend of peace stretched before her and Hal had been entirely responsible for that. Just because she was no longer suffering did not mean the need for an alliance was at an end. That would be unforgivably selfish. Fair was fair and she owed him. Taking a deep breath, Lizzie had straightened her spine and set a course to rescue her Earl.

'Oh, there you are, Hal, *darling*.' She had pushed her way through the barricade of persistent silk and wove her hand possessively around his elbow. 'I am sorry to interrupt, ladies, but I must steal him away. Your sister has been searching for you.'

His warm palm came to rest atop hers and had squeezed gratefully. Once again, her body seemed to stand to attention at his touch. 'Is she indeed? Then you had best take me to her. Quickly.'

'I shall *expect* you back presently my lord,' said Lady Arabella Farlow, a statuesque blonde with far too much of her décolleté on show and a permanent and well-practised pout which she obviously thought was attractive. 'Lady Elizabeth has monopolised you quite enough this yuletide and I am *dying* to get to know you better.' She punctuated this with a little wiggle of her shoulders which made the parts of her spilling out of her dress wobble.

Lizzie had blatantly stared at the younger girl's chest, mimicking the disapproving face her mother had used to such great effect. 'My dear Lady Arabella, I do believe you have misplaced your fichu. It might be prudent to retrace your steps to go find it.'

As intended, Lady Arabella coloured with embarrassment and Lizzie whisked Hal away before the vixen found her bold voice again.

'You might want to give Lady Arabella a wide berth.'

He sighed and squeezed her hand again. 'I have been trying to give that chit a wide berth for months, but she is outrageously persistent. Just before you saved me, she was quizzing me about the exact directions to my bedchamber.'

'I hope you did not give them to her. She's the type to visit.' Lizzie tried, and failed, to ignore the knot of irrational jealousy that clawed in the pit of her stomach, reasoning she was merely being protective of her friend. Hal *was* her friend now. Odd feelings aside, she genuinely liked him and enjoyed his company. They looked out for one another. Who'd have thought she would have befriended a notorious rake? Not her. A month ago, the very idea would have sent her into a rage.

'Oh! I gave her directions all right. The third room to the right as you go into the west wing.' Lizzie paused and stared at him in disbelief, only to watch him throw his dark head back and laugh. 'The third room to the right is not mine, you nodcock. I am not that stupid. It's Lord Hewitt's.'

Lizzie tried to maintain her outrage, but her lips were already twitching at the thought of the pompous Hewitt being awoken by the predatory and pouting Arabella. 'You shouldn't have done that either.'

Hal laughed heartily and once again her insides did a funny little wiggle and she found herself staring hungrily at his lips. 'Nonsense. Of course I should. Besides, I couldn't resist a bit of revenge on Hewitt, and who knows? They both might thank me one day. What an interesting couple they would make. I am so delighted with myself, I might stay awake all night and wait for the screams. Which one will scream louder, do you think? My money is on Hewitt.'

For the rest of the evening, they remained together wherever possible, drinking far more wassail than was sensible and laughing conspiratorially at one inappropriate comment after the next. He partnered her in charades and spillikins, and then sat, with her father sandwiched unsubtly in between them, for a long and raucous game of speculation, which he won with very little effort and to her father's complete and utter disgust. And just now, he had stared deeply into her eyes as he had bid her goodnight and then he had kissed her hand, in that slow and sensual way of his, so she practically floated up the stairs thinking a stream of silly thoughts which were most unlike her.

There should definitely be a warning pinned to his coat. Tomorrow, perhaps a brisk, solitary walk across the cold, hilly parkland was in order? The exercise might help to unscramble her wits. This alliance was not quite working out the way she had expected, because she had certainly never expected to develop any feelings for the man. Or for any man for that matter. Especially charming, handsome men with tarnished reputations and a way with women. Yet with each passing hour, a little bit of her resolve was steadily chipped away. If he hadn't been a rake, and if she was in the market for a husband, Lizzie would be sorely tempted.

And now she was lying to herself, because she was sorely tempted. Hal had reawakened a part of the girl she had been. The effervescent, witty, social young woman who enjoyed laughing and had wanted to marry her prince, then live happily ever after. Worse still, her hardened, shredded, battered heart was beating again, except it had chosen to beat for another man like Rainham. Infinitely more handsome and charming. Undoubtedly more noble, but still very, very dangerous. Twelfth Night really could not come soon enough.

After a fitful night's sleep, Lizzie arrived to breakfast deliberately late only to find the dining room filled with people, including a very dashing-looking Hal. The moment he spotted her he waved, a look of panic on his face, and numerous young ladies sat around him in the most predatory fashion. 'There you are, Lizzie *darling*! I saved you a seat.' He patted the chair next to him and she realised, in that instant, any chance of a restorative solitary walk had just flown out of the window. As he had feared, poor Hal was at the mercy of his baying hordes. This morning she would be his personal bodyguard, although pasting a lovestruck expression on her face did not prove to be as difficult as it usually did. Nor did looking jealous. She pierced Lady Arabella with such a fearsome glare that the younger woman blushed and her fingers flapped nervously at the lacy fichu she was clearly not used to wearing.

The seat Hal had managed to save was far too close to him. The baying hordes had barely left her enough space to wriggle into and, once seated, Lizzie's hip was pressed intimately against his.

'Did you sleep well?'

'Like a log.' She hoped the dark circles under her eyes were not too evident. 'You?'

'Surprisingly soundly.' His voice dipped to a whisper which warmed her neck. 'I barricaded the door with the dressing table.'

'Very wise.'

'You missed the show this morning. Lord Hewitt turned quite an impressive shade of crimson when he collided with Lady Arabella.' Perhaps that explained the fichu and the flush, yet the girl was obviously intent on still stalking Hal, as she brazenly interrupted their hushed conversation by calling across the table.

'A few of us are going riding, Lord Redbridge, and would be delighted if *you* would accompany us.' Talons back in place, she shot Lizzie a look which told her that she was most assuredly not invited.

'Lord Redbridge is otherwise engaged this morning.' Lizzie smiled tightly and took a sip of the tea which had just been placed in front of her.

'Oh, really? Doing what? Because if it is more interesting than riding then perhaps I could join you?'

'We are going into the village to shop for ribbons.'

She felt Hal instantly stiffen at the suggestion and hoped, for both their sakes, that ribbon shopping was a poor alternative to all the entertainments on the Danbury estate. There was a beat of silence, then Lady Arabella beamed. 'Perfect. I need new ribbons and I dare say you and the Earl of Redbridge are desirous of a chaperon.'

'We already have a chaperon. The Earl's sister is accompanying us and...' Surely there must be something dreadfully dull and unappealing she could think of to dislodge the barnacle-like Lady Arabella, although Lizzie's mind had gone quite blank. Then it came to her. 'And I have arranged to meet Lord Hewitt in the hall. Did I mention *he* was accompanying us as well?'

* * *

Despite the fact Hal had to walk to the village for the sake of authenticity, dragging his delighted sister and less delighted brother-in-law along, too, he had a thoroughly pleasant morning. His sister monopolised Lizzie all the way there and back, leaving him to chat to Aaron as they trailed in their wake and, aside from the distinct lack of baying hordes, it was nice to see her getting on well with his family. Especially Connie. His sister had never suffered fools gladly and her good opinion mattered to him more than anyone else's. Not that he wanted her good opinion in this case, of course, but it comforted him none the less to know that he had it.

The afternoon wafted by without incident, although he had scarcely had two minutes alone with Lizzie all day. Largely because Aaron had decided to attach himself like a leech in case Hal succeeded in stealing another kiss from her. Even the outrageous stories he kept telling about Hal's exploits, all sadly true, were directly intended to ward her off and the poor fellow was getting increasingly frustrated by her cheerful, laughing acceptance of it all.

'Surely you have heard about Hal's scandalous exhibition at the Serpentine, Lady Elizabeth?'

'My father mentioned something, but I must confess I have no idea what occurred.'

'I am not sure we need to discuss that, Aaron, *darling*. Not when I am still furious at *you* for your part in it.' Connie's voice dripped venom which her irascible husband ignored.

'It was a warm summer's day and we decided to have

a race. A lap of vigorous swimming around the lake and then a sprint to Hyde Park Corner.'

'Aaron dearest, do you want to sleep in Lady Danbury's stable tonight? Because if you do, you are going the right way about it.'

Undeterred and encouraged by Lizzie's obvious interest, Aaron took her arm. 'We found a secluded end of the Serpentine and stripped down to our drawers…'

'Aaron James Wincanton, this is hardly a proper conversation for a pleasant walk in the countryside.'

'Oh, let him have his fun, Connie.' Hal took his sister's arm, grinning cheerfully. 'The incident is hardly a secret.' At least a hundred people had witnessed it and it had made the papers and, more importantly, poor Aaron had no idea it would not make the slightest bit of difference to his alliance with Lizzie.

Aaron went on to recall, in great detail, how when they had concluded their neck-and-neck swim around the enormous lake and then heaved themselves out of the water to dress, ready for the gruelling next leg of the race, they had discovered that all their clothes had been stolen. Like the gentleman he was, Aaron had hidden in the bushes to spare the blushes of the many people in the park. Hal, on the other hand, had refused to concede and had sprinted across the grass in his soggy drawers and claimed victory.

'You ran from the Serpentine to Hyde Park Corner in just your underthings?' Lizzie stared at him dumbfounded. 'Hal, you really are incorrigible.'

'But that is not the best of it, Lady Elizabeth.'

'It gets worse?'

Aaron paused for effect. 'The water had rendered his

drawers transparent. Everybody who saw him fly past could see his unmentionables!'

Lizzie giggled and Aaron's face fell. 'As shocking as the incident was, it made him a great deal more popular with the ladies… Oomph!'

His sister's elbow rammed into her husband's ribs with some force. 'It is not too late to have our marriage annulled. Husband.'

'*Blissful* marriage, my dear. You keep missing out the word blissful.'

They arrived back at the Danbury residence just as the sun was beginning to set. Lizzie was more relaxed and contented than he had ever seen her. His sister, on the other hand, appeared ready to skewer her husband. To that end, Connie had practically dragged Aaron upstairs to 'dress for dinner', a euphemism for 'I am going to give you a sound tongue lashing', if ever there was one, and at last Hal had her to himself for the first time that day.

'Ribbon shopping? That was the best deterrent you could come up with?'

She slanted a cheeky smile up at him and something peculiar happened in the vicinity of his heart. It felt like a twang. As if some imaginary string had been plucked. 'I saved you from Lady Arabella, didn't I?'

'I cannot fathom why she is being so persistent.'

'You are an earl with a reasonably good face.'

'A good face? Am I starting to grow on you, Lizzie, darling?'

'I'm afraid your scandalous behaviour at the Serpentine has quite put me off.'

'You wouldn't be saying that if you had seen me. I look quite spectacular in my birthday suit.' Flirting was second nature to him, but flirting with her was dangerous. Probably best avoided. 'Come upstairs and I'll show you.' His voice instinctively deepened and what was meant as a naughty retort intended to shock and make her giggle sounded a lot like an invitation. His long-lost but recently found vigour was urging him on, as was his heart. 'My bedchamber is the third room to the *left* as you go into the west wing should you feel the urge to visit me in the night. Shall I leave the dressing table in its correct place—just in case?'

'You are shameless.' But she was still smiling and that twanging happened again, accompanied by his suddenly racing heart as she lent closer. Desire had never felt quite so…personal before. 'I certainly hope somebody is within earshot to hear all this outrageous flirting. I would hate for your efforts to be wasted.'

The easy smile Hal gave her was false and not easy to achieve. She assumed he was acting, as per the terms of their agreement, when he hadn't meant to be at all. Forgetting the remaining two berries, he wanted to kiss her. Badly. Kiss her until they were both senseless and then carry her to his bed. Make love to her, then talk to her all night…

Talking? Good grief! The sudden and visceral need to know her on a deeper level was unsettling.

A footman went past, carrying steaming cups of wassail, and Hal grabbed some to stop himself from touching her. She sipped hers slowly and gazed around the room. 'Lord Hewitt has not so much as looked at me all day, so I hope he has decided I am no longer potential marriage material—however, he has been casting longing glances in Lady Arabella's direction, although she still looks at you.'

Was she? Hal hadn't noticed. He was developing a worrying habit of not noticing anything but Lizzie whenever he was with her. 'Poor Lord Hewitt. I am inclined to feel sorry for him. To covet something you cannot have is torture.' Never were truer words spoken. Her lack of reciprocal romantic interest in him was painful.

'I cannot bring myself to feel sorry for him at all. Although I am encouraged to see my father has avoided him, too, so clearly the bloom is off that rose. Dear Papa has also, thus far at least, avoided trying to foist any new dullards on me.'

'Your father strikes me a good man, Lizzie. However, I fail to understand why he believes you would be happy with a fellow like Hewitt.' The more he considered it, the more improbable it all was. Lizzie was beautiful, intelligent and positively ripe for the picking. Why was Upminster determined to sell her so short when any man would be over the moon to have her?

'After so many years sitting happily on the shelf, my father despairs of me. I believe he is now getting quite desperate as the calibre of gentleman he parades under my nose has significantly declined. He has given up hope of my snaring a prince or a duke. Now we are trawling the depths of the lesser peers and sirs. Although even by those standards, Lord Hewitt was a dud.'

Hal had skilfully manoeuvred them to a quiet alcove to watch the proceedings from a distance, and—if he was being brutally honest with himself—so he could have her all to himself for a little while longer.

'Talking of duds, I see Ockendon has just arrived.' To begin with, she merely stiffened, but then colour quickly drained out of her face. The cup of wassail tilted, spilled and Hal instinctively took it from her as he followed her gaze. But it was not Ockendon who had caused the odd reaction. It was his companion. Another man Hal could not place. Whoever the fellow was, Lady Danbury did not look at all pleased to see him, because she was smiling tightly as a hovering footman took his coat. A smile so brittle it appeared likely to shatter at any moment.

'Do you know him?'

Lizzie stood like a marble statue, frozen on the spot for several seconds, her gaze never leaving the late-comer. When Ockendon began to lead his companion into the room, she backed further into the alcove, clearly distressed.

'Lizzie! What is the matter?'

Only then did she look up at him, those cornflower eyes swimming with frightened tears. 'I have to go!' Quick as a flash, she spun around and stumbled towards the French doors. Before Hal could deposit the two cups on a table to reach for her, she had wrestled open the handle and bolted out into the dark garden beyond. It was so unexpected, so out of character, her reaction made him panic, too. Something was very wrong.

Chapter Eleven

A quick glance around the secluded alcove told him nobody had noticed her frantic escape and Hal knew she would hate to be the cause of a scene, so on stealthy feet he followed her outside and quietly closed the door behind him. There was no sign of her on the terrace and, because it was close to freezing outside, no lights had been lit in the garden. Obviously, the Danburys had assumed nobody would be mad enough to go outside.

'Lizzie?' Although barely above a whisper, his voice sounded loud in the silence. She did not answer, forcing Hal to strain his ears for sounds of movement. There were none. The silhouetted shapes of clipped bushes and trees were shrouded in mist as he plunged into the garden.

Ten minutes later and his fingers were frozen and his stomach was in knots. He had kept a close eye back on the house and he was certain she had not returned there, and without a coat or shawl she must be chilled to the bone. The further into the grounds he walked, the less the pale crescent moon illuminated his surroundings; looking for Lizzie in this was like searching for a needle in a haystack. Hal doubled back, skirting around the edge of the lawn towards the stables to fetch a lantern and wanted to cheer in relief when he spied her, sat all alone and hunched on a bench.

His feet crunched on the frosty grass as he hurried towards her, alerting her to his presence. She looked up, her lovely face totally wretched, and visibly sagged when she saw it was him rather than someone else. She had been crying. Her face was wan and drawn, her eyes and nose slightly swollen. Her slim shoulders still trembled and her fingers were twisting a crumpled handkerchief nervously. Wordlessly, Hal sat down and wrapped his arm around her, pulling her closer beneath his coat to share the heat from his body. She didn't pull away. Instead she burrowed into the crook of his neck gratefully.

'I've been worried sick.'

'I'm sorry. Seeing him after all these years gave me quite a start.' Despite their close and intimate position, she was staring out into nothingness. The old, guarded expression painted on to her pale face. Pretending all was well when it clearly wasn't.

'Seeing who?' Whoever he was, Ockendon's companion was at the root of all this.

'The Marquess of Rainham… We were engaged… once upon a time.'

'Ah.' Recognition dawned at the same moment intense jealousy sliced through him and left a bitter, unfamiliar taste in his mouth. The Rainham Hal remembered had been a handsome fellow who enjoyed his pleasures. The years had not been kind. The man with Ockendon had the pallor of a man who lived hard. Imagining her shackled to a wastrel like Rainham made the bile rise in his throat. 'You had a lucky escape all those years ago, I think.'

'I thought so…' Her voice trailed off and she stared mournfully at the twisted handkerchief in her lap. 'But now he is back.' Her voice caught and she covered her face with her hands, burrowing closer into his chest as fresh sobs racked her body.

Instantly protective and desperate to ease her pain, Hal smoothed his hands over her back and hair. The bitter taste of jealousy made him frown involuntarily and he was glad she could not see his face. 'You loved him?'

'At the time I did. I was head over heels in love with him. Charles was as charming as he was handsome.' And Hal hated him with a passion. He sincerely doubted he had ever hated anyone more than he did *that* man at *that* moment. Even the loathing he had for his own father paled in comparison to this new and potentially violent hatred which burned inside. 'Everyone warned me he was trouble, but I was too besotted to listen to them.'

'But you came to your senses.' At least he hoped she had. If she still carried a torch for the man Hal might have to commit murder. 'Do you still…love him?' His hands ached to clench into fists while he waited for her answer, fists he would enjoy pummelling in to Rainham's unworthy, pale face.

He felt her head shake against his throat. 'I loathe him. And I loathe myself more for my foolishness all those years ago. I hate how trusting and besotted I was right to the last minute.'

Hal let out the tense breath he had been holding unconsciously, thankful that her feelings for her former fiancé were dead and buried. 'We all make mistakes, Lizzie. Thank goodness you realised he was no good

and terminated your engagement, even if it was at the
very last minute.'

She stiffened in his arms and he swore he felt her
inwardly go to war with herself. On a ragged sigh,
she eventually laughed with no humour whatsoever.
A bitter, harsh sound which was difficult to hear and
filled with raw pain. 'I didn't terminate the engagement.' She sat up straight, pulled away from him, her
eyes downcast. Guarded. Then she huffed out a sigh
which sounded like defeat. 'You might as well know
the truth... That day... I was actually at the church. In
the vestry. Waiting for him...like the silliest and most
trusting of fools.' The next noise was a cross between
a laugh and a sob. 'But my devoted fiancé...he never
bothered turning up.'

Her words took a few moments to sink in, she could
tell. When they did he sounded incredulous. 'You were
jilted?'

Lizzie shrugged and stared off into space, knowing
he would see the truth if she dared to look in those intelligent green eyes. Thanks to her blind panic and foolhardy decision to run, he would be able to piece together
a great deal. It was obvious there was unfinished business between her and the Marquess of Rainham. Obvious her foolish heart had been shredded into tiny pieces.
The very last thing she ever wanted anyone to see her
as was an object of pity. Least of all Hal, when he saw
her as someone else. Someone courageous and bold and
pithy and fun. She should have stayed. She knew that
now. Stood proudly. Looked the scoundrel dead in the
eye and feigned uninterest at seeing him again.

The trickle of unease had begun the moment Ockendon had arrived. His wily old eyes had scanned the room, searching for her. She had known it emphatically when they had briefly locked with hers. She had seen him smile maliciously, then slowly turn towards his companion in introduction. The satisfied, knowing smile he wore was unsettling. At first, she had not known who it was. His back had been to her as he removed his greatcoat; the coat finally gone, Ockendon's companion turned around and nausea slammed into her. Lizzie literally couldn't breathe. All the air had rushed out of her in a stinging swoosh the moment she saw Rainham, tight bands of panic wrapped around her ribs prevented her from sucking any more in and, like a frightened deer, she had bolted towards the French doors.

The dire implications did not need to be spelled out because she had feared them for five long years. Ockendon knew she had secrets. Perhaps not all of them, but enough ammunition to force his suit. Aside from her secret, her poor papa had been through so much already. Her debacle, his wife's untimely death soon after—he did not deserve to see his life's work and good name ruined, too, because of her mistake.

If only she had had the courage to put her escape plan in to action sooner. The little house was waiting for her and Georgie in the north. Had been waiting for two months now. She had wanted to give her dear papa one last Christmas, putting off the dreadful day when she had to tell him she was leaving and taking his beloved grandson with her—she knew how much this would upset her father. Suddenly, that upset seemed kinder than what was about to happen. Her carefully constructed façade, the façade her father had worked hard to create on her behalf, was on the brink of collapsing like a house of cards. Unravelling into the mother of all scandals.

Hal was still in a state of complete incredulity. 'But everyone believes *you* called off the wedding.'

'No. My fiancé had found another, richer prospect. A duke's daughter. They were bound for Gretna Green—but intercepted before her life was ruined, too. Two silly young ladies had a lucky escape that day, I think.' His hand came up to rest on her cheek and she saw the pity. The need to understand. To help. To fix. As if he could, by some miracle, make the tangled web of lies and secrets disappear. Why did he keep doing things that made her heart melt?

Lizzie turned her head away from his touch. Much as she wanted his comfort, and she *did* want his comfort, she dared not confess all. There was too much at stake to risk baring her hand completely. Even to Hal. Not yet. Not when there still might be a chance to avoid it. 'My father used his government connections to get it all hushed up.'

She also suspected he had paid a fortune and pulled all manner of high-placed strings to completely ruin Rainham and have him banished from society. Her father was not a cruel man, but as a parent herself she understood he would have done whatever was necessary to protect his offspring. She would happily murder anyone who tried to hurt Georgie. Murder them and then happily hide the corpse. She sincerely doubted her father would feel any different. He was fiercely loyal and devoted to his family. It was no coincidence that her fiancé, normally a stalwart at all society functions, had disappeared so completely. He would not have disappeared without some serious persuading. Or some serious threats. Threats which would end her papa's career in disgrace if the world suddenly found out he had abused his power in such a self-serving way. Lizzie had been so content knowing she would never see the wretch again, she had never asked her father to explain. Now she wished she had, although she doubted he would have told her even then. In her papa's mind, women needed protecting from the world. Even fallen women.

Why had Charles surfaced here? Why now? To see him with the slimy Ockendon, hot on the heels of the odious old Earl's unexpected and creepy proposal, set alarm bells ringing. And the way Ockendon had looked at her—mentally undressing her, making no attempt at even trying to charm her. Behaving as if a union between them was little more than a formality.

Inevitable.

It was all *too* coincidental.

Her mind was racing, trying to understand what the pair of them were up to and what, if anything, she could do about it. Lizzie needed to choose her next words very carefully. 'I haven't seen him since the day before the wedding.' Blithely climbing down the wisteria, his passion spent in her willing body, his traitorous lips still lying to the end as he had blown her a final kiss goodbye.

Was he now in cahoots with Ockendon?

Probably. After what he had done, she would put nothing past Charles. He was the lowest of the low. Lower. If he was in league with Ockendon, then the old Earl knew he had lain with her. What else did he know? Her mind was spinning with questions. Had she slipped up somewhere? Had Georgie been seen? Had a servant talked? One glance at the sorry excuse for a man she had nearly married confirmed categorically what she had always suspected. Her son was the image of his father. The same dark hair. The same dark eyes. It would not take a genius to put two and two together.

Lizzie needed to speak to her father.

Hal took one look at her, saw the acute sadness, the distress and the fear, and instantly went on the offensive.

'He broke your heart!' She had never seen him so furious. 'How dare he jilt you!' He shot upright and she saw his hands fist, apparently ready to avenge her for the slight and she loved him for that. 'I think that snake and I need to have words!'

'No, Hal. The last thing I want is for him to ever know he mattered.' She reached for his hand. Squeezed it. And because she wanted to hold it tight, lace her fingers with his and rest her head on his shoulder again and stay there for ever, she dropped it and went back to worrying the handkerchief she had ruined. 'Or for the world to learn of the truth.' At least that was the truth. There were more reputations at stake here than her own. Her father's. Perhaps Lord Bulphan's, too. Other good men who had helped her father erase Rainham from her life. Even the lovely, furious Earl stood quaking with rage in front of her. Earls could be rakes. In youth, it was practically expected. But regardless of his youthful indiscretions, he did not deserve to be pulled into this scandal when all he was guilty of was protecting her from her father's matchmaking attempts. She had to distance herself from him, too. Now. Before it was too late.

'I still want to kill him. But I won't—if you don't want me to.' Hal was clearly still furious, but loyally bowed to her logic.

'Seeing him was a shock. I simply needed a few minutes to gather myself together. When I greet him, I want to be dispassionate, not…not like this.'

'Then you will greet him with me. On *my* arm. I want him to know I will skewer him if he so much as mentions anything to embarrass you.'

'Agreed.' Hal would act as a shield one last time until she knew what was at play. She also needed his strength and his presence more than she cared to acknowledge. 'Just give me a few more minutes to compose myself.' Her enemies would not see her with puffy eyes, her nose red from crying. They would see only the formidable and detached Lady Elizabeth Wilding. The one the world still believed had a pristine reputation.

Hal nodded, snapped a fresh handkerchief out of his pocket and waited for her to fix her face. As she did so, he began pacing back and forth in front of the bench like a caged tiger. His angry breath sawing in and out in frozen, white puffs, his powerful long legs tearing up the ground. Gone was the erudite and charming face he presented to the world. The man who lacked both substance and purpose was nowhere to be seen. Stripped of that mask, Hal was formidable. His height and strong build had never been more apparent. There was so much more to him than the dashing rake. If anyone could intimidate her would-be fiancé and her former fiancé, it was Hal.

When she finally stood, it was on shaky legs. Her knight in shining armour smiled, although there was ice in his eyes and a hardness about his jaw she had never seen before. Physically he appeared to have grown. Devoid of his veneer of charm, he was huge. Menacing. Ready to charge into battle like one of the lead soldiers he had picked out for her little boy. 'Are you ready to step into the lion's den, fair maiden?' The charming smile was false this time. Pasted on for her benefit to make her feel better. Beneath it his temper was tangible.

'As ready as I will ever be.' At least she had a tiger on her side as she ventured forth into the lion's den. For the time being anyway. Their liaison was only ever meant to be a convenient sham, yet he was once again going above and beyond the parameters of their bargain. Ockendon and Rainham were a completely different kettle of fish to the dullards he had agreed to keep at bay. But, of course, when they had made the arrangement, she had no inkling her secrets were on the cusp of being exposed. A way to enjoy a month of peace before she began a new life.

Far away.

From everyone and everything she held dear.

With a jolt, she realised she would miss Hal, too. When this was all over, if she emerged from it all unscathed, she would still see her papa on high days and holidays when she moved north. If the scandal erupted, her dear papa would probably be forced to withdraw permanently to his estate in Cheshire, and if Georgie's existence became public knowledge, Lizzie supposed she could at least retire there, too. Either way, she would never see Hal again. The realisation rooted her to the spot for a moment as she gazed at him, pathetically trying to sear his image in her mind. Exactly as he was now. Solid. Strong. Loyal to a fault. Ready to defend her even though he did not know the half of what it was he was offering to defend.

He saw her hesitation as further evidence of her fear and wrapped her chilled hand about his arm. 'Come on then, Lizzie darling. Let's show the snake you are unfazed.'

An eerie calm settled over her as she stepped back into the Danburys' enormous drawing room. Hiding or running would not put off the inevitable. The guests had thinned out this close to dinner, all gone to change or rest or whatever people did when there was a gap in the proceedings. Her father was missing, probably frantically searching for her, and so were their hosts. The Earl of Ockendon and the Marquess of Rainham were not. In fact, their strategic position in the very centre of the room could only mean one thing. They wanted her to see them. It was why they were here, after all.

Beneath her palm she felt the corded muscles in Hal's forearm stiffen. Aside from that he was the very picture of casual male confidence as he led her on a path directly towards them. His strength prevented her step from faltering when her former lover turned to look at her for the first time. Smiled nervously, then eagerly stood when Ockendon nudged him, just in case she tried to avoid conversing with him.

'Lizzie. You look wonderful.' There was a tremor in his voice. Fear? Guilt? 'The years have been kind to you.'

She could not say the same. He appeared to have aged far more than five years. Still handsome, he was paler. The dark hollows under his eyes suggested he was a creature of the night or did not sleep well. She hoped for the latter although suspected he was too shallow to have a conscience. Although it was plain to see he was not comfortable to be in this room. There was a jerkiness about his posture—as if he was on the cusp of running away. His breathing was uneven. His face sweating. His dark eyes, so like Georgie's, watched her carefully. It was strange that one could unconditionally love and despise the same set of eyes at the same time.

Regally she inclined her head. 'You are too kind, my lord.' Lizzie feared she would snarl if she said his actual name. It reminded her that he knew her far too well. All of her. She flicked her eyes to Ockendon who, she noted, had failed to stand in her presence. There was no sign of discomfort in his demeanour. He was enjoying this. 'My Lord Ockendon.' Another polite nod, although she made sure he saw her true feelings by turning her face up partially in disgust. He would not see how much he frightened her. Not now. Not ever.

'Gentlemen.' Hal, too, nodded and then smiled lazily at her. It was the sort of secret smile that couples shared. One which warned the two men she was his. To her it said something else entirely. It said *I've got you. Don't worry.* It buoyed her to be bold. After all, there was no point beating about the bush. They were here for a purpose and one which likely included blackmail.

'Lady Danbury had assumed you were not coming, Lord Ockendon.' Lizzie was baiting him, as she feared his purpose. She also knew she could not fight against whatever he had planned unless she was appraised of the plan beforehand. If scandal was inevitable, she would meet it head on and then decide how to play it, if indeed she could. She had already decided she would do practically anything to protect her son—or her father. With a shiver, she realised, that might have to include marrying Ockendon.

He eyed her up and down somewhat lasciviously, his rheumy eyes lingering too long on her bosom again. 'Oh, I always intended on coming, lovely Lizzie. You knew that, though. Didn't you? After our last little chat, I believe I left you in no doubt of my intentions.'

She felt Hal tense and squeezed his arm to stop him replying. 'I have still not given you leave to call me by my first name, sir. Nor will I ever.'

The Earl smiled smugly. 'Oh, I think you will. One day soon.'

Hal's thumb began to slowly caress the back of her hand.

Obviously.

It drew both men's' eyes very effectively, as he had intended. 'There is something pathetic about an older man chasing a young woman, don't you think? Especially when it is blatantly obvious her affections are directed elsewhere.'

His gaze pulled her in and she was powerless to do anything except stare up into his hypnotic mossy-green eyes. Hal would think it was for show. Self-preservation in front of her two tormentors, and in part that was true, however, Lizzie also knew she was branding him into her memory. Squirrelling away the possessive gleam in his expression, wishing for once that it was more than just pretend. Wishing circumstances were so very different.

'As far as I see things, Redbridge, nothing is set in stone until a lady walks back up the aisle with a ring on her finger.' A blatant dig which told her he knew she had been left at the altar. He grinned at his companion. 'Isn't that right, Rainham?'

True to form, Charles appeared devoid of any guilt for what he had done to her. He nodded at his odious friend, too eagerly, and then vainly avoided looking back towards her. Gone was the confident rake she had fallen for and in its place was a subservient lapdog; Ock-endon was undoubtedly his master. 'The absence of a ring means a lady is still fair game.'

Chapter Twelve

Hal sensed there was more going on here than he knew—however, he knew enough to intervene. As much as he wanted to feel Rainham's nose shatter against his fist, his first duty was to help Lizzie save face and get through this uncomfortable and unexpected ordeal with her head held high. He forced the corners of his mouth to curve upwards. Forced himself to stick out his hand. Tried not to allow the revulsion show on his face as he shook Rainham's heartily and took some comfort from the slightly bewildered and obviously terrified expression on the bounder's face. Rainham was here under duress. Ockendon had some hold on him too.

'We are all adults here…this nasty undercurrent is completely unnecessary. If anything, I should thank you, Rainham. Had you not been such a thoughtless, money-grabbing scoundrel, then I would have been denied the opportunity to have my darling Lizzie now.'

He watched Ockendon's eyes narrow and forced himself to pat the man on the back jovially, too. 'I know Rainham here jilted her, old boy. Lizzie and I have no secrets from each other.' Or they wouldn't once he had got to the bottom of whatever was going on behind those guarded cornflower eyes. And he would get to the bottom of it. Of that he was determined.

Ockendon knew something about her, something dreadful if Hal was any judge, and was going to use it to snag himself an heiress. His father had been as mercenary whenever money was concerned so he recognised the signs. Locate the weakness, put pressure on that point mercilessly until it gave way, then reap the ill-gotten rewards. Whatever Ockendon had planned would not come to fruition. As soon as he got back to town, Hal was going to thoroughly investigate the man's business affairs and any other affairs while he was about it. Rainham's, too. He would dig and dig until he found dirt he could use. Their weaknesses. As much as he hated his father's methods, Hal had been well schooled in the art of forcing the hands of others from the moment he could talk. He might not usually have the stomach to sink to such dastardly depths, but Ockendon had made himself fair game. He needed to speak to Lizzie. 'If you will excuse us, gentlemen. We need to change for dinner.'

'If I might have a word with Lady Elizabeth in private...'

Hal's face came within inches of the Earl's. 'You may not.'

'I believe that is for the lady to decide.'

As she was still holding on to his arm as if her life depended on it, Hal had felt her body stiffen at the request. 'She has already decided she does not want you. Therefore, keep your inappropriate comments and filthy, impertinent looks to yourself. Tell the world your little friend here left her standing at the altar. It is in the

past and she has me now. Try to frighten her or leer at
her again and I will hunt you down and *destroy* you for
it. Better yet, take this sorry excuse for a man back to
whatever debauched and debased hellhole you found
him in. *Tonight*. If either of you has the audacity to be
seated at the table at dinner, then I will not be held accountable for my actions.'

Rainham, like the snivelling toad he was, was visibly shaken by the threat. His eyes widened; his nostrils flared. Instinctively his gaze flicked towards the
exit. Ockendon was fuming, but held his tongue. Just
as well. Hal was praying for any excuse to punch him.
They stared silently at each other for several moments,
before Ockendon finally stood and stalked towards
the door with the snake scurrying beside him as if his
breeches were on fire. As an afterthought, Ockendon
turned, walked slowly back towards them and made a
great show of pretending Hal did not exist. 'I am a powerful man. It is in your *family's* best interests to talk to
me, Lady Elizabeth. Make it sooner rather than later.'

He turned and marched towards the door Rainham
had already disappeared out of. Hal started after him,
only to be stayed by Lizzie's tight grip on his arm.
'Please, Hal, leave it.'

'Leave it? The audacity of the man makes my blood
boil.'

'They have gone. Just as you asked them to. Thank
you for saving me.'

Except she did not look like a woman who had been
rescued. 'Is there a possibility that Ockendon knows
something else about you?'

Her mouth moved to answer, then clamped firmly

shut. In the end, she ignored his question and unwound her arm from his. 'I need to speak with my father.'

'I would prefer you speak to me first. What's going on, Lizzie?'

The shutters went down. 'You saw for yourself what is going on. Clearly Lord Ockendon wants to use Rainham's treachery and the threat of a scandal to press his suit. Let him. Enough years have passed and I no longer care if the truth comes out.'

She was a dreadful liar. Her eyelids fluttered like butterfly's wings as she tried to hold his gaze. What wasn't she telling him? For the sake of privacy, he tugged her into a dark corner under the stairs. 'Is there something else? Only I get the distinct impression *there is* something else.'

Her eyes widened. Her tongue flicked out to moisten her top lip. 'Of course there is nothing else.' She was lying. He knew it in the same way he knew she was petrified. 'I am merely a little shaken at seeing Rainham again. I shall be my usual self over dinner. You'll see.'

A typical Lizzie-like pithy response, but her eyes were so troubled, awash with unshed tears, and it undid him. His fingers came up to brush her cheek and she leaned into his palm. Closed her eyes. Sighed softly. A single, fat tear trickled down her cheek, betraying her. Gut-wrenching proof that his suspicions were correct. He gently brushed it away with the pad of his thumb. When she began to pull away Hal brought his other hand up to cup her other cheek, then allowed it to slide down the delicate column of her neck. Her skin was like velvet, but her pulse beat a rapid tattoo beneath his fingers. The outer shell she was trying to portray was as much of a sham as their public *romance*. 'Please tell me what's wrong. I want to help you.'

She stared deeply into his eyes, as if she was searching the inner depths of his soul to see if she could trust him and he recognised the exact moment she decided she couldn't. He recognised it as it came with a sharp slash of pain, like a knife to the chest. Utter disappointment at not being considered worthy enough. His hands dropped ineffectually back to his sides when she took a decisive step backwards. She did not want either his help or his touch. 'Please stop worrying about me. There really is no need. My broken heart mended a long time ago.' Another lie. Another pain jabbed close to his heart.

'Rainham was a blasted fool to jilt you! Had I been in his shoes, I would have counted the seconds till I put the ring on your finger.' Where had that come from? His aching heart began to hammer erratically against his ribs. Wherever it had come from it was true.

Good grief.

'Maybe you *should* marry me, Lizzie.'

'W-what?' Her mouth hung open.

Hal's head began to spin. He had just proposed. Very badly and out of the blue. Hopefully she would turn him down. He had always avoided commitment and hardly knew this woman yet, horror of horrors, right at this moment this felt right. Even the appeal of sowing his wild oats was apparently waning. A voice in his head was making him question it. *Why would you waste time with other women when the only one your heart wants is currently stood right in front of you?* Looking at him as if he had just gone completely stark, staring mad. Which clearly he had. Perhaps Lady Danbury's wassail was off.

'You are very kind, but—'

'I am not being kind!' The annoying voice in his head told him he had to convince her it was the right course of action. 'We could announce our engagement tonight over dinner. With a special licence, we can be married by Christmas. Then you will no longer have to fear Ockendon or Rainham or the scandal of being jilted because everyone will be gossiping about our wedding.' Oh, Lord! Nonsense kept spilling willy-nilly from his mouth. He did not want to be shackled to a wife just yet. It was too soon... Far too soon. Thank goodness he hadn't given her any enticing or romantic sets of reasons to make her want to marry him.

But, the voice said, *they are sound and pragmatic ones. Lizzie might respond better to logic than the fact that your heart seems to think you were meant to be together.*

The walls tilted. Good grief! What the hell was going on? Soppy romantic ideas about two people who were meant to be together, especially when one of them was him, were ridiculous. He couldn't possibly think the pair of them were meant to be together.

Could he?

He certainly liked her and desired her. She was fun. Entertaining. Lovely to behold. So what if he had a sudden urge to wake up with her every morning? Spend his days with her. Grow old with her...

Dizziness swamped him. There had to be something in the wassail which did not agree with him, that could be the only explanation. To keep himself upright he grabbed the wall for support and hoped he did not look as blindsided as he felt. If he *hadn't* been poisoned, his current behaviour was very worrying.

'I can't marry you.'

His knees went then and he sat down shakily on an oak chest. He should be rejoicing the fact she had turned him down. His proposal had been rash to say the least and had literally come out of the blue. Instead, he was crushed. His breathing became laboured because of an acute pain in his chest. 'At least give it some thought. It's not really such a terrible idea when you consider the benefits.' And now, to top it all, apparently, he was not averse to begging.

'The benefits?' He saw bemusement and pity on her face. Both made him panic.

'We rub along well together.'

There is this odd feeling in my heart every time I am with you. It sort of swells and feels content.

'We are both cynical in nature and find the expectations of society tiresome.'

I want to spend every minute in your company.

'I do believe we have a mutual attraction to one another, which I doubt most married couples could claim, and it would save us both from the dullards and the hordes.'

Be mine for ever, Lizzie. I have a sneaking suspicion I'm a little bit in love with you.

Good grief!

Was he? How had that happened? He needed to stop speaking. Clamp his wayward jaws shut.

'I can't marry you.'

'Why not?'

'It would be totally wrong... For so many reasons.' To soften her words, her fingers came up to rest on his face and she gently brushed back his hair. He wanted to haul her into his arms, beg her to reconsider, but his pride was battered quite enough already and he was so confused by what he had just done he couldn't think of anything remotely sensible to say. If Hal was being completely honest with himself, he could not think of anything sensible to think either. He watched, as she lowered her body to kneel before him, rejoiced when she closed the distance between them and pressed her lips to his.

Home.

Those were his first thoughts before his body burst into flames and he did haul her into his arms. He wasn't sure which one of them deepened the kiss, but all the urgency, all the despair and all the longing he felt came tumbling out as he clung to her. At some point he tugged her on to his lap, let his greedy hands explore the curves of her body while his mouth worshipped her and his heart burst with joy. She wanted him, too. She *would* marry him.

It was Lizzie who tore herself away and stared up into his face for the longest time. Her fingers began to trace his features. 'You are sweet, Hal. I never thought I would ever hear myself say such a thing about a man with your reputation, but it is true nevertheless.' He could hear sympathy in her voice, feel her withdrawing back into herself. Withdrawing from him. From them!

When she stood up, stepped away, putting both physical and emotional distance between them, her expression was inscrutable. That damn drawbridge had been reeled in and she was hiding behind row upon row of battlements again, shutting him out. She did not believe in him enough. Or feel the same way. His poor heart twisted painfully in his chest and he could hear the damn voice in his head howling in protest. Hal jumped up, but before he could move towards her she stayed him with her hand. Shook her head definitively.

She smiled sadly and started towards the stairs, then hesitated and stopped. When she turned around her expression was wistful. 'Thank you for being there, Hal, and for offering to sacrifice yourself for me. It means the world. Thank you also for all you have done in the last few weeks. You have been a good friend to me and bizarrely at a time when I needed a friend the most. This silly Christmas season has been a pleasure. I will always remember it fondly.'

Chapter Thirteen

Alone in his bedchamber, still reeling from both the earth-shattering surprise of proposing and the despair at being swiftly turned down, Hal paced the floor. Perhaps the wassail had been tainted. With some sort of drug which rendered one stupid and prone to folly. His proposal had certainly been foolhardy. It was undoubtedly ill timed. The poor girl had suddenly been confronted with a man who had broken her heart, another who wanted to use that information against her and Hal had gone and sprung a proposal on her.

A pretty lacklustre and, now he came to think upon it, unconvincing proposal. *We rub along well together.* As if an intelligent and vivacious woman like Lizzie, who was plagued with dullards and wary of marriage, would be tempted by a declaration quite so bland? For a man renowned for his way with both words and the ladies, that was frankly pathetic. It was a blessing she had turned him down and an even bigger blessing she had thought his proposal was a noble, selfless gesture. It allowed him to save face even though he was feeling quite wretched at the rejection whilst still reeling from his bizarre reaction to their kiss.

Home.

That word kept haunting him. How the blazes could a woman be home? It made no sense, yet it made perfect sense. Perhaps he was going down with something? A fever, perhaps? Fevers made people delirious. That had to be what was wrong. A decent dinner, a soothing draught and a good night's sleep were probably in order. Tomorrow he would endeavour to get to the bottom of whatever was going on with Ockendon and see if that made a difference to his odd mood. Only then, if the silly voice in his addled head was still plaguing him, would he give the matter of his romantic feelings towards Lizzie some more thought and decide how to proceed with them. The sprig of mistletoe sat on his nightstand and he picked it up. This was meant to be a bit of fun. A harmless wager. Nothing serious. But that kiss had been serious. It had been significant. He plucked off another berry and tossed it into the fire.

Good grief! He was seriously considering a proper romance. What was that if not a Christmas miracle? If he hadn't been feeling so miserable, he would laugh at the cruel irony. A fortnight ago his vigour was missing and his life lacked something. Now he had plenty of vigour and his addled mind had decided what was lacking. It was Lizzie. She was home. And she didn't want him. Something he would doubtless get over as soon as he stopped feeling the urge to rescue her. He hoped, at least, that was all that was wrong. With that in mind, he probably should rescue her swiftly.

Hal quickly dressed for dinner and then headed back downstairs in search of Aaron. His friend was holding court at the refreshment table, but quickly excused himself when Hal motioned to him. 'You don't look particularly happy. Something I am going to take as a very good sign. I take it you have not made any more progress with the berries.'

'Forget the berries.' Hal had. The very last thing on his mind was the Mistletoe Wager when he suspected his heart was a little bit broken. 'What do you know about the Earl of Ockendon?'

'I know he smells.' Aaron's face wrinkled. 'And I know I've never liked him. Why do you ask?'

'I think he is trying to blackmail Lizzie.'

'That's a pretty serious accusation.'

They might be overly competitive with one another, but aside from his sister Hal trusted no one more. 'There is a scandal in her past. Rainham jilted *her*. Ockendon knows it and has brought the snake here to flaunt it under her nose.'

Aaron was silent for a moment, taking the news in in the calm measured way he did when something was important. 'At best, that news is a minor scandal now. Their engagement was years ago. The gossip will be harsh, as it always is with a titbit so juicy, but quickly forgotten.'

'That's what I would have said, but...' Hal raked his hand through his hair and shook his head. 'But my gut says there is something more to it. Something much worse. She was frightened. Ockendon was so...certain of his power over her.'

'Did you ask her?'

'Of course I asked her. She denied it.' But Hal had seen her. She had been broken. Had remained broken even as she had climbed the stairs less than an hour ago. The more he thought about it, the more it all bothered him. Which probably accounted for his ridiculous *'marry me'* outburst. 'I think she's in trouble, Aaron.'

'Then all you can do is keep a close eye on the situation and hope it either comes to naught or she confides in you.' Not what Hal wanted to hear. Whatever was troubling Lizzie he wanted to fix *now* and banish the fraught look which tugged on his heartstrings and made him make lacklustre but genuine marriage proposals on the spur of the moment. 'Unless, of course, she is embroiled in a truly awful scandal...in which case it might be prudent to distance yourself from her.'

'How can you say that!' The very thought was preposterous. 'Would you abandon Connie at the first sign of trouble?'

His friend watched him thoughtfully for several seconds. 'The last time I checked, Connie was my wife and Lizzie was a wager.' Hal felt his expression harden, then saw Aaron's change, too.

Awe and wonder.

Amusement.

An irritating grin crept over his face. 'Good Lord! I never thought I'd see the day! You're developing *feelings* for her?'

Denying it was pointless, because he was. He wasn't entirely sure what sort of feelings they were, labelling them as anything quantifiable terrified him. Hell—his hasty proposal had terrified him, although not quite as much as her refusal had. And frankly that terrified him more. Hal was starting to think they were meant to be together one day. Not yet, of course, he had far too many wild oats still left to sow. But one day he could see himself quite content with Lizzie, in the not-so-distant future... And there it went again. His addled mind was wandering down paths it had no right wandering down. Like a besotted idiot, he still hadn't answered his brother-in-law's question.

By the look on Aaron's face, any sort of response would be tantamount to an admission of guilt and Hal was certainly not ready for that either. Not when his head was all over the place and his heart hurt. 'I *like* her, Aaron. Lizzie is a good sort and I would hate to see her wronged by Ockendon. You have to admit, her former fiancé turning up here with him, after being absent from society for years, is a bit contrived.'

'It is. That I will grant you. And if Ockendon needs money, your lady-love has a temptingly huge dowry to entice him. I concede that, too. Her father has certainly made her an obvious target for fortune hunters.' Without telling him of his suspicions, Aaron's line of thinking was along the same lines as Hal's. In his head, he could hear his father's voice repeating his usual mantra. *'The world runs on coin, Henry. Nothing else matters.'*

'I will do some subtle digging on your behalf tonight, Hal, over dinner. I suggest you concentrate your efforts towards the young lady in question. Use some of that devilish charm to see if you can wheedle any more details out of her.'

With no better plan, Hal would do exactly that.

Fate, or rather Lizzie, denied him the opportunity. When she and her father failed to materialise, he went off to look for her, only to be informed by Lady Danbury's butler that the Earl of Upminster's carriage had left well over an hour before. Standing alone and confused at the bottom of the very staircase he had last seen

her on, it dawned on him. Lizzie's final words to him
had not been words of pity or thanks at all.

They had been a goodbye.

The journey home had been an emotional one. In
view of the Earl of Ockendon's thinly veiled threats and
the sudden reappearance of her treacherous fiancé, her
father waved away her concerns. Ockendon, he assured
her, was all bluster. So what if he knew she had been
jilted? There was no way he knew about little Georgie
when the boy's father had no idea he existed. At best,
all Ockendon could do was enlighten the *ton* to gossip
now so old it was not worth repeating. Besides, he had
argued, he had friends in high places and no newspaper
would dare print the story of how she had been abandoned at the altar. He would sort it all out. She wasn't
to concern herself with it. Lizzie had fervently pressed
him for details about how he had banished her former
fiancé from society and he had patted her hand and said
that, too, did not matter. His troubled eyes gave him
away even as he denied it. As always, he was exclud-
ing her from decisions which would directly affect her
in the name of protecting her!

He was delaying the inevitable. Being jilted was not
the worst of what had happened. She had been very
thoroughly, and quite compliantly, ravished by Rainham. One day the truth was bound to leak out. And
aside from the fact her pristine reputation would be
left in tatters, her father's good name dragged through
the mud in the process, her little boy was growing up
fast, and it was not fair on him to keep him cooped up
in the Grosvenor Square house for ever. If anything,

Lord Ockendon's behaviour highlighted how tenuous her situation had become.

'If you had chosen a husband, Lizzie, if you were now married as I have always wanted, then Ockendon would not be able to use the past to threaten you.'

'If you had not insisted we maintain appearances and forced me back into society, then he would have forgotten me. I have said for some time now that I should set up a household of my own and disappear from society for ever.'

'And how would you find a husband then?'

She wanted to scream, instead everything came tumbling out in an angry, frustrated rant. It was not the best way to inform him of her plans to leave in the New Year. Her papa's temper had exploded when she confessed she had already purchased a house with her own money behind his back.

'I will not allow it, Lizzie!'

'You cannot stop me. My mind is made up. I have to think of my son and his best interests. It is not fair to continue to curtail his movements in the way we do. Soon he will grow to resent his lack of freedom and will feel like a prisoner. Is that how you want him to grow up? It is certainly not the life I want for him.'

'But you will be all alone up there, Daughter. Who will protect you?'

From then on, the discussion had deteriorated in its usual fashion. They were like two angry rams, their horns locked, battling to see which one of them had a thicker skull. He would not listen to reason and accept Lizzie was long past the age when she could look after herself. Had he not faithfully promised her mother, on her death bed, that he would see her married to a good man? In desperation, he had even suggested he would allow her to marry the Earl of Redbridge, if that is what her heart wanted, which in turn led to her confessing the truth about her unlikely alliance with Hal and her frustration with the near-constant parade of dullards and her father had hit the roof. She had not seen him so angry since the day Rainham had abandoned her in a church full of lilacs and a child in her belly.

The final hour in the carriage had been spent in stony silence. Neither spoke. What else was there to say? She had done things her dear papa's way for five long years, and now, despite all the hiding, all the keeping up of appearances and his fervent quest to see her wed, what did she have to show for it? A spiteful old earl trying to blackmail her into marriage and another broken heart! What a roaring success. If the honest truth had succeeded in anything, it had succeeded in making relations between father and daughter worse than they had ever been.

Several hours later, and by tacit agreement, they were still avoiding each other. Her papa was holed up in his study, no doubt plotting how best to salvage the situation whilst still keeping his daughter in the dark, and Lizzie was sat with her son in the morning room, trying not to let him see her turbulent mood. Intense fear mixed with anger, frustration, and the unexpected sadness at having to sever her relationship with Hal. Despondent and completely broken and so very tired. Even her bones ached. Georgie was spread-eagled on the carpet, thoroughly engrossed in drawing a picture, and showed no sign of having noticed.

'What are you drawing?'

He paused, then turned to her, grinning. 'I am making you a present. Nanny said I should give you a gift for Christmas and I know how much you love my pictures. This one is going to be extra special. It is a picture of us.'

Love filled her heart. Gave her the strength she needed to do what was necessary when the time came. 'You are exactly right. I will adore it. How did you know I wanted a picture of us for Christmas?'

'Grandpapa told me. He said that I was the most important thing in the world to you, therefore you would much prefer a picture of me than the stag beetle I drew for you last week. You can have that one for your birthday instead.'

The guilt was instant and painful. Doing what was necessary did not make the doing of it any easier. 'Grandpapa is a very wise man.' Tears prickled her eyes at the thought of separating him from his grandson. The two most important men in her life were devoted to one another. They had been since the day Georgie came squalling into the world. From the first moment he had held her baby, her papa had loved him unconditionally and without judgement—just as he had always loved his daughter. The circumstances of Georgie's birth had been irrelevant. If only there was another way to keep them both safe without having to separate them.

Georgie's little tongue poked out as he returned to concentrate on his masterpiece, his chubby fingers clutching the coloured chalk too tightly, and she took a moment to watch him work whilst reminding herself she *was* doing the right thing. Society was unforgiving of babes born on the wrong side of the blanket. Had she been a man, a titled man, then things might have been different. The Regent acknowledged his bastards and they were tolerated by the *ton*. Many of the children born to the mistresses of powerful men lived openly within their ranks. People turned a blind eye. The circumstance of their birth was frowned upon, but only to an extent. Such toleration only extended so far. Men were expected to sow their wild oats. Young ladies were certainly not. Lizzie would be branded a fallen woman and cast out of their ranks without a backward glance, her innocent little boy destined for a life tainted by her shame. Her father disgraced...

The quiet appearance of the butler brought her back down to earth with a start.

'Sorry to disturb you, my lady, but the Earl of Redbridge is outside. He refuses to believe you are not at home and is currently sitting on the front step. He claims he will remain there until you grant him an audience.'

At the mere mention of his name, her heart began to yearn. She still could not believe he had offered to marry her in an attempt to save her. How sweet. How endearing. How utterly selfless and romantic. In that moment, she had realised he was nothing like the rake she had once planned to marry. Hal was noble. Too noble for his own good. One day, he would make some lucky woman a wonderful husband, but it couldn't be her. When she had turned him down he had appeared genuinely wounded rather than relieved. She had hurt his feelings and that saddened her. At the time, she had wanted to tell him the truth. He deserved to know why she had said no, yet a part of her hadn't wanted to see if his nobleness would extend that far. Would he miraculously see past her youthful indiscretions? The realist in her knew she was clutching at straws and certainly not being fair to him.

In truth, once he learned of Georgie she knew he would bitterly regret proposing in the first place, then she would have had to suffer seeing him distance himself from her. Who could blame him? He was a handsome, rich and charming earl who could have anyone. Why would he settle for some other man's second-hand, soiled goods or take on the unwelcome responsibility of a scoundrel's by-blow? Severing their acquaintance was the sensible and kindest thing to do. It protected him, at least, from the scandal which was about to erupt. Her attempt at being equally as noble.

Knowing he was but a few feet away was torture, but her mind was made up. Now that her father knew about their alliance, her too-brief relationship with the handsome, charming, all-too-lovable and heartbreakingly noble Earl had reached its natural conclusion.

'Could you give him this, Stevens?' Lizzie had written the letter as soon as she had arrived home in the small hours when sleep had evaded her. It was a cheerful missive, purposely so, because she wanted him to remember her fondly and did not want him to continue to worry about her. She thanked him for acting as her deterrent, expressed her regret that she was unable to fulfil their bargain for the entire month, but had decided to leave town for her father's estate imminently to spend the rest of Christmas and New Year with her brother. She wasn't sure when she would be coming back. She also made light of her dealings with the Earl of Ockendon and of Hal's generous offer of marriage as a consequence, reminding him that they had made a bargain to keep him *from* the parson's trap—not to snare him in it. Oh, the irony! How amusing...

She did not see any point in warning him that she might well about to be in the centre of a scandal of significant proportions. Whatever his reputation, he was her friend and did not deserve to be caught in the crossfire. Some distance now would allow him to escape largely unscathed if the truth could be kept until New Year's. Enough lives would be damaged as it was without having Hal's on her conscience as well. It did not matter that tears had been dripping down her cheeks as she had written it, or that her heart ached to know she had seen him for the very last time or that a part of her would bitterly regret not knowing him sooner, or Heaven help her, meeting him before she had met Rainham. She did not see any need to tell him she was fond of him. Very fond of him. Perhaps more than fond. There was no point.

'And if he refuses to leave?'

'Tell him I am not at home, Stevens.' Allowing Henry Stuart to get close to her in the first place had been a mistake. Allowing anyone to get too close to her was foolhardy in the extreme. She had lived by that edict for five long years—until him. Already he knew more about her than anyone outside of her family. Perhaps more. Hal seemed to understand her far better than her father. They were kindred spirits on so many levels. She felt it in her heart. There had been an honesty between them which had mattered a great deal. Growing affection. Undeniable attraction. 'Tell him...' Her voice caught with regret for all that could not be. 'Tell him I will never be at home to him again, Stevens—but I wish him all the best with the hordes.'

'The hordes?'

'He will know what I mean, Stevens.' Hopefully he would understand. Lizzie wasn't entirely sure she understood anything any more. Not when everything in her life had been tossed up into the air and had thus far failed to land. A few weeks ago, she would never have believed it if someone had told her she would have feelings for a man again, romantic and affectionate feelings, especially for a self-confessed and charming rake. Yet here she was, more than a little bit in love with the one currently sat on her doorstep.

The butler regarded her with sympathy. 'As you wish, my lady.'

A few minutes later he returned. 'He has gone, my lady.'

Of course he had. Lizzie should have felt relief. Instead, waves of pain and disappointment washed over her, when she had not thought she could feel any worse. 'Did he leave me any message?' A little something she could cling to in the dark days ahead.

'He did not, my lady. Should he have?'

Yes! Yes, he should have. Underneath the brave face she was struggling to maintain, a tiny part of her had hoped he would fight for whatever it was they had, even if it was doomed to be futile. Lizzie selfishly needed to know he would mourn the end of their association as keenly. That he felt the same pull. The same need. The same heady connection. She shook her head and gazed down at her son again. She had no right to be selfish and expect more from Hal than he had already given freely. 'No, Stevens. I was not expecting him to reply to my message.'

'I could fetch him if you wanted. His house is a short walk from here.'

Another reason why it was prudent to leave Mayfair as soon as possible, not that she needed another one. Being so close to him would drive her mad with longing. 'There is no need. That will be all, Stevens.' The little man sat contentedly at her feet, diligently colouring his mother's hair purple, was the only man she could ever permit to matter henceforth.

Chapter Fourteen

Hal had never been much good at loitering. His huge build and short attention span had made hanging about and waiting for things to happen anathema to him. However, in view of the unusual circumstances, and his current foul mood, needs dictated he must. To that end, he had been loitering in Grosvenor Square for the better part of two hours waiting for all the lights to go out in the Earl of Upminster's Mayfair fortress. Technically, he wasn't actually in the Square. An hour ago, when the stable lad on guard had briefly disappeared to answer the call of nature, Hal had sneaked around the back of the garden and scaled the ridiculously high walls. He was currently lurking amidst the shrubbery closest to the house. A rose bed, he assumed, judging by the amount of nicks he now had in his breeches. Thank heavens he had the good sense to wear his sturdiest boots and a robust pair of leather gloves. A solid suit of armour might have been more appropriate.

His hour in the cold, frigid December air had not been completely wasted because he had caught several glimpses of Lizzie—at least the silhouette was shaped like Lizzie—and was fairly certain he knew which of the many bedchambers was hers. Unfortunately, her window was firmly closed. Shouting up in anything above a whisper would likely alert the servants to the presence of an intruder and Hal did not fancy his chances up against the Wildings' giant butler. There was a solid-looking ancient wisteria climbing up the back of the house and, as he was determined to get to the bottom of whatever nonsense was going on and she had refused to see him, Hal had little choice other than to climb it.

Frankly, if it gave her a fright it would damn well serve the wench right, because he had been in a perpetual state of worry since she had bolted out of Lady Danbury's French doors. And he had proposed. Having never had cause to propose before, the occasion was momentous and the more he recalled her horrified reaction at his offer, the more upset and offended he became. He had wanted to help her. Begged her to let him help her and she had cut him out as if he did not matter at all. That stung. Thanks to her heartfelt and ground-shaking kiss closely followed by her swift and silent exit from the house party, Hal had suffered several hours being stalked by a very determined Lady Arabella, then a sleepless night worrying.

Some time in the small hours his temper kicked in and he decided enough was enough. He had been an attentive fake suitor, suffered through a painful dinner with Lord Hewitt and rescued her from the Earl of Ockendon twice. Then sent the man packing with her toad of a former fiancé so that she was spared the sight of them for the rest of the weekend! And he'd proposed, something which still caused his head to spin, because he suspected he had meant it. He deserved the truth. Not a letter! To that end he had ridden for hours across the countryside, alone, and had damn well nearly frozen to death in the process. How dare she send him a letter after all that? Especially one which told him next to nothing.

Fuelled with righteous indignation, he began to heave himself up the knotted branches. The blasted woman was going to talk to him, and if it took him all night, he was not damn well leaving without some proper answers. Why was she terrified of Ockendon? What secret did the man know about her and why had he dragged her wastrel of a fiancé into it? More importantly, why wouldn't she see him? They were supposed to be friends, looking out for one another, contractually obliged to be a deterrent until the Christmas season was over. The last time Hal checked, that was Twelfth Night.

Twelfth Night! And they were still only a few days from Christmas Eve. She owed him another fortnight. Another fortnight and some jolly good reasons why she had curtly refused his proposal without giving the matter some serious and proper thought. It was not as if he was a rancid, money-grabbing specimen like Ockendon. Hal had all his own teeth, was financially secure and was widely regarded as a catch amongst the sea of hordes who were stalking him incessantly. Lady Arabella would not have said no! No, indeed, she would have jumped at the chance. The sorry-looking sprig of mistletoe sat limply in his pocket would have been missing all five of its berries well before now, if the wager had been about Arabella, and certainly not still sporting one. Perhaps that was the answer. He and Lizzie seemed to lose their heads whenever their lips touched, so perhaps he should simply kiss her into submission and be done with it.

His frozen fingers finally gripped the deep, stone window ledge and he pulled his face level with the glass. Heavy curtains prevented him from seeing anything other than the reflected blackness of the midnight sky, and even though there was the distinct possibility he was dangling outside the wrong window, he was not going to give the minx beyond the opportunity of raising the alarm and having him forcibly removed from the trellis before he had said his piece. Surprise was the only immediate weapon in his poorly stocked arsenal. The only others were dashing good looks and bucketloads of charm, neither of which apparently held any appeal whatsoever to the confusing vixen who had kept him awake for the better part of two days.

Silently, he tested the frame. It was a sash window and to his utter delight was blessedly unlocked. Somebody was on his side. Somebody or something. Out of respect for the miracle he glanced heavenwards and quietly thanked the Almighty for giving him the means to break in, then pulled the window upwards and threw himself blindly through the aperture.

He landed on the floor with a thud and untangled himself from the curtains. 'Now listen here, Lizzie...' The room was empty. It was undoubtedly a feminine room. An abundance of lace and delicate furniture gave that away. There was a single candle burning on the nightstand, the bed was turned down in readiness and her perfume wafted in the air. Wherever Lizzie was, it wasn't far away. It was also just as well she had not been there to witness his arrival—aside from the fact it had hardly been graceful, she probably would have

screamed the place down and woken the whole house.
This way was much better. It gave him time to collect
himself.

Feeling a touch self-righteous, Hal stripped off his
gloves and greatcoat and tossed them on to a ridiculously spindly-looking chair. He did not dare sit on it.
The legs were so thin his immense bulk would likely
shatter it into matchsticks. As there were no other chairs
in the bedchamber, he eased his big body down on to
the mattress to wait. Ten minutes later and still no sign
of her, Hal plumped up a pile of pillows to rest against
and made himself comfortable.

The object of his frustration eventually came in,
clutching a book and wearing a gossamer nightgown
which made his throat constrict with sudden lust before
she shrieked a little too loudly for comfort and lunged
at him, brandishing the book like a club.

'Shh! It's just me... Hal.' He placed one finger to his
lips and held his other hand up in surrender. She skidded to a halt inches away, looking delightfully confused,
the book still raised like a shield.

'Hal?' Shock quickly turned to anger. 'Hal! What
are you doing here?'

'Try to whisper, Lizzie darling. I would rather we
did not alert the household to my presence.'

Her eyes turned swiftly to the door before fixing on
him. The candlelight made them appear darker, like the
sky before a thunderstorm. Judging from the thunder-
ous expression hovering around the edges of her confusion, it was an apt description. 'How did you get in?'

'Seeing as your henchman Stevens refused me entry
earlier—repeatedly, I might add—I had to resort to
covert methods to gain entry.' Feeling pretty pleased

with himself for circumventing the many layers of se-
curity and certain he could soften her tense mood with
his charm, he shot her his best naughty grin and settled back against the pillows smugly. 'I scrambled up
the wisteria.'

She became instantly furious. All signs of delightful
bewilderment vanished and she glowered down at him
with her hands fisted at her sides. 'How dare you! How
dare you sneak into my house. My bedchamber! And
what the hell do you think you are doing on my bed?'

'So much for whispering.' At this volume, it was
only a matter of seconds before the alarm was raised
and Stevens would eject him bodily. 'Could you try to
lower your voice an octave or two? Take a couple of
deep breaths...try to remain calm.'

'Calm!' Her finger prodded sharply into his breast-
bone. 'You expect me to remain calm when you have
broken into my house?'

'I needed to talk you.'

'I wrote you a letter!'

'Which said next to nothing!'

'So you thought the best course of action was bur-
glary?'

The accusation made him smile. 'Er... I think you
will find that a burglar enters a property with the intention of removing items from it.' He held his palms up for
effect. 'Not guilty, your honour. Now please sit down...'

'Get out.' The finger jabbed again, repeatedly, firing
his temper again. He was the one trying to be reasonable, yet she appeared oblivious to the fact her recent
behaviour had been anything but.

'Not until I get what I came here for.'

She recoiled then, seemed to remember she was

dressed in only her nightgown and snatched the eider-
down to wrap around her like a shield. 'How dare you!'
Her jabbing finger flapped ineffectually near his face.
'You are a scoundrel, Henry Stuart. How dare you as-
sume that I would climb into bed with you just because
I allowed you to kiss me?'

'Oh, for goodness sake!' He stood up then and took
some enjoyment in looming over her. She took a pan-
icked step backwards and he closed the distance, then
watched her eyes widen with indignation.

'Keep your hands to yourself, sir!'

Furiously, he waved both of them in front of her face.
'You have got completely the wrong end of the stick
and, frankly, I am insulted. I have *never* had to force
myself on a woman and I resent the accusation. What
the blazes has got into you? I came here to *talk* to you.
To get some answers. To hear the damn truth rather
than the pack of lies you have fed me!'

'You were on my bed!'

This was really not turning out as he had intended,
although he supposed reclining on her bed with his feet
crossed and his elbows thrown above his head might be
construed as a seductive position, and he supposed he
had just scared the living daylights out of the girl. 'In
case it has escaped your notice, I am still wearing my
boots and everything else for that matter. And need I
remind you that it was *you* who kissed *me*!' She had the
good grace to look guilty, but still clutched the eiderdown about her as if he were some pillaging Viking intent on ravishing her. Hal sighed and plopped his bottom
back down on the edge of the bed. 'I was merely waiting for you. Just to talk. That doll's house chair at your
dressing table didn't look like it could hold my weight.'

Her eyes flicked to the chair, then back to him before he watched her shoulders drop and her combative stance disappear. 'You still should not have come here. Not like this.'

'Did you give me any other choice?' Hal stared directly into her lovely blue eyes and she dipped her head. It was all the acknowledgment he needed. 'I called several times today. You knew that. You had your henchman give me this letter.' He tossed the missive on to the mattress and sighed. He wanted her guard down, not up. 'When it became apparent you had no intention of honouring me with a proper explanation for your odd behaviour, and because I have genuinely been frantic with worry, I had to resort to sneaking in. And I would like it noted that sneaking in was no mean feat. Thanks to you and your uncharitable butler I had to stand in the cold for hours waiting for the opportune moment.'

'A gentleman doesn't climb up a lady's wisteria uninvited.'

'A lady doesn't send a letter to a gentleman terminating their acquaintance, especially if the said gentleman has selflessly proposed to the lady hours before and then ridden across two counties in the small hours to check she was well. What the blazes is going on, Lizzie? I think I deserve to know.'

'Please don't make this any more difficult than it already is, Hal. I had reasons…good reasons for leaving Lady Danbury's.' Once again she could not hold his gaze.

'Which are?'

'Things I would prefer to keep to myself.' Her arms came around to hug herself, an unconscious action which spoke volumes. Hall reached out and tugged at the eiderdown, forcing her to sit beside him.

'You might as well know I am not leaving until you tell me. You'll have to get that menacing butler of yours to tear me limb from limb first.' He could sense her indecision, so wrapped his arm around her shoulders and whispered into her hair, 'I am your friend, Lizzie. Whatever is going on, I want to help.'

She was still for a long time and he gave her the space to decide what her next move would be. When she eventually spoke, it was in a small voice. He heard the defeat and the fear. The deep well of sadness. 'You cannot help me, Hal. I fear Lord Ockendon has learned something which will explode into a huge scandal if he shares it with the world.'

'Take it from someone who had been embroiled in many a scandal, they all blow over eventually and I doubt yours is anywhere near as bad as you think it is. I bet you have never dashed across Hyde Park flashing your nakedness to all and sundry.' He had wanted to make her smile, but the attempt fell flat.

'Oh, it's bad, Hal. So bad that it is enough to blackmail both me *and* my father with if Ockendon is of a mind to, which I am in no doubt he is. What I need to decide is whether I want to unleash the scandal, knowing full well it will ruin a great many lives, or whether I can bring myself to agree to the Earl's demands.'

Now she was making him very worried. 'Surely you cannot seriously be contemplating marrying *him*?' Something which beggared belief when she had readily turned down Hal's proposal.

'I hope it will not come to that. Lord Ockendon is

yet to bare his hand so I am hoping there is a way out of the mess.'

'There is. Marry *me*.' This proposal did not make him feel as nauseous as the first had. A worrying turn of events in itself, although like the first time, his heart told him it was right. His hand came up to touch her cheek and he traced the pad of his thumb over her lips. 'I think there is more than friendship between us, Lizzie. Don't you?' Of its own volition, his face moved towards hers. Her chin tilted up and her eyes travelled to his lips. She felt the pull of attraction, too. Her body had instinctively turned to press against his. 'We will weather the scandal together.' The tips of their noses touched. It was a strangely intimate and compelling moment which he did not feel the urge to rush. Their mouths were a whisper apart. He could feel the steady, rapid beat of her heart against his own pounding one. Their shallow breathing in perfect tandem. The warm and comforting sense of rightness. She pulled away before he could kiss her.

'I can't marry you, Hal.'

'But you can marry *him*? A man you hate and who terrifies you?'

'I won't marry him either. I shall disappear. It is not as if I am unused to hiding.'

'Hiding?' Lizzie was talking in riddles. Hal still had no idea what sort of a mess she was involved in and was downright angry at the rejection of yet another proposal without any sound reasons as to why. The woman was infuriating. He took a deep breath to prevent himself from shouting. He reached for her again, a little desperately. 'Just tell me what the blazes is...' The bedcham-

ber door opened and the angry, frustrated outburst died
in his throat.

'Mama... I had a bad dream.'

A dark-haired little boy came in, rubbing his eyes
with one chubby hand and clutching a tatty stuffed toy.
Lost for words, Hal watched Lizzie stand, the heavy eiderdown she had wrapped around her falling to the floor
as she scurried to the child. Bent down. Lifted him into
her arms. 'My poor darling.' She ruffled his hair and
kissed the top of his head. 'It was only a dream, Georgie. It cannot harm you.' Her eyes sought Hal's with
what looked like regret.

'Mama?' The word came out strangled. Incredulous.
Hal scrambled to assimilate this new and totally unexpected information.

She turned towards him proudly then, clutching the
child to her protectively. 'Yes. Mama.'

'Who is he?' The boy stared at Hal, clearly only just
registering his presence.

'A friend.' She watched him defiantly. 'He is leaving. He won't be coming back.'

'I don't understand...' Although he was beginning
to, good grief he was beginning to, and she watched his
face dispassionately as all manner of emotions skidded
haphazardly across it unchecked. Shock. Disbelief. Disappointment.

Horror.

Her cornflower eyes hardened at that. 'I am sure
you can let yourself out in much the same manner you
let yourself in.' A brittle tone, like jagged glass. 'I am
going to sleep with *my son* in the nursery. We are leaving in the morning. Goodbye, Hal.'

In a billowing cloud of linen, she turned and went.

For the first time in their short acquaintance, Hal felt no desire to go after her.

Chapter Fifteen

The snow started some time in the middle of the night. She knew this as she had watched every second of the interminable darkness tick by, worrying. About hers and Georgie's future, Ockendon's threats and the potential damage to her father's reputation and career from the impending scandal. As awful as those things were to consider, they were less painful than recalling the expression on Hal's handsome face when he had realised she had a child. All her procrastinating and avoidance in appraising him of the truth had, she realised, been as much about protecting herself from his inevitable reaction as it had been about protecting her family. She could have confided in him sooner, from the outset, in fact, and in all probability he would have still helped her and kept her secret. He was that noble beneath all the swagger. But a part of her had enjoyed the frisson of attraction between them. It had made her feel young, unburdened and gloriously alive again, even though she had known it was not something which she could ever consider acting upon. Until she *had* acted upon it and now wished she hadn't. Being held by him, feeling his passion and losing herself in his kiss had made her yearn again for all the things she could not have as a mother of another man's baby. A wastrel's son.

Watching him recoil the second after he had proposed again had cut like a knife. Lizzie had been so hideously disappointed in him then, even though she had no right to expect otherwise. Hideously disappointed in him and ashamed of herself. The guilt at feeling shame for the innocent child in her arms galvanised her. Georgie was her everything and she was tired of fearing the judgement of others. Her final words to Hal had been curt and proud. How dare he judge her by a different set of standards to those in which he had lived his own life? Hal had likely lain with more women than he could remember. She had only been with one man and had paid the ultimate price. So she had called him on it when her son had asked, inwardly daring him to contradict her.

He won't be coming back.

Hal had not denied the assertion. He had left swiftly afterwards. She knew because she had been compelled to check, just in case some miracle had occurred and he had dithered. They had shared a poignant and special moment before Georgie had burst through the door, so she hoped perhaps he would linger. What for or what she wanted beyond that was not something she allowed herself to consider. But her bedchamber was chilly and empty, much like her bruised and battered heart, so she supposed she had an answer even though it turned out not to be the one she wanted.

By the time Lizzie dragged herself exhausted into the breakfast room a little past dawn, there was a foot of fresh snow covering the ground and, by the looks of the pewter sky, it was in no mood to stop any time soon. The head coachman had already sent word he believed the three-day journey to Cheshire was foolhardy in the extreme until the weather cleared and she had to bow to his judgement. The larger roads would be difficult, the smaller ones and the narrow lanes which ran through the Peaks in the north would be too dangerous. Even the elements were conspiring against her.

To his credit, her papa did not gloat at the news she was staying, albeit temporarily. He simply nodded and patted her hand. 'I will sort all of this out, Lizzie. I promise you.' Then he had bundled himself into a heavy coat and trudged out of the front door. She had no idea where he was going and there was no point in asking him. If he was hellbent on protecting her and Georgie, he was notoriously tight-lipped about how he intended to go about it and would tell her no more than he thought she should know. For five years, he had done much the same and would continue in the same vein unless she put a stop to it all once and for all. But she had seen the tight lines of worry which pulled at his face, the heavy, burdened gait and wished he would include her in his ongoing attempts at protecting her. Being kept in the dark was soul destroying.

Sat in the drawing room impotently staring at the walls, Lizzie decided to tackle the problem head on. She went to her mother's old escritoire and put pen to paper. Her note to the Earl of Ockendon was short and to the point. She was tired of his pointed comments and veiled threats and demanded he explain himself, asking him to meet her in St James's Park this very afternoon or, failing that, to leave her alone.

As much as she dreaded the meeting, it was necessary. The young footman she sent with the note came back directly with the reply. It was shorter than Lizzie's, missive and menacing.

> *I am glad you have come to your senses. Two o'clock. Come alone.*

In five hours she would know her fate. Until then, she would force herself to enjoy a blissful couple of hours with her son. Perhaps the last blissful hours they would be able to spend in quite some time.

Stevens appeared out of nowhere and coughed politely. 'There is a caller at the door, Lady Elizabeth. The Earl of Redbridge.'

The pang of longing and pain caught her unexpectedly and she winced. 'Tell him I am not at home, Stevens. We have been through this.'

The butler frowned, clearly uncomfortable. 'He is not here to see you, Lady Elizabeth. Or your father. He says he has come to visit Master George.' He whispered this as Georgie was in earshot, drawing another insect on the floor near her feet contentedly. 'Under the circumstances, I ushered him inside. Just in case any passers-by overheard.'

Lizzie fought to keep her nerves under control. She hadn't expected to hear from Hal again and could not imagine why he had called asking to see her son. 'Where is he now, Stevens?'

'I put him in the green drawing room, Lady Elizabeth.'

'And I decided not to stay in it.' Hal's dark head popped around the doorframe and he eyed the now outraged butler warily. 'Please don't kill me, Stevens. I am not worth going to gaol over.'

Stevens looked to Lizzie for guidance and would, no doubt, cheerfully pummel Hal into a soggy mess at her instruction. He had been recruited specifically to protect her and her little boy, and took the responsibility seriously. Too seriously if his expression was to be believed. 'You can leave us, Stevens. I shall call if I need you.'

Hal edged into the room as her bodyguard glared at him murderously. 'I will be just outside the door. *Just* outside the door.'

'Message received and understood, Stevens. Whilst you are out there, I don't suppose you could rustle up some tea?' Hal grinned cheekily and she quite admired his bravado. 'Only it's dashed cold outside and I could do with something to warm me up.'

Stevens grunted and stalked out, slamming the door behind him in an obvious display of superior masculine strength. 'I don't think your butler likes me. It's most upsetting when one considers all of the cheerful little chats we have had every time I've come to call and he's merrily sent me packing.'

She would not be charmed by him, although the charm did not completely cover his discomfort. There was an awkwardness about him she had never seen before. An air of trepidation. 'Why are you here, Hal?'

His gaze travelled to Georgie, who had stopped colouring to stare back at him. She had no idea what her son was thinking. He had never been in the company of anyone other than the immediate family or the highly paid and fiercely loyal servants in their employ. This was the second time he had seen Hal in a few hours and the first had been in her bedchamber last night. Something which had hardly been appropriate, yet he had been too tired and too distressed from his bad dream at the time to question her flimsy explanation.

'I came to introduce myself to your little boy. I thought it only right and proper after...' He looked away then, clearly embarrassed. Those splendid broad shoulders of his rose, then fell on a ragged sigh. 'I realised he must be curious. Little boys are curious about most things. I certainly was. And last night was a little out of the ordinary. For all of us.'

At a loss at what to say, and more than a little overwhelmed at both his thoughtfulness and his presence, Lizzie shrugged and watched transfixed as Hal crouched down on the carpet a few feet away from her son. 'Good day to you, Master George. My name is Hal. I am a very good friend of your mother's and am very pleased to make your acquaintance.' He stuck out his big hand and gently shook Georgie's little one. A bit bewildered but accepting of the extraordinary, as children are prone to be, Georgie cheerfully gripped the strange man's palm and smiled up at him. The sight made her throat clog with emotion. Under a different set of circumstances...

No! She could not think like that. It served no purpose.

'I see you are an artist, Master George. What is that you are drawing?' As if he conversed with children every day, Hal lowered himself on to the carpet and mirrored her son's cross-legged pose.

'It is a common wood louse, sir. Did you know they have fourteen legs?' Her little boy was always delighted to have a conversation about insects.

'Fourteen! Good gracious, that is a lot of pairs of boots to polish.'

Georgie peered at him sceptically until he saw Hal smiling and realised one of his two legs was being pulled. He grinned back. 'Do you like insects, sir?'

'What's with all this sir business? My name is Hal, not sir.' He ruffled her son's hair and her heart clenched. 'And, yes—I do like insects. I am a huge fan of all creepy-crawlies. I find they are the most perfect things to scare girls with. My sister hates them and it is enormous fun to watch her run around the room screaming at the sight of something with a profusion of hairy legs. I have never hidden any woodlice in her small things—though now that I know they have fourteen spindly legs apiece I shall do so at the first opportunity.'

Always keen to help, Georgie frowned. 'I don't think you will be able to gather any till spring. Woodlice tend to hide away in winter. It's too cold for them. But once the weather gets warmer I shall help you find some. They live under stones and things. We have a big urn in the garden and when Grandpapa lifts it up for me there are hundreds of woodlice there.'

'Well, that is just grand. My sister will have an apoplexy.' Hal leaned closer and dropped his voice to a conspiratorial whisper. 'Perhaps we can hide some and scare your mother, too.'

Georgie giggled, already charmed, and playfully nudged Hal as if they had known each other for ever. 'It wouldn't work. Mama is not scared of bugs.'

'Your mama is a very brave woman indeed.' His eyes drifted up to rest on hers intensely. They were troubled. Apologetic. Lizzie had no idea what that meant and helplessly stared back. Just as it had the night before, the atmosphere became charged; the air heavy with things unsaid and emotions not acknowledged.

'Your tea!' Stevens practically kicked the door open, snapping Lizzie out of the spell, and slammed a laden tray down on the table. He shot Hal a menacing look and curled one meaty paw into a fist. 'I will be *just* outside the door!' He stomped out, leaving the door ajar this time.

'Stevens means well.'

'You do not need to explain. I might not be the most scholastic of fellows, but I think I have the gist of what is going on.' Hal offered her a half-smile. 'We need to talk, I think. When we are alone.'

She nodded, grateful that he understood what needed to be said was not for little boys' ears. Hal turned back to her son and picked up some coloured chalk and began to help Georgie colour in his woodlouse. For some inexplicable reason, her little boy wanted it all colours of the rainbow, something Hal apparently understood. Lizzie poured tea and watched them. When the masterpiece was finished, Hal joined her on the sofa and drank the cup she had poured him, maintaining a cheerful stream of childish conversation with Georgie all the while.

'Can you draw me a ladybird, Mama?'

A piece of paper and some chalk was thrust into her hand and she felt self-conscious as she sketched out the outline of the bug. This was the first time anyone outside of the household had ever witnessed her be a mother and it was disconcerting, especially as he was watching her closely. She wished she knew what Hal was thinking. What did he see? Did he see a fallen woman? A victim? A doting parent? She sincerely doubted he saw her as an attractive young woman who roused his passions any more...or a potential wife.

'I see your mama is an artist, too, Georgie.' The familiar pet name tripped off his tongue unconsciously, but then again, Hal had also casually pulled her son to sit on his lap. He appeared extremely comfortable there.

'Mama always draws the best insects. She says it is one of her greatest talents.'

'Can she build snowmen?'

'She tries, but they always end up a bit lopsided. We are going outside to build one soon.'

'Soon? When all the snow in the garden is fresh and calling to us? I think we should all go and build one now. If I do say so myself, I build excellent snowmen. It is one of *my* greatest talents. And he will be as straight as a die. Fetch your coat, Georgie boy! And gloves.'

Hal had said the magic words as far as her son was concerned. He wiggled off his lap and dashed out of the room, squealing with excitement, leaving them both alone. Lizzie was suddenly awkward, dreading the inevitable. To hide it she continued to sketch the ladybird.

'He is Rainham's?'

She nodded.

'He jilted you because you were with child?' Hal could not disguise the anger in his tone. Outrage on her behalf. Always so noble.

'No. He does not know Georgie exists—or I hope he doesn't. He jilted me before I had a chance to tell him and afterwards I never wanted him to know I was expecting his child.'

'But Ockendon knows?'

'I don't know. He has alluded to it. My *deep, dark secret* which I keep *hidden*. That's a little too coincidental, don't you think?' His silence was deafening. 'Thanks to my father's ridiculous hope that he could still find a man who would deign to marry me and the amount of money he has thrown into my dowry to practically purchase one—not that he sees that, of course—I believe Lord Ockendon intends to use the information as collateral to force me to accept his proposal.'

'Call his bluff. Your father is a powerful man.'

How to tell him what she suspected, but didn't know? 'I fear my father would be ruined by the scandal, too, else I would not think twice, but...' Lizzie stood to give her jumpy nerves something to do and began to pace. 'He had Rainham removed from society. I do not know how and for years I did not care, I was simply grateful I never had to clap eyes on the man.'

'But you suspect your father is guilty of some sort of foul play.'

'Yes. More collateral. Don't you remember what he said at the Danburys'? It is in your *family's* best interests to talk to me. Not mine. My family's. And he dragged Rainham with him to make sure I understood.' Now she thought upon it, her former fiancé had been uncomfortable. Frightened, even. He had looked ready to flee when Hal had threatened him, genuine fear on his dissolute face. If only she knew what her dear papa had done, this would all be so much simpler. 'My father is a good man, Hal. He would have done whatever was necessary to protect his family.'

Further conversation was prevented by the reappearance of Georgie, who had been swaddled in layers of warm clothes and began bouncing on the spot as she and Hal donned their own. Once outside, Lizzie toyed with the idea of telling Hal she was meeting Ockendon this afternoon, certain he would know how to best play the situation without giving too much away. However, deep down she knew he would never allow her to talk to the Earl alone and would insist on accompanying her. Ockendon would hardly bare his cards with a witness present. Instead she kept tight-lipped and tried to enjoy playing in the snow, watching her son laughing with Hal. Watching Hal patiently teach him how to build a proper snowman, then lift him giggling to push in the carrot nose and coal eyes before sacrificing his own hat and placing it at a jaunty angle on their creation's head. It was such a pretty picture. Hal had a natural way with children and would doubtless make an excellent father one day.

To his own children.

Born in wedlock.

Because he was an earl and such things were expected and she was a fallen woman on the cusp of complete ruination.

Chapter Sixteen

Hal left the Wilding house on a mission. It made no difference that he had not enjoyed a wink of sleep in three days, or that his body was drooping with fatigue. His mind was racing. It had been racing around in circles since the moment that little boy had burst into his mother's bedchamber.

At that moment, not only the rug but the entire floor had been pulled from under Hal's feet. She had a child. A child! One that nobody knew about. Something which was as unforeseen as it was scandalous. In that awful moment Hal had been instantly grateful she had turned down his proposal. Hell, the urge to run had been instinctive. He had no memory of climbing down the wisteria or of racing across the garden. His wits returned as the first flakes of snow melted against his face and he found himself stood in the middle of the Earl of Upminster's lawn, his breath sawing in and out and the pain in his heart so acute he was clutching at his ribs.

Anger, disbelief, disappointment, and shame at his own cowardly, yet perfectly understandable, disgust were like physical blows to his body. He stumbled to a stone bench and sucked in several lungsful of the frigid midnight air and began to count his lucky stars at his narrow escape. Except…

After a few minutes, he did not feel particularly lucky or proud of his reaction. Images of the moment flashed through his mind. Her lovely face. The defiance. The way she had protectively hugged her son.

Rainham's son.

The by-blow of a wastrel and a scoundrel.

A huge scandal.

He had watched her spine stiffen and her body turn instinctively to shield her child from whatever poisoned darts were about to be thrown, yet she had made no excuses or apologies for the truth.

The little boy's frightened eyes.

He knew what it felt like to be a frightened little boy. Knew, too, what it felt like to be the son of a bad and selfish man. Hardly a little boy's fault.

From somewhere, Hal found the strength to move his heavy limbs. Climbed back over the high wall into the mews; dragged himself across Mayfair to home. He drank more than a few glasses of brandy which did nothing to numb the thoughts warring in his head or the confused emotions cluttering his mind. As dawn broke, he realised it all boiled down to three things.

Lizzie was his friend.

She was in trouble.

An innocent little boy was in trouble, too.

Hasty, ill-conceived proposals and unexplainable and irrational feelings aside—as her friend, he was damn well going to help her. Whatever secrets she had kept were hers to keep. Ockendon had no right to use them for his own financial gain no matter how scandalous they might happen to be. Not if Hal could prevent it. They had made a pact to protect one another from the unwanted attentions of would-be spouses and it was one which he intended to honour because…

Because.

Hal was not ready to justify what his heart and soul wanted him to do. To quantify or analyse it any further would likely terrify him and his poor head could not take any more confusion. All he was prepared to acknowledge was that he had a burning desire to protect her. Now that marriage was out of the question, he needed to give some serious thought to how he could best do that.

If his awful father had taught him anything, he had taught him people could be manipulated into bending to your will if the incentive was right.

'The world runs on coin, Henry. Nothing else matters.'

Hal might not subscribe to the principle, but he could not deny the science behind it. His father had built up a huge business empire by using whatever means were at his disposal. To the best of Hal's knowledge, that hadn't included anything illegal, but he had sailed fairly close to the wind. Veiled threats and the right kind of incentive had been his father's stock in trade, whether that be regarding business or his dealings with his own family. As much as Hal loathed behaving in any way like his father, all he needed to do was find just the right incentive to stop Ockendon.

Of course, he could have started on his quest first thing. Probably should have. But something pulled him towards Lizzie. Perhaps it was his conscience. All he knew was he had to see her. Let her know he was on her side. That he was on her innocent little boy's side, too. It was not as if the child had any say in who his father was. So he had called on them and stayed far longer than he should have, while all the time his mind had been racing. Plotting. Trying to untangle the mess. However, to accomplish that he needed to know exactly what Ockendon had over her father.

His own father had a favourite analogy for removing obstacles. In days of yore, when an army besieged a castle, they had two choices. Surround the fortress and starve the occupants out or find the most vulnerable part of the structure and ruthlessly mine under it, then stand back and watch the impregnable stone towers collapse under their own weight. Whilst both techniques had merit, he doubted they had time to wait it out, so Hal needed to find the weakest link. In this case, his gut told him it was Rainham.

As soon as he had bid Georgie a cheery goodbye and squeezed Lizzie's hand in reassurance, Hal trudged through the snow-lined streets towards the Earl of Ockendon's house. He tempered his initial and violent need to tackle the man face to face in favour of reconnaissance. Until he understood the situation fully, Hal would keep his powder dry.

From a distance, he watched a servant wrap the knocker on the front door. Clearly his odiousness was leaving town today—or had already left—as so many did this close to Christmas. He wanted to ask the butler if his master was bound for his country estate, but didn't dare. Even though he had never had reason to call upon the Earl, Hal was too well known and preferred to not enlighten his enemy to his quest. Instead he circumvented the house and headed towards the mews.

The stable was virtually empty, save the still-stalled team of greys and one solitary groom. The fellow looked thoroughly fed up as he forked old straw into a pile, totally oblivious of the fact he was not alone. When he bent to pick up a hand brush Hal spied a significant hole in the sole of the man's boots.

Interesting.

'Good morning, my good fellow!' Hal grinned as the groom's head turned. 'I wonder if you would be inclined to help me.' He idly transferred a few silver coins from one gloved hand to another and then back again in case the lad was not too bright. He needn't have worried. The groom eyed the coins hungrily.

'What sort of help?' Not the response of a man who couldn't be bribed.

'Information. About your lord and master.' Hal watched the man's face unconsciously scowl and pressed his advantage, certain there was no love lost between master and servant. 'I am happy to pay you for your discretion.'

He propped the fork in front of him and rested his wrists on the handle. 'What do you want to know?'

'I am looking for Lord Ockendon's guest. The Marquess of Rainham. Where might I find him?'

The groom waited for Hal to toss him a coin before he answered. 'He ain't got no guest. He brought a gent back with him last night, but they went out late and only his lordship returned. Haven't seen the other fella since—and, before you ask, I have no idea where he went.'

Not what Hal wanted to hear. Rainham could be anywhere, although his gut told him Ockendon would not leave his minion left to his own devices. He was too valuable. Wherever he had gone, he would be staying away from prying eyes. 'Is it possible he has gone to your master's estate?'

The groom shrugged. 'It's possible, I suppose, but as his lordship is travelling there late this afternoon in the carriage, I'd have thought they would have travelled together. A carriage is safer than horseback and the road to Norfolk is popular with footpads and the like.'

A valid point, yet Ockendon could have hired another carriage to hide his guest quickly. 'How long is his lordship expected to stay in Norfolk?'

'One week. Two. Who knows? All I know is there'll be no wages for me again until he returns.' The groom was angry. Hal saw it in the flat line of his mouth and the hot intensity of his stare.

'He doesn't pay you when he is not in residence?' Perhaps Ockendon did have money worries?

'He barely pays us when he is, but since the mistress died he employs most of us on a casual basis when he's in town, then turfs us out on our ears when he goes off again. Which he does a lot nowadays. I don't know why he don't stay in blasted Norfolk and put us all out of our misery.'

Lizzie was the only person in Mayfair mad enough to be in St James's Park in the middle of a snow storm. The frozen wasteland before her matched the numbness of her own emotions. Hours of fear, worry and heartbreak had taken too much of a toll and now her mind had shut down to allow her to function while she had trudged past all the houses like a woman condemned. The festive door wreaths and spicy scents of Christmas mocked her. There was no joy in this season. Only fear and misery. Both emotions had left her wrung out like a dish rag hanging limply from the sink. She had arrived here a few minutes before two and had now stood so long the chill was making her bones ache, but was not surprised the Earl of Ockendon was making her wait. It added to the drama and heightened the sense of tension. He would like that.

When he finally strode out of the cover of trees, she simply stared back impassively and waited for him to come alongside. He tipped his hat in greeting, the permanent smug smirk curling up the corners of his mouth, went to take her gloved hand to kiss it and she snatched it away. 'I am tired of the games. Talk.'

'I know you gave birth to Rainham's bastard. A son.'

The news was hardly a surprise. Lizzie had been braced to hear it. 'What makes you think he is Rainham's?' Only her family had ever been apprised of that detail, although the servants probably suspected as much. Many of them had been in her father's employ at the time of her engagement and were paid well for their silence.

'His age and colouring lend themselves towards him as the sire. He has Rainham's eyes.'

He had seen Georgie? He had to have to have made such an observation. Pieced together the truth. 'Really? And how, pray tell, would you know that?'

'I will grant you, getting a decent sighting of the lad has proved challenging. Your father's house is well protected and the servants very tight-lipped. However, you, Lady Elizabeth, are a creature of habit. Every Tuesday and Thursday your carriage leaves Mayfair unfashionably early.' He chuckled at her expression, enjoying the knowledge it was her mistake which had caused her downfall. 'I confess, I stumbled across the pair of you quite by accident a month ago when I had the good fortune to be riding through Richmond Park. I was some distance away, but you are a striking woman.' His eyes strayed to her chest. 'When one is as advanced in years as I am, one recalls a great deal of gossip. I was sat in the church when the congregation were informed you had called off your wedding. It was quite the scandal at the time and the source of much speculation. I remember it clearly. Five years ago. The boy's somewhere between four and five years old, and five years is the same amount of time your erstwhile fiancé had been absent from society. Such a unique set of coincidences set my mind wondering.'

'So I have a son. Tell the world. I will still not marry you.'

Ockendon acknowledged her comment with another chuckle. 'Yes, indeed, a bastard child is a *scandal* to be sure, yet I had already anticipated it would not be enough to bring you around to my way of thinking. I had the devil of a job tracking down poor Rainham. For a little while I was certain he had disappeared off the face of the earth, then I recalled his family seat was in Cornwall.' He appeared delighted at his own industry. 'A shockingly run-down and miserable place and still no sign of your Marquess—fortuitously, he had left his usual trail of bad debt across the county and there were a great many tradesmen who were disgruntled with the fellow since his…return…but more of that later. I traced him to Bodmin Gaol and discovered he had been festering there for well over a year. He was in a dreadful state. The stress of bankruptcy had addled his mind and he was most accommodating when I offered to pay to secure his release. Told me all manner of *interesting* titbits. Titbits far more scandalous than your secret son, my lady.'

He laughed again and her temper snapped. 'Spit it out, man. Lay your cards flat on the table. If it is as bad as you are suggesting, then you already know you have won.'

'Indeed, it is bad. *Deliciously* bad. I suppose you already know your beloved had absconded with another woman rather than marry you. But do you also know the Duke of Aylesbury sought retribution? He had him tied up and dragged back to London. He wanted him dead and was happy to toss his remains in the Thames for the fish to eat. Your lily-livered father refused to consider cold-blooded murder. He was always so upright and proper. So full of his own importance. Instead, he arranged for Rainham to be chained and smuggled on board a prison boat bound for Australia.'

The gasp escaped her lips before Lizzie could stop it. 'You're lying!' Oh, God! She hoped he was lying. The Earl watched her reaction with barely contained glee.

'Isn't it marvellous? No trial, not even trumped-up charges, just the straight and highly *illegal* kidnap and transportation of a peer of the realm to Botany Bay. I wonder what the penalty for such a crime is, Lizzie?'

Her stomach plummeted to her feet. Ruination was the least she had to worry about. If this version of events were true, then her father could be facing worse than ruination. Perhaps even the scaffold. Oh, Papa! Her stomach lurched at the thought and her knees buckled momentarily until she forced herself to stand proudly. Forced her eyes to meet Ockendon's with futile defiance.

Ockendon's gloved hand came up to touch her cheek

and this time Lizzie did not dare pull away. This man held her papa's life in that hand. 'The story gets better. About a year later, your father must have got cold feet. The fool had Rainham brought back without Aylesbury's knowledge, threatened him with it. Warned the poor chap that he was now an outcast in London and, if he escaped death by Aylesbury's hand, would be thrown in debtors' prison if he dared return. Ironic, really, when *that* is where I found him. For a man who is as weak-willed and self-centred as your former beau, a life in virtual and impoverished exile in Cornwall was a more attractive option than death. And, of course, I will be eternally grateful to your father for his spinelessness, because it left me a trail of crumbs to follow. Had he listened to Aylesbury and let Rainham's sorry carcase become fish food, I wouldn't stand a chance with you. Isn't fate wonderful?'

Lizzie's mind was whirring. She had steeled herself to hear something bad, dreadful even, and was prepared for an epic scandal to erupt. At her worst imaginings, both she and Papa would have to flee to obscurity thoroughly ruined. But if the authorities were to arrest her papa, if he faced criminal charges—gaol or worse— there was no way she could stand by and allow such a travesty to happen when she had the power to prevent it.

'What is it you want?'

'I want a wife. One with powerful connections. One with a significant dowry who can give me the son my barren first marriage could not. I already know you are fertile, lovely Lizzie, although I will not condone your by-blow in my house.'

A tiny part of her died. 'I will never marry you if

Georgie is sent away. I will not leave the care of my son to strangers.'

'Georgie—so that is his name?' He waved a gloved hand dismissively as if the cruel wrenching apart of mother and child was of no consequence. 'I am sure your overprotective father will see to his needs and I am not a monster. You will be allowed to visit once or twice a year.'

'And if I refuse?' Her voice came out ragged, choked with sadness. Once a year! Death would be sweeter.

'Then I will hand your father over to the authorities and feed your family's secrets to the newspapers as fodder for the gossips. But we both know it will not come to that. I hold *all* the power now.' He took her gloved hand and tugged the soft leather barrier slowly off. 'You are a *good* daughter and would never condemn your father.' Her skin now bared, he placed his lips against the exposed flesh and tasted the back of her hand with his tongue, his eyes never leaving hers as he did so. 'And I know you will be a very *good* and very *dutiful* wife. Enjoy your last Christmas as a spinster, Lizzie. I shall be attending the Earl of Redbridge's Christmas Ball on Twelfth Night. That strikes me as the perfect venue to announce our engagement, seeing as everyone will be there—including Redbridge. In the meantime, I shall have my solicitors contact your father regarding the settlements. Do tell him I will expect the dowry sweetened, won't you? Will not settle for less than double what it is now…as a starting figure, of course. And it goes without saying he will do his utmost to bring me into those illustrious circles he moves in, seeing as I will imminently become his son-in-law. A government position in the Foreign Office or Home Office will suffice.'

He released her hand, a hand which would now need to be washed in lye to remove the stain of him from her skin, and stepped back. 'I shall also procure a special licence so we can be married immediately after, so you should begin your preparations, too. A wedding in St George's in Hanover Square might be fitting—and at least this time around you can be certain your groom will turn up.' He smiled again. A cold, malicious smile. 'And as I know how much you loathe society, you will be moving permanently to my estate. Away from… mischief.'

And everyone she loved. Georgie. Papa. Hal. The numbness which had cosseted her before she stepped into the park was gone, replaced by agonising pain. Utter devastation. Ockendon saw it and his wrinkly face split into an ugly grin.

'I believe I shall enjoy our marriage bed, Lizzie.' His eyes dropped to her bosom again, leering as if he could see through the thick layers of clothes to her nakedness beneath, leaving her feeling violated. 'Not as much as I shall enjoy spending your father's money, or utilising his powerful government connections. I am looking forward to *that* part of our nuptials a great deal.'

Chapter Seventeen

Hal had found his feet heading down Holborn the next morning as soon as the shops were open. They led him back to Hamley's Noah's Ark. A quick scan of the shelves and an even quicker purchase later, he bounded into Grosvenor Square eager to share the information he had already gathered. If his suspicions were correct, then he was certain he could find a way to rescue her.

He rapped on Lizzie's front door with peculiar butterflies flapping in his tummy and tried not to think about what they meant. Stevens opened it and his mighty shoulders slumped. 'Good morning, Stevens. Are we going to enact our usual tiresome rigmarole or are you going to let me in?'

The giant butler stood aside and gestured him into the hall whilst simultaneously threatening murder with his eyes. 'I shall see if Lady Elizabeth is at home. Stay. Here.' One meaty finger pointed to a spot on the carpet and Hal made a great show of shuffling to stand upon it.

'I shan't move, Stevens. I promise.'

The butler stalked down the hall towards the same

drawing room Hal had visited the day before and, to vex the butler as much as anything, he tiptoed in his wake.

'Lady Elizabeth, the Earl of Redbridge…'

'Is here!' Hal pushed passed the fuming servant and strode with a smile into the room.

'Hal!' Georgie scrambled off the floor in a scattering of coloured chalks and barrelled towards him. His small body crashed into Hal's at speed. Hal hoisted him up and balanced him on his hip.

'How is our snowman doing?'

'He is still standing.'

'Excellent news. How about we go and make him a lady-friend later? If this snow is here for the duration the poor fellow will get very lonely all on his own. Every upright snowman deserves a snow lady to make coal eyes at.'

With the child bouncing in his arms with excitement, Hal finally turned towards the sofa to greet Lizzie and her appearance shocked him. Dark circles ringed her red, swollen eyes. Face pale and drawn. Spirit battered—or perhaps broken. Something had happened. Something dreadful. He lowered Georgie to the ground and ruffled his hair. 'I need ten minutes alone with your mama first, young man.' He handed him the wrapped package he was carrying. 'Go and see if Stevens wants to play with these with you out in the hall.'

'Wooden swords! Yippee!'

Hal waited until the child had disappeared, then softly closed the door and came to sit beside her. 'What's wrong?'

'I met Ockendon y-yesterday.' She crumpled next to him, her hands covering her face and her slim shoulders racked by the force of her distress. At a loss what else to do, he enveloped her in his arms and hugged her close.

For an age, she couldn't speak, so Hal smoothed his hand over her hair, kissed the top of her blonde head and promised himself he would flay Ockendon at the first opportunity. 'It's going to be all right, Lizzie. I promise. The rancid Earl is in debt up to his eyeballs.'

'Y-y-you d-don't understand, Hal… My f-f-f-father…' She collapsed against him again, inconsolable for several minutes.

When she finally lifted her face from the now-sodden front of his shirt, the pain in her eyes broke his heart. He knew in that moment she was about to tell him something terrible.

'My father has broken the law, Hal… He kidnapped Rainham and had him smuggled on to a prison ship under a false name. Within a few days of my being jilted he had my fiancé transported to the Antipodes as a common criminal. He left him there to rot.'

'W-what?' His mouth struggled to form words. Kidnapped. Transportation. He had not expected to hear either word.

'It was a gross abuse of his government position.' An understatement. The kidnap of a peer of the realm was a capital offence. Even assuming the Government would not wish to throw one of their own to the wolves, or suffer the embarrassment of a public trial, Lizzie's father was potentially in serious trouble. 'Papa must have had second thoughts, as he had him returned a year later…but Charles still spent a year as a prisoner in that terrible place and suffered many more months in atrocious conditions at sea.' She was shaking, Hal realised, and not with cold. 'I have no choice, Hal. I have to marry him.'

'Over my dead body!'

'I will not see my father arrested. He meant w-well… he was trying to protect m-me… It is my fault Ockendon knows. M-my carelessness that put my family in d-danger.' She told him about her visits to Richmond, weeping profusely and quivering like a leaf in a storm. In her distraught state, it took a while to piece together the whole sorry tale. At the end of it, Hal realised the existence of a bastard child was merely the tip of the iceberg. It would have been better if the Duke of Aylesbury had had the snake murdered in cold blood. Now that Aylesbury was dead, the only witness to the whole affair was the man who had wronged Lizzie so grievously. The Marquess of Rainham, despoiler of innocent young women, libertine and jilter, was now the victim.

'I will find him, Lizzie!' Hal had to find him. One life and the happiness of a great many people, himself included, were riding on it. She allowed him to tug her close again and he buried his nose in her hair. 'Without his witness, Ockendon has no case.'

She burrowed against his chest gratefully, her voice small. Matter of fact. 'There will be other witnesses. The crew of the prison ship might be dredged up to talk. There will doubtless be plenty of others in Cornwall. His creditors, gaolers.' She sighed and pulled away and he wished she were not as intelligent as she obviously was. 'He wants to announce our engagement on Twelfth Night.'

'You cannot marry him, Lizzie. Your father is a respected and powerful man. It will take more than circumstantial evidence to see him sentenced. If I can find Rainham, I am confident I can buy his silence.' Or at least he hoped he could. He had never actually tried. This was all so tenuous and needed to be more than wishful thinking. 'We need to be one step ahead of the game. Anticipate what Ockendon intends to do. Cut him off at the knees… We have a fortnight. A great deal can happen in a fortnight.' If this last two weeks was anything to go by, then anything was possible. And wasn't that the truth. A fortnight ago, the only complication in Hal's life had been his missing vigour and the eager hordes. Now he had a terrified woman, an innocent boy, a man's reputation and perhaps even his life on the line and the most persistent and worrying pain in his own heart to consider. 'Ockendon is in debt. I do not know to what extent as yet, but I will. I promise. I will find his weaknesses and exploit them. Once I am done, he will have no case to bring before the authorities. You have my word.' And he had a sneaking suspicion part of his heart, too, as it was still aching at the prospect of losing her. A horrible, hollow feeling which made him nauseous.

The thought of her miles and miles away brought a lump to his throat, yet Hal had no earthly idea how to save her. Although he had to. Somehow, by hook or by crook, he had to stop Ockendon and seal his spiteful, blackmailing mouth shut for ever. That was the only outcome he could bear. 'I am going to need to speak to your father. He will need to be involved if we are going to avert catastrophe.' She nodded. The first signs of hope had begun to glimmer in her lovely eyes and his heart swelled. He had put that there and he could not let her down. 'And I am going to need to bring in some reinforcements. With your permission, I would like to tell my family. My brother-in-law Aaron will be an asset in our quest.'

She appeared appalled at this. Ashamed, even. Her sad eyes dropped to her hands. 'I suppose the whole *ton* will learn I am a fallen woman soon enough, Hal, so I doubt it will make much difference.'

Fallen woman? She wasn't a fallen woman. She was a brave and loyal one. A wronged one. 'Men like Rainham are practised seducers. You were young and trusting. Engaged. You had no idea you would end up an unwed mother. My family will not judge you for that.' Or at least he hoped they wouldn't. If they did, he might have to have the mother of all arguments with them until they saw things his way. Punches might be thrown, Persian carpets ruthlessly rolled. 'Between us, we will find a way.'

She nodded and attempted a smile but Hal could see she did not hold out much hope. When she bravely pulled her shoulders back as her son dashed back into the room, wielding both the wooden swords Hal had bought him aloft, her gazed fixed on Georgie and her voice came out as barely a whisper. 'This might be my last ever Christmas with my son. Whatever happens I want him to enjoy it.'

Georgie was having a whale of a time with Hal, who was attempting to teach her son the rudiments of fencing when her father came in. The sight brought him up short. As he stared at them, Lizzie noticed how old and tired he suddenly appeared. He was suffering, too, yet they had barely exchanged a single word since they returned from the ill-fated Danbury house party.

She walked towards him and threaded her arm

through his and his hand instantly came to rest on hers tightly. They were both apologising without words, yet both knew there were many things still to say. None of them was likely to be pleasant, not when their secrets were about to implode.

'Stevens informed me he visited yesterday, asking to speak to Master George. Your son seems to like him a great deal, Lizzie.'

'Hal is easy to like, Papa. He wants to help us.'

'I can sort this all out, there is no need to trouble yourself or...' Stubborn to a fault. Always trying to protect her.

'I met with Ockendon yesterday.'

The air left his body in a whoosh. 'You shouldn't have done that.'

'He knows about Georgie, too—and how you and Aylesbury had Rainham dispatched to Botany Bay.'

'I see.' She felt him wobble and guided him to a seat. He sat heavily, looking every inch his sixty-two years. 'At the time...well...'

'I do not judge you for it. If somebody tried to hurt Georgie I would happily do the same. However, as I am sure you have already worked out, he is threatening to turn you over to the authorities unless I agree to marry him.'

'Let him. I would rather that than—' She held up her hand before he could protest.

'I would rather not have to see you go to gaol or, Heaven forbid, hanged because of me. If it comes to it, I *will* marry Ockendon.' Her dear papa appeared suddenly so bereft. 'Hal is of the opinion we can stop Ockendon and I would never forgive myself if I did not at least try to prevent that man from destroying my life. You need to tell us the truth. All of it.'

His eyes flicked to the fencing match and Hal met his stare head on. He smiled, then went back to entertaining Georgie to give them some privacy. 'Do you trust him, Lizzie?'

A silly question when her heart was positively bursting with affection and gratitude for the man. 'Implicitly.'

Her son jabbed the point of his sword in Hal's belly. He clutched the imaginary wound, staggered left, then right and then proceeded to die noisily on the carpet. When Georgie giggled, he jumped up again, hoisted him into the air, flipped him upside down and marched him dangling by his feet towards them. The sight made her yearn for such a heart-warming picture every day. Her son's laughter. A happy home. One which Hal shared. If only her circumstances had been different.

'Are we making my snowman's lady-friend now, Hal?'

'We shall make her this afternoon. I have to speak to your grandpapa first.'

'What about?'

Hal tapped the side of his nose conspiratorially. 'Christmas surprises, young man. Secret Christmas surprises for nasty little boys who love bugs. Now, off with you. Go and pester your nanny, or, even better, Stevens. I will wager good money the man is loitering *just* outside the door.'

Lizzie took his chubby hand and led him out. Conscious that her days with him were limited, she did not hurry to settle him with his nanny. These moments were now too precious and she would not squander one no matter how dire things were for her. By the time she returned to the drawing room, her father and Hal were sat, heads together, in deep conversation. They had been joined by Viscount Ardleigh, who appeared a little stunned at what he was hearing, but no less engaged. They paused as she entered and for the briefest of moments she could tell her father was on the brink of dismissing her in his usual over-protective way. Hal patted the space next to him on the sofa. 'I have brought Aaron up to speed with your situation, Lizzie.'

'This is all my fault.' Her papa's voice was choked with guilt. 'I should have let the Duke of Aylesbury have him killed or left him to rot in Botany Bay.'

'Why did you bring him back?' Although Lizzie suspected she already knew the answer. Her father did not have a mean bone in his body.

'I don't know.' He sighed and shook his head. 'When I packed him off, I was careful. Nobody knew his true identity. The ship's captain believed him to be a fraudster, a man who had a reputation for impersonating people to defraud them. That way, I assumed nobody would listen to him ranting about being a peer of the realm. But of course, then I had no idea you were carrying the man's child. Once I learned that, and after Georgie was born, the guilt ate away at me. I couldn't stomach the thought of my grandson asking about his father and knowing that I had sent him to hell to die. I used my connections to have him brought back—but knew I never wanted him near you both. I threatened him with Aylesbury, his creditors…whatever I could to keep him away, and like a fool I let him go back to his estate, certain he would never darken our doors again. I shouldn't have done that. I put you in harm's way.'

'I put myself in harm's way, Papa. Ockendon saw me

with Georgie in Richmond Park, then followed me repeatedly to be sure. As he said, I am a creature of habit. Every Tuesday and Thursday...'

Hal turned towards her and took her hand. As usual her pulse stepped up a notch at his touch. 'We need to know word for word what he said to you yesterday. What do you remember?'

Lizzie remembered it all. How could she not? It had been the singularly most important and terrifying conversation of her life. She had spent the entire night recalling Ockendon's chilling words and mourning her own stupidity. Realising you had been instrumental in your own downfall was devastating. Her outings to Richmond had given Ockendon everything he had needed. Step by step, she repeated the conversation, pausing to answer the numerous questions Hal or his brother-in-law threw at her. How did he look when he said that? Did he stipulate why he needed a wife with a large dowry? Like the most thorough lawyers they cross-examined every word, every nuance in Ockendon's behaviour, searching for clues to help. She briefly considered withholding some of the disgusting insinuations the old Earl had made about her fertility and their marriage bed, but decided against it. The information might be pertinent and if there was the slimmest chance of escaping her fate, Lizzie intended to grasp it and so did Hal. Therefore, only the truth would suffice.

At the end of her testimony, Hal stood and began to pace, royally furious on her behalf. 'We need to work swiftly if we are going to silence Ockendon. Let's find his weak spot. I shall use my contacts in the city to see if our Earl has made any foolhardy investments of late or taken out any loans.' It was obvious he was keen to get started. He was in danger of wearing a hole in the carpet.

'And I shall do some digging in Whitehall.' The old fire had relit in her papa's eyes. Yet another thing she owed to Hal. 'If he has got himself into trouble somewhere, somebody there is bound to know something. You are right—the more dirt we can find on that old fool the better. He will rue the day he threatened my daughter!'

'We could probably do with some extra help finding his accomplice. I shall head to Bow Street and engage some Runners. Rainham has to be somewhere close. The weather turned nasty the night he parted company with Ockendon and the best place to hide a wastrel is London.' Lord Ardleigh stood, too, and took her hand. 'Ockendon is nowhere near as clever as he thinks himself to be. He will have slipped up somewhere. Try not to worry.' Shocked at his kindness, Lizzie merely nodded. She barely knew this man, yet he was here, loyally supporting her because of Hal.

'What can I do?' Suddenly doing nothing felt like the worst sort of punishment. She would go quite mad with worry.

'Georgie needs you.' Hal's voice was soft. Sympathetic. 'And I think you need him, too.'

It dawned on her then that this very well could be her last ever Christmas with her son. The last stretch of uninterrupted time she might ever be allowed to have with him again and the sudden tears filled her eyes and threatened to spill down her cheeks. Stoically, Lizzie turned her face towards the window, hoping for some composure. Now was not the time for either tears or panic. She had some hope and she would cling resolutely to it until it died. If it died.

'If you do not mind me saying, Lady Elizabeth, you shouldn't be alone.' Lord Ardleigh pressed a clean handkerchief into her hand. 'You need to keep occupied. I have a wonderful wife who will be more than happy to keep you company and two equally wonderful daughters who are about the same age as your son and would love another playmate. I have already sent word to Berkeley Square and expect them here presently. I'll wager they will help to take your mind off things.'

Hal stalked to the door, impatient to get started and ready to do battle again on Lizzie's behalf. His mossy eyes locked on hers as his hand hovered on the handle. 'Can you apologise to Georgie for me? Tell him I will be back to build the snow lady as I promised.'

He remembered her son.

Lizzie nodded and stared stunned at the now-closed door. Amidst all the panic and the plotting and the impending threat of scandal, he remembered he had made a promise to her little boy. The tears fell from her eyes so she closed them, lest her father or Lord Ardleigh see the tell-tale emotion swirling in them. The gratitude, the wonder, the trust, the yearning, the absolute certainty which only came from one thing.

Love.

Chapter Eighteen

The next few days passed in a blur. The men were on a quest to save her from Ockendon, so she saw her father rarely and Hal not at all. She had no idea where he had gone. All she knew was he had left London unexpectedly on her behalf and she was now worried sick about him, too. Hal had departed in such a haste that he had neglected to appraise either her papa or Aaron of his destination, except to say that he was following a rumour.

A rumour!

Did the man seriously think that was explanation enough at a time like this? However, thanks to Connie and Hal's mother, Lizzie was never left alone with her thoughts, something which was just as well as they kept turning very dark very quickly when she finally collapsed exhausted in her bed at night. The days, however, despite her inner turmoil, were filled with Christmas and the wonderful sounds of children laughing as Georgie had the time of his life with the hellions-in-training Prudence and Grace.

The Christmas part was wholly unexpected and

strangely therapeutic. Every year her father closed up his Mayfair house for a week and the family travelled to Cheshire for Christmas, so aside from a holly wreath on the door Lizzie had never bothered doing anything else to honour the season whilst in town. This year, thanks to the drama she was embroiled in, the Wildings were staying put and the Stuart family had adopted them all into their own festivities.

Hal's sister Connie had been a godsend. The first time she had visited, she had come alone, insisted on Lizzie eating something, then had sat and listened quietly to the whole sorry tale without judgement. Everything had poured out, from the first moment her fiancé had scrambled up the wisteria to the dreadful ultimatum she had received from the Earl of Ockendon. The only bits Lizzie kept private were the personal and intimate details involving Hal. Although Connie was being lovely, it was unlikely she would want to hear that a totally unsuitable woman had fallen head over heels for her noble brother, or that Hal had proposed before he had known about Georgie and undoubtedly regretted it now. Lizzie's feelings hardly mattered. To her credit, Hal's sister was nothing but supportive.

The next time Connie had visited, she had brought her daughters and her mother, and the children played boisterously while the ladies chatted. Once Connie learned that there were no Christmas plans in place, she had galvanised the whole house into action, pointing out, quite rightly, that her son deserved to have a wonderful, magical time, and certainly did not need to see his mother fretting while the menfolk sorted out the 'other nonsense'.

So that was what Ockendon's threats became. The

other nonsense. Nonsense which would all come to naught because Aaron and Hal would fix it. Connie and her mother were so certain of this fact, it gave Lizzie lingering hope they might be right. Even if they weren't, she wanted to believe it. Just for a few days. Just in case this truly was her last ever Christmas with her son and her father. The fear and stress was still there, but instead of mulling over it, Lizzie allowed the Stuart family to take over her life and force her to bring Christmas kicking and screaming into Grosvenor Square.

Now, if she said so herself, the finished article was very festive. She had never seen so much holly. Shiny sprigs decorated every nook and cranny, winter greenery was woven through chandeliers, framed every fireplace and doorway and the poor kitchen was working overtime to bake every cinnamon-and-spice-infused delight known to man. With the snow, and with two playmates close to his own age, Georgie was in his element, a smile of perpetual childish ecstasy permanently glued to his face. He was having a positively marvellous Christmas Eve.

'Stevens—we need more carrots.' The flame-haired Prudence issued this order as if she was the lady of the house and the soft-hearted butler stopped pushing the giant snowball he had been instructed to roll and brushed the sticky, fresh snow from his gloved hands.

'I shall enquire in the kitchens, my lady, although cook was complaining only yesterday about the amount of carrots which have recently been procured by the three of you.' He cast his eyes pointedly over the battalions of carrot-nosed snowmen now littering the lawn. All snow*men*. Georgie stubbornly refused to have any ladies because his new hero Hal had promised they would build one together.

'If it helps the kitchen, we could make do with parsnips.' Prudence gave the butler a regal nod. 'And we shall use Georgie's chalks to colour them orange.'

Despite the weight of the world on her shoulders, the peculiar exchange made Lizzie smile as she remembered how Hal had bragged he encouraged his nieces to be resourceful with the materials at hand. The idea of them all colouring parsnips in the snow was as ridiculous as it was charming. Oh, to be a child and have such a simplistic view of the world. If only all problems could be solved with some coloured chalks!

'Is that my daughter issuing orders?'

'Papa!'

Aaron strode across the garden in his greatcoat, grinning, and his two girls squealed simultaneously and flew at him. He picked them both up boisterously, then went to kiss his wife with a wriggling daughter tucked under each arm. The public show of family affection made her envious, so she looked away, only to see her son watching the reunion intently. She walked towards him and began to assist him in slapping snow on to the body of the lopsided snowman currently under construction.

'Where is my papa?'

That knot of guilt she always carried was worse than usual. 'Far, far away, my darling.' At one point, she now knew, Australia—and by her father's hand—now back to haunt her again. Lizzie adjusted her son's woollen hat so that it covered his ears and tried to distract him. 'I think we need more snow for his head.'

'Is Hal my papa?'

Lizzie's chest tightened. 'No.'

'Are you sure? Only he is far, far away at the moment, isn't he? And we do have the same dark hair…just like Prudence and Grace have their mother's red hair. Your hair is blonde so I must follow my father. I think Hal and I look similar, don't you? And he carries me like Lord Ardleigh carries Grace and Prudence. Better, in fact, because he carries me upside down.'

With a catch in her voice, Lizzie smiled, completely flummoxed as how to answer him and yet reluctant to crush his childish dreams—or hers—just yet. 'As it's Christmas Eve, have you made a wish?'

As she'd hoped, her little boy turned to her quizzically. 'I have to make a wish? How do I do that?'

'When you go to bed tonight, you have to close your eyes and concentrate hard on whatever it is you want the most.'

'What sort of things can I wish for?'

'Well…' She began to pat more snow on to the snowman's body, absurdly grateful Georgie was distracted by the thought of wishes. She wasn't ready to talk about his father yet and would put it off for as long as was humanly possible. For ever, maybe. 'At Christmas time, people usually wish for something they do not have. A new toy, perhaps? Wooden tops, building bricks…an entire army of lead soldiers…'

His eyes lit up. 'If I wish for it, will I get it?'

'That depends on how hard you wish for it.'

'Then I shall go to bed early and wish all night.' In view of her desperate situation, Lizzie decided to do exactly the same.

* * *

It was two in the morning by the time Hal's horse trotted wearily into Mayfair. Fortunately, the skies had remained clear for his entire journey home from Norfolk, and although thick snow showed no signs of melting it had been crisp and easy to navigate. Perhaps riding through the night had been foolhardy, but he had wanted to be able to tell Lizzie his news as soon as possible, knowing she must still be worried sick. The last time he had seen her she had been so demoralised and broken, and like her knight errant he had been determined to avenge her.

He contemplated knocking on the front door, but that would mean waking the house and he selfishly wanted her all to himself first. She probably wouldn't like it, but for a myriad of complicated reasons which he did not want to have to analyse in case he thought better of it, he was going to climb the wisteria again.

Bone weary and frozen stiff, the ascent took more out of him than it had the first fateful time, and the sash window was very definitely now locked. Hal rapped on the glass and hung on for grim death. Immediately, the heavy curtains were torn apart and Lizzie's startled face appeared in the window. She was a sight for sore eyes. Her golden hair loosely plaited. The frothy nightgown an explosion of feminine lace. Her rosebud lips slightly parted in shock. At some point in the very near future, he fully intended to kiss them as he had thought of them constantly for days, although he needed to be able to feel his own lips first. The two icy strips of flesh that framed his mouth were probably unattractively blue and completely numb. He wanted to be able to feel her when he briefly succumbed to the temptation. Feel her and taste her properly because she was like a drug he craved and had gone far too long without, so it stood to reason he needed to thaw out sufficiently first. Hal gave his best approximation of a grin, which under the circumstances was less than half-hearted, and she fumbled with the catch and slid the window upwards.

'Hal.'

This time, he heard only soft relief in her voice and he tried not to hope she had been worrying about him. She gripped his arm and helped to haul him over the sill. The second he was in she began to fuss in a very encouraging manner. The window was slammed shut, she stripped him out of his damp, heavy greatcoat and gloves and ushered him towards the tiny fireplace. For the time being, her dainty chair appeared to take his weight, although he did not dare fidget just in case it swiftly surrendered under his bulk and allowed her to wrap him in the cosy eiderdown she hastily stripped off her bed.

'You need something warm to drink. I shall call for some tea.'

She most certainly would not. Rousing just one servant would negate his decision to climb the wisteria and mean he would have to behave decently, when he was really not in any mood to although knew he must. Things were very different now. She was a mother. She was in trouble and distraught. Hal had no right to want her with the fierce, possessive passion he was struggling to fight. 'I wanted to talk to you alone first…although I wouldn't mind if you went and smuggled me a generous snifter of brandy from somewhere.'

She disappeared, barefoot, in a voluminous cloud of white linen, leaving Hal to enjoy the aroma of her perfume in private. After a few moments, he realised that all the lamps were lit in her bedchamber, suggesting he had not rudely awoken her at all and he felt guilty that she had been alone and worrying for so many days and was clearly struggling to sleep. He should have sent word about where he was or what he was doing, but up until a few hours ago he had not had anything truly positive to report. Even now, all he could really give her was more hope than she had yesterday, but at least that was something.

Yet he was quietly confident his efforts would come to fruition. As much as he hated to make his blasted father right about anything, the world, it turned out, really did run on coin. Not entirely, of course, yet the liberal distribution of it in the last twenty-four hours had yielded some splendid results. There was still over a week to locate the elusive Lord Rainham and Hal still had pots of the stuff.

Lizzie dashed back in, clutching a full decanter of brandy and one glass. 'I have brought you Papa's good stuff…from his study.'

She practically filled the balloon to the top and thrust it at him. Hal took a few grateful sips and sighed contentedly as it trickled warmly down his throat and settled to heat his empty stomach. He should probably eat something, too, he realised, as nothing solid had passed his frozen lips since luncheon because he had been in such a hurry to get back to her. Hard liquor on an empty stomach might cause him to do something rash and very definitely inappropriate.

Lizzie stood nervously in front of him, her hands in a near-constant state of animation for a few seconds until she sank to the floor to sit in a cross-legged puddle at his feet. 'Please put me out of my misery, Hal. Am I doomed?'

'I don't think so.'

'That doesn't sound particularly reassuring.'

'Then let me rephrase it. I believe I have enough information to make Ockendon think twice and shortly I hope to have enough to silence him for ever.' Hal saw the light of hope begin to flicker in her eyes and gave in to the temptation to reach out and run the tip of his finger along her cheek.

'Did you find Rainham?'

'No.' The excited glimmer in her lovely eyes dimmed. 'I met a banker who had heard a rumour Lord Ockendon's house in Mayfair was heavily mortgaged, but I could find no evidence of that in any of the London banks.'

'Would the banks impart that sort of confidential information?'

'When you invest in the city, they have a certain amount of loyalty towards you.'

'And I suppose you invest in the city?'

'A great deal more than my over-cautious father ever did. I am owed a few favours.' And Hal had called every single one in. 'It appears the rancid Earl has a habit of upsetting people. His former solicitor was very disgruntled at still being owed money for his services after twenty years of loyal service. He was very happy to tell me all manner of interesting things.'

'Such as?'

Hal wasn't meaning to be mysterious, but his thoughts kept being distracted by the silken feel of the loose tendril of her hair he had wound around his hand. Good grief, he was pleased to see her. Just sitting in her presence was lovely. Comforting. *Home.* Either he was overtired or she had bewitched him. Funny how he didn't seem to mind the latter any more. He dropped the curl reluctantly and sat forward. She had waited long enough and deserved to know it all. There would be plenty of time to ponder his odd feelings later, after he had climbed back down the wisteria and trudged through the snow again towards his own bed.

'Like the fact that he used to receive three thousand pounds per annum from his wife's family, a sum which had been agreed as a part of the marriage settlement and which would continue to be paid to her children upon the event of her death. But as you already know, the poor woman died without issue and the lady's brother refused to continue the arrangement after her demise. The solicitor was instructed to find legal arguments to force the fellow to continue his payments, but failed. Ockendon refused to pay him for his services and sought new counsel—and I now know he desperately depended on that three thousand a year. It funded his lavish lifestyle while here in town. A lifestyle he is equally as desperate to maintain—seeing as he is obsessed with the idea of being powerful and when one simply cannot wield any power from the wilds of one's country estate.' Hal took another quick sip of the brandy and watched fascinated as she took the glass from his hand and took a healthy swig of it herself. He felt guilty for sincerely hoping she was also drinking it on an empty stomach and might be inclined towards rashness.

'Then it would seem your suspicions about his money worries were correct. I assume you have learned more than that whilst you have been on your mysterious mission to God knows where? A place, by all accounts, where messengers are unheard of and letters cannot be sent.'

A chastisement, yet one which told him she cared about him. That thought warmed him more effectively than her eiderdown or the brandy. 'I've been to Norfolk.'

'Ockendon is in Norfolk!'

'Yes, he is, but his minion is not. Of that I am certain. I was careful not to alert him to my presence. I don't want the scoundrel knowing I am spying on him and would much prefer to take the wind out of his sails callously and to his face. On Twelfth Night, before I summarily have him thrown out of my house, that is.'

If he could find Rainham and convince him to switch his allegiance as well as plugging every leak which might cause her harm. At this stage, that was a problematic 'if'. 'The solicitor said he was spending more and more time at his estate. The mounting cost of staying in London and maintaining two staffs was crippling him, hence he hires the majority of his Mayfair servants on a casual basis. My investigations in the city were turning up nothing tangible, yet I could not shake the feeling he would try to hide his situation from the *ton* and what better place to do that than sleepy old Norfolk? I thought it best to travel there directly and it's only a day's ride.'

Once again, Hal's gut instinct had proved to be right. 'A year ago he *did* mortgage his Mayfair town house. To the hilt. The debt is owed to a bank based in Norwich. According to his steward, a man whose tongue becomes far too loose with the lubrication of ale, his estate has also had some financial problems of late. A large flood last year destroyed most of his grain crop. A number of staff were let go.'

'Is he on the cusp of bankruptcy?'

'Yes.' Hal watched the hope return and grinned. 'His situation is dire enough for me to know he recently negotiated a reduction in his mortgage repayments with the bank. A significant reduction in his repayments for six months only. That is all the leeway they would grant him.'

She stood then, agitated and began to pace. 'All the more reason why he needs to marry an heiress—but hardly enough evidence for us to stop him from exposing my father and Georgie to the world. If anything, it merely makes his situation more desperate and ours more tenuous. Speed is of the essence if the banks have only given him six months to…' Then she stopped and her eyes narrowed. 'Wait…how would you know what terms he has negotiated with a provincial bank in Norwich?' He adored her intelligence.

'Because, as of yesterday afternoon, I became the majority shareholder in the bank and thus privy to all of its dealings.'

'You bought shares in a bank?' Her jaw dropped. 'To help me?'

Suddenly uncomfortable, and determined not to ever tell her how much of a premium he had had to pay to secure the shares, Hal simply shrugged. 'It was a good investment, regardless of the particular circumstances. The Norwich Municipal Bank now dances to my tune. One of my first tasks will be to call in Ockendon's loan unless he agrees to maintain his silence.' Hal's fingers were drawn to her hair again. 'I won't let you marry him.'

'I will not allow him to ruin my father.'

'Neither will I—but if it comes to it, your father

would sooner have his reputation sullied than see you condemned to a life of misery with that extortionist.' She went to argue. He could see the fiery determination in the sudden set of her jaw and her instantly stiffened posture. She was so loyal. So selfless. So irritatingly stubborn and independent. So much like her proud and noble father. Always ready to do the exact right thing by others even to the detriment of herself. It was frightening how much he had missed her these last few days. How much he had thought about her. About them. Hal couldn't help but smile. 'Wouldn't you? If it were Georgie you would sacrifice your reputation in a heartbeat. Because that is what we are talking about here. Nothing but your father's reputation. I could ruin Ockendon with a single stroke of my pen. I doubt he will continue with his quest to blackmail you once he realises how dire his financial straits now are. And I shall buy Rainham's silence, as much as it galls me to do business with such a snivelling, spineless, self-preserving...' Hal stopped himself mid-flow to wince. 'I'm sorry... He is still Georgie's father and I shouldn't bad-mouth him.'

To his surprise, she rolled her eyes. 'Please do not try to spare my sensibilities regarding *that* man. He is a snivelling, spineless, self-preserving toad. I wish every single day I had chosen a better man—*any* man— to have fathered my son. But let us not waste another breath talking about him when I am more concerned about my father. What if we cannot find Rainham? Or worse, what if we do and then Lord Ockendon still exposes what my father did?'

Hal had mulled this problem over a great deal in the last few days and intermittently on his interminable ride back to London when he forced himself not to think about her. 'I doubt his Majesty's government would condone the scandal of one of their longest-serving and most respected advisors standing trial. Despite the greatest provocation, he did not kill anyone. In fact, a good lawyer would argue quite the opposite. He did what he did to stop the Duke of Aylesbury having the blighter killed. Even your cowardly fiancé would testify to that. Aylesbury is dead, so cannot be punished either way. The whole case will stand on Ockendon's word and testimony obtained under duress. Rainham was out of his wits, if you remember, after having spent an eternity incarcerated in Bodmin Gaol. A sentence he earned fair and square because he is a wastrel who cannot pay his own debts. He was desperate. Is *still* desperate. Without Ockendon's promised remuneration he is still penniless. The dissolute Marquess of Rainham is the weak corner.'

'The weak corner?'

'My father was fond of analogies when it came to business. In days of yore, when an army besieged a castle, they had two choices. Surround the fortress and starve the occupants out, whittle them down until they surrender or find the most vulnerable part of the structure and ruthlessly mine under it, then stand back and watch the impregnable stone towers collapse under their own weight. That toad is the weak corner. If *I* offer to clear his debts for him, Rainham will stand in the witness box and say anything to serve his cause. Your father sent a bad man to a penal colony for a few months to teach him a lesson, then brought him back. At the worst, he will be forced to leave society and be shunned. He will be pilloried in the newspapers. But his life will go on, as will yours. His fortune will be intact. His estate still thriving. Take it from someone with a truly dreadful reputation—it is not so bad.'

Chapter Nineteen

For a man who prided himself on always being irreverent and naughty, Hal had a habit of using logic to great effect. Lizzie plopped down on her mattress with a sigh. 'You are assuming a great deal. First we have to find him, and I doubt that will be easy. He is far too valuable to Ockendon. Even if we do, he might well have told others and then there will be no containing the gossips. The scandal will be horrific.'

Hal nodded with resignation. 'I cannot deny that.' He stood up, dragging the eiderdown with him, and came to sit next to her on the mattress and wrapping a corner around her shoulders as he pulled her head to rest against his. 'Although I remain cautiously optimistic the story can be contained. We still have over a week until Ockendon returns to town and at the very least you do not have to marry him now that I own his debt. Surely that is good news.'

'Of course it is.'

Lizzie allowed her body to relax into his. Did it really matter if the whole world knew she was a fallen woman or that Georgie was born on the wrong side of the blanket? One of these days it was bound to come out, whether by the odious Earl's hand or another's. She had always known that and had prepared for the inevitable for over a year now. Her original plan—relocate to her cottage in remote Yorkshire, assume a new name and tell the world her son's father had died in the war— would still shelter Georgie from the worst of the talk. Lizzie sincerely doubted London scandal would travel to such a rural and isolated community. She wouldn't have to give up her son. And Hal was right, her father was unlikely to be tried as a kidnapper if Rainham testified his life had been in danger and her father had, in a strange sort of way, saved him from an execution.

Unlikely. In a perfect world.

But bitter experience had taught her the world was not perfect and the current political situation was tumultuous to say the least. If the Opposition got wind of her father's actions, then they would use it mercilessly against the government. The Whigs would scream for proper justice and *proper* justice dictated a trial. Lord Liverpool might have to sacrifice his friend for the good of the nation, just as Lizzie already knew she would still sacrifice her own happiness for the sake of her papa. If she could save him that ordeal by suffering a marriage with a man she loathed, then she would say 'I do' in a heartbeat. Hal had done so much, and spent so much, to help her she did not want to diminish his herculean efforts on her behalf with a cold dose of pessimistic reality. Not tonight at any rate, when he was frozen to the bone and clearly exhausted.

Besides, she reasoned, Lord Ockendon was old. He certainly appeared much older than his years which suggested he was not in the best of health. With any luck he would leave her a widow sooner rather than later and her life would return to normal. And then again, maybe he would live another thirty years because Lizzie had nothing but bad luck when it came to men. Hal would be lost to her and would doubtless marry a pure and more deserving young lady, Georgie would still grow up without her and her ageing father... Good Lord! Her father would be dead by the time she was free. Another sobering thought and one which made her eyes watery and her chest constrict.

'Why are you crying?'

'Relief.' The lie tripped off her tongue and she forced a smile. Hal had tried. He had bought a bank and ridden halfway across the snow-covered country overnight. It was all so tragically optimistic and hopelessly romantic. 'Thank you, Hal. How can I ever repay you for your generosity?'

His thumbs came up to brush the unshed tears away. 'Don't cry. There is no need to repay me. It has just turned Christmas Day and all I want is to see you enjoy it.'

The tears fell, about to betray her. Only at the last moment did Lizzie's expression comply as she fought to maintain the brave face she wore for him. 'But you have bought a bank...'

'An investment.' Further protest was silenced as his mouth brushed across hers. 'And if you recall, we made a bargain to protect each other till Twelfth Night. You still owe me twelve days. If you really want to repay me, then stand at my side during every interminable festive entertainment I am being dragged to, especially the tiresome ball my mother is forcing me to host, and continue to keep the hordes at bay.'

She would pretend to be happy for his sake. For her son's sake. For Papa's. Whatever happened, she would enjoy this Christmas because the realist in her still screamed it might be her last with all the men she loved. 'That hardly seems enough.'

'It's enough for me.'

On a whim, she leaned over and kissed him. Lizzie had intended it to be short, a friendly gesture of thanks, only the second her lips touched his they were in no hurry to move. Nor did his. The world was instantly a better, brighter place. Soon she might well be locked into a horrendous marriage with a man she detested or an eternity away in a desolate corner of Yorkshire. Whichever fork in the road fate took her would be without him. But Hal was here now and now might be all she ever had of him. As there was no point in fighting the temptation, she kissed him again before pulling back. 'You are such a lovely man, Henry Stuart.'

'I am more than lovely. I am irresistible. It is a wonder you can keep your hands off me.'

He had meant it as a glib remark, she knew. He was playing the flirty, charming scoundrel again to make her smile, as if his selflessness on her behalf was of no matter. But the simple truth was she very much wanted to kiss him again, realising this was her last chance. *Their* last chance. With all the misery and heartbreak cluttering the horizon she deserved this memory. One which she could cling to like a rock in a stormy sea. A real memory of what it *should* be like between a man and a woman.

They were here alone, in the dead of night, sat on her bed and wrapped in each other's arms. All at once, she ruthlessly banished all thoughts of tomorrow and the direness of her situation. Lizzie would have to face that again soon enough. For now, she had tonight. And him. The man her heart yearned for. The one who made her bare skin ache for his touch and her body want. Need pulsed in her core. Her fingers traced the day's growth of stubble on his cheek reverently. To her complete surprise, her own voice came out thickly. Breathless. 'Seeing as you have bought a bank *and* climbed the wisteria, we might as well make the visit worthwhile.'

He pulled away then. Offended. 'You know that is not what I came here for.'

Lizzie pressed one finger to his lips. 'I know. You would never come up here to seduce me. You are far too noble to use your good deeds so shamelessly.' She twisted her body to sit astride his lap, watched his eyes darken and revelled in the surge of feminine need now coursing through her veins. 'I am not so noble or good. Tonight I want to be shameless. I don't want you to leave, Hal.'

'You really don't need to...' His hands came to her waist to push her away, so she grabbed them and smoothed them shamelessly over her breasts. Pushed her pebbled nipples eagerly into his palms to prove to him he was what her body wanted. That she was serious.

'Right now all I can think about is you. Only part of that is out of gratitude. The rest is pure, unadulterated lust.' Lust that would give her something to sustain her through the bleak years ahead. Memories of Hal. This man she loved.

'Every time you touch me, I want. Every time you kiss me, I want.' Lizzie leaned closer so that her lips grazed his cheek. 'I never thought I was capable of wanting a man again. I was done with all men...until

you, Hal. We have twelve days left together and I am
tired of denying myself. I'm sure a man with your reputation knows how to make love to a woman without
creating a child, so what is the harm? I'm tired of feeling frightened and miserable, and I want to fully enjoy
this Christmas. I want to enjoy you.'

From somewhere within, Lizzie became a seduc-
tress. It seemed to be an entirely natural state to be in
with him. Natural and necessary. She trailed hot, open-
mouthed kisses across his jaw and nipped at his ear. She
could feel Hal warring with his own conscience as he
sat still beneath her. Rigid. His breathing was erratic,
but his hands still cupped her breasts even after she released them and allowed her own fingers to begin to
explore the breadth of his shoulders and chest through
the unwelcome barrier of his clothing.

When she brought her lips back to his mouth, he
failed to respond, but his eyes closed and he allowed
the pad of one thumb to circle the aching point of her
nipple. When she moaned her enjoyment, then shuffled
her knees forward, her nightdress riding up her thighs
as she fought to get closer, she felt the unmistakable
bulge of his hardness through his breeches and knew
he was as desperate for the act as she was.

He wanted her, too.

All the pent-up passion and yearning she felt for
him was not one-sided. It made no difference that there
was no future for them beyond the next few days, there
seemed little point in denying the desire which burned
between them. She was long past ruined and about to
be the capital's greatest scandal. One night of passion
with a notorious rake would not make one whit of difference any more.

Lizzie traced the outline of his mouth with her tongue while her fingers quickly undid the buttons on his waistcoat. He made no attempt to stop her nor did he succumb to her ministrations. All the while, his thumb, the only part of him not being noble, still lazily circled her nipple until she thought she would scream from the wanting. Lord, he was stubborn! Why wouldn't he take what she wanted to freely give?

Like a woman possessed, she grabbed the hem of her nightgown and wrenched it over her head, baring herself fully to his eyes and then sat back, forcing him to look at her. His gaze caressed her body in the absence of his hands. His mossy-green eyes darkened further as his pupils dilated. They fixed on her nipples and unconsciously he licked his lips.

'I didn't come here to bed you.'

'And I won't let you leave here till you do.' She slid off his lap and walked brazenly to the window. Locked it. Closed the curtains. Then watched his eyes follow her naked body to the door. Lizzie turned the key and removed it from the lock and smiled like the most practised of courtesans as she tossed it aimlessly across the room; standing shamelessly with her hands saucily placed on her hips and a knowing smile curving her mouth.

His face was inscrutable and for several seconds he simply stared back at her, impassive...aside from his glorious erratic breathing. But then his eyes betrayed him and began to rake her body from top to bottom with barely concealed hunger. Imbued with a new sense of womanly confidence, Lizzie slowly closed the distance between them, her gaze never leaving his.

'You cannot compromise me. That has already happened. And I am not interested in trapping you into marriage like some of your baying hordes. I won't marry you, Hal. I won't marry anyone. When this surprising Christmas season draws to a close, and all of this *nonsense* is done, I am leaving London whatever happens and never plan to return. We shall have to say goodbye. It would be silly to deprive ourselves because of your misplaced nobility and your ridiculous notion that I am only offering myself to you because I am grateful, don't you think? Especially when I want you. All of you. And you know me well enough to know I am not inclined to do anything I don't want to. Now...' she stood inches away, her teeth grazed the warm skin just below his ear and she heard his stifled groan '... the burning question is: are you going to be a good boy, Hal, and give me what I want for Christmas or do I have to take it?'

Another groan; this one considerably more guttural. Almost angry. 'I think you are going to have to take it.' But his eyes were filled with need as they locked hotly with hers.

'So be it.'

He put up no resistance when she pushed his waistcoat from his shoulders. Sat impassively as she pulled his shirt from the waistband of his breeches. Almost. Because he moved his arms upwards to allow her to peel the linen from his body.

With impressive arrogance, he sat back on his hands while she tugged off each boot, then fumbled with the falls of his trousers, and watched her through passion-darkened, hooded eyes as she worked the buckskin down over his hips until he sat gloriously naked before her. Gloriously naked and completely aroused.

Just for her.

It was a magnificent sight.

Because she had to, she leaned down to kiss him. A thorough and decadent kiss which he took full part in, yet aside from the intimacy of their mouths, no other part of their bodies touched. It was the most erotic and intoxicating moment of her life. To be so close to him, both of them naked and eager, yet never to have experienced the touch of the other on their bare skin.

Lizzie caved first, smoothing her palms over his chest, and tracing the dusting of dark hair down his hard abdomen. As her fingers grazed his navel, Hal groaned. One large hand encircled her waist and tugged until she tumbled on top of him. 'You are going to kill me, woman!'

'Can you think of a better way to die?'

'Inside you. That would be perfect.'

She had to agree. She had never been more ready to give herself. Was desperate to give herself to him.

Hal rolled so their positions were reversed, then reverently pulled the ribbon from her hair. He used his fingers to tease out the plait, then spread her hair across the pillow to form a halo about her head. Satisfied with his arrangement, he lazily explored every curve of her body with one fingertip. The sensitive column of her neck. Her collarbone. Breast. The indent of her waist and the flare of her hip. The subtle undulation where her calf met her knee. Then back up again via a different route. It finally came to rest on the soft, golden triangle of curls at the apex of her thighs.

'I knew you would be beautiful. I never imagined you would be this beautiful.'

When he kissed her, Lizzie felt it everywhere and

sighed into his mouth. Of its own accord her body arched towards his hand—but it was her breasts he worshipped next. Loving her nipples with his tongue until she was writhing against the mattress and begging him to take her.

But still he would not be hurried. His lips followed the same convoluted path across her fevered skin his hands had already explored. He kissed every inch of her. Rolled her on her front and nipped and nibbled his way down her back and smiled smugly when she protested before they shifted position again. The intensity of his stare emboldened her and she knew instinctively he adored what he saw. To him she was beautiful. Perhaps the most beautiful woman in the world.

'I want you now, Hal.' Every sense was heightened. Screaming for release. It was she who pushed his hand towards her sex, opening for him willingly. Shamelessly. She had never felt so deliciously unashamed before. So determined to find her own pleasure. 'Touch me.'

With the same torturously gentle motion he had used on her breasts, his fingers moved in tiny circles. Every nerve ending came alive and zeroed in on one tiny spot, and all at once she realised that Rainham had not known a damn thing about the act of love. With him it had been quick and frantic and ultimately awkward. An invasion. With Hal it was a celebration. A revelation. Utter, utter carnal bliss at the hands of a true master.

Her fingers found his hardness and explored it. So hot. So hard. Touching him was addictive. Her wits were scrambled. Limbs leaden yet quivering. Her body hovering on the cusp of something wondrous yet almost painful. She had never experienced a fiery need like it. Instinct told her to curl her palm around him and caress his length in long, firm strokes, feeling powerful when she saw the effect it had on him. His breathing became ragged and his eyes fluttered closed. Her name tumbled from his lips like a benediction. Then, with an animalistic sound he pushed her hands away from him and held them pinned gently above her head on the pillow. His gaze dropped and she allowed her thighs to fall open in invitation, no longer sure who was the seducer and who had been seduced. It made no difference. They were both too consumed with each other to think of anything except what they were about to do.

Lizzie thought he would take her quickly and put them both out of their torment, but he didn't. Their faces inches apart, they watched each other as he gently eased inside. Slowly filling her until he was buried to the hilt.

Only then did he start to move. Again, with measured, aching slowness until she could stand it no more. She wanted everything and all of him. Her legs wrapped around his waist, pinning him to her core, and she used her own hips to find the satisfaction she craved, driving them both mad. At some point, he must have succumbed to the madness, too. She had no clear memory of when that was amidst the vortex of new sensations buffeting her, before she knew it they were writhing together, wordlessly lost in each other. Moaning and kissing and frantically touching until a dazzling light exploded behind her eyes and her body shattered around him.

Chapter Twenty

Hal stared contentedly at the ceiling and enjoyed doing something he never did. Cuddling up to a sleeping woman in her bed hours after he had made love to her. Usually, when it came to sleeping, he much preferred the whole bed to himself. His own bed. Wherever that happened to be. Not that he was the sort of heartless rogue to dash out of a lady's bedchamber as if his breeches were on fire the moment the deed was done. He had too much respect for women for that and enjoyed their company immensely even when his passion was spent. He always stayed for a little while. Chatted. Made them laugh. Then pretended to bid them a reluctant farewell with whatever convenient excuse worked best to extricate him from the situation as painlessly as possible. He was fairly certain none of his former paramours had been offended by his departure.

Mind you, the women he favoured tended to be the more worldly-wise widows, the younger, neglected wives of older husbands, seasoned mistresses, actresses and opera singers. Most of them knew how the game was played. They were probably as relieved to see him leave as he was to be leaving.

Yet here he was, happily still ensconced in Lizzie's bed, his arm curled loosely about her hip while his nose nuzzled the crown of her head, feeling thoroughly pleased with himself. For the first time in his life he felt totally at home, a state he had found himself in perpetually since Lizzie had seduced him on Christmas Day.

Home.

That word and this woman seemed synonymous. No matter how many times he hauled himself up the wisteria or how many times he had made love to her since that first splendid night, try as he might he could not explain away the odd, comforting glow he had whenever he was around her. His excuses always fell ever so slightly short. Having now got to know her completely, having lost himself in her delightful body repeatedly and having spent more hours than he cared to count absorbed in her company at the numerous festivities they attended, he was prepared to acknowledge it was not just his head that he had lost.

Somewhere in the last few weeks he had lost his heart to her too. Hal genuinely lived to see her smile. He had been so preoccupied with making her happy he had quite lost sight of everything else. That was a bad case of love if there ever was one—although not quite as daunting as he had always believed it to be.

It did not matter that he was still the wrong side of thirty and still far too young to settle down. There were no more wild oats to sow. Why would he consider making love to any other woman when the only one his missing vigour wanted was right here? Thanks to a silly sprig of mistletoe, fate had decided it was time

Hal took a wife. Lizzie. The most passionate, beautiful and noble woman in the whole world. Loving Lizzie, marrying Lizzie, felt intrinsically right.

Unfortunately, the stubborn wench had declared she had no desire to marry him.

Repeatedly.

A stumbling block, to be sure, but hardly an insurmountable one. When he had first met her, Hal had likened Lizzie to a fortress. Guarded. Surrounded by high battlements and with only one sturdy and unpredictable drawbridge. There were, however, no weak corners. Once the woman made up her mind, it was set. While he had basked in the euphoria of their lovemaking between bouts of fevered passion, Lizzie had talked on and on about her plans for her new life.

In the north, for goodness sake! Without him.

As if he was going to allow that to happen.

But there was no point in arguing with her when she was nobly sacrificing her own happiness—their happiness—because of the misguided belief he would be much better off without her or that the horrendous scandal she feared was about to imminently blow up in her face. Hal had even allowed her to make jokes about the future Countess of Redbridge, a woman with a reputation so pristine and shiny he would need to shade his eyes from the golden goodness radiating off her. It had soured his splendid mood until he discovered the perfect way to shut her up was to have his wicked way with her again.

As if a man like him, who had been in more strange beds than he cared to count, who was on first-name terms with the proprietors of every unsavoury gaming hell from here to John o' Groats and one who had bared himself to the amassed *ton* at the Serpentine one sunny Sunday afternoon, could tolerate an eternity with a woman so dull?

At times her determined pessimism was laughable, yet the underlying sadness he knew she masked with false gaiety for his sake—or her son's or her father's—broke his heart and, no matter how hard he tried, he could not convince her that she was not doomed because he would fix it.

She would try to distract him with passion and Hal had a talent for distracting her quite thoroughly as well. Hence she was now sleeping peacefully in his arms and he was enjoying the sight of her wistfully smiling in her sleep. Wistful smiles that he had created and that he had every intention of creating until he was dragged, kicking and screaming, from this mortal coil and buried six feet under the ground.

Fortress Lizzie was in for a shock if she seriously thought he was going to marry anyone else aside from her. And vice versa. He still had one whole day until Twelfth Night ended. One last day to breach her defences and make her see sense. In the absence of any corners to mine beneath, Hal was going to lay siege and systematically whittle the blasted woman down until she surrendered to his way of thinking. Tonight he would send the weasel Ockendon packing and they would be able to get on with their lives. It was just a shame all Hal's attempts to find Rainham had amounted to nothing. With Rainham firmly in his pocket, Lizzie would finally accept her dreadful ordeal was over and then perhaps...

He heaved a sigh and she stirred. Her face emerged from a tangle of hair and she appeared delighted to see him. Because he could, Hal ran his palm over her bottom possessively. 'Good morning. I hope you slept well.'

He watched her lips curve upwards. Neither of them had slept much last night. As the month got shorter Lizzie appeared to want to sleep less and less. Today, he knew with irritated certainty, she intended to say goodbye to him for ever at the end of his own blasted ball.

'I had a wonderful dream. A handsome rake scrambled up the wisteria and did unspeakably shocking things to me.'

'That same rake had better climb back down it swiftly before your fearsome butler wakes up and relieves him of his teeth.' Dodging Stevens had become considerably more problematic and the fellow had taken to glaring at him through menacingly narrowed eyes whenever he came to *officially* call. Hal had a sneaking suspicion he knew full well what the pair of them were up to. Knew full well, but was biding his time.

'Surely you can spare me half an hour?'

Another goodbye. Instead of grinding his teeth in irritation, Hal kissed her.

An hour later she had lost the watery glimmer of martyrdom he kept seeing in her lovely cornflower eyes—he had seen to that—and barely had the strength to wave him farewell as he gingerly lowered himself from the window.

The north! Hal wanted to shake her.

'This came for you.' Panic made him fall the last five feet and he landed with a painful thud on his bottom at Stevens's feet. The giant butler unceremoniously thrust a note in his face. 'One of your Bow Street Runners tracked you here just after midnight. I didn't want to *embarrass* Lady Elizabeth by bringing it in.'

Pride made Hal stand before he took the letter. The seal was broken. 'You opened my private correspondence?'

'You seduced Lady Elizabeth.' The butler's face was deadpan, but his nostrils still flared. 'They've found him.'

The knots in his gut Hal had carried around for close to a fortnight suddenly loosened despite being caught red-handed, practically *in flagrante*. 'Where?'

'Seven Dials. The Runners are waiting outside where he is. I presumed you wanted to speak to them first.'

'I do!' Hal was already striding across the lawn. Perhaps it would be better if he sprinted home first? Quicker, certainly with…

'I've already got two horses waiting. I'm coming with you.'

'Suit yourself.' Having the ham-fisted brick wall next to him when he confronted Rainham the snake would be beneficial. 'But I do the talking.'

'Are *you* going to do right by *her*?'

'I'm determined to damned well marry her, Stevens!'

'Then I'll let you do the talking.'

Thanks to the horses and the fact the blanket of snow which had suffocated the city now resembled a lace shawl, the main roads were blessedly clear and empty as the sun began to rise. However, there was not enough ice to mask the stench of the seething, reeking cess pool of Seven Dials. The natural habitat for a rat like Rainham. They met two Runners dressed in inconspicuous rags loitering outside a tatty-looking brothel. The dissolute Marquess was blissfully oblivious to their presence or that Hal was about to ruin his day.

By all accounts, a man matching Rainham's description was upstairs. He had been there since before Christmas, when his aged companion had paid in advance for him to stay for the next fortnight before disappearing in a 'fancy carriage' and hadn't been seen since. He had also promised to pay the proprietor handsomely to keep the gentleman *entertained* and his presence a secret. Because Hal had given the Runners carte blanche to bribe whoever and however they saw fit, the proprietor was most accommodating, even going as far as directing them to the bedchamber. Real coin always trumped a flimsy promise. More proof that Hal's father might have been right about the world and coin after all, although hardly a surprise here in Seven Dials, where poverty ruled and money was everything.

Hal did not bother knocking on the door. He strode in, with the beefy Stevens hot on his heels, then stood impassively as the two lightskirts were hastily pushed aside and Georgie's vile father pulled the sheets up to cover his nakedness. Clearly Ockendon had the measure of his accomplice to bring him here, where there was plenty to occupy someone with Rainham's debauched tastes.

'If you would excuse us, please, ladies.' He flicked two coins in their direction and waited for them to exit the room. Neither bothered dressing. They merely bundled their tangled clothes up and brazenly sauntered to the door, one winking at Hal saucily in invitation. The butler closed it with deliberate slowness, then scraped a chair across the bare wooden floor and placed it in front of it, then sat, blocking the Marquess's only escape route. He folded his arms and glared menacingly at Rainham, who looked ready to launch himself out of the single grubby window at the first viable opportunity. Hal found himself amused at the sight.

'We are three floors up, so jump out of that window if you are of a mind to. I shan't stop you. In fact, I believe I would find a great deal of pleasure seeing your broken body on the road below.'

Rainham swallowed nervously, his frightened eyes flicking between Hal's and his giant companion's. 'What do you want?'

'I think you know... Deep down.' Because it felt like the right thing to do, Hal reached down and slid his boot knife out of his Hessian. A knife which he had only used twice. Once to cut up an orange and once to slice through the impossibly knotted laces of a lusty widow's corset—but Rainham had no idea Hal had no appetite for violence. Usually. Knowing what the snake had done to Lizzie made the thought of it significantly more tempting than it had ever been. He smiled smugly as Rainham's eyes focused on the sharp blade, then casually used the tip of his knife to clean some imaginary dirt from under his fingernails. 'You've been talking, it seems, to your new friend and *benefactor* Lord Ockendon. Telling him things that are not true. Spreading lies... Malicious lies. Isn't that right?'

'I didn't lie.' But the man blanched as he spoke, his Adam's apple bobbing repeatedly as he gulped in air. 'I promise you I didn't lie.'

'That's a shame. If you are loyal to Ockendon, then you are of no use to me. Or anyone, for that matter.'

Rainham's mouth opened and closed, then opened again, much like a reeled salmon fighting death. 'I—I

d-don't understand.' Hal turned the knife so that the
weak morning light caught the blade. Smiled. 'Are you
going to k-kill me?' The snake's voice was satisfyingly
high. 'You can't kill me for telling the truth!'

The attempt at retaliation was wasted. His eyes were
darting around, seeking a way out, and beads of damning perspiration were gathering on his pale skin. Poor
Rainham. He was about to discover how talented Hal
was at calling a man's bluff. A skill he had honed to
perfection out of necessity to block his father. Just like
his father, the Marquess of Rainham was trying to bully
a woman.

Lizzie.

A woman who had been hurt enough.

He allowed the anger to ferment in his gut for a few
moments before answering and found an odd satisfaction in it.

'Do you know, old boy, I rather think *I am*. Look
at where we are. Slap, bang in the middle of the biggest haven of criminals and ne'er-do-wells in the whole
of London. You could not have picked a place more
suitable to my purpose if you'd tried. Thank you for
that. Makes everything so much simpler.' The Marquess baulked and looked ready to cry. For good measure, Stevens stood and quietly flexed his fingers as if
he had been brought here specifically to deal with the
murdered corpse, lest the blood marred Hal's fine coat.

'If you turn up here, gutted like a fish, the residents
will deny any knowledge of what happened. That is
the way of things when everyone is as lawless as their
neighbours. The horrendous poverty serves to make
the people here ruthless. They sold you down the river
for a few coins.'

Rainham gulped and the last of the air came out of his lungs in a whimper. Hal nearly had him. The man was so weak-willed, so desperate to save his own sorry skin he would be easy to completely break. What the hell had Lizzie ever seen in him?

'We will not be disturbed, by the way. The landlady was most accommodating when she learned exactly who I was and…of course… I am *very, very* rich.' Hal paused to allow his words to sink in, pressed his advantage when he saw realisation dawn. 'Tell me—who will mourn your passing in the *ton*? Your reputation proceeds you, as far as those who remember you are concerned, that is. You have been gone such a long time I doubt many will notice your passing…and as far as I can ascertain, your only friend in the world is that toad Ockendon and I can assure you he is next on my list. Whatever nonsense he has planned will be *ruthlessly* nipped in the bud. Of that you can be quite certain. With Lizzie's *powerful* family connections staunchly on my side, my fat purse and sudden determined appetite for vengeance, *you* don't stand a chance. So be a good boy and tell me what I want to hear. It really is your only chance of walking out of here alive.' The little colour remaining drained out of Rainham's face, so Hal paused for a heartbeat. 'Did I mention I will double whatever Ockendon promised you? And pay your passage to the Americas so you can start afresh.'

Snakes were so predictable. 'It wasn't my idea! I fully intended on keeping to the bargain I made with Lizzie's father. I knew Aylesbury would kill me if I dared to set one foot back in town.'

'Then why did you?'

Rainham gulped. 'Ockendon rescued me. Informed

me that Aylesbury was dead. Said I would be safe. Said he would keep me safe if I helped him.'

'So you gave him information he could use to blackmail Lizzie. A woman you claimed to have loved.' Hal could not disguise the acid in his tone or the raw hatred in his eyes. To his credit, Hal noticed Stevens wore exactly the same expression. The world might run on coin, but it couldn't buy loyalty. True loyalty had to be earned and he was suddenly grateful she had this big brute in her corner, protecting her.

'I feel bad about that. I really do... But I had people after me, baying for blood, and there was so many stipulations and caveats on the marriage settlements. The Earl of Upminster had insisted upon them. It forced me to—'

'Steal away the Duke of Aylesbury's daughter instead because she had a fatter purse and no such caveats. *This* I *know*, Rainham. I also know you failed in that endeavour, too, and it doesn't do anything to make me feel any more lenient towards you.

The dissolute Marquess appeared to shrink as he drew his legs up and his white knuckles clutched ineffectually against the blanket. Hal was happy to let the weasel squirm and sat quietly. Waiting.

'She let me seduce her!'

Like a true snake he was blaming Lizzie rather than himself. 'What a bad girl...' His voice dripped venom. 'To allow herself to be seduced by such an accomplished and seasoned despoiler. You must be right. It was all *her* fault. Your part in the proceedings was insignificant.' Hal could picture the scene. A younger, trusting, more innocent Lizzie, bowled over by Rainham's practised charm. 'How old was she back then, Rainham? Eighteen? Barely out of the schoolroom. You had a decade of experience on her and you promised her marriage?' The temptation to drag the man out of the bed and choke the life from him was difficult to ignore. But he had to.

'You have to understand—' Hal ruthlessly cut him off with his hand.

'I understand. I understand perfectly. Be under no illusion, Rainham, that I hate you, I want to kill you for what *you* did to her, and would happily tear you limb from limb if you ever malign her or gossip about her or her family again! Right now, I will do *whatever* it takes to keep her safe. What. Ever. It. Takes. Once this is done, know that you *will* die if you ever set foot on these shores again or so much as speak her name. Do you understand!'

'Y-yes!'

Chapter Twenty-One

'I don't believe it! The blighter has won again.' Her father threw down his hand of cards in disgust.

'Believe,' said Aaron matter-of-factly. 'The blighter has the luck of the devil.'

They were wiling away time until the guests arrived for the Annual Twelfth Night Ball—a Redbridge tradition and one Hal's mother was beyond excited about. For the first time in ten days they were not in Grosvenor Square, but Berkeley Square, and for the first time in Georgie's young life he was spending the night in a house not belonging to her father. He had been having so much fun with Prudence and Grace that Lizzie had relented and allowed him to spend the night of the ball in the nursery in Hal's house with his boisterous new friends. He deserved it. Tomorrow her son would have to say a final farewell to the girls and his grandpa as they finally travelled north. A journey which had lost much of its appeal now that she also had to say goodbye to Hal—and one which might be very short lived if she had to marry the man she despised.

Hal, on the other hand, did not appear perturbed by

her imminent departure at all. In fact, he had been a positive joy since his return on Christmas Eve. Thanks to the Hal and the Stuart–Wincanton clan, Georgie had enjoyed the best Christmas Day of his life. Aside from her little boy's euphoria at a whole army of lead soldiers, she had never heard him laugh so much. From the moment he'd arrived back mid-morning, Hal had taken charge of the children's entertainments and the children. For at least two hours, he organised a fearsome war between the brave and noble British and the cheese-making Frenchies, culminating in the epic Battle of the Persian Rug which everyone was commandeered to join. Hal, typically, cast himself as Wellington and forced his sister Connie to be Napoleon. Georgie controlled the Highlanders, Aaron the cavalry and her dear papa controlled the English cannons. Prudence and Grace, as hellions-in-training, were given the challenge of being the enemy as a test of their resourcefulness. Lizzie was also a Frenchie as she was a girl. Despite their best efforts, Wellington was victorious and Napoleon—or rather Connie—was ceremonially rolled up in the rug as a punishment for trying to take over the world. The children had all slept in the nursery with Georgie after collapsing from exhaustion. All three slept with smiles on their faces. Smiles Hal had put there.

Hal had since become a constant companion during the days, where he entertained the children and led them astray, and an ardent and passionate lover every night when he climbed the wisteria and stayed till dawn. He made no mention of their parting. The pair of them talked about the here and now rather than the future. The one time Lizzie had tentatively suggested he might come to visit them occasionally, so that their final goodbye was not final and that their impossible love affair might continue temporarily if he ever ventured north, his dark eyebrows had drawn together and he had swiftly changed the subject. That reaction, and the fact that he had made no attempt to renew his proposal—not that she would have said yes—probably said it all. Theirs was a transient, mutually beneficial relationship as per the terms of their original bargain and he had gone above and beyond. That had to be enough.

'I am surrounded by sore losers.' Hal stretched like a cat and gathered up the pile of coins in the middle of the card table. For some reason, he was wearing the same sorry-looking sprig of mistletoe which had adorned his lapel since the ill-fated Danbury house party. The one sad white berry was all shrivelled and deflated, yet he had a habit of touching it reverently whenever he was sat near his brother-in-law. 'Can I help it if fortune favours the brave?'

'My lord.' The Stuarts' austere butler interrupted. 'You have a visitor. The Earl of Ockendon. He insists you sent for him.'

Lizzie's spirits plunged. Although she had known this confrontation was due to happen tonight, she was not prepared to have it now. So early. When she was trying to enjoy her last night with Hal and desperately trying to pretend nothing was wrong, but apparently the ever-confident Hal had summoned him.

'Indeed. Show him in!' Hal was clearly eager to get the deed done but, like Lizzie, the rest of the family were suddenly all subdued.

Ockendon strode into the room with a face like thunder, still wearing his coat and clutching his hat. 'Where is he?'

Hal stood, ignoring the hostile tone, and inclined his head like the most gracious of hosts. 'If it is your puppet Rainham you are enquiring about, I am delighted to tell you he is safely hidden and happy to be so.' He turned and smiled at her shocked face, enjoying his surprise announcement immensely.

'You found him.' Her face, her limbs, were all frozen. All Lizzie could think was, *I don't have to marry Ockendon!* The relief robbed her of breath and she gripped the back of the chair. He'd done it. Hal had saved her. Just as he had said he would.

'Of course I found him!' Hal turned back towards Ockendon. 'And my Lord Rainham was most accommodating.'

'You think you are very clever, don't you, Redbridge.' Spittle sprayed out of the Earl's mouth as he snarled. 'But I have his sworn and signed testimony which will call you both liars!' He spun and started towards the door.

Hal sat, elegantly adjusting the fabric of his trousers as if he cared about the lay of the fabric, and crossed one long leg over the other. It was such an impressive sight to see. 'About that... I'm not sure how to break this to you, old boy, but I am going to require that document.'

'You say that as if you hold all the cards, Redbridge, when we both know I have the means to destroy the entire fêted Wilding family in one fell swoop.' For the first time, Ockendon's gaze took in the rest of the room, his cold eyes settling determinedly on Lizzie. 'Are you going to sit here and watch this buffoon make idle threats to your betrothed on your behalf? Be warned, madam, you will pay for every slight.'

Lizzie went to speak, only to feel Connie's hand on her arm. 'Let my brother deal with him. Hal obviously has the situation well in hand.' And apparently, nobody else, her own father included, appeared to want to contradict this statement.

'If you say one thing to malign Lizzie, her father or her son, I will happily destroy you.' Hal's voice was icy calm. His eyes colder. 'The Marquess of Rainham will *not* testify against Lord Upminster. In fact, he is now of the earnest belief he put himself on the boat bound for Botany Bay to escape the tangled mess he had made of his life. If you use that testimony, he will stand in the witness box and say you obtained it under duress, when he was out of his wits in a stinking gaol, and that you told him exactly what to write in order to blackmail the Wildings.'

Aaron and Connie smiled at this news. Her father visibly sagged with relief, a little overcome. All Lizzie could do was slump back into her chair.

Again Ockendon chose to ignore Hal and snarled at Lizzie instead. 'Am I to assume you will not be announcing our engagement tonight?'

'I would prefer complete ruination than a single day spent as your wife.'

His eyes narrowed. 'So be it.'

Ockendon turned on his heel and stalked towards the door. 'When I leave here, I am going to tell the world about your bastard!'

Quick as a flash, Hal was out of his chair and hot on his tail. One large hand grabbed the Earl's collar and pulled him back, then shoved him ruthlessly against the wall. 'If you ever speak to her like that again, they will be the last words you ever say.'

The older man's rheumy eyes widened in fear as Hal lifted him from the ground by his lapels, but he still spat and clawed like a cat. 'Unhand me! I do not dance to your tune, Redbridge.'

'Actually. You do.' Hal let go and stood back simultaneously, so swiftly and unexpectedly that Ockendon was not ready and dropped on to his bottom on the carpet. Instantly, Hal was all lazy charm again. 'I assume you are familiar with the Norwich Municipal Bank? You should be, seeing as you owe them a great deal of money...'

'I am sure I have no idea what you mean!' Ockendon scrambled to his feet, tried and failed to appear nonplussed.

'Come now...' Hal began to straighten the Earl's crumpled lapels '...they lent you eight thousand pounds. Eight thousand pounds you are struggling to pay back. Eight thousand pounds which would render you bankrupt if the loan was suddenly called in.' Fear made the tendons in the Earl's scrawny neck stand out. Made him lick his vile lips nervously. 'I suppose now is as good a time as any to inform you that *I* am now the majority shareholder of the Norwich Municipal Bank. I hold sixty-eight per cent, in case you were wondering. *Sixty. Eight. Per. Cent.* So you see, you *do* dance to my tune, Ockendon. And you will continue to dance to my tune. If you utter one word about Georgie or what happened to Rainham—just *one* word—I will call in that loan. I will take your precious town house and raze it to the ground and have *you* thrown into debtors' prison.' The Earl of Ockendon's face was ashen as Hal strode to the door and opened it. To everyone's surprise Stevens was filling the doorway. 'Throw this odious man out, Stevens, would you? He won't be coming back. And be a good chap and bring back Lord Rainham's testimony.'

One meaty hand grabbed the Earl by the collar and within a split second he was gone, the door clicked quietly shut behind him. Hal simply sauntered back into the centre of the room like the cat who had all the cream.

'Who's up for another hand of whist?'

The room had erupted and while they celebrated, Lizzie tried not to focus on the sad reality. This scandal might be over but, at best it was a respite. Unless she left society, Georgie and her dear papa were still at risk and that meant Lizzie still had to face the heartbreak of doing what she knew was necessary. She couldn't stay. Another stolen day, or week or month was merely delaying the inevitable—and the delay would make leaving so much harder in the long run. She had already tumbled head-first into love with Hal. With every day that love only grew deeper. If her heart was going to withstand the pain, she had to cut all ties quickly.

This was it.

Her last night with Hal.

For ever.

Their eyes met across the noisy room and she saw the pride in his at his achievement on her behalf. When she smiled back at him, his stare became even more intense and that pride turned to joy. All he ever seemed to want was to make her happy so Lizzie did not want his last memories of her to be anything other than that.

For his sake, one last time, she would sparkle. So she celebrated with everyone, and when Stevens returned with that damning document she threw it on the fire laughing, toasting Hal's victory with the champagne he had opened, enjoying the giddy relief of freedom until the first guests began to arrive and they all had to behave as if the end of the world had not just been narrowly averted.

As expected, the ball was an unmitigated success. Everyone was having a wonderful time—except Lizzie. The closer she got to midnight, the more the confused and tangled warring emotions drained her. Relief. Joy. Disbelief. Sadness. Love.

Pain.

Pain so intense she had to fight the hovering tears constantly. Every time she glanced in Hal's direction and he gave her a secret, intimate smile back, it ripped through her and she wished with all her heart things could be different.

But how could they be? Lizzie had responsibilities. She did not have the luxury of concerning herself solely with her own selfish happiness. Georgie could not be hidden away in Mayfair for ever and the alternatives were impossible. She would never allow him to be banished to the country and could see no way he could suddenly magically appear in Mayfair without his existence ruining her father. How did one explain away a four-soon-to-be-five-year-old child? Or a ten-year-old one. A sixteen-year-old one. With each passing year, fresh lies would have to be heaped on more lies and her innocent boy would have to suffer.

'Waltz with me.'

Hal's warm breath caressed her neck and the tears threatened to spill. Soon the guests would leave and so

would she. 'Of course.' Another memory to store away
in a box now full of them. One last dance to go with
the last kiss they would share in the morning before she
drove away. The last time she saw him as her carriage
would pull out of sight.

Hal led her on to the floor and tugged her into his
arms. Typically, too close for propriety, but not so close
to scandalise. Lizzie was past caring about the latter
and stepped closer still, allowing herself the pleasure
of feeling their bodies touching.

One last time.

'Where are you taking me?' He had twirled her
across the floor and was headed towards the door.

'The hall.'

'The hall. And that, I suppose, is explanation
enough?'

He smiled and slowly brought the dance to a stop.
'Come. I wanted to show you something.'

They seemed to stroll for an age. His town house was
impressive, even by Mayfair standards, the entrance hall
vast and filled with milling couples who had gathered
to escape the crowds and the heat of the ballroom. Hal
led her past all of them and then through another door
into a deserted, firelit parlour.

'Are we having a tryst? Because if we are I have already seen what you are going to show me.' Flirting
covered the pain.

He simply smiled enigmatically and went to the sideboard. He slid open a drawer and pulled out a small
box. 'I put this here earlier. I want you to have it.' He
placed it in her hand and stood back, uncharacteristically nervous, and her heart began to thud. Lizzie stared
at it and hoped it was not what she thought it was. At

her hesitation, he clasped his hands behind his back. Frowned. 'Open it.'

With shaking fingers, she did as he asked and stared mournfully at the glittering diamond nestled within. She had wanted tonight to be perfect for him and now she was about to ruin it.

'Marry me, Lizzie. Not because you are frightened or because you are grateful. Marry me because we love each other and we are meant to be together.'

'Oh, Hal…' She took one last look at the beautiful ring before slowly closing the box. He loved her? A part of her died as it clicked shut. 'I can't… You know I can't.'

He raked one hand through his dark hair in agitation and began to pace. 'For God's sake, woman! I love you!'

In her dreams, when he had said this it had been whispered, but his angry, raised voice somehow made it more heartfelt. More tragic.

'I love you, too, but my situation is untenable.'

His hands came up to grip her upper arms; despair distorted his handsome face. 'Surely you are not intent on pursuing this Yorkshire nonsense? Ockendon and Rainham cannot hurt you now. You are safe. Your father is safe. Georgie is safe…'

'Georgie is still a secret, Hal.' Lizzie broke the contact and put some distance between them. His touch would only make her falter away from what was right. 'He cannot remain a secret for ever. He deserves to live out in the open like every other child, running through fields, playing with others. If this month has taught me anything, it has shown me how he has blossomed amongst children his own age.'

'Once you marry me, he doesn't have to be a secret.

I adore the boy. Are you frightened I will want him hidden away like Ockendon threatened? You can tell the world, for all I care!'

'Because that would ruin his life, wouldn't it? Everyone would realise he was Rainham's son. *Rainham's* son! I wouldn't wish that stigma on my worst enemy. Wherever he went, whatever he did, the gossip would follow him. The whispering behind fans about his fallen mother at public engagements…the pointed lack of invitations to other children's parties, the lack of acceptance in a society which puts a woman's virtue above all else! The fact that you deigned to marry a fallen woman and take on the burden of him!'

'Oh, for pity's sake—as if I care about that? I've been a scandal all my adult life—one more will hardly make a difference!'

'What about the shame it would bring to my father and the damage it would do to the reputation he has worked forty years to achieve? He was complicit in hiding my baby. Good grief, Hal… What if the truth about his hand in Rainham's disappearance is questioned?'

'I'm paying for passage and a new life for that man in the Americas. You do not need to worry about him…'

Lizzie held up her hand and slowly backed towards the door. She had to fight the overwhelming urge to believe he could be right. 'We escaped the scandal this time. Next time we might not be so lucky. You know what the gossips are like. My way is better… I am better on my own. In the north I can invent a new past for my son, which will also protect my papa, something more noble than being the dirty secret of a fallen woman and the bankrupt, dissolute Marquess of Rainham's by-blow!'

Chapter Twenty-Two

Hal wanted to grab her and shake some sense into her. The stubborn wench! Always so pessimistic and blasted noble. She denied him the pleasure by darting out of the door. No doubt she hoped he wouldn't cause a scene. Too bad. He was going to cause one.

He stalked to the door and found little comfort in noisily slamming it open. Barging past several people, he caught her by the elbow and pulled her to face him. 'We are not done!'

'Yes, we are!'

He would not be swayed by the tears pooling on her long lashes or the limpid, brave misery he saw shimmering in those fine cornflower eyes. 'You are not better on your own. Neither am I. Any fool with half a brain can see we are better together. You and I were meant to be together. You love me! You said so.' A crowd was beginning to gather. Hal didn't care. 'And I love you. Are you going to allow a silly scandal to keep us apart?'

'Weeeeeeee!'

Another sound from above.

High-pitched.

Children, nightgowns billowing. Sliding down the banister at speed towards them.

Prudence. Grace.

Georgie.

The high colour drained out of Lizzie's face as her son beamed at her proudly. She started towards him, but Hal raced to beat her. He bent and grabbed the little boy around the waist and hoisted him into the air. 'You rapscallion. You're supposed to be in bed.'

Connie had already claimed her girls and was blinking back at him with alarm. 'I can take him, Hal.'

'Nonsense. You know full well he won't sleep unless his papa tucks him in.'

It felt like the right thing to say. Especially as the crowded hall was now as silent as the grave and all eyes were on them. Georgie was staring back at him with wonder.

'We have the same dark hair.'

Hal ruffled it. 'Of course we do. And you have my handsome face, too.'

There were gasps. Murmurs. Lizzie was stood like a wide-eyed statue, the only evidence she was not made of stone the rapid rise and fall of her bosom.

'You have a son?' A rotund matron peered at him through her lorgnette.

As Hal was making this up as he went along, he nodded. 'Scandalous, I know, but hardly a surprise when I am famously scandalous. In my defence, I didn't know about him, else I would have married his poor mother—but, alas…childbirth…' He tried to look winsome, hoping that the adults would understand because he sincerely doubted he could maintain his charade if Georgie got wind of anything involving the words death and his mama in the same sentence. The boy adored his mother.

'The poor thing!' Another matron. 'But you took him in?'

'I might be a scandal, madam, but I am a noble one. Georgie is my son and I adore him.'

Remarkably, the women in the room were charmed. She could see it as one by one their faces softened. The men mostly appeared startled—but it was different for men. Many of those in this room probably had by-blows of their own and all of them hidden or ignored. Dirty secrets. Lizzie watched Hal ruffle her son's hair again. 'Why were you sliding down the bannisters, young man?'

'I saw you and Mama arguing. We thought it might make you both smile.'

Hal placed his finger over Georgie's lips. 'It's not official yet, young man. She hasn't said yes. She has this ridiculous notion that marrying me will ruin her father's reputation—but my secret is out now, so I suppose it hardly matters.' His eyes locked with hers. 'My offer still stands. I know I'm unworthy and I know I'm a scandal, but Georgie needs a mother. One who will love him as much as I do and who will treat him as her own. And I need you. I love you, Sullen Lizzie. Will you marry us?'

Two pairs of male eyes stared back at her hopefully. One pair brown, the other the most seductive green.

'If it helps, I have given him my consent. Despite his past, I am confident he has matured into a fine young man.' Her papa's eyes were watery, no doubt from a stray speck of dust in the pristine hall. Another pair of hopeful eyes.

'And I wished for it for Christmas.'

Georgie's wondrous expression undid her. She had no words. Speech of any sort was impossible, so she walked towards Hal and placed a lingering kiss on his lips. Who was she to argue against the wishes of all the men she loved.

'Is that a yes?'

She nodded and his mouth crushed hers. A few people clapped. Many were smiling. Even more were already gossiping and that was fine, too. With everything else Hal had accomplished in the last few weeks, there was no point in worrying about her talkative son giving the game away one day. Between them they would work it out. What was a little scandal in the grand scheme of things? Hal was a glorious scandal. Besides, everybody knew rakes made the very best husbands and this one was going to be a wonderful father as well—to all their children.

Hal lowered Georgie to the floor, whispered something into her son's ear that had him clamping his lips shut and kissed her again properly. When he stepped back he grinned, then plucked the single, shrivelled berry from his sprig of mistletoe and tossed it at his brother-in-law. Aaron caught it with one hand.

'Seeing as it is a night for the truth, I think it's fair to tell you I originally sought you out and wooed you because of a bet.'

'A bet?'

'Yes—the Mistletoe Wager.'

'Aaron Wincanton!' His sister's face was like thunder. 'After the Serpentine you promised...'

'It's my fault, Connie.' Hal did not appear the least bit sorry. 'I bet Aaron I could steal five kisses from Lizzie before Twelfth Night was done. I am delighted to say that I won.'

'No. You didn't.' Ignoring his wife's glare, Aaron pulled out his pocket watch and pointed at the dial. 'It's past midnight. Twelfth Night is over. As per the terms of our original arrangement, that last kiss doesn't count.'

Hal shrugged and winked at Lizzie. They both knew he had stolen more than five kisses before Christmas Day. Since then there had been hundreds and all of them splendid. And he clearly did not know that Lizzie and Hal had made their own arrangement as well. Knowing how competitive the two men were, that news was unlikely to go down well. She was going to enjoy being part of this family.

'I suppose I've lost then... Although, ironically, I also won. Although not quite what I was expecting. But a wager is a wager.' He kissed her again. Lingered. Then picked up her little boy. After a quick ruffle of his matching dark hair, Hal twisted Georgie upside down and then sensibly carried her giggling child away from the sea of gawping people, as if neither had a care in the world and being scandalous was not scandalous at all.

'Come on, Georgie. Come and help your scandalous but noble Papa in the stables.'

* * * * *

LET'S TALK
Romance

For exclusive extracts, competitions
and special offers, find us online:

- facebook.com/millsandboon
- @MillsandBoon
- @MillsandBoonUK

Get in touch on 01413 063232

For all the latest titles coming soon, visit
millsandboon.co.uk/nextmonth

JOIN US ON SOCIAL MEDIA!

Stay up to date with our latest releases, author news and gossip, special offers and discounts, and all the behind-the-scenes action from Mills & Boon...

 millsandboon

 millsandboonuk

 millsandboon

It might just be true love...